CALYPSO DOWN

A CHRIS BLACK ADVENTURE

CALYPSO DOWN

A CHRIS BLACK ADVENTURE

JAMES LINDHOLM

CamCat Publishing, LLC
Fort Collins, Colorado 80524
camcatpublishing.com

This is a work of fiction. Names, characters, places, and incidents are either products of the author's imagination or are used fictitiously.

Hardcover ISBN 9780744307443
Paperback ISBN 9780744307450
Large-Print Paperback ISBN 9780744307467
eBook ISBN 9780744307474
Audiobook ISBN 9780744307481

Library of Congress Control Number: 2023943112

Book and cover design by Maryann Appel

Illustrations by Maia Lai
Artwork by Aerial3, Memories

5 3 1 2 4

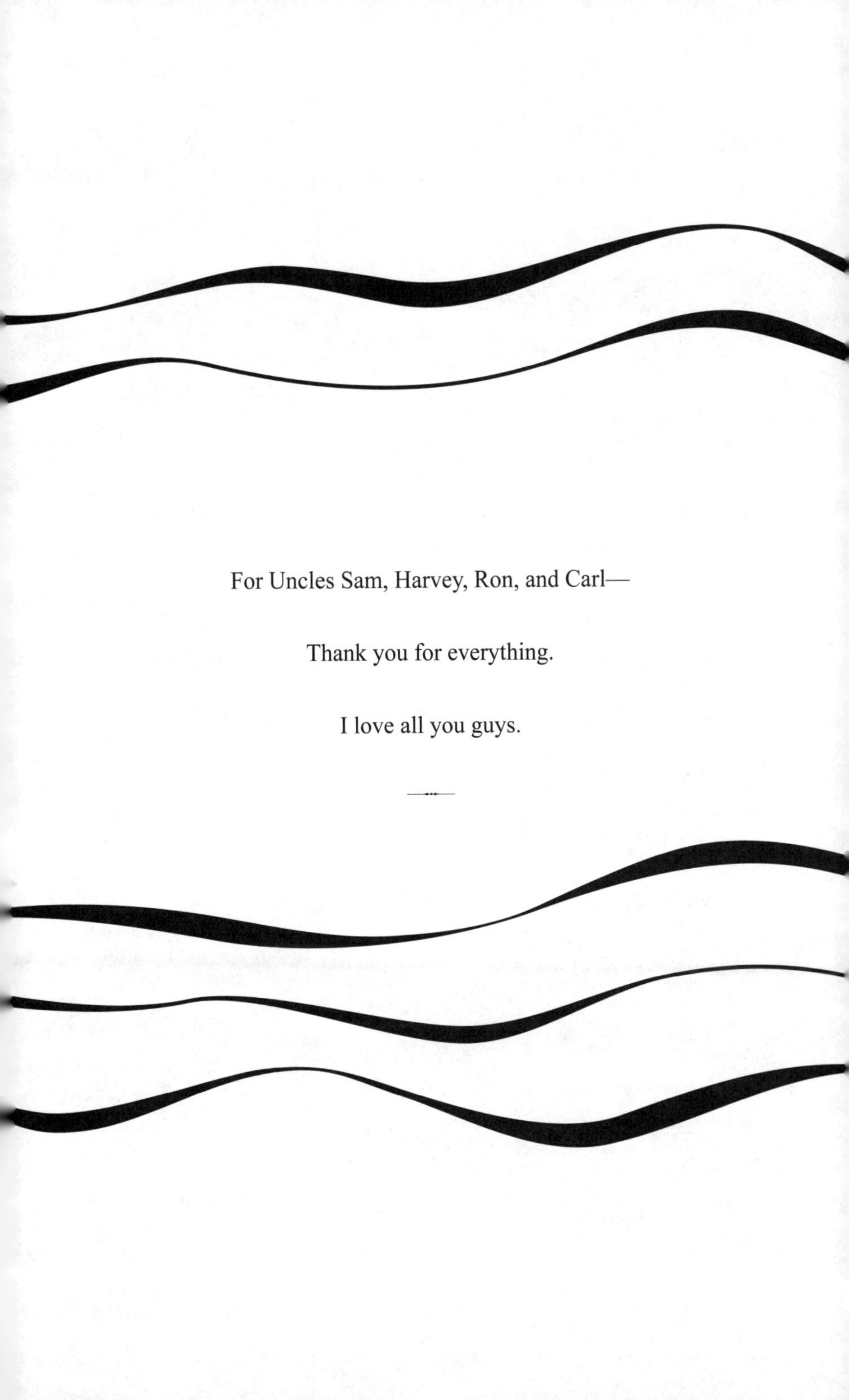

For Uncles Sam, Harvey, Ron, and Carl—

Thank you for everything.

I love all you guys.

CALYPSO I SEALAB

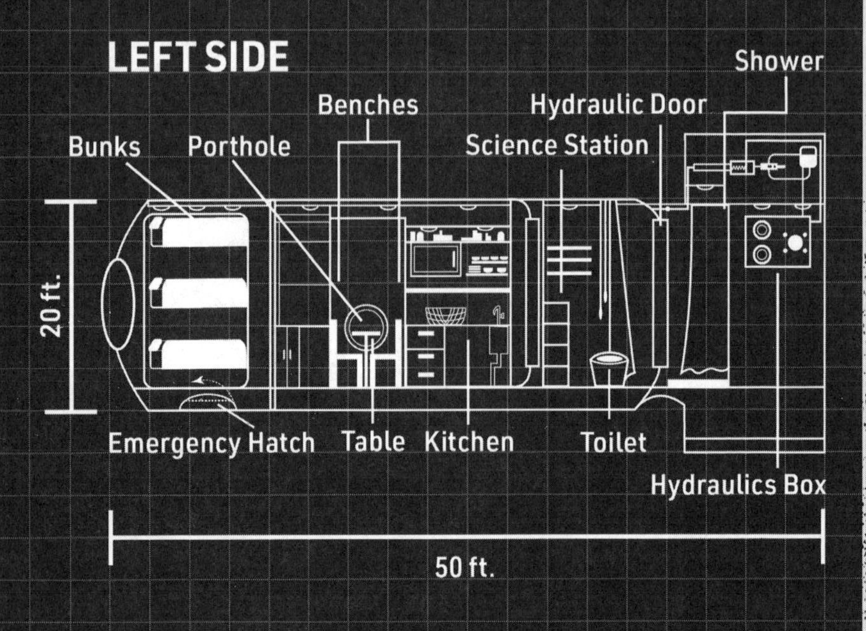

RIGHT SIDE

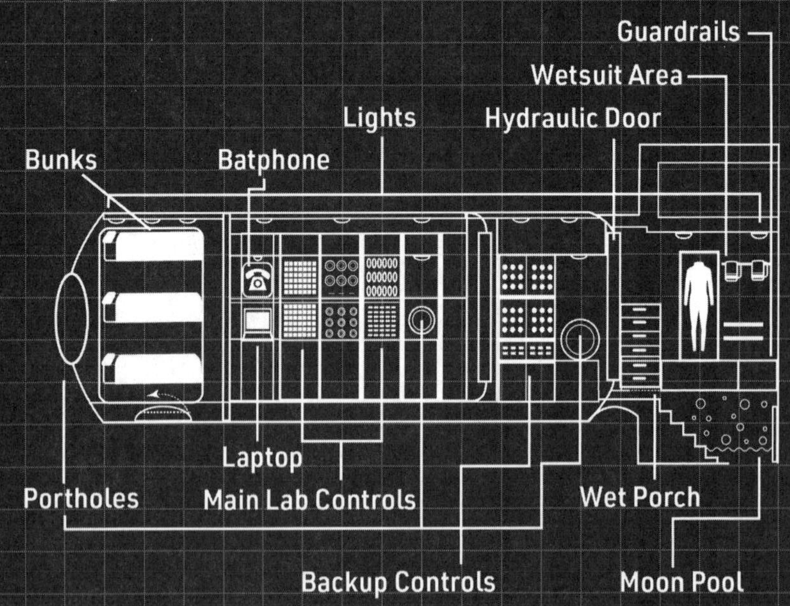

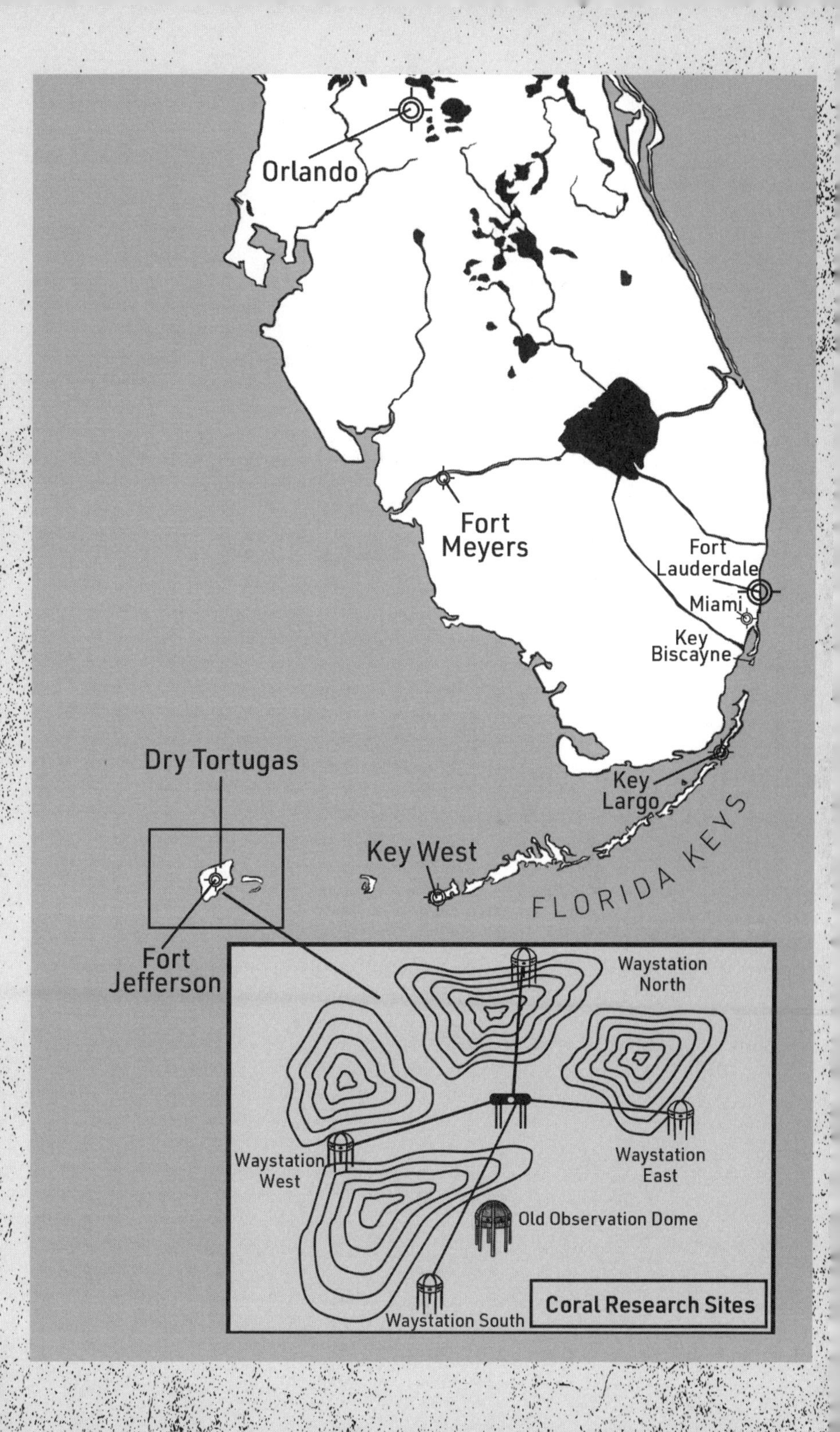
Orlando
Fort Meyers
Fort Lauderdale
Miami
Key Biscayne
Key Largo
FLORIDA KEYS
Key West
Dry Tortugas
Fort Jefferson
Waystation North
Waystation West
Waystation East
Old Observation Dome
Waystation South
Coral Research Sites

1

Deep underwater and alone, Ben Foster knew he was going to die. The cold darkness enveloped him faster than his panic. Firmly wedged into a crevice between two large boulders, he was surrounded by the utter blackness of the Floridian quarry at night. *That was strike two!*

Strike one had come only seconds before when Ben had accidentally dropped his Sola NightSea dive light into the crevice, realizing only then that he'd failed to charge the batteries on his smaller backup light. At that point, Ben's heart rate increased rapidly in the dark, his pulse pounding within the two-millimeter neoprene hood he was wearing. But then he'd spotted the faint illumination from his dive light coming from under an overhang below him, and his heart rate slowed.

Ben knew he shouldn't have been diving solo at all—not to mention at night—in a location as dangerous as a quarry. Several years earlier, a trip to Bermuda with his exotic Aunt Agatha had given Ben the chance to get certified as an entry-level SCUBA diver. His instructor had been an American expatriate friend of his aunt who used baseball analogies for everything.

"Listen, man. Diving is the way. And once you're certified, you'll be able to dive wherever you want to. But you've got to think of each dive you do as an at bat," the guy had said. "You get three strikes, but remember, with the third strike you're out. You don't want to be out while diving, man, so don't let things progress beyond strike two. Got it?"

"I think I do."

That simple analogy had stuck with Ben ever since, and so it was only natural that *strike one* was the first thing that went through his mind when he dropped his dive light. *Aunt Agatha's going to kill me*, was the second.

To celebrate the milestone, Ben had planned to make his one hundredth dive at night, from a boat, in the Dry Tortugas. It was only a four-hour drive to the Florida Keys from his house north of Fort Lauderdale, followed by a short two-hour boat ride out to the westernmost point in the Keys. He'd made the trip with Aunt Agatha the year before. *Perfect.*

But there'd been complications.

"There's a big mission starting out there next week," the dive shop owner in Key West had explained. Ben had called down hoping to arrange everything for the trip. "They've put a submerged research station down on the edge of the reef at Barracuda Key, right where you were planning to dive. Scientists are going to live there for ten days to conduct experiments. So, the entire area is closed off to any diving or unofficial boat traffic until those folks leave. You should see the social media on this thing. Hashtag something or other, a mythological name, but I can't remember what it is. It's blowing up."

Ben could not hide his disappointment, so the shop owner tried to sell him on another option.

"We've got a shop up in Lauderdale that can set you up with a boat dive if you want. It's two hundred bucks cheaper than the dive here in the Keys."

"No, thanks," Ben had replied before closing the call. He'd been wreck diving off Lauderdale before: low visibility and not a lot of fish.

Ben had fallen into a funk for just under twenty-four hours before he'd realized that he had an option much closer to home. The quarry. It wasn't as sexy as the Dry Tortugas, but it would do.

The old Piedmont Quarry was located only twenty minutes outside of Fort Lauderdale on Highway 98. The abandoned limestone quarry had filled up with freshwater decades before, creating a deep lake. It didn't have a beach, but it did have natural breaks in the steeply excavated vertical walls surrounding the lake that allowed people to enter the water. Kids from his high school and the nearby community college often came to swim during the day and party during the night.

Ben knew that entering the water at the Piedmont was dangerous. The water had slowly filled in the quarry, leaving the unexcavated bottom full of crevices and dangerous overhangs that had trapped many a swimmer over the years. In fact, so many people had drowned at the quarry that the area had been officially closed off when Ben was in elementary school.

Unofficially, however, the county hadn't repaired long-standing breaches in the fence surrounding the lake, and the sheriff's office rarely bothered to roust teenagers who strayed inside.

"There's so little to do around here," Aunt Agatha had explained. She worked in the county clerk's office. "I guess they'd rather the kids hang out somewhere nearby than drive far away to get drunk. You just be very careful if you ever go out there. Promise me."

Ben had promised. He'd been diving there with two of his friends on many occasions, but never along the south wall. When the visibility was clear, diving over the submerged boulders in the quarry was cool. Someone had stocked the lake with smallmouth bass long ago, so fish could be seen swimming among the rocks in the summer.

On the day of his centennial dive, Ben had parked his aging pickup truck in the grass near one of the breaks in the cliff and prepared his gear as the sun set to the west. The north wall of the quarry was two hundred feet higher than the south side. Dark green trees lined the ridge above bleached-white limestone cliffs. He'd waited through twilight, watching from the hood of his truck as the distant lights of Fort Myers replaced the sunset on the horizon, turning the trees a dark purple and the cliff walls a light pink.

He'd made sure to text his aunt that he was entering the water, though he'd not indicated that he was diving alone.

"You know I'm fine being the enabling aunt," Agatha had texted in reply. "But please don't make me regret that."

Fifteen minutes later, with only the stars and a quarter moon illuminating the scene, Ben had geared up and entered the glassy-calm water. He'd slipped on his fins, rolled over onto his back, and begun kicking along the south wall of the quarry with the intention of submerging after five minutes of surface swimming. Familiar with the area from a previous dive, he didn't turn on either of his two waterproof lights in order to save his night vision for a little longer.

The dive had gone according to plan until he'd dropped his Sola. He'd seen a few bluegill and smallmouth bass swimming among the boulders, and also discovered an old ten-speed bike and a large propane barbecue; both must have been dumped from the cliff above.

Now, hovering above the boulders, looking down at the narrow crevice, Ben considered whether it might just be best to surface in the dark without his lights. The luminescent face of his submersible pressure gauge indicated that he had a third of his air supply remaining. But his aunt had given him that Sola as a birthday gift, and he didn't want to leave it behind. He was pretty sure he wouldn't be able to find the same spot again, even in daylight.

Inverting himself, Ben kicked gently downward as he reached his arm out in front of him. He was initially careful to avoid touching the boulders on either side of the crevice, knowing that were he to come in contact with the bottom, the thin veneer of sediment that covered everything would be stirred up, ruining visibility. However, the deeper he swam into the crevice, the narrower it became.

The eighty-cubic-foot aluminum air tank on his back slammed hard into the boulder behind him, forcing his chest forward and into direct contact with the boulder in front. Hoping that he was only partially snagged, Ben tried to reach a little deeper for the dive light, but his right hand was still at least two feet from it. It was then that he realized he couldn't move. Not forward. Nor backward.

Ben's respirations increased rapidly as he tried to force himself upward. *He was stuck.* His attempts at dislodging himself had stirred up silt all around him.

When he became aware of the stinging pain on his chest where limestone fragments had penetrated his three-millimeter wetsuit and sliced through his skin, he screamed into his breathing regulator, expunging even more air from his tank.

Seconds passed. He realized that he could not free himself. He screamed again, kicking hard with his fins, but that only served to wedge him more tightly into the crevice.

Minutes passed, and Ben lost hope. No longer able to look downward toward the dim illumination from his light, the silty darkness around him was complete. He wished above all things to be back at his Aunt Agatha's house, watching bad action movies and plotting their next adventure. Agatha was the only parent he'd ever known. His mind rapidly cycled through moments he'd spent with her: the time she brought home his first skateboard, their first visit to Fenway Park in Boston, and the trip to California where they'd skydived together. Over and over, the events replayed in his head, bittersweet reminders of what he was going to miss.

He also cursed himself for coming to the quarry alone. It would have been so easy for him to call his two regular dive buddies, both of whom were probably sitting at home tonight with nothing to do.

I'm such an idiot.

But then Ben's left hand brushed across the dump valve located on the lower portion of his buoyancy compensator vest. As his hand closed around the plastic ball connected to the valve by a nylon cord, he prayed that pulling the cord would release air from his vest, which in turn would potentially free him from his predicament.

So, he pulled.

Immediately, Ben felt and heard air bubbles escape his vest. At first, nothing else happened, but then he detected some movement. Seconds later he could feel himself begin to float upward and away from the boulders.

He was free!

Not waiting to collect himself and forgetting everything he'd learned about the dangers of ascending too quickly toward the surface, Ben swam upward urgently. Breaking the surface in less than twenty seconds, he spit out his regulator and inhaled deeply. The calm at the surface was a welcome relief. He laid back his head and looked at the stars. Relief rushed over him.

Barely a minute after his safe return to the surface, an inflatable boat with a small outboard motor passed within inches of his head as he bobbed in the dark. Though the small boat's wake rocked him as it passed, Ben thought he could make out seven men in the boat. They were all dressed in black, and their boat had no visible running lights.

What the hell? Ben's first thought was that they were probably looking for him. He quickly became concerned that someone from the sheriff's office had seen his truck and that he was going to get into trouble.

Confirming his fears, the small inflatable came about and steered directly at him. Before he thought to react, two men sitting at the bow reached down to grab him, yanking him from the water easily despite all his SCUBA gear.

Lying on his back amid the legs of the seven men, Ben felt the boat turn north and begin motoring away from the cliff into the middle of the lake. No one spoke as they quietly motored over the rippled surface. Ben tried to sit up but was forcibly pushed back down by someone's foot on his chest.

I'm screwed.

Minutes passed. Lying on his back, wedged into the bow of the small boat, Ben's eyes had yet to adjust, and he could see very little beyond the legs around him. Only the small boat's motor penetrated the eerie silence. His air tank pressed painfully into his spine and the relief he'd experienced only minutes ago had completely dissipated.

"Can I please sit up," Ben sputtered, his lower lip trembling. This time one of the men closest to him drew a knife and held it inches from Ben's face. The blade glinted in what little light was available. *Oh, shit. These aren't cops.* He shivered as warm urine ran down the inside of his wetsuit's legs.

Looking around, he could see that all seven of the men were wearing SCUBA gear. The sheen of water on their neoprene wetsuits glimmered in the moonlight. *They'd been diving too.*

When the engine cut, silence descended over the scene, broken only by the sound of the boat's own wake lapping against the hull as it caught up. Even in the dark, Ben could feel all eyes turning toward him.

"What are you doing here?" barked the man to Ben's right, who held the knife. He was much smaller than the other five. "Who is with you?"

"Where are the others?" demanded another.

Ben struggled to process what was happening. "What others?"

"Do you expect us to believe you are out here on your own?" asked the small man. "Diving at night with no one else around?"

"I didn't, I mean, I don't—" Ben stammered. "There's no one else here."

"He's just a kid," observed the man sitting at the stern. "He doesn't know anything."

A brief animated discussion arose among the other five men.

"Who could have sent him?"

"This could fuck up the entire operation."

"We're going to have to report back on this."

Ben's eyes had adjusted to the dim light, and he could see that all seven were carrying what looked like automatic rifles. *Fuck!*

"Look," said the man piloting the boat from the stern. His neoprene hood was pulled back, and Ben could see closely cropped white hair. "Just throw him back in the water. He has nothing to report. By the time he swims his way back to shore, we'll be long gone. He is not a threat."

"I won't say anything," Ben said, beginning to feel hope.

Seconds later the small man with the knife grabbed Ben's buoyancy compensation device. He quickly sliced through both shoulder straps before moving down to slice through the cummerbund at his waist. Another man pulled off Ben's fins, and a third pulled his mask from his forehead.

"Listen, Shaw, you're just a tourist on this op," said a man to Ben's left. He pointed at the white-haired pilot with the index finger on his right hand, which was missing beyond the first knuckle. "We have to report this to Fessler. I'm not letting anyone go until we've talked to him about this."

"Jesus Christ!" the pilot exclaimed in obvious frustration. "No names. This operation is challenging enough without you all in a panic at the first sign of trouble. Get your shit together."

"I'll off him right now," interjected the small man.

"The kid clearly doesn't know anything. He's out here alone. He's got no idea who we are," the pilot defended him.

"Now that you idiots used our names, we have to deal with him. Poke him in the side with that bowie knife, Bash, and throw him over. The water's three hundred feet deep out here. No one will ever see him again."

"Wait. Please!" begged Ben, terror rising in his voice. "I didn't hear anything. I won't tell anyone anything. I promise."

"Sorry, kid," replied the white-haired man. "It looks like you were in the wrong place at the wrong time. We've got too much riding on this operation to let you go."

"Add a few more pounds to his weight harness. Without a BCD he'll sink like a rock."

Ben screamed as he was heaved by both arms onto the port side pontoon.

"Enjoy the swim," hissed the small man called Bash as he stabbed Ben in the right side, just below his ribs.

When they released his arms, Ben fell back into the water and immediately began sinking. His ears felt the increasing pressure of greater depth and he instinctively grabbed his nose to equalize his ears. The water around him got progressively colder as he sank.

Too late, Ben realized that he should be reaching down to his waist to undo his weight harness. But his arms weren't responding anymore.

Strike three, he thought, watching the moonlight disappear above him. Then his vision failed, his mouth filled with water, and he knew no more.

2

Chris Black was jarred awake as the bow of the small research vessel steered directly into an oncoming swell. He rubbed his eyes and used the palm of his hand to wipe the drool off the right side of his chin. *Jet lag sucks,* he noted to himself, not for the first time. It was only a three-hour time difference between Florida and his home out in California, but it was enough to compound his ongoing sleep deprivation.

He was sitting on a bench along the starboard gunnel, wearing his blue three-millimeter wetsuit and leaning back against his one-hundred-cubic-foot steel SCUBA tanks, which were strapped in an upright position for the ride out to the dive site. He pulled down on the bill of the blue NaMaRI hat he'd picked up in South Africa, adjusted his polarized sunglasses, and tried to go back to sleep, but the short period swell in the Atlantic resulted in a quick succession of waves slapping the hull. After banging the back of his head for the third time, Chris gave up.

Chris's colleague and childhood friend, Robert "Mac" Johnson, was sitting on the bench next to him, still sleeping. Mac's head was resting awkwardly on Chris's shoulder, mouth wide open. He and Mac had flown into Fort Lauderdale International Airport from San Francisco the day before.

As a research scientist and the assistant director for the Center for Marine Exploration (CMEx) in Monterey, Chris often found himself conducting research in remote locations. And almost as often, his friend Mac was along for the ride. They'd grown up together in Carmel-by-the-Sea. When Chris left for college and graduate school in New England, Mac had joined the Navy, ultimately earning a coveted spot with the SEALs. A wounded knee had ended Mac's military career. After completing a degree in mechanical and electrical engineering, Mac had joined Chris at the CMEx as the director of marine operations.

Around them, the rest of the divers on the vessel were a flurry of activity. The organizers of the forthcoming saturation diving mission off Key West had decided to send the team of divers north to Fort Lauderdale to participate in the day's activities with Chris, a consultant for the mission, before they started saturation training at the end of the week.

"We're still about twenty minutes out from the site. You've got plenty of time to finish getting your gear together," Chris's friend Sarah assured him with a smile when Chris tried to suppress a yawn.

Sarah Henson was a trained ecologist who now worked as a resource manager in the Florida Keys. Her blue and white hat, long-sleeve rash guard, and board shorts were all emblazoned with the logo of the federal agency she worked for. In that role, she had her hands in nearly every major marine science project in the region. She still liked to get in the field as often as possible to keep her finger on the pulse.

"Thanks," replied Chris. "We prepped all our gear last night. Couldn't sleep."

"Really? I remember you sleeping at the drop of a hat back in the day."

"Yeah, well . . . things change."

"Copy that," said Sarah. "Maybe you can set up your cameras, then."

"Also done," noted Chris.

Stretching out the shoulder Mac wasn't lying on, he added, "I guess I'll let Mac sleep. He was up even later than I was last night, talking to his new lady friend."

"My lady *friend*?" interjected Mac, without opening his eyes. "I'll have you know I was regaling an extremely accomplished woman with exciting tales of our many exploits."

"You don't have to spend all your time with Dana talking about me, you know," offered Chris, winking at Sarah. Dana St. Claire was former military and now worked with Mac and Chris's colleague Hendrix as a private security consultant.

She'd been with them in the Galapagos Islands off South America when their research vessel had been hijacked by Colombian pirates. Dana had proven invaluable to their efforts in recovering the vessel and all the students on board.

"I mean, I don't want you feeling insecure," Chris clarified, patting Mac's leg. Chris and Dana had shared a tender moment in the heat of battle with pirates, but once back in the States, it was clear that she and Mac had the enduring connection. Chris was very excited to see his friend so happy, but given his and Mac's long history together, that didn't mean he was going to make it easy.

Mac straightened his back and stretched his arms. "If it's Tuesday it must be . . . what? Florida?"

Sarah laughed and tried to speak over the engine noise. "You've done quite a bit of traveling over the past few months, I guess. I've wanted to go to the Galapagos for a long time."

"Yeah, the Galapagos," answered Mac. "We barely made it out of there alive."

"And South Africa," continued Sarah.

"And South Africa," repeated Mac. "Barely made it out of there, too. Plus, I don't think we're allowed to go back."

From behind his sunglasses, Chris watched the other divers as Mac and Sarah were talking. Joking with Mac was as natural as breathing at this point, but he wasn't feeling particularly jovial. The trauma of the incident in the Galapagos had subsided over the past months, but the guilt he felt for allowing young students under his supervision to be victimized by pirates had lingered. When he'd accepted the request to come help support the *Calypso I* saturation mission, Chris had realized that he wasn't yet ready to take full responsibility for a group of young scientists again. He needed more time to process the events in the Galapagos and his role in those events. He'd only accepted the request because he would be in a supporting role within a much larger program and wouldn't be directly responsible for anyone's safety.

"South Africa *and* the Galapagos?" asked Brian Nakasone. He was from San Francisco and spoke with a frankness Chris often associated with urban dwellers. He was kneeling on the bench with one knee adjusting his SCUBA regulator, his black hair closely cropped on the sides, and several inches long on top. "That's pretty cool. Guys, I'm diving with them."

"Take it easy, dude," replied Nat Gamal without looking up from the large waterproof camera housing that was sitting on her lap. The large acrylic dome covering the lens was nearly as big as her head. Dyed green bangs stuck out from under a thin gray hoodie she was wearing. "Didn't you hear the guy just say they barely made it out alive?"

"*Barely* is good enough for me," said Brian, reaching up to high-five Joe Bauer, the diver standing next to him, but getting no response. Joe was looking down at his phone.

"And Joe leaves you hanging!" exclaimed Nat. "I think that says it all, dude. You're diving with us."

Chris smiled and watched them put their gear together, reviewing what he'd learned from the biographies he'd been provided. Nat Gamal and Joe Bauer both worked on fishes. Nat was originally from

Egypt, but now lived in Canada. And at five feet, five inches, she was clearly the feistiest of the group in Chris's estimation.

"*Dude*," said Brian, glaring at Joe.

Joe Bauer stood at least a head taller than Brian. He swiped his finger across the waterproof case covering his smartphone and pointed it toward Brian and Nat. "Have you seen this?"

"What?" replied Nat and Brian nearly simultaneously.

Joe was considerably more reserved than Nat. He was from Miami and from what Chris observed in their brief time together, he took everything he did very seriously.

"Social media around the mission are just exploding," explained Joe, turning the phone back toward himself. "This is crazy."

"I saw that last night," said Jessica Wilson. She was sitting on the other side of Mac making notes on a waterproof slate. "I didn't see anything too extreme."

Jessica was from Texas, and she was the hardest one for Chris to read. She was very quiet, even when everyone around her was having fun, choosing to focus more on her invertebrate ID books.

"Maybe not last night," replied Joe. "But this morning it's something else altogether."

The conversation stopped as the pilot cut the engines to pull up to a large yellow mooring ball. Bright morning sunlight gleaned from the ball and the calm Florida waters around it.

Sarah leaped up onto the bow of the boat and grabbed a line from the ball using a boat hook, securing it to one of four cleats. This assured that the research vessel did not have to deploy an anchor, which could be damaging to the dive site below. She then returned to the stern and faced the assembled divers to lay out the day's plan.

They were set to dive on the wreck of the *USS Roosevelt*, a former US Navy destroyer that was intentionally sunk off Fort Lauderdale two decades before to provide more opportunities for recreational SCUBA diving.

As Sarah began outlining the details of the day's dive, Chris was distracted by a bright red cigarette boat motoring directly toward them from a thousand yards away. He could see at least three large men standing on the back deck, all holding tight to the canopy covering the wheelhouse as the boat's outsized bow plowed through the swells. *They're not messing around*, he thought, wondering if they were drug runners or drunken college students. *Tourists they are not.*

When the boat was only about five hundred yards from the divers, Chris saw a patrol boat approaching quickly on an intercept course. The red boat, however, was moving much faster and easily outpaced the patrol boat, maintaining their course directly toward the divers.

A loud siren erupted from the patrol boat, followed closely by a stern voice on a bullhorn. "Vessel *Patriot*, you are in a restricted area. Come about immediately!"

Several seconds passed, during which Chris stood up and gripped the rail behind his tank. Quickly calculating the slim odds of getting everyone off the boat safely before a collision, Chris exclaimed, "Everyone down, *now*!"

3

Senator Gwendolyn Pierce slowed imperceptibly as she approached the baggage claim area at Miami International Airport. Though she was scrolling through messages on her smartphone and carrying on two separate conversations with aides walking quickly on either side of her, Pierce still had time to spot the TV news crews hovering outside the arrivals gate.

The long walk through the concourse had been free of all press. But from what she could see in front of her, there were at least six different reporters waiting on the other side of the gate, each with associated camera operators. All the cameras were rolling, and their presence had encouraged dozens of travelers to linger at baggage claim to see what was going on.

"Shit," she muttered under her breath. "Terry, I thought you said we'd have twenty-four hours before it hit the fan in the press. I'm not ready to make a statement."

The seventy-five-year-old junior senator from Vermont was four years into her first term in the Senate, where she worked alongside the state's eighty-year-old senior senator and frequent presidential candidate. However, her long career as an environmentalist and anti-war activist on the international front had established Pierce as a clear voice in the Senate despite her relative inexperience as a legislator.

Pierce wore her gray hair pulled back in a ponytail and was outfitted in her standard "uniform" of a black fleece jacket, blue jeans, and rafting sandals. "If all these wannabe cowboys are going to be walking around the Senate in bolo ties and steel-toed boots," she'd told her incredulous aides during the campaign, "then I'm sure as hell going to stick with my own activewear. High-heeled shoes are for younger women with something to prove."

This was the senator's first official trip to Florida. She'd been to Orlando once, decades before, when her kids were young to visit all the theme parks, but she'd otherwise stayed away from the state.

"I'm not sure why they're here, Senator," replied Terry, as she frantically scrolled through messages on her own phone. "Let me see what I can find out."

"I can't stop moving now," whispered Pierce, looking down as she spoke. "Those cameras are on. I'll just have to wing it."

"Senator!"

"Senator!"

"Senator, is it true that your committee is going to recommend no further arm sales to foreign governments?"

Pierce stepped through the gate and into the middle of the semicircle created by the crowd of reporters and onlookers. The combined impact of the Miami humidity coming in through the constantly opening terminal doors and the intense glare of the camera lights instantly made her regret not removing her fleece when she stepped off the plane. She hoped that the cameras didn't pick up on the sweat accumulating at her hairline.

"Ladies and gentlemen," said Pierce as she held up both palms in an effort to slow the staccato assault of questions. "I'm not ready to comment on the committee's deliberations. We may have something for you on that later this week."

"Can you at least confirm that your recommendation will be to halt all arms sales?" asked a reporter leaning forward out of the crowd. His microphone was only inches from Pierce's face. "How do you think that's going to impact a defense industry that isn't used to such constraints?"

Pierce looked around at the reporters, noticing that the camera phones being held out by the crowd now outnumbered the TV cameras by three to one.

"Later this week, people. Or perhaps this weekend. Today I'm here to support Science Without Borders, an organization, which, I'm proud to say, is a product of Vermont ingenuity and dedication to the idea that national borders will soon be a thing of the past."

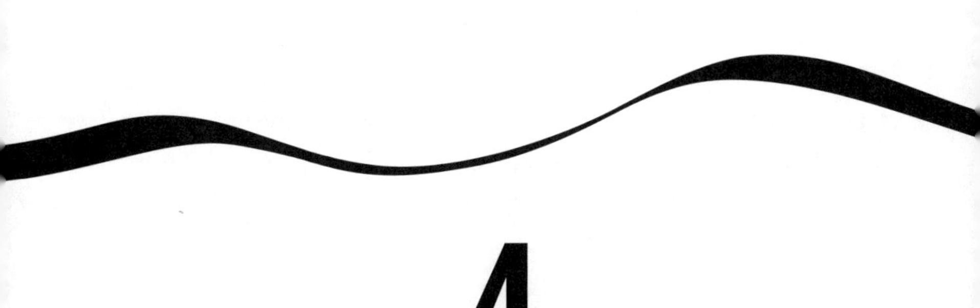

4

"Incoming!" screamed Mac Johnson, who was now fully awake from his jet-lagged slumber.

Chris Black and the other divers braced themselves for the collision that looked inevitable as the *Patriot* bore down on them. The wail of the chasing patrol boat's siren was barely discernible over the increasingly loud engine noise of the cigarette boat racing at them.

Considering his options, Chris realized that he had few. *This is not going to go well.* The horrified looks on the faces of his young research team nearly made him sick to his stomach.

Seconds from the point of no return, the pilot of the *Patriot* cranked the wheel and the vessel angled sharply to port, missing the researchers by just a few feet.

The threat of collision averted, just seconds later their boat was struck by the wake of the fast-moving cigarette boat and that of the chasing patrol boat, nearly capsizing them.

Clinging to the starboard rail, Chris briefly dangled in the air as the small research boat was hit by a wave directly abeam. Looking down he could see Nat and Brian struggling to stay in the boat below him as water poured in over the partially submerged portside rail.

Chris was greatly concerned that SCUBA tanks would break free from their mounts and crush people, but the tanks remained secure.

Then, as quickly as the threat had appeared, it receded. The research vessel stabilized with all divers still on board. Six inches of seawater sloshed back and forth at the divers' feet as the only evidence of the chaos that had just visited them.

Silence engulfed the group as Chris watched the patrol boat chase after the *Patriot* in vain.

The larger vessel was just too powerful.

"What the fuck was *that*?" exclaimed Nat as Brian vomited next to her.

No one else spoke as Chris watched as each of the divers looked around them to take stock.

"How is everyone doing?"

"I've seen some reckless boating out here," said Sarah, "but that was the first time I thought I might not survive."

The group discussed the relative merits of heading back into port or staying on site to conduct the dive as planned. A show of hands indicated that everyone wanted to proceed with the dive.

"I'm not real wild about missing this opportunity just because some *Miami Vice* jackass nearly killed us," said Brian.

"I concur," said Joe. "And I hope that enforcement patrol catches those guys."

"We'll have to find out later," replied Sarah. "Jessica?"

Jessica quietly nodded.

"Nat?" asked Sarah. "Are you sure? You almost washed over the side."

"Yeah, I'm sure," said Nat. "My apologies for the language, Dr. Black, but fuck 'em. Idiots like that shouldn't win. Let's dive."

"Okay, then let's review the plan one more time," said Sarah, clapping her hands together. "The mooring ball marks the deepest portion of the wreck. When you get to the bottom of the line, you will be in one hundred and fifty feet of water. The wreckage extends up the slope into approximately sixty feet of water where a separate line attaches to that mooring ball over there."

Chris could see another yellow mooring ball shoreward from their current position.

"We've got three buddy teams. Each team has separate objectives, and therefore will dive independently. Brian and Jessica, the two of you are looking for sponges and corals. Nat and Joe, I know you two want to study your fishes, but you agreed to help us replace some of the lines inside the deeper section of the wreck, right? And Chris and Mac, you two will be looking specifically for invasive fishes."

"Lucky," said Nat. "Can I check out your video later? I'm particularly interested in any parrotfishes you see. Obviously, they're not invasive, but it would be good to know if they've made it up here from the Keys."

"Of course," replied Chris. "We'll record everything we see. We can drop it all onto a thumb drive later, if that works for you."

"Perfect. Thanks."

"What are you looking for with the corals?" Mac asked. Though he was clear on the SCUBA logistics, he wasn't as clear on the scientific objectives of the different groups.

"Good question." Jessica spoke so quietly it was hard to understand her. "The wreck below us, because we know exactly when it was sunk, provides us with a fixed reference point to better understand the growth rate of corals that we find on the hard surfaces down there."

"That's obviously harder to do on natural reefs," said Brian. "But on a manufactured object, with a precise timeline starting when it sank, we'll be able to learn a great deal. A woman named Karen Li down in Cape Town pioneered this approach at other locations."

And I knew her before her pioneering days, thought Chris of his good friend Karen. He'd have to send her a message later describing how far her reputation had spread.

"Teams one and two will be ascending back to this vessel at the second mooring ball," said Sarah. "We'll move over there once everyone's in the water. Chris and Mac will work their way progressively shallower over the course of the dive. I will follow your bubbles in the small inflatable and pick you up at the bow of the wreck when you're done.

"Out here at the deep end of the wreck, you researchers will be the only divers in the water today. However, Chris and Mac, when you reach the shallower end near the bow, you'll likely encounter recreational divers in the area. Just pop your sausage buoy when you're ready to surface, and I'll be there. Any questions?"

"I thought permits were required to be out here. How're the recreational divers getting in?" inquired Mac.

"There are several commercial dive operators with permits to dive in the area," explained Sarah.

"What do you want us to do with lionfish if we see any of them?" asked Chris.

Lionfish were native to the Pacific and Indian Oceans but had recently expanded their range considerably to include Florida and the Caribbean. They were voracious predators and had, Chris thought, the dubious distinction of being both poisonous and venomous.

At the *Poseidon* Undersea Laboratory, which was farther south off Key Largo, Chris hadn't seen a single lionfish over his first five missions in a period of seven years. However, on his last mission, he'd seen pairs of lionfish on literally every dive he'd done. They'd gone from nonexistent to superabundant in less than a year, all because some people likely released the fish from their home aquariums for one reason or another. With few to no natural predators, their numbers had increased quickly.

"What do you mean?" asked Joe. "What would you do with them?"

"Many sites elsewhere in the Caribbean, even those inside marine protected areas, are encouraging divers to remove any lionfish they see," answered Chris. "When we were at Roatan, Honduras, last year, they actually provided pole spears and PVC tubes to help with the removal."

"Ah, I see," said Joe. "That's a good idea."

"I think some of the recreational dive boats might be doing that," added Sarah. "But today, all you and Mac must do is note where you see any of them. We think the pairs stay pretty close to particular spots, so we'll use your positional data to go back and get them later. Look, but don't touch."

"Well, we've already cheated death once today," said Chris. "But any day I can avoid contact with venomous sea creatures is a good day."

Nat and Brian both laughed as they made their final preparations to dive. Joe looked on with a blank expression on his face. Jessica said nothing, staring down at the notes on her dive slate that Chris had seen her read and then reread at least twice. *A curious bunch,* he thought. *Not a group I'd have put together. Just hope they'll get along in the undersea lab, a literal pressure cooker. There, personality trumps all.*

5

Chris plunged into the warm Florida water and immediately moved clear of the research vessel's stern to make way for Mac to enter. Floating at the surface, he reached up with his fist and tapped the top of his head, signaling to Sarah that he was okay.

Since Mac was the last diver in, as soon as he entered the water, the pair began their descent. This was Chris's first dive in Florida in several years, and the clear water surprised him once again. Looking down as they passed thirty feet, he could easily see the bottom of the mooring line at the seafloor one hundred twenty feet below. A curtain of air bubbles extruded by the other dive teams extended from the bottom all the way to the surface.

Passing seventy-five feet, Chris used the inflator hose on his buoyancy compensator device to add a small amount of air to the bladder on his back. This slowed his descent and gave him time to prepare his camera system to collect imagery of any fishes he and Mac encountered on the wreck.

The system was small and uncomplicated. So small that he'd been able to transport it in his carry-on luggage. A small, eight-inch bar was anchored on either end by padded vertical handles. At the center of the bar, he'd mounted a small waterproof digital camera. And on the underside of the bar, he'd attached two green pinpoint lasers, each resembling laser pointers used by lecturers around the world. In this case, the lasers, set precisely six inches apart, projected parallel beams of light into the field of view of the digital camera. Those beams, when positioned near fishes of interest, would allow Chris to estimate the size of each fish, a critical factor in understanding fish population dynamics.

Swimming above the wreck itself, Chris reflected on the interesting tension between the recreational dive community and environmentalists created by the placement of shipwrecks. In Florida, despite having the longest barrier reef in the continental US, they'd embraced the intentional sinking of wrecks like this one to create more diving opportunities for dive tourism, whereas back home in California, the environmentalists had successfully prevented intentional sinking across much of the state.

Looking for an area of the wreck where no divers were working, Chris could see the other two research teams below him. Farther up toward the bow of the sunken destroyer, he noticed a trio of divers he assumed were the amateurs Sarah had mentioned. Having been so immersed in research diving for more than two decades, Chris felt a twinge of discomfort knowing divers with uncertain levels of training and experience were in their midst. But he brushed off the concerns and focused on the task at hand.

Because the ship had been intentionally sunk only a few years before, the superstructure was still very much intact, creating perfect hiding places for lionfish. He used hand signals to indicate to Mac where he wanted to go and how far off the bottom he wanted to stay.

Returning the *okay* sign, Mac removed a small waterproof slate from a large pocket on his right thigh and prepared to take notes. Small golf pencils hung from each side of the slate in flexible surgical tubing. The notes, when combined with Chris's imagery, would provide a near comprehensive record of the dive and all their observations.

The pair stopped their descent at approximately fifteen feet above the wreck. At that distance, given the water clarity, they could easily observe thousands of fishes swimming above the wreck without changing the behavior of those fishes.

Checking his wrist-mounted Suunto dive computer, Chris noted that at their current depth they had approximately six minutes of bottom time available. That time would increase as they progressed along the wreck into shallower water.

Chris could hear an audible hooting in his ears as Mac pointed down an aggregation of five blue parrotfish. Though sound traveled about four times faster in water than in air due to water's increased density, Chris knew few divers who were capable of clearly audible vocalizations underwater. He didn't know how Mac did it, but he'd taken advantage of the skill on multiple occasions.

As they slowly ascended along the wreck, the two green lasers projected out from Chris's camera rig like flashlights shining through campfire smoke.

Where they encountered the bottom, the lasers provided two easily discernible green dots Chris's students would later use as frames of reference while watching the video for measuring fish sizes. They also gave Mac a guide for where to make his observations.

They crested ninety feet having encountered hundreds of fish but without observing a single lionfish. Looking back, Chris could see that they'd left the rest of the research team behind. Returning his gaze toward the wreck's bow, which he estimated was approximately one hundred yards out and thirty feet shallower, he could see scattered bubbles from other divers along the abandoned gun turrets.

Mac signaled to Chris that he had eighteen hundred PSI remaining in his primary tank, a little more than half the air he'd started with. Chris had close to the same. For a deep dive such as this one, Chris and Mac each carried additional air in smaller bailout tanks hanging from their BCDs. These forty-cubic-foot aluminum tanks had separate regulators attached to them and could be used in an emergency should something go wrong with their primary air tanks.

Chris spotted a pair of lionfish hovering under the barrel of one of the large guns. Using the lasers, Chris estimated that each of the two fish was about eight inches in length, making them either late juveniles or early adults.

He was about to signal Mac that they should go in for a closer look when the trio of divers he'd seen earlier caught his eye once again. One of the divers was carrying a pole spear. Chris and Mac watched as the guy jammed it into a crevice between a turret and the deck. When he pulled the spear out, a large fish was impaled on the tip. It was twice the size of the lionfish they'd just seen, and it was a mottled grayish brown.

Without demonstrating any precautions, the man held up the spear next to him. He didn't seem concerned by the kind of fish he had caught, although he should be, and Chris wondered if he even knew. One of the man's buddies moved in close, and the third buddy used a small waterproof camera to take a picture of the conquest. When the camera's strobe fired, the fish, likely assumed dead by the divers, convulsed madly, and struck both posing divers in their heads.

Oh, shit! Chris thought. That was a stonefish, and those divers were in big trouble.

6

Jeremiah Fessler set his rifle down on the organized workbench and sat back on his stool. His thinning blond hair hung from a dirty gray trucker's cap; his T-shirt was emblazoned with a giant American flag. He removed the prosthetic below his right knee and rubbed the end of his leg. Fessler had had some form of prosthetic for more than twenty years, having lost his lower right leg to complications from diabetes and drug use in his early twenties.

The flat-screen TV mounted above the workbench was muted, but Fessler could see the talking head from the local Orlando ABC News station speaking in front of a green screen with an image of an undersea laboratory projected behind her. Fessler clicked the volume on the remote.

". . . the mission will include four young scientists from across the northern hemisphere, Dave," said the blonde on the screen. "They will live underwater for ten days, SCUBA diving up to eight hours a day."

The camera shifted to the news anchor, Dave Roberts, who was seated behind a massive desk to the left of the green screen. Roberts had the orange complexion of a spray-on tan and hair so dark that Fessler doubted it was real. "That's pretty incredible, Maryann," observed Roberts. "And I understand that the United Nations is supporting the mission."

"That's right, Dave," said the reporter with a smile. "The undersea lab, the *Calypso I*, named after a nymph in Greek mythology, is the first of at least four similar laboratories planned to be deployed around the world." The woman paused to review her notes.

"The next mission is scheduled for the Red Sea, to be followed by Australia and then Indonesia. Senator Gwendolyn Pierce from Vermont, a major proponent of globalization, arrived in Florida just this afternoon to support the launch of the mission."

Fessler watched as the camera cut away to Pierce standing at the baggage claim down at the airport in Miami.

". . . national borders will soon be a thing of the past," said Pierce.

"Do you really believe that, Senator? No more borders?" asked a reporter from CNN.

"I absolutely do," responded Pierce. "Just think about how many of our current conflicts, both here in the US and around the world, are the result of border disputes and nationalistic fervor. I firmly believe that missions such as this will help us move toward a borderless and truly international and intercultural future."

Fessler picked up a large Ka-Bar knife from the workbench in front of him. He hefted it briefly in his palm then threw it at a wooden target ten feet away. The blade stuck two inches into the wood just left of the bull's-eye.

"Wow, that's quite a claim, Maryann," observed Dave as the camera cut back to him in the studio. "This mission will start this weekend down in the Dry Tortugas. Will the public be allowed to watch any of this happening?"

"Not directly, Dave. While I understand that they will be broadcasting some portions of the mission, public access to Fort Jefferson has been closed for the next three weeks, and unauthorized vessels will be turned away from the area around Barracuda Key."

"Oh, boy. I can see that making a few people unhappy," observed Roberts.

Fessler clicked the mute button again. "You can say that again, Dave, you lame piece of shit."

Fessler, an impressive six foot, five inches and two hundred ninety pounds, was a former high school football player from central Florida whose life had not developed as he'd imagined it would.

As the rejections from professional football teams and three separate branches of the military had piled up alongside unpaid bills on his stained yellow coffee table, Fessler had fallen into a spiral of depression, followed shortly by alcohol and drug abuse. That had only exacerbated his physical woes and landed him in the Marion County jail.

He'd contemplated suicide in his cell but was unable to muster the enthusiasm to pull it off.

It was then that complications from diabetes and drug use had necessitated the amputation of his right leg below the knee. During his time in Marion's hospital ward, Fessler met a Vietnam veteran named Bill Todd. Todd was recuperating in the adjacent bed from wounds received in a knife fight with members of a Cuban gang, Los Pistoleros.

"I seen you around, seen those tats you got. Why ain't you joined up with us yet?" Todd had asked.

"Who's us?" asked Fessler.

"The Brotherhood. You've heard of us."

Fessler remembered seeing flyers advertising meetings for the Brotherhood at the indoor shooting range he frequented regularly. He'd also overheard conversations about the group. But all he knew for sure was that it was some kind of a veterans' organization.

"We're growing, here and out in the world," explained Todd. "I'm the founder and could use someone like you to help out. You interested?"

Fessler had spent the next week asking Todd about the activities and plans of the Brotherhood. On the heels of his rejection by the NFL and the military, he'd found the invitation to join them very compelling.

"I've got things all taken care of in here," explained Todd. "But out *there*, I need help. A short timer like you? Perfect."

Todd had proposed a plan for Fessler that involved recruiting new members from his mandatory group counseling sessions. He'd been particularly interested in recruiting younger ex-cons with experience dealing with social media.

Enabled by several of those members, the Brotherhood had found thousands of supporters online from around Florida. Success with social media begat a wide range of campaigns among its members to first oppose politicians or government employees based on their established positions and/or voting records on topics like gun control and immigration, and then to actively attack those people in vicious online assaults.

The righteousness of his members' vehement complaints consumed Fessler with the same vigor that his dark thoughts once did. Based purely on member support alone, he'd hired more young guys to press the Brotherhood's focal issues, including America First, the Second Amendment, and anti-immigration, via whatever social media platform people were using at the time.

Five years back, he'd received a call from an anonymous woman offering considerable financial support if he was willing to take the Brotherhood in yet another direction, preparing for the possibility of armed conflict.

Similar groups in other states, the woman had emphasized, had taken over government offices, plotted to kidnap elected officials, and even sought to bring the entire federal government down on itself. The Brotherhood had stagnated as simply an online venue for venting frustration, she'd said. But it could be relevant again if they considered more direct action out in the world.

They didn't consider much. The Brotherhood was all in.

One of the three burner phones Fessler used to communicate with his leadership buzzed from its position on the workbench to his left, breaking his reverie.

"This is King," said Fessler, as he opened the flip phone, using the name his closest comrades within the Brotherhood had given him as an ironic nod to his leadership within a failing democracy. He listened to the voice on the other end for sixty seconds before responding.

"So, the practice run was a success?" he asked. "Good. We may not need your strike team if everything else goes according to plan. But you never know."

"I understand," said Hugo Martinez, a former sergeant in the Florida National Guard who'd been dishonorably discharged for an affair with a female cadet. He now worked as a problem solver for the Brotherhood. He mentioned the diver they'd encountered.

"We always knew there would be collateral damage," said Fessler. "Who did it?"

"Your newest recruit," replied Martinez. "He seemed to relish the opportunity."

"Bash. I thought so." Aaron Bash had been a gamble Fessler had made earlier in the year. Bash was the youngest recruit they had and was likely certifiably crazy. But his facility with weapons and his willingness to do just about anything was hard to turn away. "Shaw's position?"

"He wasn't enthusiastic about killing the kid, but agreed." What Martinez failed to mention was that they'd had no choice once the kid could potentially identify them since Martinez had carelessly used their names. Self-preservation demanded that such details were left unsaid.

7

Panic erupted among the three recreational divers. With no need for communication, Chris and Mac instantly moved toward them as quickly as a safe ascent allowed, which from forty feet below would likely take just over one minute. Through the clear Florida water, Chris saw the spearfisherman drop the spear and grab his head, writhing in pain.

The spear spiraled downward under its own weight, with the impaled fish wriggling frantically.

Stonefish. While the lionfish had received a great deal of attention as it spread around the world, largely unfettered, less attention had been focused on species like the reef stonefish. It was a solitary, ambush predator, well camouflaged in gray-brown for hiding on the seafloor. And it harbored the most lethal venom of any fish on Earth. Chris had read survivor accounts in which they'd begged to have limbs amputated to relieve the pain.

As Chris swam, he checked his wrist computer, confirming two things: He and Mac had plenty of bottom time remaining, provided their air lasted. But they also needed to make two stops as they ascended, first at forty and then fifteen feet, to allow for sufficient off-gassing of the nitrogen that built up in the bloodstream during the deeper portion of the dive. That five minutes would ensure their safe return to the surface without contracting the bends, but would complicate the rescue of the injured divers.

The spearfisherman was unconscious by the time Chris and Mac reached him, the likely victim of cardiac arrest. The injection of venom into its prey was achieved by several spines along the stonefish's dorsal line. Chris knew that while the venom did not immediately kill most victims outright, the convulsive pain caused by the venom often resulted in a heart attack. Because both victims were struck in the head, he suspected the pain would be particularly acute.

With insufficient air in the diver's buoyancy compensator vest, his motionless body began to sink. Chris swam directly to him, halting the man's descent and immediately beginning an assessment.

The other man struck by the stonefish was still conscious but was shaking violently. The photographer had at first moved in to help but retreated under assault from his panicking buddy. Mac approached slowly, holding out his palms in a gesture intended to calm the man.

Chris watched as the small trickle of air being extruded by the diver in front of him slowed, and then stopped altogether. A nonbreathing diver at forty feet underwater presented a significant challenge. The sound of the outboard motor from Sarah's inflatable boat above them gave him the best solution he could hope for. Chris extracted a small slate from a pocket on his thigh. He wrote, "STONEFISH STRIKE. LIKELY CARDIAC ARREST. *NOT* BREATHING," and attached the slate to the front of the man's BCD. He then assessed the man's weighting system.

Since every diver's weight setup was different, Chris took several seconds to figure out where the man's weights were located. Finding pockets on either side of the BCD, he used the inflator hose to add air to make him more buoyant. He then quickly removed the weight pockets and released the diver, pulling his own arms back in the process.

Unfettered by lead weights, the diver's body rocketed to the surface. Such uncontrolled ascents were very dangerous, but for a non-breathing victim of a stonefish strike, death was a distinct possibility already unless help came fast.

From the deck of the wreck, Chris could see the man reach the surface, his inflated BCD keeping him afloat. Seconds later he could see Sarah's boat begin motoring over to the diver.

Turning his attention to Mac and the other two divers, Chris could see Mac administering aid to the photographer, who'd lost his mask when trying to help his friend. Mac pulled a backup mask out of an external pocket on his left thigh and helped to put it on the photographer.

The photographer was breathing quickly in his own panic, a cloud of bubbles extruding from his regulator. Chris could see Mac check the man's submersible pressure gauge and then pass over his own bailout tank to the diver. The smaller tank would have enough air for the man to safely ascend to the surface on his own as Chris and Mac conducted their final safety stop.

Confident that Mac had the situation under control with the photographer, Chris turned to check on the status of the other spearfisherman. The man was nowhere to be seen. Chris immediately scanned the surface to see if the diver had ascended, but there was no sign of him. He looked along the deck of the wreck in both directions—again no sight of him. Chris then scanned down the slope toward the stern. No diver.

Chris checked his dive computer. At his current depth of forty feet, he had almost half an hour of bottom time remaining. However, if he were to descend farther to search for the missing diver, that available time would dissipate quickly.

Just then, Chris spotted an eruption of bubbles below him. It was coming from over the side of the wreck, approximately thirty feet below. While he couldn't see what was causing the bubbles, a panicked diver in great pain from a stonefish strike was a likely candidate. He knew that the mind responded in mysterious ways when in duress, having seen freezing and frostbitten men remove all their clothes under the misplaced belief that they were overheating. The injured diver could be doing anything down there.

Chris motioned to Mac, putting his two index fingers together, pointing to the photographer, and motioning toward the surface with his thumb. Mac flashed the *okay* sign, agreeing to lead the diver to the surface. Chris next pointed two fingers at his own mask then motioned toward the bubble cloud beneath them. Mac was slow in responding with the *okay* this time, indicating to Chris that he, too, was evaluating the risk Chris was about to take on.

Reflecting on his first training session for saturation diving at *Poseidon* fifteen years before, Chris recalled his instructor's frank assessment of a particular buddy emergency situation.

"Once you're in saturation, if your buddy is in trouble at the surface, and you go to him, you will very likely get the bends; possibly a very bad hit depending on your physiology," the trainer, John Halbeck, had emphasized. "However, if you *don't* go to your buddy, he will very likely die."

Halbeck had let that realization settle in before continuing. "Now, we can't require you take that risk, but you should know that these are the types of trade-offs associated with the mission on which you're about to embark."

The analogy only went so far, Chris realized, as he technically owed nothing to a recreational diver he didn't know, who'd been cavalier with a dangerous sea creature and paid the price. But then again, he couldn't simply leave a man to certain death.

Deciding to risk his own safety on the off chance that he could save the diver, Chris oriented himself toward the bubble cloud, which was beginning to dissipate, and began kicking hard. The strength of his kick, coupled with his decreasing buoyancy as he descended, allowed Chris to close the distance quickly. As he swam, he watched his gauges, noting that both his allowable bottom time and his air supply were declining rapidly. He also ran through his mind a few scenarios as to what he might encounter on the other side of the wreck and considered how he might deal with them. A panicked, struggling diver, for instance, would likely take a big effort to subdue, bringing both Chris and the diver closer to very serious trouble.

However, as he swam over the edge of the wreck, Chris realized it had all been for naught. Resting on the seafloor below was the diver's tank and BCD, the regulator still trickling a small amount of air as it hovered above the rig. The diver was nowhere to be seen.

8

"Look," said Chris as he paused to take a breath. "All I'm saying is—"

"Yes, what are you saying exactly?" asked Mac. "Because it sounds like you're handling me."

"All I'm saying is," Chris continued, "you know you have a history of losing yourself during the infatuation period of a new relationship. You do too much to try and endear yourself, and the women run away because it's overbearing. It happened with Beth. It happened with Susan. I don't want to see that happen with Dana. It's obviously early days, but you seem to be enjoying each other."

The pair walked through the front doors of the Ritz-Carlton on Key Biscayne still sweating from their run along the beach. Both wore shorts, sweat-stained T-shirts, and battered baseball caps.

They'd run north along the waterfront to the edge of the island, a total distance of six miles. The lobby was bustling with activity as people came and went to the pool and beach adjacent to the hotel. Families predominated, with parents herding masses of small children anxious to get in the ocean. Mac leaned against the lobby wall to stretch his calves and didn't respond.

"I'm not trying to handle you," said Chris, pushing on despite Mac's lack of response. "I've got bigger fish to fry with trying to help this mission succeed. If you relax for a minute and pull your head out, you'll see what I'm talking about."

Chris finished his hip and hamstring stretches and moved deeper into the lobby. He had stayed at the hotel twice before on previous visits to the nearby marine lab, pointing out to his university travel overseers that its proximity to the lab made sense as a base of operations despite the cost. The proximity to the ocean for long swims as well as the running path along the beach were important attributes that he kept to himself. Sarah was waiting for them in the lounge, again clad in agency-related apparel. She was sitting with a woman in a floral print dress and sandy brown hair just brushing her shoulders. Chris recognized her immediately.

"Carrie!" said Chris, leaning in to give his old friend a hug. "It has been too long."

Dr. Carrie Best stood up to give Chris a stronger hug. "Nothing like a sweaty hug from an old friend."

"Right, sorry."

"And this must be Mac," added Carrie as she reached her hand out to Mac, who'd walked over behind Chris. "I've heard a thing or two about you over the years."

"Mac, Carrie was with the seafloor mapping group in New Hampshire back when I was in Woods Hole for grad school."

"Ah, yes, I remember," replied Mac, shaking Carrie's hand. "I'll spare you a second sweaty hug. It's nice to meet you in person."

The group moved through the generous lobby area and sat down on couches situated in a corner, somewhat isolated from other guests. Chris could see that Sarah was carrying a manila folder full of what he assumed was paperwork associated with the diving incident off Fort Lauderdale two days earlier. *That stonefish took at least one poor bastard down with him.*

Sarah motioned to Carrie, who began. "So, Chris, you know I'm here to give you the latest topographic imagery we have for the area where the *Calypso I* is deployed down in the Dry Tortugas. I have that all on a hard drive here in my bag. But I don't know if you were aware that I'm the chair of the Diving Control Board here at the university."

"I knew you were on the faculty," Chris replied, "but I didn't know you were on the DCB too. I guess committee assignments find us wherever we go."

"That they do. I know that both you and Mac are well versed in the DCB's charge, so I will not belabor those details here. The board has already reviewed the incident report."

"Already?" asked Mac. "That's fast."

"Yes, well, had the mortality been among one of our divers, the process would look very different. The only reason we are involved is that the two of you were diving under our auspices on Monday and we want to make sure all the details of the incident are clear."

"And?" asked Chris, arching his eyebrows.

"*And*," replied Carrie, pointing at Chris, "you are supposed to be joining the saturation mission this weekend."

"So?"

"So we'd prefer if there were no distractions from the mission."

"Distractions? We saved some lives, Carrie," said Chris, sitting back in his chair. "What would you have us do instead? Watch as three people die? You don't think that would have been a worse distraction?"

"Of course not," said Carrie, turning her hands palms up. "The mission is high profile, Chris, and therefore has plenty of detractors. Nobody wants to give them fodder."

"Including me. I didn't have to fly all the way out here to help out, you know. There's plenty for me to do back home." Chris was incredulous, almost kicking himself for volunteering his expertise.

"I know, Chris; everyone appreciates that. The quick thinking on both your parts saved two lives, indeed." Carrie paged through the file. "Mr., um, Mr. Langton is still in intensive care, but he is expected to make a full recovery."

"Has he indicated that he learned *anything* from the event?" asked Mac, as he stood up to stretch his legs again. "It's one thing to be reckless and stupid. It's another to fail to recognize the stupidity."

"I think the jury is still out on that one," answered Carrie. "I interviewed him personally, and all I can say is that he's pretty distraught over the loss of his business partner, Mr. Hayward."

"What about the photographer?" continued Mac, sitting back down in a chair next to Chris.

"Mr. Brody is very thankful for all your help. I think his attitude is exactly what you would hope it would be. He will likely be a better diver because of the incident. And he's eager to meet you, by the way."

"I'm happy to meet him, but maybe after we're done with the *Calypso* mission. I'd hate to cause another distraction."

"Come on, Chris, no need to be so sour. This mission is a big deal for everyone involved—the students, the DCB, Senator Pierce, the UN. I know you know that the politics involved make this a public relations nightmare. Nobody is implying you and Mac did anything you shouldn't have done. On the contrary. But nobody wants the possibility of danger anywhere near the *Calypso*."

"I know, I'm sorry."

"Any sign of Hayward's body?" asked Mac, trying to steer the conversation in a different direction.

"No, it hasn't been found, despite a considerable recovery effort," said Carrie. "Chris, the real reason I'm here is—"

"Other than to tell me to lay low?" Chris smiled.

Carrie rolled her eyes. "The real reason I'm here is that we've reviewed your dive computer log." Carrie smiled at Chris. "Remarkably, it appears you were able to help the divers without compromising your no-decompression dive profile."

"Oh. Yeah, that wouldn't have helped my case for supporting the mission," said Chris, suddenly feeling bad for having pounced on Carrie. His heroics could, in fact, have sabotaged his participation. "We wouldn't let anyone get near a research dive op after getting bent."

"That's true," replied Mac. "At least not without full medical clearance from a dive-savvy doctor."

"How are both of you feeling?" asked Carrie. "No residual effects?"

"Tip-top," answered Chris distractedly, as his eye was drawn to a large-screen TV behind the bar at the other side of the lounge. "I'll be getting a head-to-toe checkup by the mission doc when I head down to the Tortugas in a couple of days." The flashing red banner at the top of the screen read "Breaking News: Key Biscayne Runners Stabbed," and he could see police and emergency personnel milling around a stretch of the running path he and Mac had just come from.

"Can you excuse me for a second?" Chris asked, standing up.

"Excuse me, would you mind turning up the sound for a minute?" he asked the bartender. The young woman produced a remote control from behind the bar and turned up the volume.

"Reports are still coming in," the talking head explained. "But it appears that two men were attacked while jogging along the beach here in Key Biscayne. The authorities have not released their names, but we have been told that both were in their forties.

"Witnesses reported a man wearing a hooded sweatshirt, possibly with short blond hair, leaped out from behind the seawall to strike at each of the men with a knife. He then fled on foot. The authorities are still looking for the suspect. Attacks like this have become more and more common . . ."

"What's up?" asked Mac as he materialized next to Chris.

"Two men were just stabbed in an attack along the beach. They were both jogging. It must have happened right after we went past."

"I guess we dodged a bullet," observed Mac.

"Well, a knife really," answered Chris. "But yeah."

"One guy with a knife doesn't really worry me," said Mac. "Those electric bikes on the running path are far scarier. They cruise way too fast, and you can't hear them coming. If they're going to get me, I predict it will be on one of those."

Chris watched the footage of the running path as it was recycled over and over. Something about the incident bothered him, but he knew Mac was right. Probabilistically, the risk was much greater from more commonplace threats like speeding e-bikes.

"Unearned speed . . ." he observed quietly.

9

Aaron Bash accelerated through a red light, one hand resting casually on the top of the steering wheel and the other on a loaded .45 Smith and Wesson sitting on the seat to his right. In his wake, a Toyota hybrid rear-ended another car as it skidded to a stop to avoid crashing into Bash's massive white pickup truck. Bash ignored the honking.

Heading northwest out of Fort Lauderdale on US Route 27, as he crossed over a bridge, Bash casually flicked a knife out the passenger-side window into the canal below. He doubted anyone would be able to ID him or his buddy for the stabbing of the two runners down in Key Biscayne, but there was no sense in keeping the knife he'd used. He had lots of knives.

For the third time in the past half hour, Bash looked down at the phone sitting on the seat next to his gun and rejected the call. *Martinez. I know what I'm doing*, he thought.

At five-foot, six inches tall, Bash was often overlooked as a physical threat to those around him. But within two years of his graduation from an alternative school for students who'd been involved with the justice system as minors, Bash clashed with the law again and had spent two sixth-month sentences in the Orange County lockup for assault and assault with a deadly weapon. Both charges derived from fights he'd started—and finished—at bars frequented by community college students from three nearby campuses. The deadly weapon had been the leg of a broken chair that Bash had used to beat a male student so severely that he never fully recovered from the multiple head injuries.

Bash had still been in lockup when a young paralegal had visited his cell, explaining that the aunt he'd been living with had died at the hands of her husband. With his uncle now in jail for manslaughter, Bash was his aunt's only remaining family member. He'd inherited a one-year-old pickup truck, three handguns, a rifle, and twenty thousand dollars.

After his release, Bash got himself a job at a fast-food restaurant, where he overhead a group of customers talking about an immigration protest scheduled for the next day at Orlando International Airport. He skipped work and joined. The small, short-lived protest had included approximately sixty people carrying signs and chanting America First slogans on the sidewalk outside the baggage claim area. A middle-aged woman had thrust a flyer into his hand as he'd stood watching. The only thing on the flyer was a single black pixelated square. He knew that the square was a QR code and that if he pointed his smartphone's camera at the square, it would likely take him to a website.

Bash had sat at home in Orlando on the couch iteratively watching dashcam videos of Russian car crashes on YouTube and studying the flyer for several days before he'd finally clicked on the QR code. He landed on a simple website that directed him to a clearinghouse, including links for multiple different social media accounts.

He'd clicked on one entitled "Take a Hostage." It featured three masked men sitting around a table in a basement discussing how they were going to abduct the mayor of a small city.

He'd clicked on another entitled "Kill the Postman First," which argued that the US Postal Service was first and foremost a vehicle for government control of its citizens. "When the civil war starts," the silhouetted man on the screen explained through a voice-masking device, "you have to stop the mail first."

Bash quit his job at the restaurant, choosing to live off the twenty thousand dollars he received from his aunt. He'd watched each of the links on the website, some of them twice. He'd clicked on links nested within links and found even more.

One of those links led him to something called the Federal Brotherhood Initiative. They were looking for new members to help wage the battles no one else could.

His phone rang again.

"Yeah, I know it was the wrong guys," Bash screamed into the phone sitting on the seat next to the .45 with the speakerphone enabled. "What can I tell you?"

Fuck. He accelerated through another stoplight.

"Wrong guys?" Martinez said. "I don't know what you're talking about. I want to know what happened off Lauderdale."

"We were close, very close," Bash explained. "But the cops were all over us. We could have rammed the research vessel easily. That's what I wanted to do. But we figured that would've just looked like an accident. Nothing like the impact we were hoping for."

"So, what happened?" asked Martinez.

"We turned at the last moment and took off."

"And the cops?"

"Once we got out into open water, their boat was no match for the *Patriot*," answered Bash. "We hauled ass out of there and turned south."

"So a fuck up, but not a total disaster," observed Martinez. "Hopefully they think it was just some drunk college students out in daddy's boat. So, what were you saying before about the wrong guys?"

"Hang on, I've got to deal with a cop pulling in behind me," explained Bash, as he spotted flashing red lights in his rearview mirror.

He clicked the phone off without listening to a reply as he pulled over to the side of the highway. He rolled down the driver's side window and placed the .45 in his lap. *This shouldn't take long,* he thought. *But I'll have to swap plates after it's done.*

10

"Dr. Black? I've really enjoyed your presentation. But this mission seems very dangerous. Am I missing something?"

Chris, now wearing a tan sport coat over a white Oxford button-down and dark blue jeans, paused to surveil the two-hundred-plus people assembled in the large auditorium, including undergraduate and graduate students as well as many from the general public. The Bill and Rose Davis Auditorium was located on Virginia Key, across the Bear Cut Bridge from Key Biscayne and immediately below South Miami Beach. It was immediately adjacent to the marine lab campus of the university, serving both as an academic and a public venue for presentations, concerts, and a wide variety of other events.

The wall to his left was covered in smoked glass. Once the sun had set, the blinds had lifted automatically to reveal the evening lights of Key Biscayne beyond. Miami Beach was just to the north.

He'd been invited to the university by the organizers of the *Calypso I* mission to give the first presentation of what would be a multipart lecture series once the mission was underway. The original plan for the evening had involved a panel discussion scheduled immediately after Chris's talk that would include Senator Pierce from Vermont as well as several local politicians. Chris had learned only five minutes before his talk that the panel discussion had been canceled and that he'd need to extend his presentation by twenty minutes to fill the time. That was fine with Chris, as he enjoyed public presentations and was happy to avoid interacting with politicians.

"Think about it this way. Years ago, I read this article in the *New Yorker* magazine on entrepreneurs. What's the first thing that comes to mind when you think of entrepreneurs?"

"Risk takers," called out a guy from the back row.

"Exactly," replied Chris. "What's your name?"

"Omar."

"Do you want to elaborate on that point, Omar?"

"Uh, no." There were some chuckles around the room. Chris joined them.

"Well, you nailed it, Omar. That is exactly what most people would say. I would have, too, had I not read this article. But the point of the article was that not only are entrepreneurs *not* risk takers, they're the exact opposite."

"What's the exact opposite of a risk taker?" asked Andrew, a grad student seated in the front row.

"Someone who only undertakes an activity after considerable research and training, both of which eliminate much of the perceived risk," answered Chris. "The activity only *seems* risky to those who know nothing about it. If you haven't trained for it, of course it seems outrageous."

As he paused, the room grew so quiet one could hear the proverbial pin drop.

"Saturation diving is effectively like cave diving—once your body has become saturated with nitrogen, you can't go to the surface quickly without getting the bends, so it is very much like having a ceiling above you. You have to solve your problems at depth, as opposed to the surface. Can anyone remind me what happens with the bends?"

"It's painful," called out someone Chris couldn't see.

"It's caused by nitrogen bubbles, right?" asked another.

"You're both right," said Chris. "The bends result from the nitrogen you inhale during a dive but don't metabolize. If you ascend slowly, the bubbles work their way out of the bloodstream into your lungs and you simply exhale them.

"But if you ascend without taking sufficient time, those bubbles can race through your bloodstream and accumulate in your joints, causing extraordinary pain and contortions, hence the bends." He paused for effect. "That sounds dangerous, right?"

"It does," replied a student named Corin who was sitting next to Andrew. "Cave divers die all the time."

"You're right, Corin. There clearly *is* danger, but saturation diving is not reckless, it's a calculated risk. Thinking back to that *New Yorker* article, the danger occurs in the context of total preparation. Which I think is different from the more abstract danger that most people fixate on. If you've received proper training, you can anticipate danger and hence avoid it. Or should a dangerous situation arise after all, you're prepared. I've done six missions to the *Poseidon* undersea lab down in the Keys, and the training has been excellent, every single time."

"But the danger still finds you, doesn't it?" Sitting behind Corin and Andrew was a woman Chris hadn't noticed earlier. Her scarf covered much of her head, but it didn't conceal her striking hazel eyes. Unlike many of the young students in the room, this woman's eyes conveyed a depth of experience that youth would never comprehend.

"I'm not sure what you mean," replied Chris.

"I Googled your name before coming to see you speak tonight," the woman continued. "And found dozens of stories from California, South Africa, and the Galapagos in less than a second. I assume there are others. How do you reconcile those incidents with your entrepreneur theory of danger?"

"Those incidents had nothing to do with scientific research," said Chris. Throughout the audience he could see people's faces illuminated by their smartphones and tablets as, he assumed, they conducted searches on his name.

"Okay, then perhaps you can tell me what your opinion is on the protests outside this auditorium right now," said the woman.

Chris looked toward Sarah Henson and Carrie Best, who were both standing to the left of the stage. "I wasn't aware of any protests. Perhaps we'll go outside and check it out."

Open conversations started throughout the audience.

"I'd be happy to talk with you after," Chris said to the woman before turning toward the larger audience. "I think I've outlived my welcome. Thank you everyone. I'm sorry the panel discussion didn't work out, but I hope you learned something about the mission. I can hang around for a few minutes if anyone has any other questions."

Following applause, Chris was immediately swarmed at the podium by people wanting to ask questions they were likely too shy to ask in front of an audience. *Were the kidnappers in the Galapagos real pirates? Did you get to keep any of the gold from South Africa? What's it like to be attacked by a great white shark?*

While he answered questions, Chris casually surveyed the room for the woman with the hazel eyes. She had not come forward to follow up on her questions and was nowhere to be seen.

However, Chris did notice two men standing at the back of the room. Their size—both were muscular—and their garb—both looked like military—stood in stark contrast to the rest of the audience. One of the men had an eye patch. They blended into the departing crowd before Chris had a chance to ponder why their presence had bothered him.

11

"What's going on outside?" asked Chris, as he joined Sarah Henson, Carrie Best, and Mac in the green room behind the stage.

"I mentioned earlier that there might be a protest in front of the auditorium," replied Sarah. "As soon as the panel discussion was announced, several groups applied for official protest permits."

"It's happening," said Mac. "I just snuck a look out the theater's side door and chaos reigns out there."

"Why protest here?" asked Chris. "Not because of my presentation, I hope."

"Not because of you per se, but the mission for sure," answered Sarah.

"The mission's happening hundreds of miles from here," added Chris. "And who protests talks by fish ecologists like me?"

"I told you this mission is a public relations nightmare, Chris. Where there is a politician, there is protest," said Carrie. "Particularly if Senator Pierce from Vermont is involved. Many groups down here in Florida absolutely hate her. Plus, I think the Keys are too far for most of these people to travel for a protest, so they came here. Given the connection to the mission, your presentation and the panel were as good a rallying point as any other."

"So, I am providing a distraction yet again?" Chris smiled facetiously.

"Oh, stop it, Chris." Carrie playfully punched his shoulder.

"Ouch."

"How did you get involved in this, anyway?" asked Carrie.

"The idea for the saturation mission came from an international NGO called Science Without Borders, which is headquartered in Vermont," explained Chris. "I'm sure that's why Pierce is involved. And maybe because of the UN connection too. I've seen her on cable news pushing for stronger international ties. I've never worked with the Borders group or the UN, so this seemed like an interesting chance to get involved."

"So, they contacted you?" asked Sarah.

"A guy named Frank Donagan first told me about it when we were in the Galapagos," Chris continued. "He works for the US State Department. And our colleague Hendrix encouraged me as well. Initially, he was going to be involved with the mission security when it was planned for the Middle East. After Frank and Hendrix briefed me on the possibility, I received a formal request from someone in DC to come serve as an adviser. With *Poseidon* currently the only undersea lab in the world dedicated to research, I'm a huge supporter of any project focused on increasing opportunities for extended stays underwater."

Donagan and Hendrix had both featured prominently in Chris and Mac's recent adventures. Hendrix had served in the Navy with Mac, before starting his own security consultant company.

"Who requested your official participation?" asked Carrie. "It seems strange that it would come from DC."

"I don't remember the guy's name. Anyway," Chris went on, "someone determined that starting in the Middle East was too ambitious.

I have to agree with that. So, the whole plan was shifted to the Dry Tortugas where things can be more easily controlled for the first go-around. One of the aquanauts from the original mission plan, Nat Gamal, is still on the team."

"A former Congressman who's serving as an unofficial representative of the US government for the mission wants to meet with you tonight before you go down to the Keys," said Sarah.

"*Tonight?*" asked Chris.

Sarah furrowed her brow and looked at Chris. "Yes, Congressman Rhodes. I forget which state he represented."

"Actually, that's the guy who invited me," said Chris.

"*Grampen* Rhodes?" asked Mac, the surprise clear in his voice. He leaned his head back and laughed out loud. "Things just got even more interesting."

"How so?" asked Chris.

"This is the congressman from North Carolina," Mac explained. "Supposedly a religious guy. Basically, he got kicked out of Congress for 'inappropriate contact' with several interns."

"Copy that," said Chris. "Pierce must really be enjoying working with someone like that. Why isn't she here tonight?"

"The company line is that she was pulled away on business," replied Sarah. "But I'm pretty sure she heard about the planned protest and decided to stay away."

"Interesting. From what I've seen on the news, she doesn't seem like someone who would shy away from a fight," said Chris. "How do you remember Rhodes?" he asked Mac.

"He used to be on the House Armed Services Committee. Big weapons enthusiast. Used to come out to our SEAL training camps for no obvious reason."

"Mac, you were a SEAL?" asked Carrie. "I don't think Chris ever mentioned that."

Mac lifted his knee and tapped it.

"Yeah, I was a SEAL for all of about four years, until my knee got shot out from under me. Now I'm just a simple ROV pilot."

"You're not a simple anything," suggested Chris. "I'd like to stick my head outside to check out this rally/protest. Mac, you coming?"

12

Leland Jones, seated at the head of the table, his gray hair closely cropped, his suit tight on his large frame, smacked a sweaty hand down on the glasstop, leaving a moist outline of five fingers behind. "Okay, everyone out! Sumner and Dirksen, you stay."

"That was a fucking awful report," he continued after the door closed behind the last man to leave. "Fucking awful."

A light rain fell outside the third-story conference room in central Florida. Water droplets collected on the reflective glass that extended from floor to ceiling along two of the four walls. In addition to being impervious to the weather, the conference room was also opaque to all electronic surveillance and the glass could withstand direct hits from even high-caliber weapons.

Jones, Sumner, and Dirksen sat around a twelve-by-four-foot table constructed from imported Indonesian hardwoods. The two walls of the room not covered with glass were adorned with depictions of military conquests ranging from a painting of George Washington's winter crossing of the Delaware River to a grainy image of the D-Day assault on Omaha Beach in World War II, to more recent images of military contractors clad in desert fatigues against the backdrop of

Afghan mountains. The room was only partially illuminated by ceiling lights placed along one wall.

"Down one hundred and fifty million a quarter?" asked Jones. "Jesus Christ. Two more quarters like that and we'll be ruined." When his father had died suddenly of a heart attack decades before, Jones had been thrust into a leadership position with the consultant company, Unity Environmental, his father had created after Vietnam.

He'd taken millions out of the company over the years to fund a lavish lifestyle. That lifestyle, which included three houses, several yachts, and more cars than Jones could count, depended on a constant income stream. He didn't relish the idea of having to tell his wife they were scaling back. In fact, he was certain that she would leave him.

"Yes, the financial news is not good," agreed Derrick Sumner, as he looked down to brush a piece of lint off his tailored Italian suit. "But that is not why you've cleared the room, is it?"

Derrick Sumner had worked with Jones dating back to their fraternity days. He'd spent his senior year of college working to keep Jones from being kicked out of the university, first for fighting, then for harassment of several women at their sister sorority. When he graduated from law school in Pennsylvania, Sumner had accepted a job from Jones Senior that was essentially focused on keeping Jones Junior out of any legal trouble that would prevent him from someday leading Unity Environmental.

Sumner reached out from his chair across from Dirksen and tossed her a spiral-bound notebook. "Have you seen this yet?"

"What is that?" Dirksen offered without touching the notebook. She was older than both men in the room, her graying hair pulled back from a nearly wrinkleless face characterized by bright blue eyes. "Something to do with your little boys' club?"

"God damnit, Sharon!" said Jones, turning back to the table. "You know I don't appreciate that characterization."

Sumner smirked. Jones was so easy to wind up.

"I apologize," said Dirksen after a moment. "Please tell us what's happening with the Florida Brotherhood Initiative."

Jones grasped the top of the chair next to Sumner with both hands, his knuckles turning white under the force of his grip. He had struggled to diversify Unity Environmental's business portfolio since taking over the company. Where his father had favored reliable income streams associated with domestic FEMA disaster response contracts and international consultations with the United Nations, Jones Junior had doubled down on weapons sales and military contracts. While the past two decades had proven lucrative for those branches of the business, the proliferation of companies with similar business plans to Unity and the end of the conflicts in Iraq and Afghanistan had resulted in a noticeable decline in revenue.

Five years prior, while attending a weekend retreat in northern Virginia, Jones had been encouraged by several colleagues to invest in the burgeoning militia movement across the US.

"People in Kevlar running around with guns? How can that possibly help my business?" he'd asked aloud, a cigar in one hand and a whiskey in the other.

"The movement is much more sophisticated than that, Leland," a colleague had explained. "*Much* more sophisticated. These groups are helping to shape policy, at both state and federal levels."

"And . . ."

"And in our business, as you know, there is a direct line from policy to moneymaking opportunities."

Jones had hunkered down with Sumner the week after that retreat to consider their options. They'd had Dirksen collect information on several of the major groups around the country. The upshot of Dirksen's research was that while in aggregate the militias were possibly leading to policy adjustments, the practices of individual groups were quite volatile. It was not clear how direct investment in any single group would work to the advantage of Unity.

Weeks had passed before Dirksen had proposed the obvious solution. "There are more than seventy militia-type groups in Florida alone, but none of them meet our needs. I think we have to create our own."

"Our own?" Jones had asked. "We create our own group? How would that help us, exactly?"

"That's actually a very interesting idea, Leland," Sumner had interjected. "Think about it. We could use them strategically to help shift public opinion on issues relevant to our contracts. Hell, we'll just be looking for headlines and TV coverage."

Sumner moved into Jones's personal space and dropped his voice to a barely audible level.

"But it would have to be delicate. We'll set up finances that will be controlled by us but that will never be traced to us."

"Exactly," Dirksen had replied. "We control what the group does, but no one knows it's us. The group itself won't even know who we are. We'll have total deniability."

"Okay. But how do we create a militia?" Jones had asked.

"I don't think we have to start from scratch," answered Sumner. "There's a group I looked into called the Brotherhood. They're not a militia, but I think they're headed in that direction. They're primarily online right now, but their membership numbers are impressive and their social media posts get a lot of traction. Perhaps a little financial push from us will prompt them to take the next step."

The broad strokes of the Federal Brotherhood Initiative were outlined within the week, and Dirksen had been tasked with reaching out to Jeremiah Fessler, the leader of the group.

The rain picked up, pelting the conference room window.

"So, explain this current operation to me," said Jones. "And why is that bitch Pierce down here?"

"They're setting up an undersea laboratory in the Dry Tortugas with scientists participating in a ten-day mission," explained Sumner.

"An international collaboration. Lots of fanfare. Training starts at the end of next week. Pierce is here to take advantage of the press. The NGO funding the mission is from Vermont."

"I wondered what brought her down here," said Jones. "It's common knowledge that she hates the south. But how does upsetting this mission advance our needs?"

Sumner knew the room was protected from any type of outside surveillance, but it still made him uncomfortable discussing the plans for the coming days out loud.

"Look, Leland. We've got five major weapons contracts waiting for approval," replied Sumner. "Like you just said, if we don't get those, the company's going under."

"But—"

"But give me a second," continued Sumner. "We need congressional approval, and to get that we really only need to sway five votes. This isn't rocket science. A little violence and some bad press, and those five votes will swing our way. This mission is happening right *in our own backyard*, and Pierce is pushing it hard. If we do this right, we can secure our contracts *and* fuck over Pierce at the same time."

"What's our risk?" asked Jones.

"We have minimal risk," explained Sumner. "So far, all the effort's been online. Fessler and his group have been ramping up social media efforts opposing the mission for more than a month now. There's a protest against the UN engagement going on tonight down in Miami."

"And once the mission starts?" asked Jones.

"That's when the shit really hits the fan," replied Sumner. "You don't want to know what they've got planned. I've tasked Shaw with keeping an eye on that part of the operation."

"So that's where he's been . . ." said Jones.

13

"Are you ready to meet with Rhodes?" yelled Sarah as she leaned in toward Chris, cupping her hand by his ear to communicate above the sound of the protesters.

"Okay," yelled Chris in reply without moving his eyes from the massive group of protesters in the courtyard outside the auditorium. The perimeter of the courtyard was ringed by a series of evenly spaced concrete bollards to prevent automobiles from entering the area. It had been empty when he and Mac arrived before his presentation, but it was now impossible to see any of the courtyard through the mass of chanting protesters.

Stepping back into the entryway of the auditorium immediately dialed down the commotion significantly. While Chris could still see the protests raging outside through the smoked glass, none of the melee penetrated the building. He heard only the footsteps on marbled floors and muted conversations of the busy staff. "I'll just hang out in the courtyard and watch the protest," Mac suggested. "Wake me up when you come out."

"*Wake* you up?" asked Carrie.

"Mac can sleep anywhere," explained Chris. "It's uncanny."

"*Okay*. Chris, I'm headed back to the hotel," said Carrie. "We have a mapping conference starting next week, and I need to keep things moving forward."

"Organize it, or I'll organize it for you," said Chris. "Isn't that how it used to go?"

Sarah laughed. "I've never heard that one, but it fits. I'll be waiting for you guys when you're done."

Chris hugged his friend goodbye. "Be careful out there. And thanks for all the bathymetric data on the study area. Looking through all of it last night, I already feel like I know the area pretty well."

"*I'm* the one who should be careful? Seriously, Chris. Watch yourself. Regardless of your favorite *New Yorker* article, the mission you're joining will be dangerous."

Chris followed a young woman down a long hallway into the interior of the massive auditorium space. She eventually opened an unmarked door to reveal a lounge area. Sitting on a couch immediately opposite the door was a large, bald man in a short-sleeved shirt with a red tie. Despite the air conditioning throughout the building, sweat-stained areas outnumbered dry areas on the man's shirt.

Rhodes. This guy looks minutes away from a major cardiac event, Chris thought.

Rhodes smiled and reached out an expansive hand. Chris was instantly wary given Mac's comments about the guy's behavior while in Congress. But something about Rhodes was engaging.

"Dr. Black. Great to meet you! I'm Grampen Rhodes. You can call me Gramp."

"Okay, Gramp. Please call me Chris."

"Sounds like a plan. Please have a seat," replied Rhodes, motioning to a chair positioned across from him. "Safe trip from the Left Coast?"

"Yes, sir. But I've already been here for several days, so I've had time to adjust."

"Not your first trip, I understand." It didn't escape Chris that Rhodes was underhandedly announcing that he had a lot of information available to him.

"That's true. I've been to Florida many times."

"Why so many visits? Research?" asked Rhodes.

"Mostly," responded Chris. "I love California, but I'm not averse to some warm water diving from time to time."

"Well, I entered the ocean once for my baptism," replied Rhodes. "And that was it for me. I'll leave the ocean exploration to young folks like yourself."

"Is Senator Pierce going to be joining us?" asked Chris, hoping to glean some insight into how Rhodes and Pierce were interacting.

"No, I think Gwendolyn takes every opportunity to avoid me." Rhodes laughed. "And I can't blame her. If there were two people less alike than the two of us, I'd like to meet them."

Two quick knocks on the door preceded Frank Donagan's entry into the room. Donagan was allegedly a State Department employee whom Chris had first met in South Africa, and then encountered again more recently in the Galapagos Islands. Chris was pretty sure Donagan was much more than a diplomat. The man had a habit of appearing when Chris least expected it, generally to help, which, however, sometimes complicated the situation.

Chris lowered his head in a slow nod, smiling at the fact that Donagan had appeared once again. He also observed that Frank's outfit—a dark suit, white shirt, no tie—rarely varied regardless of which continent he was on.

"Dr. Black!"

Chris stood to shake Donagan's outstretched hand. "Good to see you, Frank. I just had a feeling you'd be in the vicinity."

"Oh, I'm always in the vicinity," replied Donagan.

"I figured that the international angle of this mission might draw someone like you in," explained Chris.

"Correct," replied Donagan. "And a healthy slice of domestic politics as well. Senator Pierce's involvement definitely adds a potential destabilizing element."

"Destabilizing how?" asked Chris.

"She polarizes nearly every room she enters," answered Donagan. "People either love her or hate her. I haven't met many in between."

"You two know each other?" Rhodes asked with obvious surprise.

"Yes. I've had the good fortune to work with Dr. Black and his team on several occasions. Very recently, in fact."

"Ah, yes. I understand that you've had some adventures," said Rhodes, tapping a file sitting on the couch to his left. "I'll answer your questions, Chris, but I'd first like to hear what you think of the mission."

"From a scientific perspective, the mission seems tractable," said Chris. "I've met the team and they seem capable, and from what I can tell, their respective projects are doable. The public outreach side of things will no doubt be overwhelming for them, but I can help."

"You've participated in several missions like this before," said Rhodes.

"If you mean saturation missions to an undersea lab, yes. I guess some of that is in your file there. But every mission is different, each presenting its own unique challenges."

"The mission is a major international collaboration, and from my perspective, none of the scientists have the necessary experience. I want the mission to be a success, so I offered to help find the right guy. I believe I did." Rhodes smiled and Chris could see how people might fall for his charm.

But something told Chris to tread carefully.

"I'm hardly the only scientist with saturation diving experience," said Chris. "Don't get me wrong, I'm happy to help. But since I received your letter, I've been wondering about my involvement. And may I ask what you mean by success?"

"You came highly recommended," replied Rhodes, waving his hand. "And I don't think I understand your question."

"Well, any mission like this presents some extraordinary challenges. Aside from the fact that the ocean always finds a way to complicate even the best made plans—"

"That's true," Donagan interrupted. "I've seen marine weather disrupt your seagoing operations on two continents in the last several months."

"Right," agreed Chris, "but unpredictable weather aside, add in the human factor when people of various cultures and political persuasions are working together on a science project, and success suddenly has several dimensions. So, I must ask," Chris continued, "if to you success involves groundbreaking science or groundbreaking publicity. Are you hoping for peer-reviewed journal publications? Cutting-edge discoveries? Or are photo ops sufficient? Answers to these questions will help you calibrate your expectations. And it'll help me to understand how best to support the two aquanaut teams."

"Hmm. Good questions," said Rhodes, sitting back in his chair and furrowing his prominent brow. "Thanks for stopping by," added Rhodes, looking at his watch as he quickly rose to his feet and headed for the door. "We'll be in touch."

Chris watched the door close, trying to make sense of the conversation he'd just had. "Frank, what the hell was that? He didn't answer either of my questions."

"That's par for the course in the political arena," explained Donagan. "You better get used to that."

"I thought *you* were evasive," said Chris, sitting forward on his chair. "But in comparison you look positively effusive. Did you give him my name? Is that how I got into this?"

"Not exactly," replied Frank. "The State Department was asked to come up with a shortlist of names for US-based scientists who might be appropriate to support the mission. After our conversation in the

Galapagos when you'd expressed interest, I added your name to that list. But as to how and why you were picked, that is a question for Rhodes."

"A question that he evidently doesn't want to answer," observed Chris.

14

"The best stone crabs in Miami?" asked Mac excitedly over the din of the protesters' chants, which had diminished somewhat over the past half hour. "How could one even begin to know that? What is a stone crab, anyway?"

As Chris and Mac walked back toward where Sarah had parked her van, they discussed a plan for dinner.

"Just calm yourself, dude. We'll get there and you'll see. There's no sign outside, no menu available, no list of prices. Just a bunch of wooden tables and the best stone crabs you can imagine. Sarah took me there three years ago, and I haven't been able to eat any other crab since."

"Hmph. I just thought you'd given it up."

Mac continued to talk about crabs as the pair made their way through the crowd of protesters. Chris noted that no one was paying any attention to them, focusing their anger at each other. Signs called for "No UN in the Keys!" and "Climate change knows no borders, so neither should science!" One group's signs focused on "America First," while another's advocated for something like "Internationalism."

The crowd still filled the majority of the large courtyard in front of the auditorium, extending from the perimeter established by security guards immediately in front of the building and past the row of large protective bollards out to the street. As Chris and Mac reached the other side of the crowd, Chris spotted Sarah's blue van parked in a small lot approximately fifty yards east. Standing on the curb, protesters milling around and chanting immediately behind him, his eyes drifted up the street. He caught sight of an old, blue Ford pickup coming down the slight hill from the bridge. Something about its speed concerned him.

"Mac . . ."

"I see it too," replied Mac, instantly. "It's coming too quickly. We gotta get these people back. You take the people on the right, and I'll go left."

"Look out!" screamed Chris, as he turned around waving his arms. "Get back behind the bollards!" Several of the protesters close to him responded, but the larger crowd was too preoccupied with their protestations to hear him.

The truck did not slow at all. As it approached, Chris recognized the two men he'd seen in the back of the auditorium in the front seat. The man with the eye patch was driving. The passenger held an Uzi.

Chris and Mac had separated in their efforts to clear the crowd. As the truck jumped the curb between the two of them, Chris watched in horror as it plowed into the crowd only feet from him, sending bodies flying from both camps of protesters. In the chaos of bodies and fleeing protesters he lost sight of Mac.

The large bollards protecting the building stopped the truck in its tracks, folding the front engine compartment back on itself. Smoke poured from the engine, but Chris saw no immediate sign of fire. From Chris's vantage point behind the truck, it looked like the driver, with no air bag support from the older vehicle, had been knocked unconscious. But the passenger remained conscious. He leaned out the shattered passenger-side window and started shooting into the crowd with short bursts from the Uzi.

The screams of the injured and the terrified filled the courtyard. While many people from the crowd were fleeing the scene, several protesters from both sides remained behind to help the wounded. Chris saw Mac disentangle himself from the mass of people hit by the truck's initial approach, apparently uninjured. They both joined the rescue effort by pulling the wounded back behind whatever cover they could find. Those who could move freely were encouraged to run to neighboring buildings or up the street. Those who were unable to move were encouraged to hunker down adjacent to dead bodies, which on the sidewalk or street was really the only option.

Staying low and moving quickly, Chris checked the people closest to him; the first three, two men and a woman, were dead. He spotted an older Latino man helping two young women get to their feet and he jumped in to assist in moving them away from the car and out of the line of fire. One of the women dragged her misshapen left leg behind her.

Briefly protected behind one of the concrete bollards lining the courtyard, Chris could see that the man was covered in blood. He said, "Sir, you're injured. Let me get you out of here."

"No, I'm helping," said the man in Spanish-accented English, patting his chest with his blood-covered hand. "I'm Ramon."

"Okay, Ramon, let's keep going," replied Chris, peering around the bollard to see who needed help.

Moving to their left, Chris and Ramon helped a young protester to his feet. Chris could see a tire mark across the kid's chest, but he was somehow alive and breathing.

Still working in the path the truck had cut through the crowd, the pair next moved to help a man who was crawling away from the vehicle, pulling himself along the flat concrete sidewalk with the palms of his hands. The man's legs were broken.

The repeated shots from the Uzi were deafening. Chris could see the gunman's range was limited by the truck's position and his awkward angle from the broken passenger-side window, so most of his bullets were hitting the downed bodies of people who were likely already dead.

Detecting new movement out of the corner of his eye, Chris looked right, half expecting to see some new threat. But instead, he saw a photographer approaching several yards behind the vehicle, shooting images of the scene as she gingerly stepped over dead protesters while crouching to avoid flying bullets. He was simultaneously horrified by the risk the woman was taking and impressed by the obvious resolve she was showing in the face of considerable danger.

The woman paused, lowering her camera briefly. In that instant she looked directly at Chris. The penetrating eyes staring out at him from within the scarf were the same he'd seen at his lecture.

Briefly ducking down to avoid being shot by the terrorist, she yelled, "Where is security?"

Good question, thought Chris. But the situation was developing too quickly to linger on that concern. Leaving Ramon, Chris started to move toward the other side of the truck to find Mac when the woman screamed out, "He's got a bomb!"

Chris followed the woman's finger and realized she was pointing at the truck's driver. The guy with the eye patch had revived and was holding his left arm straight out the driver's side window. In his hand was an activation switch. The man was chanting something Chris couldn't understand, but the intention was clear. He was going to blow himself up and take everyone else with him.

Despite the chaos and continuous danger at the scene, a small group of people had followed the journalist back toward the car. "Get back!" screamed Chris as he prepared to make a run for it.

A young Latino man, his white T-shirt covered in blood, emerged from the group and ran right past Chris. The collision with the bollard had elevated the front end of the Ford, leaving the driver's arm approximately eye level with the teenager. He grabbed the terrorist's extended arm by the wrist and yanked downward, screaming loudly at the terrorist as he did so.

As gunfire began from the police officers responding from near the front of the auditorium, the metal plinks of bullet impacts to the truck's cab reverberated in Chris's ear. Watching the scene in front of him, he calculated the teenager's chances of success were minimal, and a calm settled over him. This was not how he expected to go, but as much of life had run counter to his expectations, perhaps that wasn't too surprising.

The terrorist struggled against the young man's assault, but the teenager held tight to the man's wrist, continuing to yank hard in a downward motion. To Chris's surprise, the man's hand opened, and he released the trigger mechanism. It dangled in the air, still wired to whatever type of bomb he had inside the truck.

"Help me!" screamed the teenager, still holding tight to the now clearly broken arm.

Chris lunged to grab the trigger, worrying that the man would have some other means of detonating the bomb. Those concerns, however, were short-lived as Chris could hear—and feel—bullets pierce the windshield and strike the driver.

In the relative quiet that descended over the scene, Chris could hear the cries and moans from victims in the crowd. He could also hear the distinct clicking of a camera's shutter very close by.

"It's okay, guys. I can take it from here," said a police officer arriving next to Chris and the teenager.

Chris handed the trigger to the officer and placed a hand on the teenager's shoulder. "What's your name?"

"I'm Rafael," replied the teenager through labored breathing.

"Rafael, I'm Chris. Why don't we find someplace to sit down for a moment?"

Stepping away from the truck, Chris collapsed to the ground, leaning backward against one of the large bollards protecting the auditorium. Rafael sat down next to him. The adrenaline that had been so helpful only moments before now left Chris shaking and exhausted. He was relieved to find Mac joining them on the curb, looking similarly worse for wear.

"You okay?" asked Mac.

"Yup. This is Rafael. He saved all our butts back there."

"Nice work, Rafael," said Mac, patting the teenager on the knee. "I wondered why we weren't blown up."

"Are you alone, Rafael?" asked Chris, as he watched emergency personnel begin to arrive on the scene.

"No, I came with my grand—"

"Rafael!" Ramon, the man who'd been helping Chris pull the wounded away from the car, knelt down in front of them. "You crazy, crazy boy! Let me look at you. Your mother is going to be very unhappy with me."

Two paramedics arrived to attend to Rafael and his grandfather. They were led away to one of the many ambulances that had arrived in the minutes after the shooting ended.

"What's your situation?" asked Chris as he adjusted his position from the bollard to lie back flat on the concrete. "It sounded like there were a lot of bullets flying over there."

Mac took a second to survey his body before reporting, "It looks like they missed. My knee hurts, though."

Closing his eyes, Chris listened to the myriad sounds around him: approaching sirens, the squawk of emergency radios, moans of injured protesters. Amid the cacophony he could discern the clicking shutter of a camera close by. Propping himself up on one elbow, he looked up toward the sound of the photographer, using his other hand to shield his eyes from the blinding lights of the approaching emergency vehicles. The woman holding the camera stopped taking pictures and looked down at Chris with the same striking hazel eyes he'd noticed earlier. It was the woman from his presentation.

"I don't think I got your name," he stammered.

The woman cracked a half smile. Chris could tell she was about to speak when she was forcibly pushed to the side by a man lunging from out of the growing crowd behind her. The man wore a black tactical vest and a bright red baseball cap. Reaching to a holster on his belt, the man extracted a pistol and immediately pointed it toward Chris and Mac.

Militia. "You end here," said the gunman.

Chris could only close his eyes and cringe behind his already raised hand. When the three shots came in quick succession and didn't strike him, he instantly feared the worst for Mac. But opening his eyes, Chris saw the gunman drop to his knees in front of them, blood streaming from his open mouth. The man's eyes dulled and he collapsed.

Behind the fallen man, her weapon still drawn, stood Dana St. Claire. She said nothing as she kicked the dead man's weapon away and spun to observe the crowd.

"Hi, honey," Mac said.

The photographer looked from Dana to Mac to Chris and asked, "Who *are* you people?"

15

"The scientists survived."

Two hundred fifty miles north of the attack at the Davis Auditorium, the leadership of the Federal Brotherhood Initiative met on the second floor of a nondescript condominium building. Jeremiah Fessler had determined months in advance of their current operation that secrecy was the best course of action given what was about to happen.

"They survived," Fessler repeated. He had been worried that the scope of the group's activities was getting out of control. But he'd come to realize that the chaos and confusion, even within his group, served the ultimate end of destabilization. It was also going to make it harder for anyone to trace anything back to him.

"How?" asked Martinez.

"Does it really matter?" Robert Shaw replied, his aging but still muscular body clad entirely in black. He was leaning backward with one arm casually hooked over the back of his chair. His eyes scanned the other men sitting around the table.

"It does to me," replied Martinez. "I'm here to see a mission through, not to indiscriminately kill civilians. I thought we were planning strategic attacks."

Fessler scratched his graying beard before replying. "They survived the initial attack. Then someone from the crowd assisted them before Terry Enterline was able to fire his weapon. And Pierce wasn't even on site."

"Amateurs," noted Shaw as he let a seemingly casual gaze wander around the room. "The primary target wasn't even *there,* and they missed the secondary targets. Did anyone get a body count from among the protesters? No doubt people who *were* killed also share your interests."

Fessler responded angrily. "Those three men died for the cause. We will not speak poorly of them here. And besides," Fessler continued, "why were you not with them? My understanding was that *you* were going to facilitate the assault."

"I had other business—" replied Shaw.

"There is no other business." Fessler cut him off. "Your employer, our funder, made this mission a priority, and I expect you to do the same. In fact, I demand it."

"Do you." It was not a question.

"A woman stepped out of the crowd and shot Enterline," Fessler continued, ignoring Shaw's provocation. "The woman was clearly an operative."

Sitting up straight and leaning in to face Fessler, Shaw replied, "No, *clearly* she had a weapon. *That* is all we know. The fact that the attack took place in front of a large auditorium, which, if I may remind y'all, I advised against, means she could be anyone. Maybe she works for the police. Maybe she's a Fed who was watching the crowd. The point is, we don't know."

He leaned back in his chair, yet his eyes remained focused on Fessler.

"And if you think I was going to show my face outside the auditorium, then you're even dumber than I'd imagined. There's more to this operation than your little attacks, and I'm not going to compromise myself for issues of tangential importance."

Fessler pounded on the table. "You had better learn to respect the members of the Initiative! I do not care who you work for."

"I'd be careful about that, if I were you, *King*," said Shaw, glaring at Fessler. "You're not nearly as vital to this plan as you might think."

"I will feed you your own testicles before this is over," threatened Fessler.

Shaw removed a large knife from his belt and calmly placed it on the table in front of him. "You can certainly try."

Martinez spoke up again, addressing Shaw quietly, "Doesn't it strike you as odd that the woman happened to be at the right spot at exactly the right moment?"

"Look, I understand that hitting Pierce has PR value. But I'm still not convinced that these other two *need* killing, at least not them in particular. One of them was a SEAL, for God's sake. And the other's an American scientist who by all accounts does good work. I've yet to hear an explanation from anyone as to why you keep trying to kill them." Shaw stood up and stepped away from the table. He stretched his arms and then leaned on the back of the chair he'd been sitting in. "But if the goal is to disrupt and/or destroy the mission, and people have to die to make that happen, fine. Just wait until the mission starts so you get the biggest bang for your buck. Killing people associated with the mission beforehand is a waste of time."

Fessler regarded Shaw with a stern glare. "Of course that's the goal. It's always been the goal. And we have many assets in place to make sure that it comes to pass."

"Yes, I've seen the list of assets. And I agree that the goal is still attainable. That's why I'm here," said Shaw. "Speaking of assets, where's Bash?"

"He's up on the roof waiting for you," replied Fessler.

"Did he actually shoot a state trooper during a traffic stop, in broad daylight, from his personal vehicle? Do you people know anything about operational security? I'm surprised this place isn't surrounded by cops right now."

"Yes, he did kill the trooper," answered Fessler, closing his eyes. "We're dealing with that. Bash is a necessary evil. I recommend caution if you approach him."

Shaw pushed the chair in front of him back to the table. "Right."

16

A police perimeter was established around the Davis Auditorium, allowing only emergency medical service personnel to enter. As the news crews arrived outside the perimeter, including English- and Spanish-speaking contingents, the scene quickly became more chaotic. Situated at the southern end of Virginia Key, the auditorium was surrounded on three sides by water. The flashing red and blue ambulance, fire, and police lights, and the bright white lights of the news vans reflected off the water in an endless cycle.

After being cleared by paramedics, Chris, Mac, and Dana were escorted back into the auditorium by an armed SWAT team. Chris glanced back before entering through the glass doors, surveying the crowd for the photojournalist he'd encountered during the attack. He spotted her easily. She was sitting on an improvised chair holding an ice pack to her head, staring straight at him.

Chris turned to walk back toward the woman but was grabbed by his upper arm and ushered through the large, glass doors. "Please come with me, sir."

"Look," responded Chris, pointing toward the photographer. "The attack is over. I need to talk with that woman."

"I have strict orders to bring you inside, sir," said the officer in a state trooper's uniform as he tightened his grip on Chris's upper arm.

Once inside, the trio was led to the same lounge deep in the interior of the auditorium where Chris had met with Rhodes less than an hour before. "Please wait here."

Immediately after the trooper left, Mac walked back to the door and opened it. One of the two additional troopers stationed on either side of the door asked, "Can I help you, sir?"

"Uh, no," replied Mac as he closed the door.

"Guards?" asked Chris as he sank into one of the leather lounge chairs in the room, assuming correctly that Mac was evaluating the extent to which they were being monitored.

"Confirmed."

"What the hell is going on?" asked Dana, sitting forward on the edge of a chair across from Chris.

"Where do we start?" exclaimed Mac, hands in the air as he paced back and forth in front of the door. "Almost getting run over by a boat full of drug runners? Narrowly avoiding getting stabbed while on a run? Or nearly being shot *and* blown up outside this building?"

Turning toward Dana, Mac added, "Plus, while it's great to see you, I thought I was talking to you in *London*."

"You were," replied Dana as Mac sat down next to her. She placed her hand on his shoulder. "Then Hendrix called."

Dana explained that she'd been on a weeklong assignment in London, with several days remaining on the job, when Hendrix called. "He ordered me to get on the next flight to Miami. I did, and here I am."

"And? Nothing more?" asked Chris. "You arrived out front just in time to take that shooter out before he killed both of us. Was that just lucky?"

"We make our own luck," replied Dana, "but essentially yes. I was working my way through the crowd to find both of you when the shooter showed himself. Fortunately, one of Hendrix's guys picked me up at the airport and his SUV was well provisioned with arms."

"Why'd Hendrix send you?" continued Chris. "We have no idea what's going on here yet. How could he know anything?"

"You both know Hendrix much better than I do. You should probably wait until he calls to hear it directly from him," replied Dana, pointing at her ears and then up toward the ceiling.

Chris stood up and patted his pants and sport coat pockets, front and back. "Actually, I don't know where my phone is. Great."

"I'm sure he'll find a way to get through to you."

"Do *you* have a phone?" asked Chris.

"I think it's better if you wait for Hendrix," said Dana.

"What about you?" Chris asked Mac.

"My phone's in the van," said Mac.

Chris raised his arms in defeat and sat back down in the chair, leaning back and closing his eyes. "The aquanauts told us that social media was blowing up around the mission. Really nasty stuff. I've just been too busy and tired to look. But I'm pretty sure they mentioned militia. And the guy you took out sure looked the part. *And*—"

The door behind the couch opened and Grampen Rhodes strode through. Frank Donagan followed him into the room.

"And what?" asked Rhodes.

"And I think I saw the two guys in the truck at my presentation earlier. The driver with the eye patch was hard to forget."

"First, Dr. Black, I'm so glad to see you're all right," said Rhodes as he remained standing. "Mr. Johnson, it's nice to see you again. I'm sorry it's under these circumstances. I don't think I've met this little lady."

Chris could see Mac reacting quietly to the fact that Rhodes had remembered meeting him, thinking to himself that Rhodes either had a politician's memory or he'd done his homework.

"Call me *little lady* again," said Dana, her voice steely, "and I assure you the outcome won't please you."

Rhodes dropped heavily into one of the remaining chairs in the room. "My apologies, Ms. St. Claire. I'm just an old Southerner."

Sitting down in a chair next to Rhodes, Donagan said, "Chris, we seem to be picking up right where we left off in Ecuador."

"I think it would be a stretch, even for you, Donagan," Chris responded, "to blame this on us."

"No one is blaming you," inserted Rhodes. "You people are the heroes in my book."

"Of course we aren't blaming you, Chris," said Donagan. "But this attack is related to the *Calypso* mission somehow. I would not be honoring our relationship if I let it go unnoticed that we're now amid our third violent encounter, on a third continent, within a year's time."

Chris had been at the beginning of an extended research trip to Cape Town, South Africa, when they discovered the wreck of an old fishing vessel on the seafloor in the area they were studying.

They quickly discovered that the wreck was filled with millions of solid gold Krugerrands, which ultimately lead to several pitched battles with former apartheid officials who'd lost them thirty years before.

That trip was followed by a research excursion to the Galapagos Islands aboard Chris's university's vessel, the *MacGreggor*. Little did the research team know as they motored out to the most isolated of the islands, they were being shadowed by a group of Colombian pirates, who ended up hijacking the *MacGreggor* along with all the students on board. Chris and Mac, joined by Dana, had been launched on a frantic search for the vessel, before it was too late.

In both instances, Donagan had arrived on the scene with the espoused interest in helping, and Chris did not doubt that. But what he didn't like was the continually mysterious nature of Donagan's employment and his well-timed arrivals.

"Chris, are you saying that one or more of the assailants attended your lecture earlier this evening?" asked Donagan. "That's news to me."

"As I asked earlier, are these other circumstances related?" asked Rhodes, who appeared to Chris as though he was trying to reassert control over the conversation.

"To the Galapagos and South Africa?" replied Chris. "I can't see how. And this situation is already complicated enough without indulging in conspiracy theories."

"What exactly is your role here, Mr. Rhodes?" asked Dana. "My understanding is that you left office some time ago. We should be speaking with the police."

Chris watched as Rhodes's affect lost all pretense of geniality.

"I'm here at the request of our government, little lady."

"That's interesting," replied Dana, her voice a steely calm as she stood up and approached Rhodes. Leaning down, her face inches from the old politician's, she continued, "My understanding is that Senator Pierce is the official US representative to the mission. But *you* requested to be part of all this. Or perhaps my information is inaccurate?"

The room was quiet as Rhodes and Dana stared at each other.

"The events are related only insofar as Chris and Mac were central players," Donagan replied to Rhodes's earlier question, moving closer to Dana and calmly resting a hand on her shoulder. It had the intended effect. Dana took a deep breath and stepped back.

"Well, then, let's move on," said Rhodes, his eyes still trained on Dana. "What do we know?"

Donagan opened a folder in his lap and read, "A total of three assailants were killed; the two in the vehicle were killed by security guards, and the third taken out by Ms. St. Claire here."

"Do we think there were others in the crowd?" asked Mac. "I didn't see anyone else involved while the shooting was going down, but maybe the guy Dana shot had colleagues."

"We don't know for certain, but the police are investigating," explained Donagan. "And the FBI should be here soon. Attacks like this, where gunfire is coupled to a suicide bomber, are exceedingly rare in the US."

"Frank, in the last two days, we were nearly run over by a speeding boat at sea, and someone knifed two joggers not long after Mac and I had run past along the same path," explained Chris. "And now this. I'm not saying they're connected; in fact, they're probably not. But coincidences are starting to pile up."

Donagan looked up from his file. "I was not aware of these other incidents."

"Chris is right, Frank," said Mac. "They're probably not connected. But we've all be through enough in the last couple of years to warrant concern."

"I don't have a lot of time, so I'm going to cut right to it," interrupted Rhodes. "If tonight's attack is connected to all the online threats against the mission, I'm hopeful that ramped-up security will allow the mission to move forward. But Chris, I think you're going to get pulled."

"What do you mean?" asked Chris. "Why? By whom?"

"Rhodes may be right," said Donagan. "The local FBI supervisor is going to come down here in a few minutes to tell you more. This was a major terrorist attack and the three of you played a central role in thwarting it. I think they'd rather debrief the three of you at headquarters, or at least a regional field office. I don't know how long that will take."

"Of course, they will!" said Chris. "So, the question I have is what the hell are we doing here talking to the two of you?"

"Listen," said Rhodes. "What I want to know now is whether or not *you* want to go or stay. Because if you want to stay, I'm going to fight to make that happen."

"Why?" blurted Mac.

"Because I want this mission to succeed. The public relations opportunities are extraordinary, and I think Dr. Black here—and you as well, Mr. Johnson—will be a big part of making that a reality."

"You realize that we're just part of the surface support team, right?" said Chris. "I'm not one of the saturation divers."

"I do," answered Rhodes. "But my assessment stands. The mission's success depends on your participation."

"I still don't get it," said Mac, shaking his head.

"Neither do I," said Chris. "I don't see how we're central to anything at all. The mission doesn't depend on our participation. But regardless, I *do* want the mission to succeed."

"So, you'd be willing to stay?" asked Rhodes.

Chris used his thumb to point toward Mac, who replied on cue, "Our mommas didn't raise us to quit."

"Then no matter who might argue to remove you, I will ensure that you will continue," Rhodes said, then stood up and left the room.

17

Aaron Bash stood on the rooftop of the condo building looking west toward downtown Orlando. The evening sky was now dominated by the flashing lights of the many amusement parks that had come to dominate the city. He leaned heavily on the railing in front of him, taking a long drag on the cigarette in his mouth as he watched the lights alternate from red to blue and back again.

Feeling the presence of the other man at his side, having heard neither the rooftop door opening nor any sign of footsteps on the gravel covering the roof, Bash fought to conceal his shock.

"You offed a state trooper?" asked Shaw. "You, my friend, are a loose cannon. I don't care how useful Fessler thinks you are, you're not worth it."

"You were supposed to help with the attack at the protest," said Bash. "I could kill you right now, old man."

Shaw snorted at the threat. "Come on now, Aaron, you can do better than that. Your men are dead because they were incompetent. It's as simple as that, and I suspect you know that. Which is why you're up here brooding. I suspect you also know that if I perceived any real threat from you, you'd be dead already."

Bash glanced back toward the door to the stairs.

"That goes for the group downstairs, as well," said Shaw. "This Brotherhood of the incapable."

Bash was not used to being threatened, and his irritation briefly won in a fight with his fear. "Maybe I have people watching us right now," he suggested. "Maybe only one of us will leave this rooftop—"

Bash was cut off midsentence as Shaw's hand closed around the back of his neck like a vice and forced his torso out over the rail.

"I won't kill you now, Aaron, because that isn't in my job description . . . yet. Now, I'm going to let up on your neck. But if you go for that gun in your waistband, or say anything that I don't like, you're going over, whether it's approved or not. You know I'm not joking."

Looking down thirteen stories to the concrete pad beneath him, Bash nodded.

"What was that?" asked Shaw.

"I understand!" croaked Bash, feeling relief rush over him as the hand released its hold on his neck and pulled him back up by his shirt collar.

"Now, Aaron. Let's take stock. First, you and your men were almost caught taking a boat into the protected area off Fort Lauderdale. I'm not sure what you were planning on doing there anyway. Then you stabbed the wrong two runners on the beach in Key Biscayne." Shaw paused to laugh out loud.

"The *wrong* fucking people! That was an impressive move. Your team did slightly better over there at the auditorium. Even though Pierce wasn't there, at least the secondary targets were threatened that time, however briefly."

"They had help," whispered Bash.

"Yes, from a woman. We went through that downstairs. Who cares. By the way, I'm still not at all clear on why you and your band of militants have chosen to focus on these two. A scientist and a former Navy SEAL. It just doesn't add up. And Fessler's got nothing to say. Why don't you tell me what's going on?"

Bash said nothing.

"Silence, eh? So, there must be something going on after all," said Shaw. "Fine, I'll figure it out myself. So, what's the next step?"

Bash stood quietly.

"Nothing? Okay. Well, I'll tell you what. You have my number. When you have a plan, call me."

"What are *you* going to do?" asked Bash. "You talk a lot, but I haven't seen you do a single thing to advance our cause."

"Your *cause*?" laughed Shaw. "You're a goddamn juvenile delinquent. You're a hard-on running around half-cocked. What do you know about causes?"

"Shut the fuck up, old man!" yelled Bash, pulling out the pistol and pointing it at Shaw. "America First! No more fucking immigrants. No more lost jobs. No more UN. The country as it should be! We're going to change all of that."

"Words, Aaron. Just words. Do you recall how it felt just a minute ago when you were hanging over the edge?" asked Shaw, as he took a step toward Bash. "Why do you want to experience that again?"

With nowhere to move, Bash leaned back hard against the rail but kept his weapon pointed toward Shaw.

"It doesn't matter what I'm doing next, and I don't care what your assessment of my job is," said Shaw. "I really don't. You just complete the fucking tasks assigned to you, and the rest of the group will take care of itself."

Shaw departed as silently as he'd arrived. Bash felt his fear gradually wane. He turned back to look out over the city. No one spoke to him like that! No one. The man would pay for every snide comment he'd made. He would kill Shaw before this was all done.

A voice emerged from the darkness behind Bash, causing the hairs on the back of his neck to stand up.

"Oh, and Aaron? I know what's going through your head right now. Don't get carried away in my absence. Tonight, you get a pass. But just remember, there are a lot of ways to kill a man, and I know every one of them."

18

"John? John, listen to me. We are *not* canceling the mission because of a few rednecks with guns and their online minions. Do you understand me? That is *not* going to happen."

Senator Pierce's three staff members all stopped what they were doing in the hotel room and watched her pace back and forth on the small balcony. Her earbuds were in, so they only heard one side of the animated phone conversation.

"Yes, that was a horrifying attack in Miami. Yes, they are threatening more. Fine, hire more security. Hire whatever you need," said Pierce, emphasizing her points by jabbing her finger in the air in front of her. "Once the mission starts, everything will be miles offshore, right? What could the rednecks possibly do out there?"

Helene Economakis, the Senator's chief of staff, stepped out through the sliding door.

"Hang on a second, John. What is it, Helene?"

"Senator, the balcony isn't private," explained Economakis. "Perhaps it would be better if you continued the conversation inside."

"Fine," replied Pierce, as she stepped back into the room. "Listen, this is your show, John. But I didn't stick my neck out to get the UN on board to support the mission only to have you panic at the first sign of trouble. We've got a lot more riding on this than just a mission in the Florida Keys, John. If you can't pull this off here, *in our own waters*, what chance is there that you'll make it work in Israel? The goddamned *Middle East*. They kill each other every day over there, John. If we can't do this here, the UN will walk away. They'll walk away. And the whole thing will go tits up."

Pierce grabbed a banana from a basket in the room's kitchenette and sat down at a bar stool as she peeled it.

"Okay. Okay," replied Pierce with a mouth full of banana. "That sounds good. Do that and keep Helene in the loop. We'll be down there for the mission launch once they've finished the training. Until then, we'll be up here in Miami. Now, what's your other problem?"

The senator nodded her head twice and then her back went rigid.

"Grampen Rhodes is a clown, John. He's old news, but he just doesn't know it. I don't care what he says. He's there to make suggestions, and that's all. We added him just to make a few of my colleagues across the aisle back off. And for now, they have. I know, he thinks I'm intimidated by him. Fine, let him think whatever he wants. We've got more important fish to fry than Rhodes. Okay, John? Good. Bye."

The staff watched from behind as Pierce rubbed both palms across her face and then ran her fingers through her hair. She swiveled on the stool to face them.

"What's the body count up to in Miami now?"

"Seventeen dead, with another fifteen seriously injured," replied Economakis. "At least five of the injured are in really rough shape and may not make it."

"Conversations about mass shootings are simply happening way too frequently these days," observed Pierce. "I don't know how we're going to break the cycle here domestically, but perhaps we can do something to prevent this horror from being exported internationally."

"What did Lefevre have to say?" asked Economakis.

“John Lefevre did not contribute enough to the campaign to warrant this much attention,” she said after several moments. “We better tag him for a lot more this next time around.”

“What loop should I be in?” asked Economakis, her tablet and stylus poised to take notes.

“He’s calling in some extra security,” explained Pierce. “He’ll explain it all to you later. It’s fine. I just want him used to reporting to our office. We’re going to need him working with us if we’re to meet our international obligations down the road with all the other missions.”

“Of course, Senator. And dare I ask what’s going on with Rhodes?” asked Economakis.

“Nothing. Bloviating. He wants to keep this scientist from California involved for some reason. I don’t care. Once we get through this mission and move on to international venues, we won’t have to worry about Grampen Rhodes any further. Now what’s next?”

19

"What's our ETA?" asked Mac.

"If you don't drive us off the road into a ditch?" replied Chris. "We should make it to Key West by eight thirty or nine in the morning, so about three hours from now."

"Dana will save us if I drive us into a ditch," replied Mac. "At least, I hope she will."

In the side-view mirror, Chris could see the headlights of Dana's SUV following as closely behind them as the low light conditions allowed.

The early light that preceded the sun's rise began to show along the horizon of the Atlantic Ocean as Chris and Mac drove south from Miami toward Key West. Both early risers, they'd decided to spend the previous evening in the city before driving down to Key West in time to arrive for the first training day for the mission. That had allowed them to eat dinner with Rafael and his grandfather at their family's restaurant after a day of debriefs with the FBI and other law enforcement.

Following the conversation with Rhodes and Donagan, Chris had gone back out to the scene of the attack and found Ramon and Rafael before an ambulance had taken them away. Ramon, who'd not been wounded as badly as Chris had feared, had invited them to eat at the family restaurant. The Cuban tamales had been some of the best Chris had ever had.

Mac drove the rental van as they navigated one bridge after another in the pouring rain.

Despite the hint of sunrise, the Keys were very dark. Chris watched the mile markers pass by in the van's headlights. He recalled his first trip to the Keys years ago.

Unlike California's big sky and generally open coastline, in Florida and the Keys, the combined impact of the flat topography and abundant trees meant that you often couldn't see anything from the road. You had to have local knowledge to find your way around the best beaches and dive sites.

"Yes. She's very experienced with that at this point. Saving us, that is," added Chris. "Let's just hope you don't push her away before she has a chance to save us again."

Mac stared ahead as he drove.

"Sorry. Too soon?" asked Chris.

"What about the FBI supervisor? What did he have to say?" asked Mac. Immediately after the meeting, Donagan had taken Mac and Dana into a side room while Chris spoke to the FBI. They hadn't had a chance to compare notes until now.

"Even less," answered Chris. "And he was a she. They're all cut from the same mold as Donagan. They don't know how to communicate things in a straightforward manner, or they choose not to. I'm not sure why she wanted to talk to me given that we were going to spend the next day briefing everyone."

"It's the machine," offered Mac. "It's why I'm not unhappy being free of the military. Agency heads and spooks like Donagan are all part of a monstrous machine that frequently takes too long to come around to the right thing to do. And if you're not part of that machine, however talented you might be, you're an outsider. I much prefer our small team of rogue actors."

"Rogues, that's us all right. Your turn. What did Donagan have to say?" asked Chris.

"I think he's definitely connected the truck attack at your presentation to the mission, he just isn't saying that out loud," explained Mac. "We spent most of the time talking about the stabbing and the incident with the boat. He sure didn't like that he hadn't heard about these incidents. And he hasn't yet said out loud that they are connected."

"I'm not sure they are," said Chris, reaching behind him to grab the seat's headrest and stretch his arms. "The truck attack was obviously targeted at the *Calypso* mission," Chris continued, bringing his arms forward and grabbing the dashboard. "The other two incidents may be nothing. I mean, apart from the truck attack, this drive south has been the most danger we've encountered. We've been cut off in traffic several times this morning, twice fairly violently."

"But you and I both know that coincidences have a way of turning into something more," he added, slumping back into his seat. "Did Donagan have any intel on the attackers?"

"At least two of them are associated with a group called the Florida Brotherhood Initiative," explained Mac. "But I gather that was determined from a preliminary review of their social media activities. No one has claimed responsibility." Pausing briefly, he then added, "And that is part of what was spooking Donagan, I think."

"Some new player?"

"Maybe. No one likes dealing with that kind of uncertainty. What are you doing?" Chris had pulled out his smartphone.

"Nothing, I guess," said Chris. "Thought I'd look up the Florida Brotherhood Initiative. But there's no signal."

"We *are* on a road to nowhere. Perhaps your expectations for connectivity are a tad too high."

"Possibly," agreed Chris, while tossing his smartphone onto the dashboard.

"I noticed you didn't mention that photojournalist in our meeting with Rhodes and Donagan," said Mac.

"And?"

"And," Mac continued, "I assumed you had a reason for keeping it quiet. What's the scoop?"

"I really have no idea," admitted Chris. "It's just a feeling, I suppose. She was clearly focused on me, or us. And I'd like to know why."

"Do you think she's on the side of the angels?" asked Mac.

"Hah!" exclaimed Chris. "You and I hardly qualify as angels, by even the lowest standard."

"Speak for yourself," said Mac.

"Either way," Chris added, "I think she has something to offer us. I just don't know what."

Several minutes passed as they drove onward through the Keys, silently.

"Can I make an observation?" asked Mac.

"Is it going to bug me?" replied Chris with a sigh. "Sure, go ahead."

"You haven't been yourself lately," observed Mac.

"What are you talking about?"

"I mean, what are we doing here?" asked Mac. "Sure, it's a cool mission, and getting involved is definitely in your wheelhouse. On paper, this all looks great. I guess it feels like you're just going through the motions."

"Going through the motions," said Chris as he glanced out the passenger-side window into the dark.

Chris and Mac had known each other since the early years of elementary school in Carmel-by-the-Sea in California, where they'd ridden BMX bikes all over town when they weren't playing Dungeons and Dragons or exploring the marine environment. Their adventures together had only expanded as adults, including many brushes with death on multiple continents. Mac had seen Chris through the worst experiences of his life.

So, he was not surprised that Mac had picked up on his hesitancy to fully commit to this mission.

"Am I wrong?" asked Mac after several minutes.

"No, you're pretty much on point as always," replied Chris. "I think it's the legacy of the pirates."

"What do you mean?"

"I mean, we both had a lot to process after that incident," explained Chris. "And I didn't realize until we got here how far I still need to go to recover."

"How so?" asked Mac.

"Guilt, I think," said Chris. "I can't seem to get past the guilt I feel for leaving the students vulnerable to kidnapping. We should have been there. *I should have been there*."

"Right," said Mac. "I totally understand what you're saying. But as we've discussed before, our presence on the *MacGreggor* when the pirates first struck would very likely not have changed the outcome at first. We would have been captured too, or worse. And then we wouldn't have been available to save the day later."

"Yep. I know you're right," said Chris. "I'm not saying it's logical. I just can't seem to shake the guilt. And now, even though I'm definitely interested in helping the mission, I can't look past the danger to the young aquanauts. I don't want anything bad to happen to them."

"Yeah, I understand. I guess the only thing we can ask at this point is for you to do yourself a little kindness. Recognize that you did your best in the Galapagos, just like you're doing now. And that that's all anyone can possibly ask of you."

"A *little kindness*?" said Chris, now smiling. "Where did *that* come from?"

"I guess a little bit of Margaret rubbed off on me," observed Mac.

Chris's mother, Dr. Margaret Black, was a psychologist with a practice focused primarily on kids. Both Chris and Mac had been the beneficiaries of her insights many times since they were kids.

"It's been a rough year," observed Mac, as he tried to get the wiper settings to match the volume of rain hitting the windshield. "I wouldn't blame you for wanting to bag this mission and go home. Give me the word, and I'll turn this thing around."

Chris sat quietly for several moments, listening to the rhythmic beat of the wipers.

"Let's hope that from here on out, things will be peaceful," said Chris.

"He that lives upon hope will die fasting," said Mac. "Benjamin Franklin."

"I knew there was a reason I brought you along," Chris said.

The morning rain clouds dissipated before them, exposing the rising sun in the east and opening up the wider horizon. Seconds later, Chris's smartphone vibrated on the dashboard.

Seeing Chris's furrowed brow looking down at the phone, Mac asked, "What's up?"

"It's a message from the woman we were just talking about, the photojournalist. No idea how she got this number. But she's coming down to Key West and wants to meet up this evening."

20

Leland Jones sat at his desk, looking up at the large painting of his father hanging prominently on the wall of his office. He wondered if the company the man had created would survive the next six months. *Fucking peace*, he thought as he stacked two pieces of bacon on his scrambled egg sandwich.

"Come in," he answered between bites as a soft knock sounded at the door.

Sharon Dirksen entered the office carrying a cup of coffee in one hand and her omnipresent tablet in the other. "Good morning. I thought you might be ready for some caffeine, and I'd like to go over our communication schedule with the, um, Brotherhood Initiative."

Jones and Sumner had considered the potential blowback, both financially and legally, if either of them was found to be directly influencing activities related to the militia. But they were not comfortable looking outside the company for assistance, so they tasked Dirksen with any direct communications with Shaw primarily, and with Fessler if necessary.

Dirksen had always been a reliable employee. But ever since her husband, an accountant with a large firm in New York, died in the

South Tower on 9/11, she'd fixated on work. With no kids to help her mourn the loss of her husband, she'd sought solace at the office. There'd been no weekend that she wasn't at her desk, no job too time-consuming, no request too challenging.

In those early days, Jones had not planned to engage her in the less overt aspects of his activities. But Dirksen had accidentally been copied on an email that included documents describing the company's dealings in North Africa. Her analytical mind had taken no time to see the bribes and other payouts, both received and distributed, nested within the accounting documents from operations in Libya and Egypt. Jones had quickly realized that tying her more closely to the business, in particular its potentially nefarious operations, was the move that would ensure her loyalty. And he'd not regretted it over the ensuing decades. Dirksen had proven invaluable in countless dealings throughout the world. Her frank, no-bullshit approach had often shocked, and periodically infuriated, the dozens of men she'd dealt with over the years.

"What's Quint got to report?" asked Jones, referring to Robert Shaw by the nickname he'd received years before.

"He's not exactly pleased with how things are going," explained Dirksen. "I gather not all members of the group are equally capable."

"Right, but what did he *report*? I haven't had my coffee yet and I'm not up to playing twenty questions."

"Shaw reports that operations thus far have gone more or less as we expected," explained Dirksen as she watched Jones take a large bite of a meaty breakfast sandwich.

"Meaning what, for God's sake?"

"You shouldn't get too excited, Leland. You know the doctors are concerned about a potential coronary."

"Right," Jones said, waving his hand in the air. "They're worried I'm going to go just like my dad did, with a massive heart attack while sitting right here at this very desk. Well, maybe I will. But you don't want to cause it, so just tell me what Quint said."

Dirksen summarized the interactions that Shaw had described with the various players in their complicated scheme, including the mistakes made so far and the general volatility of all involved.

"The Brotherhood of the Incapable," said Jones, chuckling. "That's pretty good. Look here, though. I know he's a tough guy, but Shaw's also a wildcard. He's gone way off script before."

Two years prior, Jones had tasked Shaw with project oversight in El Salvador, where Unity Environmental was contracted to supply security to the newly elected president and his cabinet. Working in close proximity to the cabinet ministers and their families for months, Shaw had become enamored with the wife of the defense minister. As the months wore on, it became clear to Shaw that the minister was regularly beating his wife for perceived infidelities. When the wife arrived for breakfast with a black eye and a pronounced limp, Shaw had walked into the couple's bedroom and beaten the minister to within inches of his life, including punching the man in the eye so severely that he lost vision, and breaking his left leg to the extent that he would always carry a limp.

"Shaw also reports an apparent focus on killing, um, Chris Black and Mac Johnson. That authorization didn't come from us, at least not through me. Is there something going on I don't know about?"

Dirksen watched as Jones appeared to consider his answer.

"I don't know," he replied. "Maybe it's that crazy kid they have working for them. What's his name? Ash?"

"Bash. Following up on your earlier observation," said Dirksen. "I get the distinct impression that Shaw is going to kill Fessler and/or Bash before this is all over."

"I don't really care. You and Sumner got me into the mess with the militia," said Jones. "I don't see how it's helping us, and the update you just provided me highlights at least a dozen ways this will blow back on us. So, perhaps having Shaw kill everyone would make things easier all around."

21

Chris Black stood at the rail on the upper deck of mission control, a one-hundred-foot-long barge, and took in the frenetic scene around him. Sixty feet below him, anchored to the seafloor, sat the *Calypso I*, a portable saturation facility. Two decks below Chris, dozens of technicians and communication staff were moving about, getting ready to spend the next three weeks keeping the *Calypso I* operating safely.

From his left, he could hear the steady drum of the two massive air compressors that provided a continuous flow of fresh air to the facility below. To his right he could see three separate antennae systems that connected mission control, as well as the *Calypso I* itself, to the larger world with cell phone, internet, and satellite connectivity. Amidships in front of him was a large A-frame crane and winch configured to provide an elevator back and forth to the seafloor. Immediately behind on the other side of the barge was a separate crane through which the air supply hoses and the communication array cables were routed down to the *Calypso I*.

"Pretty impressive operation, isn't it?" said a young man approaching Chris. The kid had a large afro and a goatee, and a smiling yellow banana slug greeted him from his T-shirt. He also held an open notebook in one hand and a pen in the other.

"Reporter?" asked Chris.

He laughed. "The pen and pad give it away? I prefer digital of course, but those compressors provide too much ambient noise to record anything. Name's Malcolm Alexander."

Chris offered his hand. "How's it going, Malcolm? I'm Chris. Are you by any chance from my neck of the woods?"

"What? Oh, you mean the T-shirt. No, I'm from Boston, but my younger brother goes to school in Santa Cruz. I told him I couldn't understand a university that has a shell-less snail as its mascot. But then he told me how much money he's going to make in Silicon Valley when he graduates, and as a poorly paid reporter who still drives a twenty-year-old Saab, I shut up."

Chris laughed. As a scientist, he too had known many people, including his own students, who'd opted for work in the computer industry because of the high salaries.

"I sat in on the briefing downstairs and thought I'd catch up with you," Malcolm continued. "I work for *The Globe*."

"I haven't read *The Globe* much since my grad school days. How can I help you?" said Chris, wondering if this interview was part of Rhodes's grand communication plan. There had been dozens of reporters lurking around seeking information about the attack in Miami. But nearly all of them had been held at bay by the mission security team.

"First I have to ask about the incident after your presentation."

"Of course, you do. But can we stick to the mission, for now?" asked Chris.

"Uh, sure. I heard them say that you've done several of these missions before. Can you tell me exactly how this all works?"

"All of it?"

"Well, first tell me about the *Calypso I*."

Chris considered his reply for a second. "Do you remember when you were a kid playing in the bathtub? I bet at some point you held a cup or glass upside down and submerged it, right?"

"Sure."

"And what happened to the air?"

"It stayed there until I turned the cup sideways, and it would flood."

"That's basically all we have going here," explained Chris. "In this case it's a fifty-foot-long tube with a door at one end. At that end the designers added an additional space called the wet porch. It contains the moon pool, which is essentially your upside-down cup. Just like you could poke your finger up from under the cup and wiggle it around in the air, divers can come and go into the *Calypso I* through the moon pool. Those compressors you hear are providing a continuous flow of air to the facility."

Chris pointed to the sea surface directly in front of them. "See all those bubbles coming to the surface? That's just the extra air being 'burped' out from the moon pool."

"That's not a bad analogy," observed Malcolm as he took notes on his pad.

Chris laughed. "Every once in a while I come up with a good one."

"So why do this? Why live in a tube with a burping moon pool?"

"Are you a SCUBA diver?" asked Chris.

"Nah, I prefer the snow."

"Okay, but you know that there are limits to how long people can stay down at various depths, right?"

"Sure."

"Well, in a facility such as *Calypso I*, those rules still apply. But as long as you come and go from the moon pool, instead of coming back to the surface, you can basically stay down there indefinitely and dive as much as nine hours a day."

Malcolm scribbled more on his pad. "And that's more than you could dive from the surface?"

"Depending how deep you dive, it can be as much as ten times the amount of dive time that you'd have if you were diving from a surface vessel. Further, you must factor in all the time getting on the boat and motoring out to the site. Down there, they'll just get up in the morning, get their gear on, and start their work."

"What's the rub? There's got to be a rub, or this would be happening everywhere, right?"

"Good question," observed Chris. "Saturation diving isn't for everyone. Once you've been down at depth, which here is about sixty feet, for twelve hours, your body is completely saturated with nitrogen. If you stay down for five more minutes or ten more days, it will take you about fourteen hours to decompress."

"Nitrogen saturation? What exactly is that?"

"Right. The air we breathe is about seventy-six percent nitrogen, but our bodies don't metabolize it like we do oxygen. So, the nitrogen just accumulates in our bloodstream as we breathe underwater. The dive limits we were talking about a minute ago are based on how long it takes for nitrogen to leave the bloodstream."

"Right, if you come up too quickly, you'll get the bends," said Malcolm. "I've heard of that. Also, a minute ago, you said *they*. Aren't you going too?"

"No, not this time. They've got the four scientists they need. I'm just here as an adviser. I *will* be training with the other aquanauts as an alternate so in the unlikely event that one of them can't complete the training, there's a fifth member available and the mission can continue."

"Why is four the magic number?"

"The *Calypso I* holds six people—two technicians and four scientists. No room for anyone else; at least no one else living down there. Guests come and go during the day all the time."

"Does the alternate get used very often?" asked Malcolm.

"Not in any of the missions I've participated in so far. The trainers are really solid, and the other scientists seem very capable."

"They're young. Did you know any of them before this?"

"I know one of the trainers really well from my work in Florida," said Chris. "The other I know by reputation. I just met the science team for the first time in person earlier in the week, though there have been some emails going back and forth for several weeks. I was about the same age as they are now when I did my first sat mission."

"Isn't this kind of dangerous?" observed Malcolm. "I mean, it seems like a lot of things could go wrong."

"Of course, putting six people in a tube on the seafloor for ten days might produce some challenges. But as you see around you, there is a large team of people who will be working twenty-four seven to keep the mission running smoothly."

"Have you ever had any problems underwater?"

Chris laughed openly at that question. "Are you staying around for the mission, Malcolm?"

"Yes, I'm here for the duration."

"Then let's get together after everything's over, and I'll tell you a few stories over a beer."

"Sounds great. One more question. Once the divers are saturated, they really can't come to the surface?"

"Well, eventually they'll come up, of course. As I said, decompression takes fourteen hours at the depth they'll be working, and they'll complete that process on the last night of the mission. If they come up faster than that, they will almost certainly contract the bends. And that can kill you."

Malcolm seemed speechless, but only for a moment. "So, if problems arise, they can't just get away."

"No, in a very real way, saturation diving is like cave diving. You have to solve your problems at depth."

22

Hugo Martinez looked around the crowded bar. It obviously catered to tourists, he thought, complete with gratuitous pictures of Ernest Hemingway on the wall and a Jimmy Buffet cover band performing on the small smoky stage. The tables around him were populated by overly loud, sunburned white guys in Hawaiian floral print shirts and shorts.

He had more than once encouraged his wife to shoot him if he ever ended up looking like that. He smiled, recalling her immediate retort, "Looking white is the least of your problems, honey. And your stomach is as tight as it ever was."

"Martinez."

He looked up to see his contact standing across the table from him.

"You spacing out, man?"

"No, just remembering something," said Martinez, reaching out to shake the man's hand. "Good to see you, Spence."

"The missing knuckle," replied Spencer Harwood, looking down at Martinez's hand as he gripped it. The right index finger was missing beyond the first knuckle.

Harwood had served in the National Guard with Martinez years before. The men of their unit had aged very differently over the ensuing decades, with some ballooning, some withering away, and a few, like Harwood, looking like he could jump back into his uniform any minute if called upon to do so. He now worked as a construction worker and sometime security consultant down in the Keys. Though he stayed in touch with Martinez, he didn't want anything to do with the Brotherhood.

"Can I buy you a drink?" asked Martinez.

"Sure."

Martinez signaled to the waitress for two more beers and turned back to Harwood. The conversation at neighboring tables was loud, and nobody was paying any attention to them, but he leaned in to avoid being overheard nonetheless. Harwood did the same.

"I appreciate your help with this, Spence."

"I don't know what you and your Brotherhood have planned, other than what you've told me," replied Harwood. "But I don't want to be involved any further. I owe you one, Hugo. So, I made this connection for you. Now I'm out."

"I understand."

On the last day their unit had been deployed in Afghanistan, they'd been involved in an ambush on the roadside outside of Kandahar. Martinez had pulled Harwood from a burning Humvee, getting half his finger shot off in the process. Martinez had been rotated stateside immediately after the incident.

"Now we're even. Don't let this blow back on me."

"I won't," confirmed Martinez. "No one knows you're involved but me and the person you contacted."

Harwood narrowed his eyes and surveilled the room. "I don't know why I'm doing this. Way too much to lose."

The waitress arrived with new beers, setting down bottles without glasses. When she left, Martinez took a sip and leaned in again.

"I heard you got married again," said Martinez. "And there's a stepdaughter in the mix now. I'm happy for you. I won't let anything come back to you. Fessler has this thing all squared away."

"You and I have been a part of enough ops to know nothing is ever truly squared away," said Harwood, pointing the neck of his bottle at Martinez. "But you know there's a Charlie Foxtrot on your horizon, don't you? Probably more than one."

Martinez leaned back in his chair and exhaled. He knew Harwood was right. And if he were sitting on the other side of the table, he'd be having the same concerns and saying the same things.

"Roger that," he said. "But I'm all in at this point. You remember how that felt, don't you? We don't back out in the middle of an op."

"Fair enough," replied Harwood. "I just want us all to be clear. You lost your finger for me, but I'm no longer in a position to do the same for you."

"Just tell me what you were able to set up."

"I'm not going to name names here."

"Got it."

"Okay," said Harwood. "My contact asked around. I told him what you were offering."

"One hundred thousand dollars."

"Right."

"Yeah. So?"

"So, he asked around. He needed to be careful. He doesn't want any blowback either. No one wants to touch this."

"I *understand*," said Martinez. "Did he find someone or not?"

Harwood took a long swig on his beer. He put it down and wiped his mouth with his hand.

"He did."

"Tell me," demanded Martinez.

"He found someone on the inside, someone deep in the inside."

Holy shit! thought Martinez. "And?"

"And this person will be in a position to bring it all down."

"I need you to be specific here," said Martinez, his palms sweating. "Bring what down?"

"The *Calypso I.* Just to be clear. We're not talking just stopping the mission. We're talking downing the undersea lab itself. If you want it destroyed, this person can make it happen."

23

The city of Key West is located at the southwestern terminus of the main Florida Keys, sandwiched between Gulf of Mexico and the Caribbean Sea. To Chris, the city itself seemed like the rest of the Keys: a mix of gaudy tourist traps, a few remaining authentic houses and eateries, and a great deal of natural beauty. To the north, the shallow waters were a deep green, while to the south lay the impossibly blue waters of the Caribbean.

The hotel where Chris and Mac had set up was midway through town on the outer shore, facing the Caribbean. One of the larger hotels on the island, it consisted of a five-story main building and several single-story cabanas. Chris walked through the expansive atrium that served as the hotel's entrance and into the restaurant that bordered one of the hotel's several pools. The evening crowd was just starting to appear, and tiki lights surrounded the restaurant. He took the opportunity to grab a table with as much privacy as the restaurant allowed. He was early for his meeting, so he hadn't been looking for the photojournalist as he came, expecting that she would find him once he sat down.

Minutes after sitting down, she did.

"Dr. Black," said the woman.

Standing, Chris offered his hand. "Yes, and you are?"

"My name's Anna Cortez. Thank you for taking the time to meet with me."

"Well, I'm quite curious what this is about."

They both sat down and remained quiet as an attendant came by the table to pour water and remove the extra place settings.

"How's your head?" asked Chris.

"What?"

"I saw you being treated after the truck attack," Chris explained.

"Oh. Feeling better, thanks. I was too busy taking photos and got pushed over by someone in the crowd."

"You came to my presentation," said Chris as soon as the coast had cleared. "Then in the midst of the attack outside, I turn around and there you are again. That's not a coincidence."

"No, it isn't," responded Cortez. Nodding her head to her left, she added, "But before I continue, would you like to invite your two colleagues to join us? I recognize both from outside the auditorium."

Chris cracked a slight smile at the realization that she'd picked Mac and Dana out of the crowd. But even exposed, they were serving their purpose. "No, we can let them dine in peace. They're there just in case I'm wrong about you."

"Wrong about me?"

"I'm fairly sure that the two attackers in the truck were also at my lecture. And we were told that other potential attackers were likely in the crowd. So, I just need to be sure that you're not one—"

"First of all," Cortez interrupted, "I was not in Miami to see your presentation. I was responding to a tip from a source about extremists who are planning some kind of big attack."

Chris raised his palm. "Okay, wait a second. Let's take a step back. Who are you exactly?"

Exhaling, the woman sat back in her chair. "As I said, my name is Anna Cortez. I'm a journalist."

"Who do you work for?" asked Chris.

"I work freelance out of LA."

"You work freelance out of Los Angeles and attended my lecture in Miami based on a tip about extremists."

"Yes."

"Did this source tell you about the attack at the auditorium? Or were you following the guys from the lecture?"

"Good question," responded Cortez. "I was told that a high-profile target in South Florida, a location at which a protest was planned, was going to be attacked. I don't know if you're aware, but the *Calypso* mission is the focus of a lot of online vitriol."

"I've seen some of it," said Chris. "But I admit that I'm not looking at social media very much."

Cortez extracted a digital tablet from her bag. "Check this out."

Chris read the major headers as she scrolled through different social media platforms. The UN connection to the mission, which Chris knew to be minimal and largely in name only at that point, had nonetheless drawn a great deal of negative attention. Science Without Borders was also being condemned as anti-American. Senator Gwendolyn Pierce was the focus of the most extreme attacks.

"This is nonsense," said Chris. "But aren't those just Internet trolls spinning their wheels? As I said, I don't do social media. But from what I read, this kind of venomous exchange has come to define online discourse."

"That's true," agreed Cortez. "But even given that, the mission is receiving a lot of negative attention. As you can see, Pierce attracts a great deal of negative attention. I don't know how much of this hate would be focused on the mission without her involvement, but she's involved, so we'll never know. And then there's this." She clicked on a link and turned the tablet back toward Chris.

Chris felt his stomach muscles tighten as he saw the names of the mission participants, including his own, being singled out. Some group called Earth Last was suggesting the participants should be targeted personally. Reading more closely, he saw the names of the two hotels the mission personnel were using in Key West during training.

"Jesus," Chris whispered. "This is *not* good. What's Earth Last?"

"An anti-government hate group? A band of patriots? Depends on your perspective. But as far as I can tell, it's just the latest vector for this type of online ranting," said Cortez. "Anti-government groups use different names online and change them constantly. It's not easy to figure out who's behind any single group."

"Which I'm sure is the whole point," observed Chris. "What can you tell me about your source?"

"Not much, I'm afraid."

"Are you often led around like this?" asked Chris.

"Led around? Are you implying I was being misled? I don't think I was. In fact, I'd say that I followed a rather promising lead. After all, I got great pictures of an attack during a protest against a high-profile and controversial international diving mission. And now I am sitting face-to-face with a participant in that mission." Cortez smiled. "I never understood why Americans are so suspicious of investigative journalists. All we are after is the truth. The truth is not suspicious, is it, Dr. Black?"

Chris laughed. "No, not to me. I look at scientific facts to determine truth, but I fear in the political arena, facts can support several truths."

"Touché."

"You implied that you're not American?"

It was Anna's turn to laugh. "I did? Didn't I merely say that Americans are suspicious of investigative journalism?"

Chris squirmed and was about to apologize for his presumptuous comment when Anna continued. "I am, in fact, American. Now." She leaned in and whispered playfully.

"I'm not in the habit of explaining myself to the people I interview—after all, I am not the target of my investigation—but I sought you out, and you seem reluctant, so I'll make an exception."

Chris sat back in his chair and took a drink of water. "It's not that I am reluctant to speak to journalists, it's that I've been the target of too many unsavory individuals in the past."

"I can assure you that I have no unsavory agenda, Dr. Black."

"Fair enough."

Cortez nodded. "I'm originally from Mexico City," she began and explained that her Mexican upbringing had been deeply religious, but that studying abroad in the US had changed all that. She'd studied journalism at Stanford University, where her secular colleagues were a big influence on her perspective on objectivity. She'd then done an internship with the Associated Press. The AP had leveraged her familiarity with Mexico to investigate the drug cartels. As those stories had run their course, she transitioned into the growing militia movement in the US, focusing on extremism in a different form.

"A focus on extremism under your byline must make you a pretty big target," observed Chris. "That can't be easy."

"Dr. Black, I'm a female reporter in one of the most male-dominated regions on the planet. Being a target is just part of the job."

"Please call me Chris. So what do you think is going on?"

Cortez glanced around before she answered. "All I know for certain is that I've been pointed toward militia operating here in Florida. And that while following up on those leads, I've noticed the massive social media campaign against your mission. And while following militia members, I've twice run into you. Like you, I don't believe in coincidences."

24

"Dr. Black!" came a bellowing voice from Chris's left. He turned to see his friend John Halbeck, the *Calypso I* mission's trainer and one of the two technicians who would saturate with the scientists, walking toward him with the other mission technician, Trevor Boseman, in tow. "Sorry I missed you after the briefing earlier. Too many things going on."

"Nice to see you again," said Chris, as he stood up to shake hands with the two men.

"I'm sorry for interrupting ma'am." Halbeck turned to Anna and bowed politely. "We're colleagues of the esteemed Dr. Black."

"I apologize, I should have made the introductions." Chris stepped in. "This is Anna Cortez, a fabulous journalist. Please meet John Halbeck, a diver I've worked with on many occasions. And Trevor Boseman, the engineer on many a mission."

"Nice to meet you both," observed Cortez. "An exciting mission you are about to launch."

"Indeed, we are all truly looking forward to it."

John "Otter" Halbeck was a former Navy diver who'd been working exclusively at the *Poseidon* Undersea Laboratory in the Florida

Keys for the past two decades. He was the lead aquanaut trainer and had served as one of the technicians on four of Chris's six missions to *Poseidon*. He hadn't changed a bit since Chris had seen him last. He was wearing his standard outfit—Hawaiian shirt, shorts, and flip-flops. His gray-blond hair was tucked under a weathered Miami Dolphins cap. Chris's experience with Trevor Boseman was considerably less by comparison. Boseman had worked on saturation operations associated with oil and gas exploration in the Gulf of Mexico for two decades. They'd met once when Boseman visited the *Poseidon* during one of Chris's missions. He, too, had been a Navy diver. But he'd also trained briefly for the astronaut corps, which had fascinated Chris. And when Chris asked about the difference between his experience as a diver and an astronaut, Boseman's response had surprised him.

"The astronaut corps is a different level. Totally different thing. That isn't to say that it's more physically taxing or more dangerous than a saturation mission. No, it's harder because there's so much more pressure surrounding it. Dozens of movies have been made about it. Presidents talk about it. It's a real mind fuck if you aren't ready for it."

As Boseman now stood before Chris, his outfit a perfect counterpoint to Halbeck's—a short-sleeved button-down shirt, slacks, and steel-toed wing-tip shoes—Chris reflected on that long ago conversation, certain that Boseman brought a unique sensibility to whatever challenges they faced.

"What time are we rallying tomorrow?" asked Chris. "Oh eight hundred?"

"That's correct," confirmed Halbeck. "I understand you got to dive with the aquanauts already."

"Yep," replied Chris. "We dove the *Roosevelt* together up off Fort Lauderdale. They seem like a good team."

"I was worried that they might not be wild about support from outside," explained Halbeck. "Even if your presence was requested at the highest levels."

"Sure, the same thing occurred to me," said Chris. "They're young and ambitious. I might be wrong, but I think we made some headway on that front by diving together."

"Well, you're a better man than I," responded Halbeck "We'll move on to bother someone else for a while. Nice to meet you, Anna. See you tomorrow, Chris."

"Yes, you will."

After Halbeck and Boseman had moved out of earshot, Chris said, "Sorry about that. You were saying?"

"Okay, look," said Cortez. "I'm convinced something is coming."

"That really concerns me," said Chris, again leaning in and lowering his voice. "You confided in me, so I'll do the same for you. *I'm* worried too. *Very* worried. I recently had my students and my boat abducted by pirates, and I'm not ready to have that happen again. If these militia are coming for us, I want to be ready. Can't you tell the authorities?"

"I've tried," explained Cortez. "But they aren't really enthusiastic in this state about getting intelligence from journalists. Particularly not from a woman."

"Got it. I've got contacts who can help us. Maybe you feed me intel and I'll push it up the chain?"

"That's not usually the way I work," replied Anna. "But I'll think about it. Until then, watch your back."

"You do the same," said Chris. "Following your leads could put you in just as much danger."

"I can take care of myself," said Anna.

"I believe that," replied Chris. "I heard your camera clicking while bullets were still flying."

"As I said, comes with the job."

25

Sitting on a couch in the dark of his office, the only illumination coming from his laptop computer, Jeremiah Fessler propped his prosthetic leg up on his desk and looked at a badly framed picture from his senior year in high school. The young face smiling back at him, the body with both legs still attached, were distant memories.

His phone buzzed with an incoming call from Bill Todd. He recognized the phone number from the prison. Fessler had remained friends with Todd since the older man had first encouraged him to join the Brotherhood.

"King here," announced Fessler as he answered the phone.

"I don't know why you persist in using that handle," said Todd.

"Did you call to hassle me, Bill?" replied Fessler. "I've got a lot going on."

"You can hang up whenever you want to," said Todd. "But I'm checking up on you."

"Why?"

"I saw the report of the attack down in Miami," said Todd. "And the kid from the VA who brings me my meds told me there's a lot happening online."

"And?"

"I'm no genius," said Todd, "but isn't all that attention going to create legal problems for us, or you. I mean, I'm in jail already. You're not. And you're not exactly a secret to the authorities after that stunt in Tallahassee last year. How're you going to keep yourself out of jail and running my Brotherhood?"

The previous year Fessler, who had up to that point led the Brotherhood from beyond the public eye, had stepped out of the shadows to lead a protest on the front lawn at the state capitol. A dozen legislators had scheduled a press conference in front of the capitol building following the sinking of a raft of Cuban immigrants the week before. Sixty people had died before they'd reached the Keys.

The legislators were angling to leverage the incident to relax immigration laws they perceived as too strict, even though the state legislature would never approve a change. The Brotherhood, along with several other similarly motivated groups, had mobilized to protest any relaxation in the laws at the press conference and a counterprotest of pro-immigration supporters formed.

The combined protests soon degraded into screaming, and once that had begun, it wasn't long until blows were exchanged. At that point, with TV news crews covering the event from multiple vantage points, Fessler had spontaneously drawn a handgun and pointed it at the nearest opposing protester to him. Half the crowd had immediately begun chanting "Stand your ground! Stand your ground!" referring to Florida's controversial self-defense statute. The other half had started demanding that the cops intervene.

Fessler had been milliseconds from squeezing the trigger at a Hispanic woman who was screaming at him. She'd been so close to him that he could easily discern the pores on her face. The capitol police had tackled him to the ground.

He'd spent a night in jail before anyone realized he was an ex-con. Despite unambiguous evidence of his having drawn a weapon on at least ten separate news cameras, the case was dropped for lack of evidence, and Fessler had been released.

"Are you still there?" asked Todd.

"I'm here," Fessler responded.

"How long until they're traced back to you?"

"That shouldn't be an issue," said Fessler. "We've been using guys who participate in multiple groups. The Feds might poke around, but they won't find anything."

"That's what people who get caught by the Feds always say," suggested Todd. "I'd shut the kid down."

Martinez had told Fessler the same thing earlier in the day. He was not pleased to have his personnel decisions questioned. Besides, going after Pierce and attacking this undersea mission was the best thing he'd done in years. Looking down at his prosthesis, he realized that were he in better physical shape, he'd want to be down there in the Keys pulling the trigger himself. That would be a solid way to go out.

"I've got everything under control," he replied. "Don't you have anything better to do than to give me shit?"

"You're going off the rails, son," said Todd. "This militia bullshit has to stop."

"Have you lost your nerve, old man?" asked Fessler. "When did you become such a candy ass? You're the one who got me started in all of this. You. So don't back down now. We're going to strike back against the system, and it's going to shake the government down to its foundation."

"I hope you like the look of your old orange jumpsuit, 'cause that's all I see in your future, if you survive," said Todd before he hung up the phone.

26

Chris Black remained at the table for ten minutes after Anna Cortez departed. They'd been too busy talking to eat, and Mac and Dana had long ago finished their meals and left, so he ordered dinner and began to review his notes from the conversation.

If the last two years had taught him anything, it was the value of vigilance in the face of potential dangers. During downtime at sea, he and Mac had often joked with students about the many bad horror movies they'd watched over the years, and how the common thread woven through all of them was the failure of the protagonists to recognize the threat in a timely fashion.

"If you hear a disembodied voice scream 'Get out!' in the middle of the night, you leave!" Mac had argued. "You don't wait around until your daughter is possessed or your dog is impaled in the front yard."

But the line between vigilance and unreasonable obsession was thin, Chris knew. It was rarely clear in real life when and from where threats were forthcoming.

He finished dinner, yawned, and realized he'd been up since four thirty that morning. It was time to head upstairs to his room for the night.

Winding his way through the restaurant, Chris spotted Jessica Wilson sitting at a table in a corner forking at a meal. The table was nestled so deep behind two massive plants that he nearly missed the aquanaut trainee from Texas.

He waved when Jessica looked up. Though she waved back, Chris got the impression that she was uncomfortable for some reason. He could see another meal sitting across from Jessica and he briefly wondered if one of her fellow aquanaut trainees was with her. But he was too tired to check in with her and moved on through the restaurant.

As he walked past the pool and out through the open lobby, Chris noticed a man sitting in a lounge chair drinking a beer. The white man had short gray hair and was wearing shorts and a polo shirt, much like other tourists in the hotel. But whereas no one else was looking at Chris, this man was doing so conspicuously.

Behind the man, Chris could see a large flat-screen TV mounted above the bar. It was showing a radar image of the northern Caribbean. He could see the spiral clouds of a tropical storm working its way through the Virgin Islands.

The storm had been the subject of great discussion at the morning's first mission briefing. All the seven-to-ten-day meteorological models had the storm track moving northward well east of the Keys. Some mission staff wanted to delay the mission, but the majority, including all four of the aquanaut trainees, had agreed that keeping an eye on the storm while the training proceeded made the most sense.

With the social media threat to the mission's participants and the hotels in the front of his mind, Chris proceeded out the main door of the lobby and down two steps to the pool level. The hotel featured a series of circuitous paths leading out from the main lobby, around the multiple pools and cabana areas, to the other portions of the hotel and down to the beach. The paths were paved to accommodate the ubiquitous golf carts transporting people and their often-considerable baggage to their rooms. The paths were lined with bamboo trees and shrubs, with overgrown archways marking the location of side paths and other hidden nooks.

Chris paused at the base of the main path and considered his situation. His room was at the far end of the left building. In the daylight, he'd been captivated by the view from his front deck. But in the dark, at the end of a very long day, he was not enthusiastic about the circuitous walk through the paths around the pool. He was also too tired to return through the lobby and try to find his room that way.

The dark path was illuminated by lights nested within the trees every fifteen to twenty feet on either side. That left alternating dark patches in between the lighted areas. The path was crowded as Chris slowly began working his way toward the south wing of the hotel, with smiling couples walking by arm in arm. The farther he moved along the path, the fewer people he encountered. It was in the relative calm of the outer reaches of the path that he first heard footsteps behind him.

He glanced backward over his shoulder and could not see anyone in the illuminated areas of the path. However, as he resumed walking, the sound of footsteps resumed as well.

Chris considered his options as he continued to walk. If he *was* being followed, he was going to have to solve his problem on his own. There was no one else around. Stepping into the next dome of illuminated area, he paused and pulled out his smartphone. Turning the volume down with his finger, he put the phone up to his ear and pretended to be receiving a call from a colleague.

"Yeah, this is Chris. Oh, Officer Snelling. How can I help you?" Chris asked of the fictitious officer as he glanced back down the path. There was no one to be seen, but he could hear footsteps.

"Really? I'm on the path right now. I imagine that if I wait here, I'll run into them within minutes." He began to see the outline of a man approaching from down the path.

"No problem, I'm happy to wait." Chris's voice nearly caught when the gray-haired man who'd been staring at him in the lobby emerged into the light. The man looked strong, thought Chris. This could be challenging.

The man made eye contact with Chris, but continued past him and up the path as Chris continued his feigned conversation. "Perhaps just have them meet me at my room. I'll be there in a minute."

Chris resumed his walk up the path. Within forty feet he spotted the man waiting for him just out of the light in the area immediately in front of his room. Tensing his muscles for the attack he knew was coming, Chris prepared for a fight, which would have to be conducted with fists alone in the absence of any type of weapon.

"Dr. Black?" said the man as he thrust out his hand for Chris.

"Yes?"

"I apologize for stalking you. My name's Brody. Chuck Brody. You and your friend saved my life last week up in Fort Lauderdale."

"Wait a minute. You're who?" asked Chris, without yet taking the man's proffered hand.

"Brody. You rescued us during the dive along the *Roosevelt*. My two dive buddies were struck by a stonefish."

Chris took one step back to get a better look at the man in the light. "Oh, you're the photographer?"

"That's right! I was taking the picture when the stonefish struck both Hayward and Langton."

"What are you doing down here in the Keys?" asked Chris.

"Well, to be honest I heard that you and your colleague, Mr. Johnson, were down here for a mission, and I really wanted to thank you. No one would tell me your room number, so I staked out the lobby. Sorry if I caught you off guard."

"And how did you know the right hotel?" asked Chris.

"I didn't. I Googled your name. A social media post listed hotels associated with the mission, so I gave it a shot. Just got lucky."

"Look, man," said Chris. "I appreciate your enthusiasm, but this is *not* how you approach people."

"I'm sorry."

"That's okay," said Chris. "I'm going to leave now. Best of luck to you."

"If you ever find yourselves in upstate New York, please give me a call. We have some surprisingly good quarry diving near me."

"Yeah, I'll do that." Chris walked away, shaking his head in disbelief over the encounter. Several steps later he turned to confirm Brody was no longer following him.

27

"*What*?" barked Mac Johnson as he opened his hotel room door. His hair was plastered to his head on one side and there was drool crusted on one cheek. His T-shirt read "I'm a Ray of Sunshine!"

"Sorry. I need my dive gear," explained Chris, looking around. "No Dana?"

"What time is it?" asked Mac as he made way for Chris to enter.

"Seven o'clock. Time to rise and meet the day," said Chris.

Mac said nothing, so Chris added, "I ran into Chuck Brody last night."

"You did *what*? Who the hell's Chuck Brody and why am I talking about him at this ungodly hour?"

"Late night? He's the photographer you rescued up on the *Roosevelt*. He Googled my name and found us down here," replied Chris, as he looked through his dive bag to confirm all his gear was there.

"Oh. Well, that's nice. I wish him well," said Mac. "Have you heard from Hendrix? I know Dana said he was going to reach out to you, and all I've heard is radio silence."

"Nothing yet. What about Dana? Where'd she go?"

"She left early this morning to work on some other project nearby," replied Mac. "I guess the thinking is that we're now under the umbrella of protection for the *Calypso I* mission, so she's free to work elsewhere."

"I'm sure that's the thinking," said Chris. "But after my conversation with Anna Cortez last night, I don't think we should rely on that protection."

"Tell me," said Mac, instantly becoming more alert.

Chris briefed him on the conversation.

"That definitely doesn't sound good," agreed Mac. "What's the call?"

Chris zipped his dive bag closed and slung it up over his shoulder. "Just stick to our plan. Hang out at mission control today and help where you can."

When Chris had agreed to help support the mission, he'd asked whether the mission could benefit from the support of a marine engineer. The response had been an enthusiastic affirmative.

"Maybe you can start by making sure they have all the reef maps that Carrie provided us loaded up into their spatial database," suggested Chris. "Once you've demonstrated your can-do attitude, I'm sure they'll leverage your presence for all sorts of fun jobs."

"Copy that. I'll see what I can do," said Mac.

"And I know it goes without saying, but watch yourself," noted Chris. "We don't know where or how they'll strike next."

"Got it," said Mac.

Chris threw his gear in the back of their rented van and drove the quarter of the mile down the road to the coastal marine lab where the training was going to take place for the next five days. A security guard checked Chris's identification before allowing him to enter the parking lot. Another one checked it again as he approached the lab's main door. Chris walked down a spiral staircase to the lower level of the lab. The lounge where researchers decompressed after long days on the water was empty, but through the glass doors he could see Halbeck out on the dock prepping the equipment for the day's training.

"Happy you volunteered for this?" asked Chris, as he stepped through the sliding doors.

Without turning his head, Halbeck replied, "You think I volunteered for this gig? Not exactly. With *Poseidon* down for the next two months for maintenance, the director thought 'it would be good for my spirits' if I came down here to help out."

Chris looked around briefly to confirm they were alone before he asked, "How do you like working with Boseman? You guys have a different . . . style."

"I don't get accused of having style very often," said Halbeck. "But I know what you mean. He's a little less jovial than our regular colleagues, but he knows his stuff."

"Less jovial?"

"He's not a fun guy," explained Halbeck. "Very little small talk and no jokes. He's all business."

"Do you know anything about his history? I know he worked in the Gulf."

"I probably don't know much more than you. His résumé is impeccable," replied Halbeck. "The technical aspects of this short ten-day mission should be a breeze for him compared with keeping those oil rigs working. But the interpersonal element may prove more challenging. I think it's going to be a long mission for me."

"Well, at least you'll have the aquanauts down there," observed Chris. "Nat's a live wire. Brian too. Together they should keep you going. Not sure yet about Joe, and I can't say anything about Jessica."

"From my limited observations so far," said Halbeck, "Jessica makes Boseman seem chatty by comparison. I don't have any concerns at this point. But . . ."

Chris finished the sentence, ". . . but there is always the Davenport scenario lurking in the back of your mind."

"I think we've worked together too long," observed Halbeck.

Years ago, during Chris's fourth mission to *Poseidon*, they'd tried to broaden the awareness of the undersea program by offering an opportunity for an amateur diver to participate in the mission. Applications had come in from around the country. They read and then reread countless résumés. They conducted interviews by phone and in person, and even contacted references for an informal background check. Chris recalled that the process had been exhausting but that everyone felt good about the final selection of a diver from New Jersey named Ron Davenport.

Davenport's diving résumé had been impeccable. He'd had more than three hundred dives, which was an impressive number for an amateur. He'd accumulated a wide variety of specialty certifications, and his references had all sung the man's praises. All was well with the world, Chris recalled thinking, until the diving commenced.

The real Davenport was considerably different from the Davenport on paper. Expecting a capable assistant for the mission, Chris had found an extremely nervous diver who vomited after every dive. Somehow none of the nervousness had manifested during training, but the mission had ended two days early due to the ongoing challenges of having such an uncomfortable diver on the team.

"You never really know, do you?" asked Chris.

"No, never," replied Halbeck.

"Let's hope for the best with Jessica. And with respect to Boseman, well, it's only ten days."

28

Sharon Dirksen was at home in Kissimmee, just outside of Orlando, riding her stationary bike late in the evening and thinking through the day's events. She often used exercise at the end of the day to process what she'd learned and to prepare for the anticipated onslaught of new challenges for the coming day. She recognized the number of the incoming call and picked up the phone immediately. "This is Dirksen."

"Shaw indicated that you wanted to talk with me," said the caller. "So, I'm calling. Why are you breathing heavy?"

"I'm on my exercise bike. And yes, I did want to speak with you. Thank you for reaching out."

"Time for exercise. That's nice. I've got a lot to do." The caller's irritation was palpable. "What is it you want?"

Dirksen made a mental note to complain to Jones. Shaw, by comparison was easy to deal with. This conversation with their 'friend' was something else altogether.

"I've been asked to check in with you. Shaw is going to be increasingly busy as the mission begins, so I will be your primary contact from here on out."

"Fine. What else?"

"There have been multiple unplanned strikes against the two Californian advisers to the mission," said Dirksen.

"And?"

"And no one here at Unity ordered such strikes and we're wondering where the orders are coming from."

"Why do you care?" asked the voice.

"I'm sorry?"

"Why do you care? We're going to muck up the mission just as we all discussed. I don't recall there being any specific requirements from Leland as to how that was achieved."

"That's not entirely correct," explained Dirksen. "You were engaged to *muck up the mission* as you suggest, but the focus was to be on Gwendolyn Pierce and her agenda of internationalization, which would include her interest in curtailing international arms sales. It was *not* on specific personnel."

"I don't see it that way," said the voice.

"I'm here to help you see it that way," countered Dirksen. "You don't have carte blanche here."

"Listen. I know damn well why you want the *Calypso* mission to fail. Your company's hemorrhaging money and weapons contracts are hanging in the balance. So don't tell me you're going to cut off funding to me. I know too much, little lady, and you don't want me going off the reservation. If you or Shaw want to tell the other participants in this shit show what to do, go right ahead. But I'm going to proceed as I see fit."

He paused. "Is there anything else?" asked the caller. "No? Fine."

The line went dead, leaving Dirksen to stare at her reflection in the window beside her.

29

Chris was relieved to get through the first three days of aquanaut training without incident, barring the continued stream of aggressive social media posts. After the tumult of the previous week and a half, it was nice to see the team move through the rigorous technical training with ease, including a considerable amount of dive time practicing the skills they'd require in event of a problem once the mission began.

Despite the wide variety of personalities, all four aquanaut trainees worked together well. Having worked underwater alongside the trainees for every dive, and sitting through every surface interval with them, Chris had formed a much better picture in his mind as to how the mission would proceed. Nat and Brian were performing well, as expected. It was hard to miss how well they were doing because they made sure to vocalize each success. Joe and Jessica were much quieter. But both had accomplished the tasks assigned to them without issue.

"The tropical storm we've been watching may affect us after all, at least on the last couple days of the mission," said Mac, as he and Chris reclined on the couches.

"Yeah, I saw that when I checked this morning," said Chris.

"We'll keep an eye on it topside," said Mac. "It's not likely to interfere with the aquanauts once they're in saturation, but our surface diving operations may be disrupted for one or more days."

"It would be a pity to mobilize all this effort only to have to end the mission after two or three days. I've had to do that before."

"People in mission control are monitoring," explained Mac. "But I haven't heard any serious discussion of cancellation or early departure from saturation, at least due to weather."

"Understood," replied Chris. "I've yet to have a saturation mission that wasn't challenged by nature. Perhaps you and I can work overtime from the surface for the first few days if it looks like the weather will cause a problem."

"Regarding other potential challenges to the mission, I did overhear an interesting conversation in the afternoon yesterday while you were diving."

"Tell me," said Chris, looking around the lab. "But make it quick. We should have aquanauts in here any minute."

"The CEO of Science Without Borders, John Lefevre," explained Mac. "He's been hanging around the mission control barge, for reasons that are not entirely clear."

"His company *is* funding the mission," suggested Chris.

"Sure," replied Mac. "But my understanding is that he's more of a businessman than a hands-on science or engineering type. His presence on the barge is more of a distraction than it is helpful."

"Okay."

"Well, he basically talks on his phone wherever he likes, with no apparent concern for who might be listening," said Mac. "Yesterday, while I was helping with maintenance of the decompression chamber on the barge, Lefevre walked past, and he was yelling into his phone. I couldn't tell who he was talking to, but he was not happy."

"And what did he say?" asked Chris.

"He indicated that his security folks have wanted to pull the plug for days. They're really concerned about the online threats in light of the attack at the auditorium. He wasn't surprised to be getting pressure from Grampen Rhodes to keep going with the mission. But he said Gwendolyn Pierce *ordered* him to proceed with the mission *regardless* of the threats.

"He's getting crushed on both sides, and he isn't happy about it."

30

"The divers haven't been near the *Calypso I* yet, so today they'll get a look from the outside," explained Chris. At the sound of people coming in the door upstairs, he and Mac had quickly adjusted their conversation to the plans for the day. "The training plan doesn't call for the first visit inside until tomorrow, but today's lost line drill will allow them to swim around the lab before we head out onto the line highway."

"Remind me what the line highway is again." Malcolm, the reporter from *The Globe*, had come down the stairs and stood behind Mac.

While Mac and Malcolm chatted about the plans for the day, the four aquanaut trainees entered the lounge amid an animated discussion. Jessica dropped her bag, threw down her towel, and stormed back out the door.

"Look, Joe, that isn't what I meant, and you know it," said Brian. "And Jessica can stand up for herself if she's offended by something I say."

"She doesn't see it that way," replied Joe. "You heard her tell us what happened to her family, and who stepped in to help. She doesn't see militia the same way we do, Brian. You need to back off."

"Let's just calm down," suggested Nat. "No need to put on a show for a reporter."

"Hi, team," said Chris. "Everything okay?"

"Everything's good," replied Nat.

"Joe?" asked Chris

"Yes, everything's good," said Joe as he fist-bumped Brian.

Chris stepped out the sliding door onto the dock. The swells gently rocked the boats tied up alongside. He found Jessica leaning on the rail. She rubbed her eyes as he approached, but he could see evidence of tears.

"How're you doing, Jessica?"

"I'm fine."

"Is there anything I can do to help?" asked Chris.

"No," she replied. "I don't need your help. You can't fix everything, so you shouldn't even try."

Surprised at this somewhat confrontational reply from the thus far quietest and most compliant member of the team, Chris decided to tread lightly.

"I'm not trying to fix everything," said Chris. "I just want to help everyone get through the mission successfully. In my experience, living in a tube underwater with five other people for ten days is not going to make your interactions with your fellow aquanauts improve. It might be best to air things out while you're still at the surface."

When she didn't respond, Chris probed further. "What were you guys arguing about?"

"Nothing. It was stupid," said Jessica. "Can't we just focus on the research?"

"Sure," replied Chris. "But only if you're ready to come back into the lab and join your fellow aquanauts."

"Fine."

Chris followed Jessica back into the lab and looked over the group, still trying to discern how concerned he should be about whatever the trainees were arguing about when they came in. Hoping it was just the type of minor disagreement that always arises when people spend days on end in close proximity to one another, he moved on.

"I think you've all met Malcolm already," said Chris. "And you'll remember Mac from our dive on the *Roosevelt*, right? He and I will be diving from the surface during the mission to image the reef around the *Calypso I* so that your observations can be properly georeferenced."

"Cool." Joe smiled at Mac. "You were at the auditorium attack, too. I saw you on the video."

"What video?" asked Mac.

"Someone filmed the attack on their phone and posted it," explained Nat. "It's pretty jerky, but it's received more than one point eight million hits since it posted."

"I don't know why we have to keep talking about this," mumbled Jessica.

"What was that?" asked Brian.

"Look, we aren't going to solve these bigger issues today, but we *do* have to move forward with your training," said Chris, trying to keep everyone's attention on the mission rather than the life under the public eye they found themselves in. "Malcolm, these guys have all spent the last three days learning how to solve their problems without coming to the surface."

"The surface is *not* an option!" said three of the four trainees in unison, though they were each sitting in different places around the lounge. Jessica remained quiet.

"Exactly. So, today is a biggie. We also must be able to find our way safely back to the *Calypso I* if the, excuse the idiom, shit hits the fan. Like it always does."

Chris reached over the back of the couch and grabbed a small whiteboard and a dry-erase marker. "Otter's going to go over all of this in a few minutes, but here are the main points, Malcolm. This rectangle is the *Calypso I*. Since the surface is not an option, diving in saturation is very much like cave diving, which is defined by its overhead environment."

"And cave divers use lines set up throughout the caves to navigate," said Mac.

"That's right. Like *Poseidon* off Key Largo, the *Calypso I* has been set up with these four excursion lines that each extend out onto the reef at least four hundred feet in each of the cardinal directions. And borrowing again from cave diving, every sixty feet or so, a plastic arrow is zip-tied to the line. The arrows all point in the direction of the *Calypso I.* If visibility were to go to zero, or if you were to get disoriented on a dive, finding an excursion line, and then an arrow, will allow you to literally pull yourself back to the *Calypso I* safely."

"And that's where I come in," said Halbeck who, having just come in from the dock, leaned over Chris's shoulder. "Gear up aquanauts, we're heading out."

Chris asked Nat to stay behind for a moment as the others filed out of the lounge.

"Nat, what's the story with Jessica?" asked Chris. "I think I understand you and Brian, but I still don't understand her at all."

"It's a pretty sad story, actually," replied Nat, quietly. "Jessica's parents and her longtime boyfriend were all killed several years ago. They were living in Texas, down near the Mexican border. Someone entered their ranch and knifed all of them. No suspects were ever found. Jessica was away on a research trip when it happened."

"That's terrible," observed Chris. "I wondered why she was so quiet."

"Jessica's quiet, sure. But there's actually a lot of animosity there."

"What do you mean?"

"She's still very unhappy with the way the US government handled immigration along the border. That's what we were arguing about. Brian was railing against the private militias down in Texas that are patrolling the border with no jurisdiction. Basically the same kind of people attacking this mission online. Joe was trying to support Jessica, who thinks it was illegal migrants who killed her family. There's no evidence that it was migrants, but Jessica says it was only the militia down there that helped her."

"So, she was defending militia?" asked Chris.

"More or less," said Nat. "But I don't think she would have brought it up without Brian being Brian."

31

Thirty minutes later, Chris swam behind as the four aquanaut trainees followed Halbeck in a descent toward the *Calypso I*. The large stream of bubbles coming from the moon pool clearly marked the position of the undersea laboratory from a distance. But it wasn't until they approached within thirty feet that the details of the *Calypso I* came into clear relief. Chris could feel the trainees' excitement through the water. Even Jessica, he noted, seemed to be captivated by the reality of the *Calypso I*.

Out of water, the *Calypso I* was bright yellow. Under sixty feet of seawater, where all colors of the spectrum were muted by the depth of light penetration, it looked closer to white. The main hull of the lab was a cylinder close to fifty feet in length with an outer diameter of twenty feet. The wet porch structure containing the moon pool was attached at the stern of the main lab, and the entire structure was supported twenty feet above the seafloor by four large legs, each with a diameter of four feet.

The most striking difference between the *Calypso I* and the *Poseidon* was the near total lack of biofouling on the hull. Both structures were surrounded by fishes. Schools of small fishes swam in coordinated fashion around the legs, thousands more around the main hull, and above both structures, larger predatory fish hovered, waiting for an opportunity to strike. But whereas the *Poseidon* had been underwater for more than two decades, and was consequently covered with invertebrate growth, the *Calypso I* had been submerged for less than a month, and its hull was nearly as clean as the day it was deployed.

Halbeck led the team on a circumnavigation of the lab, pausing at one of the portholes to let everyone wave at Trevor Boseman, who was inside preparing all the systems for human habitation. Boseman was in the midst of his first of three hour-long dives down to the lab that he'd complete over the course of the day, as well as the next, to make sure the *Calypso I* was ready to receive the aquanauts.

Halbeck then directed everyone to follow him out along the east-facing excursion line. After swimming several hundred feet, the team reached one of the waystations set up at the end of each excursion line. The waystations were inverted, bell-shaped structures that allowed aquanauts to stand up inside to talk to each other in fresh air, report back to the technicians at the *Calypso I*, and have a snack or a drink. Halbeck had explained that they wouldn't be going into a waystation until the next day. He pointed to sand flats on either side of the line, and then held out his open palm.

Chris knew this was possibly the most challenging of the drills required during training, having completed it himself on six separate occasions up at *Poseidon*. The trainees were required to give up their masks. Halbeck would then lead each team, with their eyes closed, to specific locations several yards away from the line. He would then grab each buddy by his or her tanks and shake the diver around until total disorientation had set in. At that point, Halbeck would set them free, and the teams would use the line reels that they'd each been provided to conduct a coordinated search for the nearest excursion line.

Each search was initiated by securing one end of a line reel around a coral head. The team would then wind the reel three times around the coral head in a clockwise direction. Next, they would spool out approximately twenty feet of line, positioning one diver at the end of the twenty feet holding the reel, and the other stationed halfway between his/her buddy and the coral head.

The team then had to work together to slowly begin a search for the nearest excursion line by swimming counterclockwise. With each successive pass around the coral head, the search would broaden until one of the divers would locate the line. The drill didn't end until one of the divers found one of the arrows mounted on the line and pointed in the direction of the *Calypso I*.

Brian and Jessica, Chris could see, initiated their search in the wrong direction. By swimming clockwise around the coral head, the line would tighten rather than extend their search radius as they wound it around the coral. Chris was pleased to see that Jessica spotted their error first and motioned to Brian to swim in the other direction. His eyes burned with sympathetic pain, recalling how brutal it is to look around in salt water without a mask on.

Turning to his right, Chris could see Nat and Joe well along on their way to finding the line highway. But he also noted that Joe was swimming with some urgency, outpacing Nat. Joe was first to find the line and almost immediately found one of the arrows. Seeing Joe struggling, Halbeck quickly gave him back his mask.

Shortly thereafter, all four trainees queued up along the excursion line. Both Halbeck and Chris made clapping motions to honor the team's efforts, then Halbeck moved in to confirm that each diver was okay.

All four divers were blinking fast to try and remove the salt from their eyes, but Chris could see that they were all very excited to have successfully completed the task. When Halbeck reached Joe, who was positioned closest to Chris, Joe was able to give Halbeck the okay sign. But almost immediately Chris saw Joe's eyes roll back in his head as he passed out. Seconds later the regulator fell out of his mouth.

32

Bob "Quint" Shaw drove south on US Route 1 through the Florida Keys at speeds reaching ninety miles an hour. He wasn't in any hurry to get to Key West, that was simply the speed at which Shaw drove anywhere. At six foot two and two hundred and twenty pounds, he felt comical squeezed into his small rental car. But he adapted.

Adaptation was what had kept Shaw alive through three tours in Afghanistan, two in the Marines and one as a contractor. Named after his parents' favorite actor, Robert Shaw, he'd been quickly tagged by his fellow soldiers with the nickname Quint after his namesake's famous role in the movie *Jaws*. He didn't mind the nickname, and eventually came to call himself Quint wherever he went.

He didn't like working with the militia. He came out of every meeting with them feeling dirty. He understood his employer's rationale for the current objective, and he even agreed with it. Not that it mattered, as he would have carried out his tasks either way.

But then there was Bash. Jeremiah Fessler was an idiot, and he was kidding himself if he thought he was leading this shit parade. But Shaw reserved his highest disdain for people like Bash who killed indiscriminately, showing none of the experience derived from actual combat. He didn't need to reach under his shirt to feel the multiple scars on his back and shoulders. The fabric brushed against the raised tissue differently, constantly reminding him of the many gunshots and shrapnel that had penetrated his body over the years. Even with his newfound maturity, Shaw knew that in another life he would have killed Bash and found some other way to accomplish the larger mission.

Killing the scientists associated with the undersea mission was not a major concern to Shaw. He understood the desperation that was driving Leland Jones. It was business, and collateral damage always occurred in business. It didn't, however, please him to think about killing Black and Johnson, particularly given that Johnson had once been a SEAL. Shaw had not been ordered to do it, but for some reason Bash and his cronies had fixated on it.

His phone buzzed on the seat next to him. Since his rental car didn't have an integrated dashboard, he answered the call and pushed the button for speakerphone.

"Quint here."

"I'm never going to get used to calling you that, Robert," said Sharon Dirksen. They had worked together for more than a decade. Whether she actually cared about him or not, he felt better thinking that she did. Shaw had very little other female contact these days.

"What's the sitrep?" he asked.

"There's been an incident at the *Calypso I* site. I don't know yet if it had anything to do with us or not."

"Was somebody KIA?"

"No, well, not yet anyway," said Dirksen. "One of the scientists went unconscious underwater and had to be resuscitated. I'm waiting for more intel and will report back."

Shaw quickly cycled through his mind how Fessler's contacts could have orchestrated a dive emergency, but wasn't familiar enough with who had access to the SCUBA gear to know if that was possible.

"Are you still en route?" asked Dirksen.

"That's affirmative," responded Shaw. "I'm about one hour out from Key West. Any changes to my next task?"

"I'm not sure yet. It depends on how the next forty-eight hours develop. We may require you to make a return trip to Miami. Also, it may be that Black, the scientist from California, will take the place of the injured diver on the mission."

"Copy that. It will be a shame if he dies along with everyone else."

33

"Mr. Halbeck, please walk me through what happened as you experienced it," said Special Agent Greene. She'd boarded the training vessel as soon as it had tied up back at the dock. Chris was asked to remain on board as well.

Halbeck first described the tasks assigned to the divers, along with the water depths involved in the dive and the periods of time the divers spent at each depth.

"Here's Joe's dive computer," explained Halbeck as he handed the agent the large, rectangular, forearm-mounted computer that each trainee was issued. "I looked through the dive profile and it looks unremarkable until the emergency ascent to the surface."

"Thank you. Continue, please," said Greene.

"All four divers had completed the assigned search patterns to locate the adjacent line highway. The drill is set up so that ultimately every group achieves the task. This group was no different. I'd queued them up along the line so that I could run Dr. Black here through the task, but after flashing me the okay sign, Joe went unconscious and expunged his regulator."

"Okay, and your response was what?"

"I signaled to Dr. Black to keep an eye on the rest of the trainees, and I initiated an emergency ascent."

"Is Dr. Black a trainee too?" the agent asked.

"Technically, yes," replied Halbeck. "But he's a veteran of six saturation missions and has logged something like four thousand dives to date, so I had absolutely no concerns about turning over the divers to his care. In fact, that's why he's here, to help make the mission a success."

The agent looked at Chris as though she were assessing him and then returned her gaze to Halbeck.

"Once at the surface, I inflated Joe's BCD, removed his mask, and assessed his vitals. As soon as I determined that he was not breathing, I yelled to the barge to activate the EMS, and I began in-water CPR."

"EMS? The Emergency Medical System, correct?"

Halbeck nodded in response.

"After they activated the Emergency Medical System, did anyone from the barge assist you?"

"Yes, they quickly deployed an RHIB." At the agent's furrowed brow, Halbeck explained, "A rigid hull inflatable boat—its speed and capacity work best in these situations. We were able to get Joe in the boat, at which point I continued CPR."

"What happened next?" asked the agent.

"Joe regained consciousness and vomited into my mouth as I administered a rescue breath."

"Yikes." Chris had not yet heard that detail, but he was not surprised. "CPR is never pretty."

"No, it isn't," agreed Halbeck. "At that point, the helo had landed on the upper deck of the barge, and Joe was evacuated."

"Thank you, Mr. Halbeck. It appears that you saved Mr. Bauer's life. Now, I understand that neither of you are physicians, but do you have any thoughts on what may have caused Mr. Bauer to lose consciousness?"

"That's awfully hard to tell," replied Halbeck. "As I said, it was an unremarkable dive profile. We were well within safe diving parameters, and everyone was diving air, as opposed to mixed gas. I filled the tanks myself, and no one else has reported any problems."

"Are there any possible technological explanations for what might have happened?"

"Are you asking if anyone tampered with the equipment?" asked Chris.

"Please, let me ask the questions, Dr. Black," said Agent Greene. "Where were the tanks kept last night?"

"All the tanks were secured behind locked doors right down the dock from where we're sitting now," explained Halbeck.

"And who would have had access to that storage area?" asked the agent.

"That's a question for the lab director. I think he's around here somewhere."

"Do you have anything else you'd like to add, Dr. Black?"

"Not really," replied Chris. "I think Otter covered the incident just as it happened. I will say, however, that I've been part of incidents in which SCUBA gear was sabotaged, and if it's done well, it's very difficult to determine after the fact."

"Did this sabotage happen within the US?" asked Agent Greene.

"No, the incident I'm referring to happened in South Africa."

"Yes, well, the FBI lab will be giving all of Mr. Bauer's equipment a thorough review. Thank you both for your time. We'll be back with more questions if we have them."

After the agent left, Halbeck leaned into the pilot's chair and exhaled.

"Nicely done, Otter," Chris observed. "A textbook rescue."

"Thanks."

"Do you think anyone tampered with Joe's rig?" asked Chris.

"You mean like sabotage? It's possible, I suppose," replied Halbeck while vigorously rubbing his eyes. "But *why*? It's a *science* project. I know what you and Mac faced up in Key Biscayne and that there've been threats against the mission. But it just seems so unreal that someone would be sneaking around sabotaging gear. We're not exactly curing cancer here."

"Actually, Jessica's work could end up curing cancer someday," noted Chris. "But I see what you mean. Tweaking gear is a lot more nuanced and sophisticated than what these militia guys generally do."

"So, are you ready to be an aquanaut again?" asked Halbeck. "Because with Joe out, it's either you or no one at this point."

Chris sat back in his seat. Once Halbeck had initiated the emergency ascent with Joe, Chris had coordinated the rest of the trainees for a safe ascent back to the vessel they were using for the training dives. Then once at the surface, they'd all been focused on how Joe was doing. Amid all the action, he'd completely overlooked the fact that as the alternative aquanaut trainee, he was now going to have to saturate with the rest of the team. For better or worse, he would be living underwater for the duration of the mission.

"I'm in," replied Chris. "Didn't think I'd get a chance to saturate with you again. Hopefully we can have some fun despite everything that's going on."

"Fun sounds nice," said Halbeck. "But I'll settle for safe. I just want to get everyone else through this in one piece."

34

Chris sat on the marine lab's couch the next morning among the remaining three aquanaut trainees.

He used a bathroom cleaning sponge to erase the writing from his dive slate in preparation for the final training day's dives. He noted a distinct difference in the clamor around him, as everyone sat quietly. The incident the day before had been scary and unsettling, and the entire group seemed hyperaware that the mission harbored dangers.

The characteristic banter between Brian and Nat was missing, while Jessica was avoiding eye contact altogether. Malcolm chatted quietly with Trevor Boseman in a corner.

"Joe's going to be okay," explained Halbeck as he came in from the dock. "He aspirated a small amount of seawater yesterday, so they're going to keep him in the hospital for another twenty-four hours to monitor his recovery. But he should be back to one hundred percent very soon."

"That's great news," observed Chris.

"Do we know what happened to him?" asked Brian. "I mean, he looked fine right up until he didn't."

"I don't think we know much. He'll get a full workup at the hospital," said Halbeck. "And that will include a review of how he'd been feeling the day or two before the incident."

"So, we have no idea what caused the problem?" asked Malcolm. "Could it have been mechanical? Something wrong with his equipment?"

"Anything is possible at this point," replied Halbeck. "Joe is a solid diver, just like all the rest of our team. We wouldn't start the mission if we thought differently."

"This is a good reminder," added Chris, "that anything can happen to any of us at any time, so we need to be ready."

"Is it true that he threw up in your mouth?" asked Nat.

"Way to cut right to the heart of the matter, Nat!" Halbeck laughed. "Let's just say that Joe and I now share a special, eternal bond and leave it at that. Now, I know that we all had a rough day yesterday with one of our own experiencing difficulties. But we knew such a situation might arise, and we added a backup aquanaut into the schedule just for that reason."

Halbeck paused and motioned toward Chris.

"Dr. Black has agreed to saturate in Joe's place. I think he and Joe have worked out a plan to get the fish data Joe was going to collect during the mission."

Chris scanned the divers for reactions. "I know this isn't what we planned to happen, but I hope that I can help each of you during the mission."

"I say, welcome aboard," said Nat, slapping Chris on the thigh. Brian and Jessica nodded their heads.

"Okay, we are moving forward with today's dive, and the mission, as planned. Any questions?"

"We're going into the *Calypso I* today, but just for a short visit, correct?" asked Brian.

"That's right. Until we start saturation, any time spent in the lab will have to follow a normal dive profile. We'll have about fifty minutes, surface to surface."

"But you want our supplies by tonight?"

"Correct," answered Halbeck. "You need to deposit anything that you want to go down to the *Calypso I*, including clothes, data sheets, toothbrushes, etc., right here behind this couch by seven p.m. Please limit yourself to the two white garbage bags you've been issued, and make sure to write your name on the bags. Everything will be transferred down to the lab early tomorrow morning, so that when we finish our first dive, it will be waiting for us."

Nat, Brian, and Jessica immediately put their heads together to discuss what supplies they should bring. Nat produced a list of her gear on a clipboard and shared it with Brian and Jessica.

"How many pairs of socks are you bringing?"

"Are you going with fleece for warmth or sweatpants?"

"Is anyone bringing deodorant?"

"Chris, what do you wear in between dives?" asked Nat.

"I've got a magic pair of red fleece long johns that I've worn on every saturation mission I've been a part of," explained Chris. "And I brought them on this trip just in case."

"That's it?" asked Brian.

"And wool socks," added Chris. "Remember, the lab will be kept cool to maintain the humidity level. And you'll never fully dry off. So, I like to be as warm and as dry as possible. Fleece and wool socks are the best solution I've found."

"Jessica, can you show us where we can do some shopping later," asked Brian. "I think I need to revise my supply list a bit."

"Yes," said Jessica. "We can head over to the mall once we're back on shore. It's not far from here."

"Okay, hearing no other questions," said Halbeck. "We've got one dive left. Let's go so you can get back and do your shopping."

35

The boat ride out to the location of the *Calypso I* was two hours from Key West. From the mooring point adjacent to the mission control barge, Chris could see dozens of people walking about the barge's decks in frenzied preparation for the mission.

After a short safety briefing, the aquanauts submerged and once again approached the *Calypso I.* This time, rather than swim around it, Halbeck led the divers directly to the moon pool entrance, which was a slot measuring eighteen feet wide and three and a half feet high. He had briefed everyone on the short boat ride out about how to best enter the moon pool, including the need to swim in as low as possible to avoid bashing their tank valves on the outer portion of the lab.

Chris hovered in the water column and watched as each of the aquanauts found their way into the moon pool for the first time.

Entering the moon pool himself, Chris popped his head out of the water and kneeled on the deck below him. The water level hit him about mid-chest. Sitting back on his heels, he took in the very familiar smells and sounds of the moon pool as he recalled his first trip to the *Poseidon* lab many years before. His nose picked up the slight sent of mildew. And even with minimal current, the seawater sloshed back and forth within the small area of the moon pool, requiring the aquanauts to raise their voices for every conversation.

The *Calypso I* had been modeled on the *Poseidon*, so everything was immediately familiar. Chris observed to himself that it was very much like going to Disney World in Florida for the first time after having spent a lifetime going to Disneyland in California, in that everything looked and felt very familiar but was still not exactly the same.

The main body of the *Calypso I* was a fifty-foot-long pressure cylinder. The main-lock door opened onto the wet porch, which was a two-story rectangular structure that was built onto the stern of the lab. The lower level of the structure provided direct access to the sea, with the ocean coming and going constantly. That resulted in the continuous sloshing of water, which was amplified significantly in the enclosed space.

Kneeling in the water next to his three fellow aquanauts, Chris listened to Halbeck struggle to speak over the sloshing water. He noticed the divers looking everywhere other than at Halbeck as they took in every detail of the moon pool. Brian elbowed Chris gently and pointed down, where together they watched several small reef fish swim between their knees.

"This rack over here is where you'll stow your tanks at the end of each dive. You enter the pool, and then kneel like you're all doing right now," yelled Halbeck. "Watching the low overhead, you will each move over in this direction and then back your tanks into the rack. Once you feel them securely sitting in the rack, you can slip out of your harness. What's everyone looking at?"

"Fish!" exclaimed Nat.

"We're living underwater?" exclaimed Brian. "Very cool."

"This is much different from what I imagined," said Jessica, barely audible above the sloshing water.

"Ah, yes. You're going to have a lot of new and exciting stuff to experience. But right now, our time is limited," said Halbeck. "*Please* remember to do two things every single time you stow your tanks: First, turn around and wrap one of these bungee cords around the tank valve so your tank doesn't wash away in the night. We've had that happen before at *Poseidon*.

"Second, and this is important too, make sure to wrap both your primary and secondary regulators up around the tank valve so they are out of the water. Chris, do you want to explain what might happen if they forget that step?"

"Sure," replied Chris. "As you can see, there's an abundance of marine life moving through the pool around us. One of my fellow aquanauts once left his regulator floating underwater. During the night, a bristle worm moved into the opening of the regulator, and when the diver took his first breath the next morning, he got a mouth full of bristle worm."

"I'm a fish person," said Nat. "What's a bristle worm?"

"*Not* something you want in your mouth, believe me!" yelled Brian.

"Google it tonight," added Chris. "It isn't pleasant."

From the lower level of the wet porch, there was a three-foot by five-foot space to climb up two metal steps from the moon to the next level. The main level of the wet porch served as the primary staging area for all pre- and post-dive activities. Here the divers would stow their mask and fins, strip off their wetsuits and dunk them in a special cleaning solution before hanging them up, and then shower with fresh water before entering the *Calypso I* proper. The wall opposite the shower contained the air compressors used to fill all the tanks after each dive.

"Chris, do you want to point out things to avoid here on the main level?" asked Halbeck.

"I can think of two things," replied Chris. "First, don't, under any circumstances, overestimate the power of that wetsuit cleaning solution. After we've all spent the next ten days peeing in our wetsuits every dive, the air in the wet porch is going to get pretty rank. If you don't believe me, just wait and see, or I should say, smell."

"That's gross," noted Nat. "But then again, I've already peed twice on this dive!"

"And second," continued Chris, "note the presence of a shower curtain and the placement of that camera over in that corner to the left. We're going to all be in each other's business for the next ten days, but the curtain will provide us with a little bit of privacy during our post-dive showers."

Everyone's eyes went to the camera, and eyes widened as the realization sank in that on the *Calypso I*, privacy was a luxury.

"As you become more comfortable with the arrangements down here, you may be inclined to rip open the curtain post-shower, just like you do back home, without first toweling up. If you do that, know that that camera provides a direct, live feed to mission control above us. They don't always respond well to, shall we say, full exposure."

"Ewww, they watch us shower?" said Jessica.

"That's the point, Jessica. They don't really want to see what they shouldn't. So don't inadvertently make them," added Halbeck.

"Oh, I'm going to give those peepers a show!" said Nat. "What else are they going to do up there in mission control?"

36

Standing on the balcony of his lavish hotel room, Aaron Bash stared out into the ocean below. He'd rarely had the opportunity to stay in such accommodations, and never for more than a day. The couple in the room next door had been arguing for more than two hours. Bash contemplated whether he should intervene, as it reminded him of a similar occasion in his youth.

His first kill had been with a knife, a kitchen knife he'd borrowed from his grandmother. His family had been living in their third apartment in a year, and the neighbors next door fought continually. With his father away so frequently trying to earn money to support the family, it was just Bash living with his mother, grandmother, and three sisters. The man next door had not been impressive in any way, but he'd been bigger than all the women around him. That had granted him the freedom to beat them without consequence, which he'd done nearly every day.

Watching the waves gently lapping along the shore, Bash recalled that night clearly despite the passage of so much time. What he'd eventually come to understand as futility had racked his young mind: his father unable to support them, his mother and grandmother suffering, but everyone he'd seen on TV seemed to live on quiet, tree-lined streets, with kids playing outside. And then there was the asshole next door.

The man had never actually bothered Bash's family directly. No, he'd focused his attention on his own. So, it wasn't so much protection that had been on Bash's mind. It had just been clear to him that the man deserved to die.

"Don't fire until you see the whites of their eyes." Bash preferred the satisfaction of a knife or gun fight to explosives. One of the movies he'd seen on his neighbor's TV when he was a child was a film in which this phrase was emphasized several times. He remembered sitting on the dusty rug, holding a 'knife' he'd ground down from a discarded piece of wood.

The notion that killing should be direct was sensical to him. It wasn't so much about honor, but more about pure toughness. You had to be tough to kill someone after making eye contact. Anyone could blow someone up.

One night at dinner, the beatings had begun. Thunderous crashes had rocked the kitchen wall as the man threw objects against the wall on the other side. Bash's mother had tried to keep a conversation going despite the women's screams, but it was just too loud. Bash had stood up, grabbed his grandmother's carving knife from the dish rack, and headed down the hall.

His family had been petrified. They'd begged him not to go. But Bash went anyway. As he gripped the knife in his hand like he'd seen actors do on TV, he'd felt power surging within him. The door to the neighbor's apartment was unlocked. Bash entered and simply followed the screaming to the kitchen. The layout of the apartment was identical to his. As he walked down the hall, he passed three closed doors, behind each of which he could hear quiet sobbing.

Bash found the man standing over the woman, a rolling pin in his hand. She was lying on the kitchen floor bleeding from her nose and mouth, the dinner she had no doubt just prepared was spread on the floor around her, as were several broken dishes.

"Get up!" screamed the man. "You useless pig. Get up and make the dinner I asked for."

Wasting no time, Bash walked right up to the man and plunged the knife deep into his back.

The man spun around, shock and anger visible in his eyes, and hit Bash harder than he'd ever been hit. He was knocked into the kitchen table, which collapsed under his weight.

Bash curled up into a ball in anticipation of the attack that was about to come. But that one punch was all the man could muster, for the wound from the knife caught up to him quickly. Gurgling blood from his mouth, the man took a step toward Bash and then collapsed face first onto the floor.

Bash, his hands shaking from the adrenaline, struggled to pull the knife from the fallen man's back. When he'd finally done it, he went to the kitchen sink and washed the blood off before returning it to his grandmother.

Yes, the knife was the best way, Bash now thought. But then he'd lost three reliable recruits in the attack at the auditorium, and his options for striking back were limited, at least for the time being, as a result. They needed a different plan.

Fortunately, the Brotherhood had trained him to deal with explosives. And whomever Fessler and that asshole Shaw were working for had provided the cash to acquire explosives and to rent expensive hotel rooms.

They would place the explosives tonight, and tomorrow sounds of flying nails and screaming victims would be all anyone would hear.

37

Chris Black stretched his legs as he waited for Anna Cortez to meet him on the beach of the Fort Zachary Taylor Historic State Park. The day's diving was complete, and the other aquanauts were off putting together their supplies for the start of the mission the next day. Though he looked like a man about to join the masses for a day at the beach, that was the furthest thing from Chris's mind. His legs ached with the special kind of soreness that four dives a day, for seven consecutive days, can produce. He chuckled at the realization that the next ten days, including up to eight hours a day of diving, would soon eclipse his current level of discomfort.

The beach wound along the southwestern corner of Key West, bordered by trees and an occasional coffee shop. The beach was overflowing with families as the air temperature continued to hover around eighty degrees Fahrenheit.

Cortez had messaged him while he was still out on the boat asking for a meeting before the mission began the next day. He'd been quick to defer any interactions with the press to the mission's media coordinator. But those were all focused on details about the mission, not about a potential terrorist plot. They agreed to meet in a public place, preferably one where they could move freely, to discuss her latest revelations. That meeting time was still twenty minutes away, so Chris slowly ambled along the beach trying not to go too far in either direction.

The volleyball courts on the sand were being used for a round-robin foot-volley tournament. Chris had only seen it played one time before, on the beach in Israel, and found it fascinating to watch. The six-player teams on either side of the net used only their feet to pass around a modified volleyball, with rallies lasting as long as any volleyball game he'd ever seen.

The final game of the tournament was well underway as he watched.

He pulled out his phone and called Mac, who answered immediately. "What'd she have to say?"

"We haven't met yet. Still five minutes away. I'm watching foot volley," said Chris.

"Sounds fascinating," said Mac. "I've worked out access to a vessel for the next few days at least. So, I should be able to get the habitat imaging work we planned done from the surface while you're playing down below with the aquanauts."

"Excellent," replied Chris. Spotting Cortez on the beach, he added, "Gotta go. Black, out."

"Blackout, I like that," replied Mac as he clicked off.

The crowd around the courts erupted in cheers as the final game was completed.

As Chris approached Cortez, her body language suggested tension.

"Hi, Anna."

"Hi, Chris. I just got back from looking into a lost diver up near Fort Lauderdale."

"On the wreck of the *Roosevelt*? Was his name Langton, by any chance?" Chris couldn't understand how that incident would have attracted Cortez's interest.

"What? No, it was in a quarry. The Piedmont Quarry, northwest of the city," answered Cortez. "The kid's name was, or is, Ben Foster. He was diving at night and alone in the quarry. They found his truck and his SCUBA equipment, but no body."

"A kid. That really sucks," replied Chris. "Quarries can be very dangerous places. And diving alone, at night, in a quarry, is particularly dangerous. I'm not completely surprised that something happened. Why is an accident on your radar screen?"

"Because I don't think it was an accident," said Cortez. "My source said it relates to a threat to the *Calypso* mission."

"How?" asked Chris.

"He didn't say exactly, only that it happened during a trial run of something. The same guys that have been stalking you and Mac were involved."

Chris looked down at the sand and considered the implications of this information.

"Did you find anything when you looked into it yourself? Something your source didn't give you?"

"I did," replied Cortez. "A county sheriff dive team found a BCD with both the shoulder straps sliced clean through. Does that sound like an accident?"

"Do you mean torn?" asked Chris. "Maybe he got hung up on rebar or an old car someone dumped in the quarry and tore the straps. They really are dangerous places."

Cortez pulled out her smartphone and swiped her index finger across the screen.

"Here it is. The sheriff said, 'The straps were cut clean through. Uniform slices, not tears.' He was confident it was done with a knife."

"Maybe the kid got caught on something and used his own knife to cut himself out," suggested Chris. "Without his BCD and tank, he'd be in trouble unless he really knew what he was doing."

"Okay, maybe. But the fact remains that my source directed me to the incident. And everything he's told me so far has come to pass in some way or another."

"That leaves two questions, then," said Chris. "What are you proposing that I do with this information? And what did your source indicate would happen next?"

"Look, as I said, I don't have the best history with authorities. I've written too many stories critical of federal law enforcement responses to extremist actions. Many of my former sources won't talk to me anymore. No one wants a tip from me. And I think I mentioned the locals' negative attitude about women reporters."

As he listened to Cortez's explanation, Chris scanned the crowd around them. When his scan reached the area behind where he'd been standing, a man in a black hoodie turned and started to walk away. The man looked back once, right at Chris, and then started to run, knocking over two people in his way.

"Stay here!" yelled Chris as, driven by instinct, he started running after the man.

Cortez followed him anyway.

38

The first few steps in the soft sand hurt, but the adrenaline quickly took over and allowed Chris to pump his diving-weary legs. He began closing the distance on the man, whose hoodie had fallen back to reveal closely cropped blond hair. Bobbing and weaving through the dense, early evening crowd, it was not hard to track the only other person running. The closer Chris got, the more gray he noticed among the blond. He was not chasing a young man.

The man ran into the trees between the beach and a huge parking structure used by the park. Chris followed the man into the forest, out the other side, and down a ramp into the structure. Taking a moment to let his eyes adjust from the sunshine to the poorly lit cavern of the garage, he heard the sound of running footsteps to his left, and launched himself in that direction.

Chris spotted the man rounding the ramp to the next lower level. But as he followed down the ramp, a van full of foot-volley enthusiasts accelerated upward. Jumping up on the curb that lined the outer perimeter of the ramp, Chris narrowly avoided getting run over. Hands flat against the garage wall, he fought to stay as flat as possible along the concrete.

The van's slipstream threatened to pull him off the curb, while one of the passengers in the last row of seats actually brushed Chris's shirt with her hands as they passed.

Scanning the lower level of the parking lot, Chris could see taillights of at least ten separate vehicles flash white as they backed out of their parking spots. The first two cars that drove past him were full of more foot-volley people, yelling and cheering as they left. The third was different. It was a small white rental car, judging by the sticker on the windshield. Even in the low light of the garage Chris could see a large man awkwardly filling the front seat, his elbows angling outward to avoid a steering wheel that was too close. As the car neared, he recognized the hoodie while simultaneously making eye contact with the guy.

The man accelerated toward Chris, causing pedestrians to dive for cover. Chris easily dodged to the right and briefly considered jumping onto the hood. Instead, he leaped at the open driver-side window as it passed. He hit the man hard on the left side of his face, grabbed a fistful of his shirt, and hung on.

Being pulled along as the vehicle built up speed, Chris struggled to keep his feet under him to avoid letting them get dragged under the small car's rear wheel. The two men exchanged blows that were significantly constrained by the tight quarters of the front seat. Chris grabbed for the gear shift but failed to get purchase. With nothing firm to hold on to, and seeing several potential hazards ahead, Chris fell back from the car, barely managing to maintain his footing as it moved on without him.

Walking back up the ramp and out of the garage, Chris found Cortez waiting for him at the entrance.

"Who was that?" she asked.

"I have no idea. Did you—"

"Get his license plate? Of course, I did. Who do you think you're dealing with here?"

Still out of breath from the exchange, Chris motioned toward a nearby bench.

"What's your next step?" he asked.

"I'll get someone to run the plates on that license number. Maybe that will tell us something," said Cortez.

"Did you get a good look at the guy as well?" asked Chris.

"I did."

"Anything strike you about him?"

"He looked like military, or at least former military, if that makes any sense," said Cortez.

"I had the same feeling," noted Chris. "Do you think he followed one of us?"

"I don't know," said Cortez, thinking out loud. "You have to come and go from the facilities associated with the mission. So, he could have picked you up there."

"Sure. But you've also been asking questions," said Chris. "What if he picked you up in Fort Lauderdale looking into the missing kid?"

"Are you worried about *me*?" asked Cortez.

"What? No," said Chris quickly. "Well, maybe a little. Your dogged determination is growing on me."

"You like my dogged determination, do you? Hmmm."

"Well, I—" Chris interrupted himself with a smile, then added bashfully, "Let's stay focused."

"Showing a little dogged determination ourselves, are we?"

Cortez reached into her bag and removed a taser, which she pushed into Chris's thigh but didn't trigger. "This won't be the first time I've been in danger, you know."

"Oh, I don't doubt it," he said. "Okay, here's what we do. I'm going to text you two numbers; one is for a guy named Donagan. You'll find him up in Miami at whatever facilities the State Department has up there. He's got his hands in all sorts of things. I want you to call him and tell him everything you've told me, and what just happened here. The other is for my colleague Mac Johnson, whom you saw in action at the auditorium. He will be working from the surface while I'm underwater and will be able to serve as a contact. He's a former SEAL, FYI."

"Donagan won't just ignore me like everyone else up there?" asked Cortez.

"Not if you tell him I sent you," replied Chris. "But be careful, please."

"You're about to move into a metal tube on the seafloor for ten days with five other people you barely know, while likely being in the crosshairs of terrorists," said Cortez. "And you're telling *me* to be careful?"

39

Derrick Sumner mixed two cocktails and sat down in an easy chair across from Leland Jones. "Here you go. Maybe this will help."

"Shit, I'll need at least three of these before they start to kick in," replied Jones, as he leaned back, rested his head, and looked up at the ceiling.

He moved his feet up onto the coffee table in front of him, knocking an ashtray onto the carpet.

"Fuck."

They were seated alone in the company's executive lounge. Sumner regarded the thick cloud of cigar smoke hovering above them and concluded that Jones had been sitting there for quite a while before he walked in.

"So, what's bothering you today?"

"What's bothering me? Company's going under. Wife's leaving me. And that's just for starters!"

"Okay, what's bothering you this afternoon?" asked Sumner.

Jones used the glowing embers of a cigar nub to light another. "This militia thing has gotten out of control."

"What do you mean?" asked Sumner. "My understanding from Dirksen is that the chaos we talked about is underway. Shaw is performing as expected."

"He is," agreed Jones. "But I wasn't convinced that he would be enough, so I contacted our 'friend' to help out. And I didn't exactly tell Shaw about that."

"Compartmentalized operations. We do that all the time," said Sumner, finishing his drink and rising to pour another. "What's the problem?"

"The problem is that I think a lot more people are going to die than I expected, including a lot of innocent civilians," said Jones. "Shaw cultivated several assets to sabotage the mission just as we asked him to. But it looks like our friend has contracted two of those assets on the side to significantly expand the scope of the operation."

"How do you know this?"

"Doesn't matter," replied Jones. "I just know. The coming carnage is going to be horrific."

"But carnage was always the goal. People are going to have to die for this plan to have the impact we need it to. How has that changed?"

"It hasn't," said Jones. "But I was not planning on killing so many civilians."

"Fine. I understand," said Sumner. "But this was always going to be an issue. So I ask you—even if I could stop it, would you want me to?"

Jones puffed on his cigar.

"There's no stopping it, or them, now," he said, pinching the bridge of his nose. "The question is, how and when will it blow back on us?"

40

"Senator Pierce," asked a reporter standing on the main deck of the mission control barge, "what did you and Congressman Rhodes tell the four aquanauts in your meeting with them this morning?"

"They're already well-trained and ready for this adventure," said Pierce. "They certainly don't need old politicians telling them anything. We really just wanted a few minutes to encourage them and wish them well."

"Is that how it really went down?" whispered Mac as he and Chris stood well back from the press corps watching the chaos.

"Not really, no," said Chris. "My fellow aquanauts asked a lot of questions about mission security. Pierce and Rhodes basically fought to see who could be more authoritative in their responses."

"Who won?"

"I'd call it a draw," replied Chris. "Neither of them has actual constituents participating in this mission. But Pierce clearly has invested a lot of political capital in the portable sea lab concept, which is being spearheaded by a constituent. And it felt like Rhodes has the former politician's desperate need for relevance. He really didn't have anything substantive to add. Ultimately, they both deferred to John Lefevre, the CEO of Science Without Borders. He explained that security will be present twenty-four seven throughout the mission."

"Comforting," said Mac.

"I thought so," said Chris.

"Did anyone buy that?"

"I think they're all very excited about starting their research," explained Chris. "They asked about security, received an answer from people in authority, and it's on with the mission."

Climbing down to the deck below, where the aquanauts were prepping to begin the mission, Chris met Brian's parents and his fiancée, as well as Nat's partner Denise.

"What do you think will be the hardest part about living underwater for almost two weeks?" asked Brian's mother. "Brian says you have a lot of experience."

"Do you want the official answer, or the not-so-official one?" asked Chris.

"Can't we have both?" replied Brian's father.

"Well, officially I will miss the sun on my face and sleeping in a real bed. But unofficially, chocolate chip cookie dough! I think we'll have cookies down there, but nothing compares to fresh dough."

"Oh, you and Brian are going to get along well, I should think," observed Brian's mother.

Chris had realized earlier that Jessica didn't seem to have anyone seeing her off and so, during a lull in the conversation, Chris pulled Nat and Denise aside.

"Is nobody here to send Jessica off?" he whispered.

"I told you she's got no one left in her immediate family, but I think there might be an aunt and uncle around," whispered Nat. "And what about your peeps, Chris? Where are they?"

"Oh, they used to come to these sorts of things back in my earlier days. But this mission is far away from California, and I wasn't supposed to be saturating anyway, so nobody thought they needed to come here to watch me train people. But now that I'm going underwater after all, I'm sure my mom will be following the live stream."

"But where's your pal Mac?"

"He's up there listening to the press conference," explained Chris. "I expect not having me around for ten days will be a relief!"

41

"Okay, aquanauts," said Chris, putting his SCUBA mask on and reaching for his primary regulator. "See you at the bottom!"

The primary objectives for the aquanauts' first dive were preliminary data collection and familiarization with the waystations located at the end of each of the four excursion lines. Jessica and Brian were paired, as were Nat and Chris, based on the similarity in their respective research methodologies. Pairing the dive buddies in such a way would allow for each of the four projects to advance simultaneously. This first dive would allow the teams to figure out how to make that work.

Each buddy team would also have to stop at one of the waystations during the dive, to report back to the *Calypso I* and to practice filling the double one-hundred-cubic-foot steel tanks on their backs.

The waystations were configured to allow for both simultaneously. The communication line in each remained continuously open. All a diver needed to do was stick their head up out of the water to speak, and one of the techs in the *Calypso I* would respond.

Given the required check-in every two hours, the remote communication saved the divers the time and effort of having to swim all the way back to the lab to report in. And by engineering a special system for filling tanks on the divers' backs, a team could stay out on the reef for at least four hours at a time.

Precisely at noon, three hours after initiating their first dives, both dive teams entered the moon pool on schedule, formally beginning the saturation mission. They exchanged high fives all around and stored their tanks on the racks. Chris noted with satisfaction that regulators were secured out of the water.

This would be the only time during the mission in which both buddy teams occupied the moon pool together. Beginning with the second dive that afternoon, each buddy team would enter and exit the water at least ten minutes apart to minimize congestion, particularly in the single freshwater shower.

Chris demonstrated how to clean wetsuits before hanging them up. Though the wetsuits would never fully dry in the high humidity of the wet porch, he explained that it was much easier to put on a marginally dry and minimally clean wetsuit for each successive dive than a smelly wet one.

"You sound like you've just inhaled a balloon full of helium," said Brian, referring to the impact of the pressure on Chris's vocal cords at depth. "But wait a minute, so do I!"

"Hello, darkness, my old friend," sang Nat, "I've come to talk with you again. This is amazing!"

"Luke, I am your father!" said Jessica, catching everyone off guard with a well-delivered *Star Wars* reference. Brian and Nat both high-fived her.

"Do you guys want to hear something gross?" asked Chris.

"No," said Jessica.

"Yes!" exclaimed Nat.

Chris looked to Brian. "I guess you're the deciding vote. What do you say?"

"Definitely."

Reaching up into the piping running over their heads, Chris grabbed a light blue camping towel. "Whose is this?"

"I think that one's mine," said Brian.

"You better be sure," admonished Chris. "This is another thing they don't tell you until you get down here. Ever heard of contact dermatitis?"

"Sure," Nat replied. "That's diaper rash. My nephew gets that regularly."

"Right," agreed Chris. "Diaper rash. It comes from close, prolonged contact between urine and skin. In the case of Nat's nephew, it's caused by the diaper that traps the urine. For divers, it's the wetsuit. And for aquanauts, it's a wetsuit you wear for up to eight hours a day, which is never fully cleaned between dives."

"Oh, that's fantastic. Thanks," said Nat.

"So, what's with the towel then?" asked Brian.

"Oh, no," said Nat.

"Yes," explained Chris. "Contact dermatitis is highly contagious. If it gets on your towel, you can give it to yourself . . ."

"And if you accidentally trade towels, you can give it to someone else," concluded Brian.

"Bingo!" said Chris.

He then went on to explain an incident that occurred during his second mission to the *Poseidon*. The other buddy team had accidentally switched towels mid-mission, leading one of the buddies to develop diaper rash over most of his body.

"The only thing worse than a bad case of diaper rash," clarified Chris, "is a case of diaper rash you caught from someone else."

"That's disgusting," observed Jessica.

"It is," agreed Chris. "But the story gets better. Remember the camera set up above the mission control station? Well, the unfortunate buddy was walking back to the bunk room late one night in his boxer shorts. Forgetting he was being watched, he stopped right below the camera to inspect his rash. Unfortunately for him, and I won't name names here, his friends had been watching the live feed right at that moment and were able to make a screen capture of the event. It now lives on in infamy."

"I won't be peeing for the next ten days," said Nat.

42

Still reeling from implications of Chris's diaper rash story, the aquanauts were caught off guard when the main hatch to the *Calypso I* opened, sliding on its rails under hydraulic power, to reveal Halbeck and Boseman, both of whom had entered the facility two hours earlier while the aquanauts were out diving on the reef. "Welcome, aquanauts! If you are all dried off, come join us."

"One important thing," said Halbeck. "Please note that while this hydraulic door may make a familiar sound to some of you, the door is not a toy and should not be opened and closed more than necessary."

"Familiar sound? What do you mean?" Nat furrowed her brow. "Close it one more time. I missed it the first time."

Halbeck complied and Nat tried hard to recognize the sound. But it was Brian who figured it out. "Oh my God! It's the *Enterprise*! The door to the bridge on the original *Enterprise*. That is very cool!"

"Right!" exclaimed Nat. "Let's hear it again."

Chris had long adjusted to the coolness of hearing the door open many times a day at the *Poseidon*.

But he still enjoyed rediscovering it through this new team of aquanauts.

"You are correct," said Halbeck. "I think it's even more interesting to realize that the hydraulics in this door somehow replicate the sound created by two on-set technicians back in nineteen sixty-five."

The change in atmospheric conditions from the wet porch to the main body of the lab was significant. Whereas the wet porch remained continuously warm and humid through direct contact with the warm seawater of the northern Caribbean Sea, the interior of the lab was kept much cooler to minimize moisture as much as possible. Wrapped only in towels, and instantly chilled, the aquanauts moved quickly through the lab to the bunk room at the bow, where the clothes they'd sent down waited for them on their bunks.

"This is going to be cozy," noted Brian, as all four aquanauts sought to find their clothes and get dressed simultaneously in the small space provided by the bunk room.

Chris grabbed his red fleece pants and hoodie and stepped back into the main lab area to put them on. He heard the VHF radio squawk. "Otter, pick up the Batphone."

The Batphone was a primary way of communicating with mission control above, along with a laptop computer configured for continuous chat mode. There was always someone on the other end of the phone, just like the phone Adam West used to call Commissioner Gordon in the old *Batman* TV series.

Mounted directly overhead of the communication station was a camera like the one in the wet porch. This camera also provided mission control with a live-feed visual of the main lab extending to the outer door to the wet porch. But unlike the camera in the wet porch, this camera also was viewable by the rest of the world online through the mission's website. Though the image was lagged by ten seconds when transmitted to the world.

"Otter here," responded Halbeck into the phone. "Where?"

The ominous tone of Halbeck's voice immediately drew the attention of Chris and the other aquanauts.

"How many killed? Oh, man. Okay. We'll stand by here."

Halbeck hung up the phone and faced the rest of the group. "There's been an explosion at one of the hotels along the beach. Twenty people have been confirmed dead, but they're still sorting through the rubble."

"Oh, no," said Chris. Thinking back to the social media post listing the hotels associated with the mission and his encounter with the gray-haired guy the day before, he asked, "Which hotel?"

"It was the Ritz-Carlton Key Biscayne," said Halbeck.

"*Key Biscayne?*"

43

The early risers—including joggers, open-water swimmers, and yoga enthusiasts—had been on their way back from the beach, mixing with the families just coming down to play in the sand, when the explosion hit. The explosive device had detonated somewhere on the second story, immediately above the main pool.

The main building's facade facing the beach had collapsed, covering the pool area with debris. The force of the explosion had propelled debris out of the hotel like a cannon, sending shrapnel out onto the white sand beach as far as the waterline. The beach volleyball courts adjacent to the hotel had been empty, but the pool area and the adjacent beach had been full of tourists out enjoying the sunny day.

"My God," said Nat.

Brian sat down at the lab's only table and hung his head. "I bet it's the same people who drove into the protesters with guns. Fucking extremists—those militia crazies that are attacking us online."

"What do you mean militia crazies?" Jessica nearly screamed, causing everyone to turn toward her.

"Jessica, I didn't mean to—" Brian tried to apologize, his hands up as if in surrender.

"What's it going to take," she added, "to get people to understand the threats we deal with every day in this country? The militias are the only thing keeping us safe!"

"Come on," Brian responded, less conciliatory now. "Why are you getting so exercised about militias? You know some of them attacked Chris and his friend Mac up in Miami. And they're all over us on social media."

"Have you ever lost anyone in your family?" Jessica hissed. "No? Then you should stop talking. My family was *killed,* and the government did *nothing*! But the Bordermen guarded the house for months after it happened. They arranged a food train for us. *And* they tracked down the killers and brought them to justice. All while the local cops barely even interviewed me."

"We're sorry about your fam—" said Nat.

"Have you been reading any of this social media shit, Jessica? Have you seen what they're proposing to do to me because I'm Asian? Are you okay with that? Or what about their plans for Nat? An Egyptian lesbian? Fuck!" interjected Brian, as he paced back and forth in the minimal amount of space available to him. "We've been treading lightly around you for too long. You're like a ticking time bomb. If you want to be quiet, fine. But keep all your righteous comments to yourself. You are in no position to lecture me or anyone else down here."

The lab was very quiet, the silence broken only by the muffled burping of air in the moon pool.

Chris stared out the porthole in front of him. He was stunned by the attack and Jessica's vehement response to it. Aware that he was an interloper in the team dynamic, he fought the instinct to help calm the situation.

Eventually, Nat said quietly, "Jessica, we're very sorry about your family. And we don't want to bring up old wounds."

Jessica sat at the table looking out the porthole.

Chris turned around. He didn't relish being the "old man" on the team, but he was there to offer insights from his experience. His experience told him that the unique team dynamic that saturation diving provides was the best way to unify them. *It certainly worked for me back in the day*, he thought.

"Team," he said. "Each of you has impressed me so much over the past week and a half. You really are a capable team of scientists. But I think it has been watching the four, well now three, of you interact that has really blown me away. I know we've been focused on the science and leaving the big picture of this international effort to the communications team. But think about what you're achieving here. You three have come together from three very different parts of North America. And you've done it seamlessly. It won't necessarily be easy, but I have every faith that you can pull this off. I'm truly proud to be a part of this effort."

Nat put one hand on Brian's shoulder and the other on Jessica's. "We can do this."

"I'm sorry for screaming at you, Brian. That wasn't fair," said Jessica, turning away from the porthole. "I know you weren't trying to argue with me."

"Why don't we use the workstation over there to see what information we can find on the explosion, and then we can get something to eat," said Halbeck. "We can see if everyone wants to do a second dive later this afternoon."

44

While the rest of the aquanauts called their families and friends, Chris set up a live chat with Mac at the surface. He'd learned that the Ritz-Carlton was the target. And when he asked whether Carrie Best, his friend from graduate school who was hosting a conference at the hotel, was among the casualties in Key Biscayne, he learned she was fine. Dana had checked in with Mac to confirm that everyone was okay in Key West.

"Have you connected with Donagan yet?" Chris typed.

"Yes. No claim of responsibility yet, just like the truck attack at the auditorium. But commentary online is out of control."

"Did Anna Cortez contact him?" asked Chris.

"Apparently. She briefed him on everything she's learned from her source and more."

"Did you talk to her?" asked Chris.

"Yes. She's pretty intense. I think she left for Miami as soon as the news broke."

"Keep in contact with her if you can. It's hard to know what's really going on here."

"Will do."

"Thanks. Let me know as soon as you find anything. You know where I'll be. Black, out."

"Damn, that's still good."

Chris hadn't known Cortez for more than a week, but he could see her rushing into the fray in Miami with little concern for her personal safety. He couldn't do much to help from sixty feet underwater.

He sent his mom an email letting her know that he was okay. Then he turned his attention back to the group.

"How are everyone's loved ones?" he asked.

No one's family was directly impacted by the event, though Jessica's uncle was one of the first responders on site immediately after the explosion. She'd learned this from her aunt, as her uncle was still very much in the thick of things.

"I know this might come off as self-centered," said Nat. "But does the fact that the attack was up in Miami suggest we aren't the target after all? Denise and I were just talking about it."

"My parents asked the same question," explained Brian. "Feels like wishful thinking, but who knows?"

"Otter, what's topside say?" asked Chris.

"They're very concerned about additional attacks centered on the mission somehow. But the consensus is that we are safer down here than at the surface. The mission can continue as they monitor the developing situation in Miami, provided the aquanauts are interested in continuing. They'll leave it up to us."

"Team?" asked Chris.

"I want to continue," said Brian.

"So do I," offered Nat.

"Me too," said Jessica.

"Well, in that case, and although it may sound crazy at a time like this, I think we should eat," suggested Chris. "We've got to take in calories to support all the diving we're going to be doing. Otter, what time can we get back in the water?"

Halbeck checked the log on the mission control computer. “You clocked in at eleven forty-five. If you want a three-hour dive this afternoon, you’ll need a four-hour storage interval. That puts you back in the water at three forty five p.m.”

The storage interval was the equivalent of the surface interval that surface-based SCUBA divers were used to. The dive tables that tracked the rate at which the human body expunged nitrogen had been worked out years ago. Living underwater added considerable dive time, but still required some time in between dives to off-gas.

“What’s the story with the toilet back there? Is it functional?” asked Brian.

“It is, and it isn’t,” said Halbeck.

“What’s that mean?” asked Nat.

The group had become accustomed to Halbeck pointing to Chris for explanations. This time they turned toward him without bothering to ask Halbeck.

“Well, there are three potential scenarios with the toilet, two of which are pretty bad,” explained Chris. “First, the toilet uses suction to flush your, um, waste. If the valve were to stick in an open position, it could suck all the air out of the lab, allowing the water from the moon pool to rise, flooding the whole place.”

“That sucks,” observed Nat.

“Not bad, Nat,” noted Chris. “Second, the toilet flow is reversed, and you get explosive backwash. Now, recall that we weren’t allowed to bring deodorant or any highly scented things with us. Why was that again?”

“Because the atmosphere in here is very dense,” answered Jessica. “The impact of strong scents is amplified.”

“That blows,” said Brian.

“Eh, you’re getting there,” said Chris. “That’s right. You don’t want explosive backwash of fecal matter in our home for the next ten days.”

"So, what are we supposed to do?" asked Nat. "Go outside?"

"For the record," explained Halbeck, "you are all more than welcome to use the toilet. However, you'll find Trevor and me, and I assume Chris, tending to our business outside. The waystation located immediately outside and adjacent to the moon pool works well."

"Wait a second," said Nat. "I've already sworn off peeing in my wetsuit. Now you're saying that if I need to go to the bathroom, I have to put on my bathing suit, enter the water, leave the moon pool, and poop in the waystation?"

"That's about the size of it," said Chris, grateful that the topic of going to the bathroom had allowed the group to relieve the tension. "And don't forget avoiding the attack of voracious fishes and showering before you come back inside."

"*And,*" finished Halbeck, "we have to report to mission control every time anyone leaves and comes back. Day or night."

"I think I'm just going to hold it," suggested Brian.

"Well, you don't want to do that," explained Halbeck. "Because that military doc who conducted all your pre-mission physicals last week? She's up on the barge right now and will be monitoring the frequency of everyone's bowel movements."

"No fucking way!" blurted Nat.

"I'm afraid so," said Halbeck. "Impacted bowels are a huge concern down here. Make sure to keep drinking water, or she'll make a trip down here to make certain you relieve yourselves."

"I can't imagine why you didn't tell us this beforehand," noted Jessica.

"Yeah, that's pretty shitty," said Nat.

45

"What do we know, Quint?" asked Leland Jones. He was sitting in the boardroom at Unity Environmental, with Sharon Dirksen to his right and Derrick Sumner to his left. The painting of Washington crossing the Delaware had been lowered electronically to reveal a six-foot flat-screen set back into the wall.

"It was definitely Bash and his cronies," replied Robert Shaw, his face filling the screen. "I spoke to one of them earlier. He was quite proud of himself."

Dirksen gasped.

"Why did he target the Ritz-Carlton?" asked Jones, his hands flat on the table, his head lowered. "We've held meetings there every year for as long as I can remember."

"Two reasons as far as I can tell. First, they wanted to draw attention away from the Keys and the undersea mission. To that extent they are doing what we're paying them for."

"And second?"

"I think that was a not-so-subtle *fuck you* directed at us."

"How can he know who we are?" asked Dirksen, quickly. "He can't know."

"Okay, it was a *fuck you* at me," clarified Shaw. "He may be crazy, but he's not an idiot. He could have directed attention away from the mission through any number of diversions. But I think he deduced that I'm representing someone with money, so he chose a target that would send us a message."

"Did Fessler green-light the attack?" asked Sumner.

"I haven't confirmed that yet," said Shaw. "We have something else going on here that wasn't discussed at our meeting in Orlando."

Shaw's initial charge from Jones had been to cultivate multiple avenues of attack against the undersea mission, with a three-fold goal of undermining Gwendolyn Pierce, hammering a mission billed as the first of an international effort, and swaying votes for Unity's contracts. To do that, he'd drawn the Federal Brotherhood Initiative, as well as several similar groups, into a tentative and volatile conspiracy. The plan was to leave an unambiguous trail of evidence pointing to multiple sources.

"What do you mean by *something else*?" asked Jones. "Sharon said you mentioned this earlier."

"I was referring to Bash's strange fixation on killing the two advisers to the mission from California, Chris Black and Mac Johnson," explained Shaw. "I never even mentioned the two of them to anyone in the group, but Bash orchestrated at least three attacks against them."

Shaw picked up on Jones and Sumner exchanging a knowing look.

"You know I can serve you better if I understand the entire picture. So, it doesn't serve you well to keep things from me."

"We're not sure what's going on either," said Jones after a pause. "But if we learn anything we'll let you know. What's your next step?"

Shaw looked out from the screen but said nothing.

"I asked you a question." Jones was visibly impatient.

"I heard you."

"Then what's your next step?" asked Jones again.

"I'm going to clean up a few loose ends before we proceed to the final part of the plan."

"In Key West?"

"I'm not in Key West at this time but will be back there soon enough."

"Is your dive team assembled?" asked Sumner.

"They are. Fessler's 'cleaner,' a guy named Martinez, organized the group. They're not soldiers, but they'll do."

"Shaw, we're going to mute ourselves for a second. Stand by," said Jones, as he turned off the boardroom's microphone and camera.

"Our 'friend' has been busy, I would say," said Sumner.

"Just as I suspected," agreed Jones. "What do you think, Sharon? You've been noticeably quiet."

"Our 'friend' was pretty dismissive when we spoke," observed Dirksen. "Rude and dismissive, like I'm a peon when compared to someone in higher office."

"Marvelous," said Jones. "This just keeps getting better and better."

46

The morning dive on day two went off without a hitch for both dive teams. Jessica and Brian focused their efforts on studying reef-building corals, with Jessica studying competition for space between adjacent corals and Brian taking physical samples of coral polyps to better understand their resiliency to global climate change. They were able to work immediately adjacent to the excursion line running north from the *Calypso I,* nearly within sight of the lab, where live corals were abundant.

Chris and Nat, on the other hand, were more actively swimming as they studied fish behavior, with Nat studying the biomechanics of parrotfish feeding and Chris observing social interactions across fish species.

Following fish required that the divers tied off to the westward excursion line with a reel, and then took turns unspooling the line as they followed individual fish. When they reached the end of the line, they were forced to stop following the fish of the moment, return to the main excursion line, and then repeat. Chris was grateful that no one was observing them out on the reef, given that fish swimming patterns had the buddy team following them in often circuitous routes.

Each of the buddy teams had identified the night before where on the reef they'd be working for the morning. This allowed the technicians and the staff in mission control to understand where all the aquanauts were supposed to be at any given moment. They were essentially free to work anywhere within the line highway, the one exception being that the two teams were not allowed to work at opposite ends of opposing lines. In the event of an emergency faced by one of the teams, the first responders to any emergency would be the other buddy team. Thus, it was important to have both teams no more than a short swim apart.

While the aquanauts were out working on the reef, members of Science Without Border's communications team came down to the *Calypso I* from the surface to set up equipment for on-camera interviews scheduled during the day's storage interval. The plan involved four, fifty-minute windows during which four separate journalists would dive down, enter the lab, and interview the aquanauts on camera.

"This is crazy," observed Brian, as they'd prepared to enter the water from the wet porch that morning. "We've barely been down here for twenty-four hours, and we've already done outreach events on four different continents! How're we supposed to get any work done?"

The night before, the aquanauts had participated in a Zoom meeting with Malcolm and several of his colleagues back in Boston. That meeting had taken forty-five minutes. And then they'd been live streamed to classrooms in Australia, Indonesia, and Japan, which had taken another two hours.

"Dude, don't you remember what Chris told us last night?" Nat admonished. "The science is really *not* the story here. Those kids we talked to last night don't care how many samples you collect, or how many fish I count. The story is about all of us working together in this strange environment where we can't poop in the toilet."

"And under constant threat from attack by militia groups," added Brian. "Don't forget that."

The loudspeaker mounted near the shower squawked with Halbeck's voice, "Correction, aquanauts, you are free to use the toilet at any time. That is all."

"Creepy," said Jessica. "I forget the techs can hear everything we say out here."

The loudspeaker squawked again. "Everything."

The two technicians ran on a very different work schedule than the aquanauts. Protocol required that at least one person be awake and monitoring all activities from inside the lab during daylight and/or any nighttime hours in which the aquanauts were working. To minimize cabin fever and to monitor the impact of corrosive salt water on the *Calypso I*, the technician not on duty usually spent as much time as possible outside working on simple maintenance tasks.

Unlike the aquanauts, who wore paired SCUBA tanks on their backs, the technicians working immediately outside the *Calypso I* relied on a *hookah* dive system, which used an air hose rather than tanks. While the technicians did wear a small tank on their backs as an emergency backup, the hose was connected directly to the air compressor in the wet porch, providing a continuous air supply for nearly unlimited dive time.

The only real challenge was managing the one-hundred-foot air hose, which tended to get entangled on the *Calypso I's* superstructure very easily.

Chris and Nat had worked their way out the western excursion line for much of the dive but found that they had to turn back before reaching the end of the line in order to return on schedule. The waystation at the terminus of the western line was located adjacent to a particularly high-relief section of the reef that was covered with fish.

As they swam back toward the lab, they communicated via dive slates, agreeing that for the afternoon dive they would swim straight to the end of that line and work there for the entire dive. They entered the moon pool on schedule at the end of their dive to find the wet porch full of technicians working to set up the cameras for the interviews. Ten minutes later, when Jessica and Brian appeared in the pool, neither Chris nor Nat had moved.

"Who are they going to interview if we're all stuck down here in the water?" asked Brian.

As he said that, the heads of four more communication technicians appeared in the moon pool. Similar to the aquanauts' visit to the lab prior to the start of the mission, every technician team was limited to fifty minutes before they had to depart for the surface. That meant that they had to enter the lab, dry off, set up their comms gear, and then leave. That process required a succession of dive teams to complete tasks that would have taken only minutes at the surface.

Chris was struggling to maintain his calm demeanor in the presence of poorly implemented communication strategies. He asked the guy closest to him, "Does anyone up there in mission control realize the other team of technicians hasn't cleared out of the lab yet?"

"We're behind schedule," replied the technician, gruffly. "Everything is taking more time than we planned. We're replacements for the team above us. Excuse me." The man stepped up onto the first step and yelled, "You guys are minutes from going into decompression. Just leave everything where it is, and we'll pick up from here."

Halbeck peered down from overhead. "We're going to get the aquanauts up here and dried off before the rest of you come up. Chris, you guys should come up now."

After drying off, Chris had to step gingerly as he entered the main lock from the wet porch to avoid stepping on the communication cables scattered across the deck.

Entering Calypso's main lock area, he immediately noticed that someone had placed communications gear all over the science station. "They put their fucking gear all over our data sheets from yesterday, and I have nowhere to put the data we just collected," he whispered to

Halbeck. "I'm really trying to stay calm for the team, but I've got to tell you, Otter, it's getting harder and harder to do so."

"I understand," Halbeck whispered in return. "You and I have been present for some real circuses, but this may be the biggest Charlie Foxtrot I've seen since leaving the Navy."

47

Sitting at the hotel bar, watching morning TV coverage switch back and forth between the attack at the Ritz-Carlton and the approaching tropical storm, Hugo Martinez looked at his message twice before he pressed send. His operative would be in a position to implement part of their plans during a short operational window over the next hour. He needed to get the message out now.

He felt uneasy about working directly with Shaw on some aspects of this operation, going around Fessler altogether. But Martinez was beginning to see Fessler's leadership of the Florida Brotherhood Initiative as lacking. The man wasn't really leading at all. It was more like facilitating. Bash was a perfect example. The kid was completely unhinged in Martinez's estimation, but Fessler kept letting him do whatever the hell he wanted to. He'd killed that state trooper on a whim, for fun.

Shaw, on the other hand, treated his operations much more methodically. He'd clearly served in the military for years and knew how to juggle multiple objectives simultaneously. Perhaps Martinez would find a way to work with Shaw after this was all over. Fessler was losing it, and he had his wife to consider.

The message would arrive from a fictitious email address linked to a legitimate news broadcaster, contact@ABCnewsFlorida.com.

From topside. Note that window is now open for sixty minutes. Focus is on team two. Airtime later today. Please confirm.

Martinez pushed his laptop back and took a swig of beer. He glanced around casually to see if anyone was watching him but didn't see anything unusual.

He sat at the bar and watched the news, clicking refresh on his web browser every minute or so.

The storm was not expected to develop into a hurricane, but it would bring strong winds and a lot of rain. The rain was expected to hinder the rescue work still ongoing at the Ritz-Carlton site.

After five minutes, Martinez received the reply.

Copy. Team two on air this PM.

48

Six and a half hours after returning to the moon pool from dive one, having completed four hours of interviews from inside the *Calypso I* and then another two and a half hours of diving in the afternoon, Chris and Nat entered the waystation at the end of the west excursion line with approximately half an hour of dive time remaining. This would give them ample time to fill up their tanks, report back to *Calypso*, and eat a snack before heading for home.

Standing up inside the station, at six foot, two inches tall, Chris had to hunch over a bit. The water level was just above his waist. At five foot, five inches, Nat had considerably more space to move around.

"Great dive! So many fishes," said Nat. "As I watched them all swimming around, I kept returning to that line you used in all your interviews earlier."

"Which one?"

"We know that fish eat each other. And that they compete with one another. But they *also* work together."

"Ah, yes, that was a good one."

"Yes, I'm starting to see cooperative group foraging all over the place. Did you see all those wrasses following that goatfish right before we entered?"

"I did!" answered Chris.

He looked out the small porthole next to him.

"I can see that fish still out there on the sand patch. Before we start swimming back, want to take a few minutes to observe the group foraging more closely?"

"Definitely," confirmed Nat, as she plugged the air hose into the special adapter connected to her tanks. She pointed to the mesh bag with two energy bars hanging from the ceiling. "I guess Jessica and Brian came by while we were out on the reef."

They'd both made it for just over two hours on the original fill of their tanks, so they now had to spend a few extra minutes filling the tanks up for the return trip to the *Calypso I*. Chris snacked on an energy bar he'd brought out in a Ziploc bag, while Nat drank three small apple juice packets. She shivered.

"Strange to feel cold in water that's eighty-five degrees Fahrenheit," she commented. "But I'm getting pretty chilled."

"I know you guys all thought I was crazy," replied Chris, "when I wore this thicker wetsuit with a hood. But eighty-five degrees is still almost fourteen degrees cooler than our body temperatures. Over these long dives, the ocean just wicks away our heat."

Nat handed Chris the air hose so that he could fill his own tanks. "Can I ask you something?"

"Sure."

"Just before we staged out for this dive," said Nat, "when we were in the wet porch getting ready, Brian came out through the main hatch, and I saw Trevor talking to Jessica."

"Okay."

"I feel stupid bringing this up, but they were standing really close together as they talked. It looked like they were whispering."

Chris had noticed the same thing several times over the past two days. It only happened at the beginning or end of a dive, when everyone's attention was focused on other things. Every saturation mission Chris had been on had been coed. Everyone was always so busy, there was rarely time to think about the other divers as anything other than divers. But he'd heard stories of relationships starting underwater. He'd thought about bringing it up with Halbeck but hadn't yet found the time.

"What do you think's going on?"

"I don't know," said Nat. "Maybe they knew each other beforehand, but I didn't get that impression. Seems kind of fast to develop a relationship."

"Stranger things have happened," said Chris.

"Sure," agreed Nat. "I guess Trevor's just not my cup of tea, that's all. But who am I to judge? I've been living with Jessica twenty-four seven for almost two weeks now, and I have no idea what she's thinking."

"Yeah," agreed Chris. "That one's a mystery. Well, Otter and mission control will be watching, and they aren't fans of personal relationships forming during missions. So, they'll likely nip it in the bud."

"Got it. Sorry I brought it up."

When they were finished filling tanks, Nat contacted the lab. "Aquanaut Nat reporting in. We are going to spend three to five minutes checking out some fish here next to the waystation, then proceed back to the *Calypso I*. See you soon."

"Copy that," Boseman replied.

The duo submerged and kicked gently toward the sand patch nearby. In the short time that they'd been in the waystation, the sun had nearly reached the horizon. Chris could clearly feel the change in water temperature and ambient light.

He spotted the goatfish almost immediately and slowed his progress to observe from ten feet away. As Chris watched the wrasses—

small reef fish that swam in groups—eagerly follow the goatfish around, the air in his regulator began to feel odd: It tasted a bit like he imagined shoe polish would taste. Seconds after coming to that realization, he felt an urgent tap on his shoulder from Nat. He turned to see her vehemently pointing back toward the waystation.

Chris immediately followed her, noticing as he swam that his head was beginning to hurt. Once inside it was clear that Nat couldn't stand up. She tried to pull herself up along the inside of the waystation but didn't have the strength to do it. At the same time her legs collapsed under her, and her head went underwater.

"Nat!"

Seeing Nat begin to slide underwater, Chris knelt on the deck at the base of the waystation, using his left hand to grab hold of her tank and his right to keep himself above water as well. He estimated that she probably weighed at least sixty pounds less than he did and that whatever was in their air went through her much more rapidly than it did him. But even with her being much lighter, it quickly became a challenge for Chris to support her.

"Nat, can you hear me? Stay with me, please."

"Can't . . . can't stand . . . up. Scared."

"I know. I've got you," said Chris, before reporting in. "*Calypso I*, *Calypso I*, *Calypso I*, this is Aquanaut Chris. We have a problem. We seem to have some bad air. Tastes like shoe polish. Need help."

"Copy that, Chris," came Halbeck's reply. "We're on it. Stand by one second."

As the seconds passed, Nat drifted in and out of consciousness and Chris began feeling increasingly bad himself. When minutes had passed, Chris could see through the waystation's porthole that the sun had set. Darkness had fallen. They were stranded, in the pitch black, several hundred yards from help, and whatever was in their air was overwhelming them.

"*Calypso I*, we're not doing so well out here. Better hurry."

49

Two hundred miles to the north, Anna Cortez pulled over to the side of the road and rolled down the driver's side window. A car following right behind her honked its horn, and she waved it past.

In one hand she held the address associated with the rental car of the man who'd followed them in Key West. Her contact in the Florida Highway Safety and Motor Vehicles program had produced the address by the time she'd arrived in Miami. In her other hand she held her smartphone with the mapping app opened to the same address. The trouble was that there was no longer any structure there. In its place lay a pile of rubble behind a construction fence.

On the drive north, Cortez had been on the phone as continually as cell coverage allowed. She'd reached out to a colleague who was on the scene of the explosion at the Ritz-Carlton to see if any new information had developed there. The biggest development was that no one had claimed responsibility for the attack, which had the authorities scratching their heads. It was common for such attacks to receive near-simultaneous claims.

And on a whim, Cortez had contacted the press office at Science Without Borders to request the biographical information for everyone saturating on the mission. A nice young intern had promised to send her the digital press packet right away. She wasn't clear what she was expecting to find, but perhaps she'd know it when she found it.

She'd also called Mac Johnson three times, but repeatedly got his voice mail. That the gray-haired man had given a false address to the rental company was not a surprise. In fact, she'd have been more surprised if anything had turned up. But dating back to her earliest days as a reporter, Cortez knew that some stories hung on even the smallest detail. You just never knew which detail it was.

"What did I expect to find?" she said out loud.

"I don't know. Maybe me?" said a voice.

Cortez spun in her seat. The man in the hoodie she and Chris had chased in Key West stood right next to her car.

"I hate reporters," said Robert Shaw as he reached in and punched Cortez hard on the side of her head.

Cortez fell forward against the steering wheel, stars filling her peripheral vision, her head throbbing, and her consciousness wavering. She knew that if she let him get the upper hand, she was likely going to die.

Shaw reached over her back to grab her bag from the passenger seat. As he rummaged through it, Cortez rested her right hand on the taser which, out of habit, she'd removed from her bag for the drive north. It was sandwiched between her right thigh and the seat cushion.

"What, no gun? I'm disappointed. Don't you reporters know that it's dangerous out here?"

Cortez's head throbbed, but the initial shock of the encounter was beginning to wear off.

Leaning closer to the window, Shaw said, "So now you have a nice welt on the side of your head to match the one your friend Black gave me the other day. That only seems fitting."

Cortez turned her head to face her attacker but remained leaning against the steering wheel. "You're former military."

"No shit. What gave it away?"

Cortez tried to organize her thoughts. "Why would a former American soldier partner with a group of Florida militia?"

"Those idiots? It's less of a partnership than a convenient temporary alignment. But it isn't easy. I have to wash my hands to get rid of that unclean feeling."

"You must have dealt with similar people in Afghanistan, or perhaps Iraq," observed Cortez.

"Wow, you're really doing nicely," said Shaw. "Of course, I did. And it usually ended with my killing them. What else can I help you with?"

Cortez slowly wrapped her hand around the taser as she asked, "Nobody I ask knows anything about this militia."

"You really do ask a lot of questions. And some of them are pretty good," observed Shaw. "That's why I picked you."

"*You* picked *me*?" asked Cortez, turning to see the man's face. "What are you talking about?"

"Who do you think has been tipping you off for the past month? A concerned citizen? It's been me all along. Nobody knows anything about these idiots because we extracted them from obscurity. They are here to do a job and serve a larger purpose."

"But—"

"But nothing. *It was me*," continued Shaw. "The tip about the operation in the quarry? Me. The tip about two militia guys showing up at a lecture in Key Biscayne? Me. The attack outside the auditorium? Me."

"I don't understand," said Cortez.

"Your job was to follow these idiots and *write* about it," said Shaw, pausing to let a car drive past. "I needed them to do their militia thing, but I wanted you to make sure they got caught, *publicly*. You were supposed to write online blogs, contact the authorities. Generally, get the word out. That was the point."

"You wanted them caught?" asked Cortez. "I definitely don't understand."

"Unattributed violence doesn't help me at all, see? The boss wants people freaking out on cable news, people occupying government buildings clamoring for justice for their persecuted militia brethren. But instead, you went into big-time investigative reporter mode and didn't report anything to anyone, except to Chris Black for some reason. And then, instead of focusing on the militia, you homed in on me. I guess I own that one."

Cortez's mind raced as she considered her options. She knew that getting out of the car would not end well. Staying and fighting also had an extremely low probability of success. But the man was acting overconfident, so perhaps she'd find an opportunity to exploit that.

"But now you've served your purpose. All you can do from here on out is make my life more difficult by directing the authorities toward me. So, c'mon, let's go," said Shaw as he leaned closer to grab Cortez's shoulder. As he pulled her off the steering wheel, she spun quickly and tasered him in the throat. He fell backward onto the pavement, dropping her bag.

Cortez was briefly stunned that her improvised plan had worked. She thrust open the door and jumped out of the car. Kneeling next to Shaw, she tasered him again in the center of his chest, holding the device in direct contact with him as his body shook.

Satisfied that he was not getting up any time soon, Cortez grabbed her bag, then checked his pocket for an ID. Finding his wallet, she stuffed it in her bag and sped off, leaving him lying on the pavement.

Once she felt comfortable that she was safe for the time being, Cortez called in a report to the local police about an attacker at the address she'd just left. She made one additional call, then she turned the car east toward the Ritz-Carlton attack site.

50

Chris Black leaned his head against the inside wall of the waystation, his chin just below the waterline. He tried to focus his thoughts but kept failing as a multitude of memories flashed through his mind. He was fading fast.

His thoughts kept returning to his dog, Thigmotaxis. The soft-coated wheaten was at home in Carmel with his mom, where he knew she was happy. But he missed her. They'd once been inseparable, but his research schedule of late had taken him away from her almost more than not.

Chris recalled a course he'd taken as an undergraduate on folklore and comparative religion. He remembered being extremely interested at the time, but many of the specifics had been lost from his memory, save one. He vividly recalled the professor describing the cross-cultural importance of dogs and men. The narrative varied by culture, but the upshot was that the connection men shared with their dogs was widely believed to continue in the afterlife, where dogs became very powerful stewards and protectors of their associated humans.

He'd always assumed that Thig would precede him to the afterlife. But kneeling there in the pitch-black ocean, trying to keep both

Nat and himself alive, he wasn't so sure. It took him several seconds to understand that he was seeing light approach through the porthole. By the time his thoughts had coalesced around that realization, the heads of Brian and Halbeck surfaced in the waystation.

"How we doing here?" asked Halbeck as he took over supporting Nat from Chris.

"Bad," Chris struggled to speak. "Bad air."

Brian handed Chris his backup regulator. "Here you go, Chris. I've brought the good stuff."

"Help Nat," he said, unable to take hold of the regulator.

"We will," said Halbeck. "But we need you feeling better too, buddy."

Chris's head was hurting so much it was difficult for him to keep his eyes open. He was also losing his ability to hold his own head out of the water.

"Try this, Chris," said Brian.

When he felt the regulator's mouthpiece brush his lips, Chris summoned the strength to grab the regulator from Brian, purge it of water, and take three increasingly deep breaths.

The fresh air was an immediate relief. After several more breaths, he was able to open his eyes. Nat was also breathing on a regulator provided by Halbeck.

"We've got a limited supply of air until we get back to Calypso, and a long swim ahead of us," explained Halbeck after several more minutes. "But we won't get started until the two of you feel up to it."

"I think we should go for it," said Nat, visibly shivering. "I'm freezing out here and pulling myself along the line highway should help warm me up."

"Copy that," said Halbeck. "Chris, if you're ready too, let's go."

The elongated hoses on the backup regulators let Chris and Nat breathe easily as they pulled themselves along the line, kicking their fins when they felt up to it. Swimming along next to them, Halbeck and Brian kept close watch over their charges.

Their progress was slow. Chris had encouraged Nat and Halbeck to lead off, and Nat was not moving quickly. Pulling himself along the line behind her, he watched as Brian's light illuminated the nearby reef. The diurnal fish community had hunkered down for the night, but he could see several nocturnal species beginning to move about the reef. A green moray eel silently navigated along the edge of the reef, probing every crevice for hidden fish.

Twenty minutes after the two buddy teams left the waystation, the group returned to the moon pool. Twenty minutes after that, everyone was safe and dry in the lab.

Both Chris and Nat showed demonstrable improvement as the minutes passed. Chris noted that while the impact of the bad air had incapacitated Nat more quickly, she was also recovering more quickly than he was. He was no longer feeling like vomiting, but his head still hurt.

"We recalled your teammates here as soon as you contacted us," explained Halbeck.

"I think I heard that recall alarm," said Chris. "Thanks so much for coming to get us."

"What about a response from the surface?" asked Nat. "Why didn't they come?"

"Oh, the doctor should be along any minute," confirmed Halbeck. "But it was clear that mobilizing a team from the surface was more complicated, and slower, than our response from down here. Once we confirmed that the air inside the *Calypso I* was fine, we decided that I would join Brian on the swim out to get you."

"What do you think happened to our air?" asked Nat.

Halbeck shook his head. "We don't know yet. While you were showering, I sampled air from both your regulators, and I tasted what you described as shoe polish. We'll have to send your rigs up to the surface for testing. We'll also have to evaluate the air in each of the waystations. We know the air in the main compressor here in the lab is okay, which means it's not a problem with an intake valve on the compressors up topside. It must be something between us and the waystation."

"That was too close for comfort. If we hadn't decided to stop and observe the goatfish, we would've started swimming back right after leaving the waystation," said Chris. "We would've been somewhere between the *Calypso I* and the waystation before being overcome by the bad air."

He stopped and looked at Nat. "Think about it. There's no way we would have made it back."

"Jesus," said Nat. "You're right."

"Otter and Trevor, have you ever experienced anything like this before?" asked Jessica.

"Not on my end," said Halbeck.

"Nor mine," seconded Boseman. "This is a new one."

"Are they letting us keep diving?" asked Nat.

"That depends entirely on you two, provided your checkups from the doc go well. You don't have to decide right now. Let's just take it one step at a time. Chris, are you still with us over there? You're being noticeably quiet."

"I'm with you," said Chris, rubbing his face. "I'm just not with you."

"Obviously," replied Halbeck, raising both eyebrows.

The doctor arrived within an hour, escorted by Mac Johnson. While she checked out Nat, Chris and Mac moved into the bunk room to confer.

"You look like crap," said Mac. "I'd stay away from any mirrors."

"Thanks. At least I'm consistent because I feel like crap too."

51

Chris Black reached back into his cubby to pull out a second fleece jacket and a pair of wool socks. He also slipped on a red knit cap.

"You okay, man?" asked Mac, who was wearing only a T-shirt and a pair of shorts.

"Yeah, I'll be fine," replied Chris. "That was just a long time underwater, and the bad air didn't do anything for me. I'm freezing."

"What do you think happened?" asked Mac.

"I don't know," answered Chris.

"This *is* a newly deployed lab," suggested Mac. "Plenty of kinks to still work out. I think it's a miracle that this place got operational so quickly."

"That's true. Have you heard from Anna yet?"

"Nothing prior to my coming down here," observed Mac. "But I've been pretty busy. I did talk to Hendrix. You probably haven't had a chance to check your email yet today. But when you do, you should see messages from him."

"Just give me the high points, then," said Chris. "My head hurts."

"Hendrix and Dana are on their way here from somewhere in Central America," explained Mac, raising his palms. "And before you ask, no, I have no idea what they were doing down there. Wouldn't have told me even if I'd asked."

"That's good news," said Chris, talking through a yawn. "I've got to get some sleep."

"But check your email first."

Chris moved past the doctor, who was still examining Nat, and booted up the general use laptop. Jessica and Brian were standing in the small kitchen area drinking tea and talking with Trevor. Opening the email browser, he could see Jessica was still logged on. He logged her off and opened his own inbox. Chris was immediately alerted to the fact that three hundred unread emails had accumulated in only the past twenty-four hours.

"Ugh."

He was too tired to do service to most of the messages, and he could feel his blood pressure rising as he read through the subject lines. Fortunately, the message from Hendrix stood out from the rest, so Chris navigated directly to it.

The subject line read *Top Secret* followed by a poop emoji. Chris reflected, not for the first time, as he clicked on the message, that he was glad the head of a global security business was so professional.

The email opened to a short message. "Greetings, Dr. Black. Johnson tells me that you have found yourself in another 'situation.' I'm en route from points unknown as I type this. A contact in DC sent the image below, captured from a security camera in Miami. If you encounter this man, proceed with great caution. Will explain further when I arrive. Hendrix."

The grainy black-and-white image depicted a stern-looking man leaving a parking garage in a rental car. It was quite clearly the man Chris had chased in Key West.

Mac, who'd been watching over Chris's left shoulder, said, "Is that the guy?"

"It is."

"Hang tough, brother," said Mac, patting Chris on the shoulder. "We'll figure this out. We always do."

"We *sometimes* do, and usually only after great pain and suffering," corrected Chris.

"Yeah, that's what I meant."

52

Jeremiah Fessler sat at his desk in the dark, his latest burner cell phone in front of him. He could barely discern the outlines of the picture frames arrayed around the edge of the desk, but the photographs themselves were not visible.

A gentle breeze fluttered the curtains through an open window. The TV weather person had said a tropical storm was coming. While his neighborhood was quiet, the urban sounds from the larger city around it were discernible in the background. He drank directly from a bottle of whiskey.

He'd seen the horror of the bombing in Key Biscayne replayed several times on TV. In this age of ubiquitous camera phones, there were eyewitness accounts accompanied by imagery. While the still photos of the devastation were exactly what he would expect from such an explosion, the video of the explosion itself was gut-wrenching. In one case, a parent was filming five teenagers forming a human pyramid on the beach when the explosion erupted behind them. A moment of extreme joy was instantly transformed into one of extreme terror. The dust cloud created by the structural collapse of the hotel had quickly obscured the camera's view, but the audio continued to capture the human agony in great detail. The death toll had risen to forty, as people who initially survived the attack had succumbed to their injuries. Countless others were being ministered to at area hospitals.

The attack was reminiscent of the bombing at the Boston Marathon years before, where the nails and shrapnel from the bomb had done irrevocable harm to many of those who survived. Fessler recalled being shocked by the violence in Boston but sitting there in the dark, he'd plumbed the depths and found no such personal sense of horror this time around.

At the meeting of the leadership earlier in the week, Shaw had tasked Bash and his associates with creating a diversion to direct attention away from the undersea lab in Key West. However, after Shaw left the room that night, Bash had returned shortly after with the suggestion of a major tourist target.

And then the Ritz-Carlton attack had happened. Politicians on both sides of the aisle were demanding responses, but as no one had claimed responsibility there was yet to be a specific response identified.

Fessler had come home that evening to find emails from Martinez waiting for him. Someone had corrupted the air supply of two divers on the mission, but both had survived. There were no details as to exactly what had happened, or how the divers had survived, so Fessler had a tough time picturing the situation. According to Martinez, that failure had triggered the next stage in the plan, two stages really, that would result in the loss of many lives above and below the surface.

Sitting in the dark by himself, Fessler sipped the whiskey and reflected on the pending success of all that he'd worked for.

"To a job well done," he said as he raised the bottle.

Then something caught his eye. A strange red dot worked itself across his desk and up onto the center of his chest.

53

Robert Shaw stood on the roof of an apartment building in east Orlando, a laser-driven nightscope attached to his rifle. The streets below were populated by late-night bar hoppers finding their way home.

Shaw had awakened on the pavement in Miami, surrounded by bystanders who'd come upon his unconscious body lying in the road. He was initially very confused as to where he was and why he was there. But once he regained his bearings, he remembered being tased in the throat by Anna Cortez. Given the incredible soreness in his chest, he surmised that she must have tased him again once he was down. He had important tasks ahead of him in the next two days, but he would be sure to fit time into his schedule to find and deal with her.

The wail of sirens had been coming closer as he'd struggled to sit up. Getting involved with the police at that point was not an option, so he continued to struggle to get to his feet. Two of the bystanders had helped him to reach his car. The bitch had taken his wallet, but she hadn't thought to take his keys. Against the protestations of many in the crowd, Shaw started the car and drove away. He'd turned a corner before the police arrived.

Knowing that the car he was in would now be on everyone's radar, Shaw drove east looking for options. The second construction site gave him an idea. He parked the car down the road and tossed the keys into a nearby drainage ditch. He then climbed the fence surrounding the large site and reviewed the range of vehicle options. Breaking into the foreman's trailer had been easy, and the keys to the truck he needed were hanging right where he'd hoped they'd be.

His hope was that the truck would not be reported stolen until sometime the next day. By that point he would have already switched to a different vehicle.

The view in his scope slowly advanced along the apartments in the opposing building, allowing Shaw sneak peeks here and there inside units that he wasn't targeting. When he got to Fessler's apartment, he found the man sitting in his study in the dark with the window open.

Shaw briefly wondered what Fessler was thinking about sitting there in the dark. Was he feeling guilty or emboldened? But Fessler's thinking was not relevant for the next step Shaw had to take.

As he adjusted the resolution of the nightscope, he centered the laser on the man's chest, exhaled briefly to steady his body, and pulled the trigger.

54

The morning after the incident at the waystation the louder-than-normal sloshing coming from the moon pool suggested that the weather was taking a turn for the worse. Halbeck was on the Batphone for ten minutes talking with mission control while the aquanauts were huddled in the galley area preparing breakfast. Boseman was working in the wet porch.

Chris and Nat were slower to rise than other mornings, still feeling the residual effects of the bad air the evening before, though the doctor had cleared them both for diving. Brian, Nat, and Jessica each used the instant hot water faucet to add water to packets of freeze-dried hiker food. Chris made a breakfast burrito out of black beans, vegan cheese, and sliced peppers and stuck it in the microwave. All four aquanauts drank hot chocolate from special mugs with their names printed on them.

"How are you two feeling?" asked Brian.

"A *lot* better," answered Nat. "A good night's sleep was super helpful."

"I feel better, too," said Chris. "But maybe not a lot better."

Jessica sat at the table by herself reviewing a book of invertebrate identifications.

"Okay, team, as you can hear, it looks like the weather is not behaving as planned," explained Halbeck after hanging up the phone.

"That's a big shocker," replied Chris. "Have we ever worked together, Otter, when the weather didn't create challenges for us? I assume the storm veered farther west than predicted?"

"That's essentially the case," said Halbeck. "It's nothing we can't handle down here, but it's going to be sporty for everyone up topside."

Nat, Brian, and Jessica crowded around portal, looking upward toward the surface.

"Mission control had considered pulling us out in advance of the storm," continued Halbeck. "We would have completed our decompression in the chamber on the barge as they moved it into the harbor, but the chamber is nonfunctional right now. We'll have to go through deco down here, and then swim to the surface."

"The chamber is down?" asked Chris. "That's a little surprising given how many people they've got working at mission control."

Halbeck mouthed "later" to Chris.

"We knew this was a gamble. If the storm comes through quickly, as predicted, we will be able to return to the *Calypso I* and resume the mission."

Since midway through the first day of the mission, the bodies of all six divers had been completely saturated with nitrogen. This presented no danger to them as long as they dove within their limits each day and made sure to conduct the appropriate storage interval between dives. However, a safe return to life at the surface would require a fourteen-hour decompression to slowly off-gas the accumulated nitrogen. Prior to the start of the mission, the plan had been to bring everyone to the surface and immediately move them into a specially designed hyperbaric chamber on board the barge.

"How are we supposed to do that?" asked Brian.

"Think of it this way, Brian," said Halbeck. "The *Calypso I* is essentially a decompression chamber with a box added on at one end for the wet porch. All we have to do is close the main lock door and then slowly adjust the pressure over the course of fourteen hours. When we finish, our bodies will have expunged all the nitrogen and we will be at a pressure equivalent to the surface."

"Once we're ready, we'll simply repressurize the cabin to a pressure equivalent to sixty feet. *Then* we'll be able to open the door and leave through the moon pool. It will just be like conducting a short dive."

"But didn't you say it's going to be *sporty* at the surface?" asked Jessica. "That doesn't sound good."

"Right. In all likelihood we would be fine down here throughout the storm. But the powers that be would rather not take any risk leaving us saturated without the support of the barge above us. So, they're pulling us. We'll have to deal with a few swells at the surface."

"We are approved for a morning dive," continued Halbeck. "But I wouldn't stray too far from the lab. If you can get some work done in close, do that. We don't want you way out at the end of one of the excursion lines if conditions degrade quickly. Also remember that the waystations are currently out for filling your tanks. Until we know what happened to Chris and Nat, you can use the waystations to take a break and to check in with us. Just no air fills.

"We'll assess the conditions this afternoon to determine whether a second dive is doable. Let's go!"

Chris hung back while the other divers moved into the wet porch to gear up. "The chamber is *down*?" he asked.

"Likely sabotage," whispered Halbeck. "Think of all the so-called tech and communications people who have come through in the past two days. It could have been anyone."

"Taking down a hyperbaric chamber beyond repair is no easy feat," said Chris. "The question is, was tainting the air along the excursion line also planned? I've been fixated on threats from outside based on my conversation with this journalist, but what if we also have internal threats to worry about?"

"You're right," agreed Halbeck. "It would be much easier to sabotage from within."

"Can you get a list of all the personnel associated with the mission?" asked Chris. "And can you do it without calling attention to yourself? I trust you and Mac, but everyone else is potentially suspect."

"I think I can do that. But we'll have to be careful; as you know, we're being watched twenty-four seven via those cameras and they can monitor all our electronic communications. Depending on who we're dealing with, they could be watching us right now."

"Watching yes, but they can't hear us unless we use the phone," said Chris. "But then again, if they can put someone in mission control, what's to say they don't have someone down here."

"*Down here?*" said Halbeck, his eyes widening at the thought. "That's a *very* short list."

"I trust you, and you alone," said Chris. "But I also don't think Nat or Brian are involved. It's just a feeling, but it's a strong feeling."

"And that means . . ."

"Right," said Chris. "Jessica and Trevor. Maybe one or both of the quietest people on this mission are working against us."

"Be careful out there today," suggested Halbeck.

"Will do," replied Chris. "You too."

55

Tropical Storm Nancy originated in sub-Saharan Africa, then began its northwestward trajectory across the Atlantic Ocean, through the Caribbean Sea, and into US waters off the east coast of Florida. Drawing energy from the warm surface waters, Nancy grew to nearly six hundred miles across and produced winds in excess of sixty miles an hour. When it reached the straits between Florida and the Bahamas, it slowed its pace, cycling in a counterclockwise direction over much of south Florida. In the Dry Tortugas, the storm brought fierce, but intermittent, rain squalls throughout the morning. However, the wind remained a constant, blowing at up to forty knots. Wind swells at the surface reached eight to ten feet high.

Stepping out into the wet porch, Chris found his fellow aquanauts meandering slowly through their preparations for the dive. Both Brian and Jessica had their wetsuits pulled halfway on, but Nat had yet to put hers on. Boseman had been working over by the fill station but moved back into the main part of the lab as soon as the aquanauts arrived.

"How're we doing, team? Moving a little slowly?" asked Chris. "I know we said Nat and I would hit the water first, but perhaps we can switch?"

"That works for us," said Brian. "Right?"

"Yes, we can do that," agreed Jessica.

After Brian and Jessica submerged, Chris sat down on the step into the moon pool.

"I guess I'm still a little freaked out about last night," said Nat after a minute.

"I understand," said Chris. "We don't have to dive. We can just hang out here."

Nat sat down next to Chris, nudging him to the side to give her room.

"Aren't you freaked out at all?"

"Not freaked out, per se," said Chris. "But not blasé either. I think I've just had more experience with these close calls."

"I'm not imagining the closeness of it, am I?"

"No, that was a legit close call," said Chris. "We're both very lucky."

"That's what I thought. So, it's up to me if I want to go forward?" asked Nat.

"It's always your decision as to whether you want to dive," said Chris. "And this situation is no different. Well, maybe it's a little different, but you know what I mean."

"What were you and Otter just talking about?" asked Nat. "You were concerned that the chamber isn't working on the barge."

Chris considered his response. There was no point in getting everyone worked up about his concerns. However, he had a growing feeling that trouble was coming, and he wanted to share with his buddy. Judging by how Nat had handled herself so far, he had full confidence in her.

"In all honesty, Nat, I don't know what's going on."

"But?" said Nat.

"But there's a fair amount I haven't shared with you about things going on at the surface," explained Chris.

"We've seen all the social media craziness," said Nat. "I've been getting some pretty nasty messages through several platforms."

"Yeah, I saw some of that," said Chris. "I'm really sorry."

"I guess I check all their boxes; a strong female, lesbian, non-white, *and* foreign," said Nat. "I'm genetically engineered to piss those America First fuckers off."

"You certainly are," said Chris. "Are you deleting the messages?"

"No way," said Nat. "I've learned to keep track of all that stuff. Who knows what might come of it someday."

"I can tell you more about what I've learned, but first we should decide whether we want to dive or not this morning."

"Fuck 'em," said Nat, as she stood up to put on her wetsuit. "Let's dive."

Minutes later, as the pair kicked away from the lab, the underwater surge resulting from the swells at the surface was clearly more pronounced than it had been the day before. Chris was immediately aware of an eerie feeling.

It took him several seconds to realize what he saw, or rather, what he didn't see. No fish.

He motioned to Nat, who indicated that she, too, was stunned by the difference.

The reefs in the Dry Tortugas were at the western end of North America's longest barrier reef. Because they were sixty-seven miles away from the rest of the more developed Florida Keys, the reefs were doing comparatively well. Normally the reef would pulse with activity from dawn to dusk, with fishes of all sizes swimming below, within, and above the reef.

Swimming over a gradual rise in the reef, Nat motioned to Chris to look to his left. Sitting on a sand patch between reef heads, no farther than thirty feet off the excursion line, was an older version of their waystations. It was twice the size of the *Calypso I's* waystations and consisted of a large acrylic dome reinforced by a steel frame.

They could see from the outside that the structure still held air. Chris motioned with his hand that they should enter. Standing up inside, he removed the regulator from his mouth and pressed the purge button, venting fresh air into the space. Nat followed suit.

"This is very cool," she observed. "What do you think it's doing out here?"

Thinking back to the topographic data that Carrie Best had provided, Chris said, "I don't think the placement of this mission was random. I imagine that studies have been happening on this site for years. This must be an observation station from some previous project. It really is much nicer than our waystations, isn't it?"

"And what's going on with the fishes?" asked Nat. "Where'd they all go?"

Chris was about to answer when he spotted a massive school of hogfish moving over the reef toward them. "Check this out! What the hell?"

The school contained thousands of fish, all moving in unison across the reef. Seconds after it passed, a similarly sized school of blue tangs moved past heading in a different direction.

"This is incredible!" observed Nat. "Have you ever seen anything like this?"

"No. Both those species are usually solitary, or swim in pairs. I've never seen that many together," responded Chris.

"What do you think's happening?" asked Nat.

"It must be some kind of aggregative response to the storm conditions," said Chris, thinking out loud. "Think about it. Fishes living on shallow reefs might be responding to storms like this all around the world, but nasty conditions at the surface prevent anyone from conducting normal SCUBA ops."

"*Amazing*. If we hadn't been in saturation, we would never have seen this."

56

Mac Johnson stood on the dock at Key West, in the howling wind and rain, and looked skyward. His bright-orange foul weather gear kept the rain off, but it was still miserable. He'd not been pleased when the decision was made to evacuate the mission control personnel from the barge onto the mainland, but he'd understood. The conditions on the water had deteriorated quickly once the storm arrived in full, and mission control could not be run by a crew incapacitated by seasickness.

He was standing near the newly established, land-based mission control in the Key West harbormaster's office, assessing the seaworthiness of the vessel he'd been assigned. A particularly heavy rain squall was moving through.

"You know, they say turkeys drown staring up at the rain with their mouths open like that," a familiar voice said from behind him.

"Is that some folksy wisdom from wherever you just were?" asked Mac.

Hendrix approached on Mac's right, wearing black waterproof pants and a jacket. "Wasn't there long enough to soak up much wisdom. What's the situation here?"

Hendrix and Dana had been in a small town on the Honduran–Nicaraguan border when Mac had reached them the day before. They were meeting with several other international firms to discuss how extragovernmental entities could help stabilize the region. They'd left the meeting within minutes of the call, and Hendrix had mobilized a flight from Tegucigalpa to Miami. By the time they'd reached Miami, an SUV was waiting for them. What would have been a seven-hour trip had they flown commercially was reduced to two and a half hours aboard a collaborator's private jet.

"Not great. They've evacuated mission control to shore," explained Mac, pointing to the small harbor office down the dock. "The weather's arrived early, and the authorities are focused up north because of the Ritz-Carlton attack. Where's Dana?"

"She's securing us some firepower," explained Hendrix. "Is this our boat? Quaint."

"It'll do," said Mac. "As I said earlier, there's evidence of sabotage from within."

"Topside or at depth?"

"Likely both." He explained the bad air event that Chris and Nat had experienced, as well as the scuttled decompression chamber on the barge.

"At depth? That's a short list of potential saboteurs," said Hendrix. "A very short list."

"We know. Chris is keeping an eye on the situation."

"Well, you guys have stepped in it once again."

"Wait a second!" Mac interjected.

Hendrix raised a palm. "I know, I know. I'm the one who suggested this fiasco to Black in the first place."

Chris, Mac, Dana, and Hendrix had all still been in the Galapagos recovering from the encounter with pirates when Hendrix had alerted Chris to the possibility of a saturation mission in Israel. At that time, Hendrix was going to be involved in the security effort. Much had changed in the intervening months. By the time Chris and Mac landed in Miami, Hendrix had long since left the project altogether.

"Think about it," Hendrix continued. "Who do you know who's got more experience in saturation missions than Black, at least from the research side of things? No one. He was an obvious choice to lend his support to the mission. And I think he knows that, which is why he stayed on even after I was no longer associated with the mission."

Mac saw Dana walking down the gangway, hefting two large duffel bags. She was clad in a similar outfit to Hendrix.

"Well, you're in it now, too," said Mac, jumping on board the boat. "Dana's here, so let's get moving."

"What's the op?" asked Hendrix.

"We're going out to the mission control barge to take a look around," said Mac, reaching out to grab the gear bags as Dana handed them down from the dock. "If sabotage was indeed what shut down the compressors, I'd like to know. And I'd like to make sure nobody does anything else."

"No one else is joining us in an official capacity," asked Dana. "Who's running this mission?"

"It's true, they're not exactly the A team," replied Mac. "They weren't prepared for any of this, but at least they aren't getting in our way for now. Let's get out of here before they do.

"Buckle up," he added, "because it's going to be a little sporty out there."

It took ten minutes to clear the jetty protecting the harbor. The conditions deteriorated instantly once they cleared the entrance. Waves rocked the boat, and wind lashed the deck.

Mac piloted the boat, with Dana and Hendrix hunkered down with him in the wheelhouse looking through the gear that Dana had acquired. Visibility at the surface was less than a quarter mile.

"Can you remind me of the plan?" asked Dana, as she strapped on a shoulder holster.

"Hopefully, we can dock on the leeward side of the barge," replied Mac, without taking his eyes off the horizon. "Then we'll jump on board and see what we see. They left two technicians out there to monitor all the life support equipment on the barge."

"That can't be fun," observed Dana. She braced herself in the corner of the wheelhouse as the vessel dropped into the trough of a large passing swell. "This is definitely—what'd you call it? Sporty?"

Mac was standing at the helm with his legs spread wide to stabilize himself as the boat rocked. "Once we're on board the barge, we'll—*hold on*!"

The boat dropped into a deep trough. Mac expertly guided the bow into the oncoming swell, which engulfed the front third of the vessel. Water washed over the wheelhouse, but the structure held.

"That was close," said Mac. "Once we're on board the barge, we'll help the techs as needed and keep an eye out for any more trouble."

57

Hendrix and Dana steamed over the swells in silence for two hours. Hendrix went below often to contact his people on the mainland. Mac nearly missed the mayday call on the radio.

"Mayday, mayday, mayday, this is the mission control barge for the *Calypso I* mission. We are under attack. I repeat, we are under attack."

"Copy that, mission control," replied Mac. "This is Mac Johnson from the surface team. We are minutes away from your position. How many attackers are there?"

"I don't know, I saw two for sure. They just blew up the compressor and I heard shooting in the communications facility. *Calypso* is down. I repeat, *Calypso* is down!"

Mac tried to raise the man again on the radio but received only static.

"Vessel ahead!" yelled Hendrix, sticking his head in the wheelhouse. "I think I just saw two people leap onto the barge."

"I didn't think they were sending anyone else out here," said Dana, joining them.

"They aren't," answered Mac. "I just received confirmation from the barge that an attack is underway." He surveyed the equipment

Dana had brought before adding, “Okay, new plan. I’ll drop the two of you on the barge then go after that boat.”

“Both of you have more experience with the technology on the barge,” said Dana. “You go and I’ll take the boat.”

“You sure?” asked Hendrix.

Automatic weapons fire sprayed across the wheelhouse, but no one was hit. Dana took over the wheel from Mac, who slung several weapons over his shoulder before following Hendrix out onto the back deck.

“This is going to be dicey, watch yourselves back there,” said Dana.

“You complete me,” said Mac over his shoulder.

“*Shut up*,” said Dana. “Go!”

Mac watched from the back deck as Dana maneuvered the boat up to the rail of the rocking barge at its midpoint on the leeward side. He knew this was the most stable position on the vessel, which would give them the best shot of boarding without incident.

Without any need for encouragement, Hendrix leaped onto the barge with ease and turned to watch Mac, who followed immediately behind.

“Okay, let’s find the guys you saw jump on board.”

“Copy that,” replied Hendrix. “You go left, I’ll go right, and I’ll meet you on the other side.”

58

Aaron Bash had left Key Biscayne within minutes of the explosion at the Ritz-Carlton. Emergency vehicles were speeding toward the hotel from all directions, but no one paid any attention to him as he motored across the bridge in his dead uncle's truck. His work had been done and he had much more to do.

"Homestead," he dictated into his smartphone. "Meet me in the Wendy's parking lot. Thirty-forty minutes."

In Homestead, south of Miami, he'd stopped the truck just long enough for his friends Shane, Hank, and Manny to jump in the extended cab. Manny carried an aging duffel bag full of guns.

The four men had spent the night at the one-bedroom apartment of a guy Bash had met in jail. Banks had grown up in Key West and had agreed to finding them a boat.

A text from Martinez had indicated that the mission's primary decompression chamber was already disabled. Now it was his team's turn to go in and cut off all life support for the laboratory below, before Shaw made the final move. The storm had worked perfectly into their plans. Once the *Calypso I* was cut off, with minimal personnel on the barge above, rescuing the people in the lab would be impossible.

The two-hour ride out to the barge was rougher than Bash or any of his colleagues had imagined. Banks, the man piloting the vessel, had worked on his grandfather's fishing boat off the Keys for years, but he'd never been out in conditions such as these. Motoring parallel to the wave crests risked flipping the boat, so steering directly into the swells was the only way to safely navigate. Each cresting swell would lift the bow of the small boat, and then drop it down into the trough on the other side. More often than not, this resulted in the bow plunging directly into the next swell, submerging the entire front of the boat before popping back to the surface.

After only five minutes, three of the five men were vomiting. By the time the boat reached the Dry Tortugas two hours later, two of those three were lying on the back deck dry heaving and begging for the rolling to stop.

The next problem became clear as they approached the barge. There was no easy location to off-load people, or to tie off the boat, with such high wave action. The first attempt to approach the barge resulted in the two hulls crashing into each other. The fishing boat's wooden hull splintered against the massive wall of steel. Banks backed away, and then reapproached, trying to anticipate the swells such that one person at a time could jump onto the barge.

Manny, a friend of Bash's since they were very young boys, pulled himself up off the deck and leaped on Banks's command. Physically drained by seasickness, Manny's leap was poorly executed and badly timed. A swell brought the barge up at a steep angle just as Manny's feet left the deck. He slammed into the barge's hull like a rag doll, hitting his head and then dropping into the small void between the fishing boat and the barge.

Hank, another friend of Bash's, moved to the rail as quickly as his wobbly legs would allow to help Manny get back on board. He leaned far over the rail trying to reach his colleague who was flailing in the turbulent water below. As the next swell brought the two hulls crashing together again, both Hank and Manny were crushed to death.

Bash screamed in a combination of agony, frustration, and anger as the fishing boat backed off from the surging mission control barge. He was now down to only himself and Shane, with Banks needed to drive the boat.

He ordered Banks to approach the barge again.

"We can't pull this off!" screamed Banks over the howling wind. "I think we're taking water on at the bow. The controls are less responsive than they were five minutes ago. We've got to abort and make for that fort over there."

"No!" yelled Bash. "Get me over there, now."

"We are *sinking*!" exclaimed Banks.

"I don't give a shit," responded Bash, as he clung to the boat's wheelhouse to avoid falling overboard in the swells. "Put me next to that barge, now!"

Timing his leap correctly, Bash landed squarely on the barge's deck. Repeating the same movement, Shane followed successfully on the next swell. Banks then backed the boat away from the barge.

Looking back, Bash could see the bow of the fishing boat riding dangerously low in the water. He wasn't sure how they would get back to the mainland, but he pushed that concern out of his mind.

Bash and Shane quickly made for the nearest hatch. Once inside, free of the lashing from wind and rain, they nevertheless had to fight to find their bearings with the constant heaving of the barge in the swells. After stopping to vomit twice, Bash pushed forward, finding his way to the compressor room with Shane in tow. Inside, the sound of two massive compressors was deafening.

They found the control panel with little trouble and set one of the charges Bash had brought along in his backpack. Closing the large steel door behind them, Bash saw the door across the hall labeled as communications.

He opened the door to find two very surprised technicians staring at him.

Bash grabbed a pistol from his belt and quickly shot the man nearest to him in the stomach. However, the barge lurched violently just as he was aiming at the second man. Falling to the floor, Bash was unable to stop the man from leaping over him and running out the door. Shane ran after the man, leaving Bash alone in the room.

Looking at the large monitors on the wall, Bash could see Black and Gamal, the foreigner, getting ready to dive in the wet porch. Anxious to get off the barge before the technician could trigger some response from shore, Bash turned his pistol on the panel of computers and fired eight shots randomly. He then fled out the door and up the hallway to the nearest external door, hoping to help Shane corner the remaining technician. A muffled explosion behind him, followed by a cessation in the compressor noise, signaled that their charge had been successful.

Stepping back out into the wind and rain, Bash looked for Banks and the fishing boat. He thought he saw another small boat disappear over a swell, but he couldn't be sure. Turning to his right, he walked right into a bearded man with the wildest eyes Bash had ever seen. The man also had a massive scar across his neck as though he'd been hanged.

Shocked by the encounter, Bash gaped as he saw a second man dragging an unconscious Shane by the back of his shirt.

"Where're you going, fuckstick?" asked the man with the scar.

59

The afternoon dive had been canceled by unanimous agreement. The swells at the surface were resulting in significant bottom currents, and visibility had dropped to nearly zero as the currents stirred up sand everywhere around the *Calypso I*.

Chris and Nat sat at the table reviewing video they'd taken during the morning's dive. Brian was asleep in his bunk, while Jessica helped Trevor with work in the wet porch. Halbeck sat at the mission control computer entering details about the day's activities and the conditions outside the lab.

"This is awesome," said Nat. "Check out how the fish in these huge aggregations maintain a nearly constant position relative to each other and to the reef."

"Right," agreed Chris. "And these are non-schooling species that—"

"Uh-oh," said Halbeck.

The sound of the compressors had cut out and the screen on the mission control computer had frozen in place. The lights went out throughout the interior of the lab but were instantly replaced by emergency lights.

"I think we just lost our connection to the surface," said Halbeck.

"Is it the storm?" asked Nat.

"Possibly," said Halbeck, as he got up from his stool and made his way toward the wet porch. "But not likely."

"What does *that* mean?" asked Nat.

"Better go wake up Brian."

Twenty minutes later, connections to the surface had not been reestablished. Chris assembled Brian and Nat in the main lock while Halbeck brought Boseman and Jessica in from the wet porch.

"Otter, what's our status?" asked Chris.

"Without comms, we can't reach out for help," said Halbeck. "But hopefully someone on shore has already figured out that we've been isolated down here. Either way, we still have to decompress, and the chamber on the barge is not an option."

"Do we have enough time to pull off decompression down here?" asked Chris.

"We do, but just barely," interjected Boseman. "I estimate that we've got about sixteen hours of life support without the surface compressors supplying us with air. And decompression is going to take fourteen of those hours if everything goes according to plan. But please note, these are estimates. We could burn through the air much more quickly."

"Is there really even a decision here?" asked Chris, looking from Boseman to Halbeck. "We've got to secure the lab and start decompression. If connections are established in an hour, great, but we should move on deco right away."

"I concur," said Halbeck.

"But the storm is still raging outside," noted Brian. "We can't go to the surface under these conditions."

"You're right, Brian," said Chris. "We have major challenges to overcome. But if we don't go through decompression, our options are going to be very few."

"Let's do it," said Nat. "What can I do to help?"

Halbeck looked at Boseman and Jessica. "Are you two on board?"

Boseman nodded his assent.

Jessica looked down, but said, "Yes, I'm on board."

"Okay, Trevor and I need to conduct a short dive to secure the lab for decompression."

"You're going out? In this?" asked Nat, waving her hand toward the porthole.

"We are," replied Halbeck. "There are external valves at three locations on each side of the lab that have to be closed so that we can begin decompression. If we don't close them, the lab's hull won't pressurize.

"We'll stay close to the external superstructure and should be fine. We don't have time to mobilize the AGA masks, so while we're outside, we won't be able to communicate with you."

"Otter, let me dive with Trevor," interjected Chris. "That way you can be in here prepping the oxygen and getting everything ready."

Nat looked out the porthole into the dark. "The currents are ripping out there and it's *dark.* Are you sure we want to put anyone in the water?"

"It has to be done," said Halbeck. "But it should only take five minutes if it goes according to plan. You won't be able to use the hookah system, obviously, with the compressor down. But all our tanks are filled."

"Won't we need those tanks to surface?" asked Brian.

"Yes, but there's also the air in the compressor banks. Even though the compressors at the surface are disconnected, we've got stored air that we can leverage."

Chris and Trevor moved out to the wet porch to prepare for the dive. Trevor explained what he was going to do and how Chris could help as they prepared. Chris noted with interest that Trevor wasn't making any eye contact as he talked. He figured that the man was self-conscious due to his apparently budding relationship with Jessica.

But he had much bigger concerns to deal with, so Chris ignored it. Incentivized by the lab's decreasing air supply, they were ready to dive and enter the water within eight minutes.

The current moving through the moon pool was stronger than anything Chris had ever seen during a saturation mission. Stepping down into the water, he instantly felt the draw of the current, watching as fish washed past him struggling to fight the fast-moving water themselves. Each of the divers attached a nylon safety line to their harnesses. The line would guide them back to the moon pool should they lose their hold on the *Calypso I's* superstructure.

As soon as the pair moved out of the pool's protection, the currents worked ceaselessly to peel them away from the safety of the lab. Both divers had to pull themselves along the superstructure using their hands, for kicking was futile against the currents.

Chris spotted the first of four panels they needed to visit and moved in to access it for Boseman. As he worked on the cover, he suddenly was yanked violently downward as though something were pulling on him. Holding on to a narrow rail, Chris felt something heavy bump the back of his legs and realized that Boseman had just attached a bag of backup lead weights to his tanks. He watched in vain as Boseman took out a knife and sliced through both of Chris's regulator hoses and his safety line. Boseman then bent down to peel off Chris's grip on the rail. Chris reached for Boseman's arm but missed getting a grip.

He fell into the darkness, headed for the bottom twenty feet below.

60

Huge banks of emergency lights lined the beach below what remained of the Ritz-Carlton Key Biscayne, bringing near-daylight to the site of the explosion for round-the-clock rescue and recovery operations. The hotel had been fully evacuated following the explosion for fear that structural damage to the foundation and lower two floors may cause additional portions of the hotel above to collapse. From her position in the parking lot nearby, Anna Cortez watched as hundreds of emergency personnel carefully combed through the rubble, assisted by trained search dogs. She knew from previous experience at such sites that half of those dogs would be searching for human remains, while the other half would be seeking additional explosives.

Cortez took only a few pictures, choosing to focus her thoughts more on the coming conversation.

"Ms. Cortez?"

She turned to find a tall man with closely cropped gray hair and a dark suit approaching her.

"I'm Frank Donagan, US State Department. I believe we have a mutual friend."

"Hello, Mr. Donagan. Thank you for meeting me."

"Please call me Frank. Now what can I do for you?"

"Well, Frank, I can tell you that I don't make it a habit of divulging information to government employees, regardless of the government. But I trust Chris and he seems to trust you, so in the interest of urgency I will tell you what I've got."

Cortez spent several minutes describing the trajectory that brought her into contact with Chris Black, omitting nothing from the story. Donagan simply listened, without asking questions or taking any notes. When she got to the part about the two encounters with the man she now knew as Robert Shaw, Cortez extracted his wallet from her bag and handed it to Donagan.

Donagan accepted the wallet and thumbed through the contents, settling for several seconds on Shaw's driver's license and work credentials.

"Are you familiar with Unity Environmental?" asked Cortez.

"I am. Are you?"

"I wasn't before one of their employees tried to kidnap me, but I've spent some of the last hour reviewing their website. They're huge, aren't they?"

"They are," agreed Donagan. "They have their hands in security and military contracting around the world."

"Can you think of why one of their employees would be following Chris and me, and then try to kidnap me?"

"No, I can't. But you can be sure I'm going to investigate. Is the number you called me from the best way to reach you?"

"It is," said Cortez. "Can you move on this quickly? I'm concerned that the *Calypso I* mission is at risk."

"I'll do what I can," said Donagan. "You've been forthright with me, so I'll return the favor. It's going to be tough to focus our assets away from this attack and the earlier one at the auditorium. The undersea mission is simply not a high priority when dozens of people are dying in other attacks."

"Is that your position?"

"Not necessarily," said Donagan.

"What if the attack at the hotel was a distraction?"

"From the real target? Which you think is the *Calypso I*?"

"It could be. Look at all the chatter on social media."

"There may be something to your concerns. The targeted social media deluge is certainly happening. But I'm just one cog in a large machine. I'll see what I can do."

While Donagan described his next steps, Cortez's eye was drawn to one of the dogs below. It had found something in the rubble. The handler called over several other people and they slowly removed chunks of concrete until a body was discovered.

As the team worked to clear the body from the rubble, a stretcher materialized out of nowhere and was wheeled over to the location of the body.

She watched as a quartet of people slowly lifted the body up onto the stretcher and covered it with a blanket. Cortez thought about using her camera to capture the delicate effort the emergency personnel were making with the body. But she decided to simply watch instead.

As a duo began to wheel the stretcher back through the rubble field, another dog approached the stretcher and became quite agitated. Everyone on the site froze, as the dog zeroed in on the body as it barked.

The dog's handler pulled back on the dog as someone else yelled, "EVERYBODY DOWN!"

Seconds later the body exploded, sending new shrapnel directly into areas crowded with emergency personnel.

Donagan pulled Cortez down, producing a microphone from somewhere up his left sleeve. "Secondary explosion at the Ritz-Carlton site. Repeat, secondary explosion at the Ritz-Carlton site. Send assistance immediately."

Cortez removed her camera from around her neck as she sloughed Donagan's hand off her shoulder.

"Anna, we have to get you to safety!"

"This is my *job*, Donagan. I'm not leaving until the sacrifices of these first responders have been fully documented. They raced into the fray to help, and now they're victims themselves. Now let's get down there to help!"

61

Trevor Boseman had plans, and he rarely deviated from them. They included long-, near-, and short-term goals, right down to the details of his daily activities. Breakfast, for instance, was consumed at precisely five a.m. each day, and usually consisted of one cup oatmeal, one teaspoon honey, and five fresh raspberries. He also drank a cup and a half of black coffee. He allocated fifteen minutes to the meal, and then proceeded with the rest of his agenda for the day.

When Boseman was on travel, he found ways to replicate key elements of his routine. Six weeks before the start of the *Calypso I* mission, he'd left the oil platform he'd been working on off the Texas coast to come to South Florida to assist in preparations for the saturation mission.

He'd spent the first three days in Miami, where the brand-new undersea laboratory had arrived on a container ship from New Jersey. From there, he'd sailed with the *Calypso I* aboard a massive naval troop carrier to the deployment site off Barracuda Key in the Dry Tortugas. Working with Navy divers and surface personnel, they'd used a massive, one-hundred-and-ten-ton lift bag to slowly lower the undersea laboratory to the seafloor.

After the arrival of the mission control barge, it had taken four additional days, working round-the-clock, to successfully power up the *Calypso I*.

All of the non-Navy personnel associated with the mission were rotated back to Key West for two days off each week. The free breakfast provided by the hotel didn't start until seven a.m., so Boseman had adopted the habit of walking down the street to the nearest Starbucks coffee, carrying his raspberries and honey in a small, insulated bag in case neither were available on site.

Sitting in the same seat he'd used the day before, Boseman had been scrolling through his smartphone and eating his oatmeal when a man he didn't recognize sat down at his table.

"This seat taken?" asked the man wearing a baseball cap as he sat down. He wore sunglasses, despite the early hour.

"Actually, I'm just trying to eat my breakfast," replied Boseman, as he looked around at all the empty tables around him. He could see cars queuing up outside for the drive-through pickup, but there'd been no other customers inside.

"I can see that," said the man. "Is the food any better here than it is out on that platform?"

Boseman looked closely at the man. The thick blond hair sticking out below his Florida Marlins cap looked as though it were a wig. The ends were too uniform.

"Actually," added the man. "I guess what I'm really interested in knowing is whether the food is any better than up there at the juvenile detention center in Panama City."

Boseman let the smartphone drop out of his hand onto the table. It had been twenty-four years since he'd left that hellhole, and the court records had been sealed. There was no way for this stranger to know about it.

"Who are you, exactly?" Boseman had asked, recovering from his shock.

"Who I am doesn't really matter," answered the man, looking around. "Keep eating your breakfast.

"Let's just say I'm here to remind you where you come from, who your family is. You might have gone off to be a fancy as-tro-naut trainee and worked on oil platforms all over the world. But the fact is, you're also the brother of two of the meanest men I've ever met."

The mentioning of his brothers, Kale and Big Bill, had also been stunning. No one knew his background. At least, that's what he'd thought.

Boseman and his two brothers had spent their youths in and out of foster care and the Florida juvenile detention system. Their father had been killed by federal agents when the triplets had been eleven years old. Their mom had died in childbirth.

The Boseman trio had survived the years by supporting each other and through their willingness to do whatever each situation required to survive. If a foster father had sought to touch any of the three boys, all three responded in unison. If a bully at school had targeted any of them, the others stepped in, and the bully had ceased to bother anyone ever again.

When they'd reached eighteen, Kale and Big Bill had moved out into the woods to live off the grid. Trevor, having had the best grades of the three, went to college and then grad school. But he never lost touch with his brothers, no matter how far away his work had taken him.

"Okay, you've got my attention."

"Let's just say that your brothers and I share a mutual acquaintance," the man had explained. "And that mutual acquaintance wants to see this undersea mission fail."

Boseman was familiar with his brothers' forays into armed extremism. They'd started with a small group outside Panama City. That had been followed with a series of increasingly extreme affiliations with state and national militia groups. He would have joined them in a heartbeat if his career hadn't required him to downplay those affiliations in order to succeed. The money he'd made went directly into a shared account that the brothers had set up years before to support all three of them.

The distance he'd maintained from his brothers' activities had been a mutually agreed-upon necessity. But he'd always known that eventually maintaining that distance was going to be impossible.

"You a member of federal law enforcement?" Boseman had asked. "That's a lovely wig you're wearing. You realize, of course, that entrapment is crime."

The man had smiled.

"They told me you'd be a suspicious customer. They weren't wrong."

"Who told you that, exactly?"

"I've never met Big Bill," the man answered. "But I've spoken with Kale more than once."

"Prove it."

The man pulled a business card from the breast pocket of his shirt and slid it across the table to Boseman.

Boseman picked it up. There was nothing on it except a phone number printed in a very small font.

"What am I supposed to do with this?"

"Just call it," the man said. "I'm going to go up to the counter to buy a doughnut. When I get back, we'll talk further."

Boseman had flipped the card around in his fingers for twenty seconds as he watched the wigged man approach the counter. He dialed the number.

"That you, Trevor?" said a familiar voice.

"Hi, Bill. What is it, exactly, that you want me to do?"

62

"Hey, fuckstick!" yelled Hendrix through the wind and rain. "I'm talking to *you*."

Bash had tried to speak through his surprise, but Hendrix had dropped him with a massive jab to the face before any sounds left his lips.

"You won't—" muttered Bash, lying on the barge's deck as he tried to pull a gun out of his belt.

"No . . . *you* won't," interjected Hendrix, knocking Bash into unconsciousness with a punch to the temple.

Mac had dragged Shane Brimmer away as Hendrix dealt with Bash. After a brief interrogation he'd tied Brimmer up using zip ties from Dana's bag of goodies. He then found Hendrix just as he was waking up the man they now knew as Bash with a hard slap to the face. Mac could see he'd secured Bash's wrists and ankles, and then tied him against a wall in what Mac hoped would be an uncomfortable position.

"Hey, fucko! It's time to get up. My name's Hendrix, your name's Bash, and those are my friends you're messing with. You're going to tell me everything you know, or pain is going to take on a new meaning for you."

"I'll kill you, old man!" said Bash.

Hendrix hit him again. "Oh, I don't think so, fuckwad. That's because when I'm done with you, you won't be a danger to me or anyone else. But let's move on to more important things, shall we?"

"Where is Shane?" demanded Bash.

"The other guy?" said Mac. He'd left the man tied up and unconscious in the hallway. "He won't be joining us, or you, ever again."

Bash shook violently, but Hendrix easily maintained control.

"I will kill both of you for this," hissed Bash.

Mac leaned in close to speak when Bash tried to head butt him. Easily dodging the head butt, Mac grabbed Bash by the front of his hair and slammed the man's head back against the wall.

"I'm worried that the compressors are both toast," he explained to Hendrix. "They really did a number on them. I'm going to work on comms, while the surviving technician works on the compressors, unless you need me here."

"Solid plan. My friend and I will be fine out here. What's Dana's status?"

"She took out the boat these two arrived on," said Mac, patting the radio on his shoulder. "Now she's just keeping our ride afloat and standing by to come pick us up. The storm is picking up steam."

"What do you mean *took out*? Where is Banks?" demanded Bash.

"It means destroyed, shitbag," said Hendrix. "Your friends are no longer with us."

Bash erupted in a string of expletives. "I will kill all of you!"

Hendrix punched Bash hard in the face. "No more threats from you.

"Why don't we start with pain first, then we'll move on to questions," added Hendrix, as Mac stepped out of the galley and slowly navigated his way down the hallway to the communications room.

The communications room, Mac observed, was a shambles. It looked like one of the terrorists, standing right where he currently stood, had opened fire with an automatic weapon. Looking up at the wall of screens, the situation looked dire to Mac. At first glance, it appeared to him as though the comms were beyond repair. He saw six large displays, and each had been shot out. But as he looked more closely, he realized that the displays were only monitors connected to two desktop computers mounted in a stabilizing frame below.

And one of those was undamaged.

63

"We've known for a long time that an infusion of pure oxygen molecules in the blood is key to diver decompression. The oxygen facilitates the faster removal of nitrogen in the bloodstream, which in turn shortens the total time required for decompression."

Inside the *Calypso I,* Halbeck had enlisted the three aquanauts in helping him set up the oxygen regulators at the head of each bunk. Once decompression was initiated, each of the divers, including Otter and Trevor, would lie down in their bunks and breathe pure oxygen.

"But we also know that pure oxygen is toxic to divers at depth," said Brian. "As undergraduates, we always enjoyed yelling at the screen anytime a Hollywood movie depicted divers using oxygen."

"That's right," agreed Halbeck. "Even some of the movies that are accurate on many counts still make that mistake. Lucky for us, the science of saturation diving has come a long way over the past twenty years. We now know that three short periods of breathing pure oxygen at the start of decompression will expedite nitrogen gas removal without risking oxygen toxicity."

"That sounds dicey," observed Nat.

"Compared to everything else you've experienced on this mission, Nat, this will be a walk in the park," said Halbeck. "Trevor and I will walk you through it. You'll just lie in your bunks with all your limbs straight and breathe off the regulator for three, fifteen-minute periods."

"Why limbs straight, again?" asked Brian.

"*Again* implies you listened the first time," observed Nat.

"Shut up, Nat."

"Nitrogen bubbles tend to collect at the joints, causing the pain we call the bends. We'll keep all our limbs straight to allow as much nitrogen to leave our bodies as possible," clarified Halbeck.

An audible increase in sloshing came from the microphone in the wet porch. "Good, they're back. We need to secure the door to the main lock and start the process as soon as they're ready."

"And once we close that door, it won't open again for fourteen hours?" asked Nat.

"That's correct," responded Halbeck. "You'll want to make sure you're on *this* side of the door once everything begins."

Minutes passed before Boseman stepped through the main lock door, closing it behind him and locking it in place.

"Where's Chris?" Halbeck asked.

Boseman turned from the door to face the group. "Gone. Chris is gone." His hands shaking, he brushed back his hair.

Nat gasped, while Halbeck fell backward against the control panel behind him. "Come again?" he demanded. "What the hell happened?"

"We were working on the first panel when he lost his grip on the structure. His safety line must not have been attached properly because it detached almost instantly. The storm is raging out there. He was carried away by the current."

"What are you saying?" demanded Brian. "Chris is still out there? In this current?"

"You didn't grab him or look for him?" Halbeck yelled. "You seem awfully calm. Did you expend any effort at all?"

"Of course I did. But the current was too strong."

"And why didn't you alert us immediately? What were you doing out there in the wet porch all that time?"

"I'm sorry, I needed to collect myself. Figure out how to tell you guys."

"We can't just leave him out there!" said Nat. "Maybe he was able to grab hold of the reef and is sitting out there right now trying to find his way back."

Halbeck looked at his watch. "We've got twenty minutes before we have to start deco. I'm going to go look for him."

Trevor moved to block Halbeck. "Otter, you can't. He could be more than a kilometer away at this point. And the same could happen to anyone who goes outside right now. We've got to ensure the safety of the rest of the group. Chris would be the first to point this out, you know that."

No one spoke.

"We've got to face it," Trevor added. "Chris is gone."

64

Robert Shaw rubbed his eyes. It had already been a long night, and it was far from over. He'd met his crew of four handpicked divers, along with Hugo Martinez, at a convenience store parking lot on the outskirts of Miami. Before that, he'd swapped the stolen truck for a van in which the group could drive down through the Keys and gear up in secrecy.

It was still the early evening, and the storm was continuing to blow outside. While the crew waited, they listened in on radio communications associated with the mission. It was clear to Shaw from the panicked chatter that Bash and his group of incompetents had somehow succeeded in destroying all connections to the underwater laboratory.

Shaw had not believed success was likely given the security around the mission. He'd assumed the most likely outcome was that Bash would be killed or captured.

Fortunately, there'd been no discussion of any captures. That would have created other problems for Shaw, which he didn't need or want right now. Particularly not given that the reporter had stolen his wallet.

"So, what's our plan, boss?" asked the guy they called Blue.

At six foot, four inches, he was the largest member on the team. Shaw had only worked with him for the trial run they'd conducted outside of Fort Lauderdale, but the man did what was asked of him.

The original plan had been to time the undersea assault to correspond to the attack on the barge above. With assistance from the inside man down below, Shaw's team would have swept into the lab, killed the remaining scientists, and blown up the lab itself. The weather had forced a change in plans, but it was not, Shaw realized, entirely unwelcome. So far, the weather had kept mission control and the associated security on shore, freeing them up to dive without complications at the surface.

"We're going to hold tight here until sunrise is three hours out," explained Shaw. "Then we'll motor out to the site and splash the five of you before dawn. I'll stay topside to pick you up once you've finished the job."

"Copy that. What are surface conditions right now? Any intel on bottom currents?"

"We still have surface waves reaching eight feet, and that's predicted to continue through midday," Shaw explained. "I don't have a reliable report on currents, but given that the lab is in only sixty feet of water, you should expect current. If you drop quickly, you should be on the *Calypso* with little effort."

"What about resistance at the surface or at depth?" asked Green. He was nearly a foot shorter than Blue, but his biceps were as large as his thighs.

"There's a security presence at the harbor office we passed by earlier," said Martinez. "That's where they set up shore-side mission control. But since they decamped from the barge, they haven't mobilized any vessels. We don't expect trouble from the barge.

"The attack up in Key Biscayne has drawn away a great deal of attention. I think the weather's a factor too, but we should expect activity after sunup. That's why we'll head out predawn."

"And in the lab?" Green asked again.

"Minimal," said Martinez. "We've got a man down there, one of the technicians. But once the surface connection was terminated, all comms stopped. He may have cultivated a second contact within the science team, a woman. But we won't be bringing anyone out."

"Not even your contacts?" clarified Blue.

"Where would we take them?" answered Shaw. "They're in saturation. We bring them to the surface without a decompression chamber available, they'll take major deco hits and die anyway. No, if they haven't already realized, they soon will get that this is a one-way trip."

"If they figure that out before we arrive," said Red, a former British special forces diver, "we may have a problem there."

"You were each handpicked because we don't want to worry about these kinds of issues," said Shaw. "Just do your job. Rescue *no one*."

65

Chris Black hit the seafloor hard, as stunned by Boseman's betrayal as he was by the impact with the sand.

However, the anxiety and lingering doubts that had preoccupied him off and on since the Galapagos incident had dissipated instantly. Trevor Boseman, in trying to remove Chris from the picture, had inadvertently given him just the push he needed.

Looking up at the *Calypso I* above him, Chris took stock. The lead weights Boseman had connected to his tanks had made it impossible for Chris to swim back to the habitat, but they had also likely saved his life. Had Boseman simply cut the safety line and knocked Chris out into the current, he would have been drawn out over the reef, never to be seen again. But the weights had pulled him straight down, which now gave him a chance.

Considering his options, few and risky as they were, Chris quickly freed himself from the harness connecting him to the tanks. The ambient light from the still-illuminated *Calypso I* above gave him ample light to work with. Boseman had cut both his regulator hoses, both of which were spewing air wildly. Staying low to the seafloor, with one arm through his tank harness, Chris grabbed both hoses and kinked them. This slowed the flow of air to a trickle of bubbles, saving a critical reserve he'd need to survive.

Breathing every thirty seconds from one of the two severed hoses like a straw, he scanned the area above him looking for a solution to his current situation.

Apart from his dwindling air supply, the primary challenge would be to return to the lab without being drawn away by the currents ripping past him. As strong a swimmer as Chris was, he knew that unaided he would stand no chance against the current. Lying prone on the seafloor, he was safe. But as soon as he swam upward, he would immediately be grabbed by the current and drawn away from the *Calypso I*.

One thing was clear: he needed to go back to the lab to deal with Boseman and, more importantly, prevent him from doing whatever he planned to do next.

It was also clear that Boseman was part of whatever extremist plot had been brewing. Chris kicked himself for not investigating the team members before he'd come to Miami. Despite his bad experiences in the past, which had shown him that everyone could be compromised at the right price, he wanted to believe that scientists stood above politics and were immune to financial temptation. He was wrong. But he did not have time for these considerations now. He needed to go do what he could to save the mission—and likely the lives of everyone aboard the *Calypso I*.

A plan took shape in his mind. He unclipped the carabiner that Boseman had used to connect the weights to his tanks and removed half the weights from the mesh bag. He then took several long breaths from the regulator hose and moved toward the down-current side of the nearest leg supporting the lab, using the weight belt to keep himself close to the bottom as he went.

At almost four feet in diameter, the leg provided protection from the heavy current. Safe in that lee, Chris removed additional weight from the bag, leaving enough to allow him to kick upward with his fins while also keeping him from launching on an uncontrolled ascent to the surface. He then slowly followed the leg up to the platform that ran under the moon pool.

That's where he would be in the gravest danger. He had to move horizontally across an exposed area where the current could grab him at any moment. Continuing to rely on the weights, he dragged them along the platform with one hand, using the other hand to hold the rail at the platform's edge.

Inching along the platform's edge, Chris felt fatigue building from his fingers up into his hands as he struggled to maintain his position.

The currents threatening to rip him off the *Calypso I* were the strongest he'd ever experienced while diving. He'd crossed nearly two-thirds of the distance when the bag got fouled on the platform and wouldn't budge.

Running out of air, he'd paused briefly to shake the strain out of his fingers and hands. He then released the weights and relied on his little remaining finger strength to keep himself connected to the lab, kicking as hard as he could with his fins to keep himself from washing away.

Making it to the moon pool, and desperate for air, Chris knew that he had to be careful not to be recorded by the microphone. There was no way to know what was going on inside the *Calypso I*, and any loud noise could alert Boseman to his return. He inhaled as quietly as possible, and then slowly removed three of the aquanauts' SCUBA rigs from the rack on the lower level.

Submerging himself, and breathing off one of the regulators, he bound the tanks together by interconnecting the harness straps. Protected by the *Calypso I's* superstructure, he swam the tanks to the bow, immediately below the bunk room.

Chris had not known for sure if the hatch would be there but had hoped the modeling of the *Calypso I* on the *Poseidon* had included that detail. Finding the hatch as expected, he anchored the tanks to the external structure using a free harness strap, right next to two underwater scooters.

Pausing in the well beneath the bailout hatch, he formulated his plan.

66

Just inside the main hatch door, Mark Halbeck moved in close to Trevor Boseman, his nose only inches from the other man's. "There is no fucking way we're going to begin decompression without first looking for Chris. You got that, Trevor? *No fucking way*."

Halbeck looked down at Boseman's clothes. "Wait a minute, you took time to change into dry clothes? With Chris out there?"

Boseman leaned away from Halbeck, "Otter, I—"

Boseman was interrupted by the sound of splashing from the wet porch microphone.

A garbled voice yelled, "Hey!"

"Is that Chris?" exclaimed Nat, who was standing closest to the communication station they'd used throughout the mission. "We've got to get to him."

Halbeck pushed Boseman out of the way to gain access to the small porthole that looked out into the wet porch. Grabbing the hand-wheel on the hatch, he said, "I can't see anything. Let's get out there."

"No, stop!" exclaimed Boseman.

"Why not?" responded Halbeck.

"Quiet!" yelled Nat, holding up her hands. "Listen."

Everyone inside the lab froze. The sound of metal hitting metal emanated from the bunk room at the other end of the lab.

Three loud metallic clunks signaled that a hatch was being opened. The thin patch of carpet on the bunk room deck began to rise up as a hatch door was lifted from underneath. A figure climbed up out of the hatch still wearing a SCUBA mask, water dripping off his wetsuit.

Chris Black removed his mask and focused his glare on Boseman as he moved quickly out of the bunk room toward the lab's main lock. Boseman pulled a dive knife from a thigh pocket on his blue jumpsuit and grabbed Halbeck.

"If you come one step closer, Black, I'll kill him," said Boseman, moving his knife to Halbeck's throat.

"What the hell?" exclaimed Halbeck.

None of the aquanauts moved. Only the sloshing water in the moon pool penetrated the silence. Chris continued moving forward.

"Stop right there, Black," demanded Boseman. "I knew that I should have done you earlier. It would have been so easy."

Chris calculated his options. He knew that one wrong move on his part and Halbeck might die. And given Boseman's position next to the *Calypso's* environmental controls, two wrong moves and they would all be gone. *Keep him talking*.

"Okay, okay," said Chris. He edged past the aquanauts, who were frozen in place at the table, stopping next to the sink and putting his palms up. "But what are you doing, Trevor? You don't want to hurt Otter, do you?"

"No, I don't want to," replied Boseman. "But I have to. You, on the other hand, will be easy."

"You said that already. Why do you have to hurt anyone?" asked Chris. He was looking directly at Boseman but briefly made eye contact with Halbeck. He saw defiance in those eyes.

"To end the mission, of course," said Boseman. "Didn't that reporter tell you anything? We are not going to let Pierce and her liberal fantasy of international collaboration take place in our own backyard."

"Who's we?" asked Chris. "The militia kooks posting on social media? The ones who drove a truck into the crowd and blew up a hotel in Miami? You can't buy into that crap. You were almost an astronaut, for God's sake."

"I wouldn't expect you hippies from California to understand," Boseman spat. "Your self-righteousness makes me sick."

"Fine," said Chris. Venturing a guess, he added, "Look, you've already wrecked the mission. You fouled our air, and we're cut off from mission control, which I am sure was part of your plan as well. The mission's over, Trevor. You've succeeded. Nobody needs to die to make your point."

Chris took a step closer. Boseman pulled back.

"But now we're facing this storm, and if we don't start decompression soon, we're all going to die, including you. You don't want that, do you?"

"I'm prepared to die to end this country's love affair with globalism," said Boseman. "I've had it with supporting the whole fucking world! And when this mission ends, with all hands lost, the government will think twice about collaborating further."

"We aren't going to let you kill everyone, Trevor," said Chris. "No way."

"Get him!" yelled Boseman, directing his attention to the aquanauts.

Nat stood up immediately, but Jessica, who'd been sitting closest to the porthole, violently pushed her to the floor as she moved toward Boseman. From the pocket of her sweatpants, she pulled out a dive knife.

"Jessica, no!" said Chris. "You don't want to hurt anyone."

Simultaneously, Boseman shoved Halbeck to the deck, slicing through his upper arm, and then dashed toward Chris just as Jessica did the same. Chris grabbed a large coffee mug from the dish rack next to him and prepared to fend off Jessica's knife attack.

Jessica lunged forward. Without making a sound, Brian, who'd been sitting with his back toward Chris and Boseman when the confrontation began, leaped from his seat, hitting Jessica hard from the right and sending her crashing into the instrument panel on the starboard side of the lab. She cried out and dropped her knife.

Spinning back toward Boseman, Chris saw Halbeck thrust out his bleeding arm in an attempt to slow Boseman's progress. Boseman stumbled but stayed upright. He redirected his attention from Chris and lunged toward Halbeck with the knife.

Chris ran straight at Boseman. Though the technician was an inch taller and at least twenty pounds heavier, the speed and ferocity of Chris's lunge lifted the bigger man off the deck and sent him hurling toward the main hatch door.

Jessica screamed again and reached for her knife as she struggled to get to her feet. Brian kicked the knife away from her with his right foot, while hammering at Jessica's back with both his arms extended. She fell, crashing her head against the bulkhead, and slumped to the ground.

"Otter, are you okay?" asked Chris, keeping his eyes on Boseman.

"I'm okay," replied Halbeck, as he used his left hand to stop the bleeding on his right bicep. "Don't let him get to that instrument panel," he added, his voice low so only Chris could hear him.

As if on cue, Boseman moved to the alternative instrument panel that was normally used in the case of emergency.

Chris resumed his forward momentum and was on Boseman before the man had a chance to regroup. He used his left foot to crush Boseman's forearm, taking the knife out of play.

Grabbing Boseman by his fleece vest, he then used his right fist to deliver three rapid jabs to Boseman's face, breaking his nose and splitting his lips.

Chris paused briefly to evaluate Boseman's condition, and when Boseman looked up toward Chris with anger in his eyes, Chris hit him one last time, knocking him unconscious.

Pausing to catch his breath, Chris asked, "Is everyone okay?"

67

Grampen Rhodes's private jet touched down at Orlando International Airport. The flight from Miami had taken just half an hour. He was met by a matte-black SUV and escorted to the compound north of the city run by Unity Environmental.

He found Leland Jones sitting in the executive lounge, smoking a cigar.

"Gramp, what damn game are you playing?" asked Jones, without rising from his seat.

"I'm sure I don't know what you mean, Leland. It's nice to see you, however. May I fix myself a drink?" Rhodes loosened his tie.

"Go right ahead," said Leland, waving his hand toward the bar. "While you're at it, better make me another too."

"How's Trixie?" asked Rhodes.

"You know damn well how she is," said Leland. "She'll probably leave me within a year, sooner if the company goes under."

"I'm sorry to hear that. You two were always the center of attention back in our fraternity days."

"And how's, um, well, I guess I forgot the name of the latest one," said Jones. "How old is she this time?"

"She's mature beyond her years, Leland," replied Rhodes. "And she keeps me young."

There was a knock at the door and Sharon Dirksen walked in.

"Sharon, my dear, aren't you a sight for sore eyes!" exclaimed Rhodes as he moved to hug Dirksen. "I've never seen you in the lounge here before."

"Oh, I never come in here," replied Dirksen, avoiding Rhodes's hug. "Too much cigar smoke and testosterone."

Rhodes and Dirksen joined Jones in separate lounge chairs.

"Your lovely messenger here told me I had to come. Now how can I help you, my old friend?" asked Rhodes, leaning over to remove a cigar from the gold case sitting on the table in front of him.

"You can start by telling me what you've done in Miami," stated Jones. "You deviated from our plan."

Rhodes sat back and lit the cigar, taking long drags and puffing out a cloud of blue smoke.

"I'm serious, Gramp. I need to know what you've done."

"I like to think I bring a little southern flourish to the game," replied Rhodes. "Otherwise, why would you use me at all? Shaw could easily have handled the operations. We both know that."

"You were an additional safeguard in case Shaw was unsuccessful. But why the attack on the Ritz-Carlton? There were many Americans on the casualty list."

"That was a shame, I agree," said Rhodes. "But I thought it was necessary. Fessler and his people wanted to do more than Shaw was demanding of him, so I just gave him a little more rope, as it were."

"I can't believe you were so willing to take American lives. Have you seen the images from the site?"

"Now just you wait a minute," said Rhodes. "Don't you lecture me about casualties and consequences. Mobilizing the militia was your plan. I just augmented. You wanted less international amity to secure your arms trade contracts, and I think you're going to get that.

The undersea mission will fail, and so will Pierce and Science Without Borders. At least for a while."

Jones sat back in his chair and stared at the smoke above him.

"All that aside, Mr. Rhodes, why the focus on that scientist, Chris Black?" asked Dirksen. "He wasn't part of our plan. Why did you go out of your way to get him there? And then you had Bash try to kill him multiple times."

"Well, let's just say I have my reasons," explained Rhodes. "And those reasons are none of your business. No matter how the rest of this turns out, Chris Black will not survive the week."

68

"Otter, what's your status?"

"Irritated," replied Halbeck. "Help me get this bleeding under control and then you can tie up Boseman."

Chris was kneeling next to Halbeck to help him control the bleed on his arm when Halbeck suddenly yelled, "Look out!"

Chris spun around awkwardly to find Jessica charging at him with Boseman's knife in her hand. She had not been out cold after all. He reached for anything to throw at her, with his hand settling on the plastic dish rack by the sink. Grabbing the rack by its edge, he swung upward to deflect the knife. Plates and plastic cups went flying in all directions.

The force of his blow knocked Jessica sideways, but it didn't dislodge the knife and slowed her for only a moment.

Chris could only stare into Jessica's enraged eyes as she prepared to launch herself at him again. "Jessica, no!"

Before Jessica could strike again, Nat came charging out of the bunk room with the metal first aid kit. Holding the metal box along its long axis like a battering ram, she reached over Chris and Halbeck, connecting squarely with Jessica's forehead. Jessica's eyes blinked as blood from a gash across her brow poured down, clouding her vision.

Brian followed behind Nat, using a fire extinguisher to hammer Jessica's hand against the metal rim of the counter. The sound of cracking bones was followed by the metallic clatter of the knife falling to the deck.

"Thanks, team," said Chris, slumping back against the counter. "Jessica, what the hell is wrong with you?"

"Why in God's name are you attacking your fellow aquanauts?" asked Halbeck. "Are you working with Trevor?"

Jessica said nothing, didn't look at anyone.

"Well, whatever led to this debacle doesn't matter. We need to create a modicum of safety," replied Chris. "Let's watch those two while we get your wound dressed."

Nat kneeled next to Chris and extracted dressings from the first aid kit while Brian stood watch over Jessica and Trevor.

The knife had grazed Halbeck's bicep, but the wound was not deep.

Chris quickly dressed it, sticking two fingers under the dressing to make sure it wasn't constricting blood flow. "How's this? Is it too tight?"

Halbeck moved his arm around. "No, this is perfect. Thanks."

"We've got to work a few things out," said Chris. "I'm worried about decompression."

"Yeah," agreed Halbeck looking at his watch. "If we don't get started within fifteen minutes, we'll run out of air before we can safely leave *Calypso*. We've got to get moving immediately."

"How do we help?" asked Chris.

"Here, help me up and I'll show you the checklist," said Halbeck, reaching up to Chris.

Halbeck stood and made his way to the technicians' comms station. He extracted a white three-ring binder.

"Where do you guys keep the tie wraps?" asked Chris.

Five minutes later, both Boseman and Jessica were secured at the wrists and ankles by large tie wraps.

"What's next?" asked Chris.

Before Halbeck had a chance to answer, the Batphone rang.

69

Chris Black joined the rest of the aquanauts in staring at the phone sitting on the counter, wondering to himself, *Did that thing just ring*? A second later, the phone rang again. He picked up the phone while Halbeck made final preparations to begin decompression. "Black, here."

"Chris! It's Hendrix. What's your sitrep?"

"Hendrix? Where are you?" asked Chris.

"On the barge above you with Johnson," replied Hendrix. "Two extremists took out the compressors. We've taken care of them. Fortunately, they didn't do as well with the comms equipment. A technician up here who survived the attack, he's been a huge asset."

"What a coincidence—we have two extremists down here as well. Took a little fight, but they are secured now. But listen, we're in big trouble down here. If we don't start decompression ASAP, we're not going to make it," reported Chris.

"Copy," said Hendrix. "We'll take another look at the compressors and get back to you."

Halbeck walked past Chris to confirm that the emergency hatch was secured.

"Conditions are still extremely sporty up here," added Hendrix. "I wouldn't expect support from the surface anytime soon. Other than us, that is."

"Are you in touch with mission control?" asked Chris.

"No, but we can be," responded Hendrix.

"Tell them we're going to run decompression down here, which should finish just before sunrise. We're going to be out of everything by that point, so someone needs to come up with a plan to get us out."

"Will do."

"And Hendrix?"

"Yes?"

"Watch yourselves up there. Our two saboteurs down here were not working by themselves. I'm pretty sure they had at least one person helping them in mission control."

"Copy that," replied Hendrix.

Chris hung up the phone. "Ready to start?"

"Yes," agreed Halbeck. "What about Boseman and Jessica?"

"Brian, help me move Boseman to one of the bunks," said Chris. "And Jessica, I'll untie your legs so you can get to your bunk." While cutting her ankle ties, Chris noted that her eyes bore into him, confirming that if looks could kill indeed, nobody on the *Calypso* would survive.

He wanted to ask her so many questions, most pressing among them why she was willing to sacrifice a science project and the scientists involved for a cause that would do nothing to ease the pain she must have felt when she lost her family. Did pure hatred fuel her? But there was no time.

"Otter, can you run us through the oxygen treatment while you're doing it yourself?" Chris knew from experience that under normal circumstances, a seventh person would come down from the surface to oversee decompression.

"I think I can handle it," confirmed Halbeck. "Let's do it."

The three fifteen-minute oxygen treatments required just over an hour to complete, allowing for ten minutes in between each treatment. At that point, the aquanauts were free to move around the interior of the lab, though to conserve air everyone agreed to stay in their respective bunks.

"The pressure is going to be decreasing gradually for the next twelve and a half hours. Make sure to keep clearing your ears regularly, even if you don't feel the pressure change," Halbeck reminded everyone. "You don't want to get an ear block now."

Nat, Brian, and Halbeck all got up to move around. Chris climbed down out of his top bunk, pulling the curtain closed as he did so. Boseman was still unconscious on the lower bunk, but Chris planned on talking to him anyway. He scanned Jessica in the bunk above Boseman to confirm she was secure, and grabbed the tie wraps around Boseman's ankles. Pulling the technician out and onto the deck below shocked him back into consciousness.

"Boseman, tell me what you had planned next," Chris said in hushed tones.

"Nothing."

"Bullshit," replied Chris. "We've still got many hours down here. If you want to spend all of them in pain, just keep it up. Now what comes next?"

"Hurt me all you want, Black. I'm a patriot, and my conscience is clear."

"Ah, so that's how they got you," observed Chris. "A zealot, are you?"

"There is no course other than what you call zealotry where the nation is concerned. You should heed my words."

"Right. The attacks up in Miami? Was that you? And there was a guy shadowing me down in Key West before the mission. Do you know who he is?"

"Another patriot."

Chris thought about Cortez's information on the militia, and the confirmation from Hendrix that the guy he'd chased back in Key West was former military. A larger group had to be behind all of this. These militia wouldn't recruit sea lab technicians. They wouldn't have those kind of connections. Something else was going on. But he knew all he'd get out of Boseman were platitudes.

"Okay, good talk."

70

Chris Black woke up with a start and immediately checked his dive watch. There was less than one hour to go before decompression was complete. He'd slept, but fitfully. Dating back to his earliest saturation missions, Chris had never slept well during decompression. He'd spent his whole life preferring to sleep, as Mac once put it, "like a demented pretzel," with limbs all wrapped up and tangled around pillows and blankets. The requirement that he keep his arms and legs straight to allow nitrogen bubbles to flow unimpeded out of his limbs made sense to him but didn't lend itself to deep sleep. He hopped down from his bunk and stepped out to confer with Halbeck. The two of them had been alternating watches in two-hour shifts throughout the night in the hopes that they'd both have the energy to deal with whatever challenge was coming next.

"Anything happening?" he asked.

"We're looking good, I think," said Halbeck. "Comms went down again an hour ago, so I have no idea what's going on at the surface. Hopefully, it's just the storm and not some new attack."

Pointing back toward Boseman, whom they'd returned to the bunk, Chris asked, "Any movement out of him?"

"None that I've seen, but I haven't been watching too closely."

"I wasn't able to get anything out of him about what else he'd had planned," said Chris. "Which suggests to me that we should be wary. And Jessica had nothing to say either, even with the peer pressure from her colleagues."

"Frankly, I'm still trying to wrap my mind around the whole thing," admitted Halbeck. "The attacks and sabotage are shocking enough, but to think that two of our own team would be working against us is really . . . well, really fucked up."

"Yes, it is. Boseman didn't flinch when I suggested potential connections to the attacks in Miami or the guy following me around."

"I've known Boseman for years," said Halbeck. "This is the first time we've worked together, but I've seen him at conferences, eaten dinner at his house in Pensacola."

"Were you aware of his extremist streak?"

"Nope," replied Halbeck. "He's been working in and out of government for years. He must've kept it pretty deep."

"And then you have Jessica," added Chris. "Obviously we've seen her intensity starting to show, but her attack is something else altogether."

"We really never know what's going on behind the curtain, do we?" observed Halbeck.

"Very true."

Suddenly the air compressors returned to life.

"Looks like your friends have us back up and running!" said Halbeck enthusiastically.

Brian and Nat came out of the bunk room looking tired but also excited.

"Is that the air back on?" asked Nat.

"That's great," said Brian. "But what does this mean for us?"

Halbeck explained that with communications down again, they had no way to communicate with the team on the barge or mission control back on land. But at least the urgent need to get out of the lab in the middle of the storm had been relieved.

Ten minutes later, Halbeck announced that they'd formally reached the end of decompression. "You may notice a difference in the sound of our voices because we are now at a pressure equivalent to the surface. We'll stay at this pressure until we've come up with a solution for how we're going to get out of here."

"How long," asked Nat, "will it take us to pressurize back down to sixty feet?"

"Basically, the same amount of time it would take you to descend down to that depth on an actual dive. So pretty quickly."

Nat and Brian worked on making breakfast. Diving seven to eight hours a day could burn thousands of calories, so aquanauts had to eat continually. The food shelf was stocked with all manner of snack items, including a large variety of freeze-dried hiker meals. Cooking in the high-pressure environment of the *Calypso I* was not an option, but the aquanauts did have an instant hot water faucet and a small microwave. The instant hot water could be used to transform the hiker food into complete meals, while the microwave was always useful for melting cheese and beans on a tortilla.

"Having the air back on is great, but I've been thinking," whispered Halbeck, as he pulled Chris away from the others. "When Boseman came back after leaving you in the water, he spent an unusual amount of time in the wet porch. It didn't occur to me then because I thought both of you were out there. But for a single diver who'd just lost his buddy, Boseman took his time."

"What are you thinking?" asked Chris. "A trap of some kind?"

"What would you do if you wanted to sabotage the mission for good?" asked Halbeck.

Chris looked down at Boseman and then stepped quickly over to the porthole that looked out onto the moon pool. "I can't see anything from here, but I guess I'd rig something to blow."

"And since he entered through that main lock hatch, it would have to have armed itself after he entered," continued Halbeck.

"Oh, crap," said Chris quietly. "We finish decompression and open the hatch to go home and whammy."

"That's right, whammy," agreed Halbeck. "One of us has to go out there to see what we're facing."

"I think that's got to be me," said Chris. "We need you in here, and we shouldn't push it with your busted arm."

"OK."

"What would we do? Repressurize so that I can leave through the emergency exit hatch, swim to and from the moon pool, and then as soon as I get back we repressurize? We don't want to go into deco again."

Now that the aquanauts had expunged the nitrogen from their bloodstreams, they were okay to ascend to the surface. But once they pressurized the lab back down to the equivalent of sixty feet so Chris could open the emergency hatch, they would immediately begin accumulating more nitrogen. If they wanted to avoid having to go through decompression again, they'd have only about fifty minutes to work with.

"That sounds about right," said Halbeck. "Or we stay put until someone comes down from the surface to help us out."

"I'm not a big fan of staying put," said Chris after a moment.

"Neither am I," agreed Halbeck. "But since you're the one going out there again, I thought I'd let you say it first."

Fifteen minutes later, Chris was suited back up in his wetsuit and waiting by the emergency hatch with his mask and fins. He'd also added a belt with sufficient weight to keep him from either rocketing to the surface or being drawn away by the storm currents. "I stowed three of our rigs down here below the hatch so no one could mess with them. I'll get some air from one of them and then make the swim to the moon pool."

Chris could feel the pressure building in his ears as Halbeck took them back down to a depth of sixty feet. When they reached the equivalent of the bottom, Chris opened the hatch.

"Just keep it open for me this time. I'll be back in a few minutes."

He took two deep breaths and then submerged. It was still dark out, and the current was still moving quickly, but not as fast as it had been earlier.

Chris pulled himself along the bottom of the lab's main body and surfaced in the moon pool in less than thirty seconds.

"Okay, I'm here," he announced in the direction of the microphone.

He pulled off his fins and stowed them with his mask, then climbed up to the next level. He could see Halbeck looking back at him through the porthole.

Looking closely at the outer hatch, Chris's first pass around it yielded no evidence of any explosives. He saw no mysterious electronic devices mounted anywhere, and no strange wires leading to strategically planted blocks of C-4, or whatever people used these days. But he also wasn't an engineer, so he knew that someone like Boseman could have used his superior knowledge of the hydraulics that operated the hatch to rig a trap.

Following the conduits that led out of the hydraulics box up onto the ceiling of the wet porch, Chris realized he wouldn't be able to check that area thoroughly without standing on something. His only choice to gain some height was to stand on two of the five-gallon buckets they were using to wash their wetsuits after diving.

And that's when he saw it. Sitting inconspicuously next to the three buckets they'd used every day of the mission was a fourth bucket. Boseman had haphazardly placed a pair of booties and a hooded wetsuit vest on top, but when Chris nudged them gently to the side, he found the blocks of light brown explosive he'd seen so many times in the movies. Slowly replacing the hood and booties, Chris now spotted two wires extending from under the bucket, beneath the floor mat that covered most of the second level, and briefly up the outer hull to the steel rail along which the door moved when opened.

The hydraulics wouldn't set it off, Chris realized, but opening the door would. Boseman had planned for the possibility that the lab wouldn't have hydraulic power. In that event, they would have used a crowbar to pry open the door. And that would have been it, Chris realized.

"I found it," announced Chris, looking at his watch. He'd taken just eleven minutes to find the explosive. They had less than forty minutes to make a decision.

"Chris," said Halbeck over the loudspeaker. "You'd better get back in here. We've got a bigger problem."

71

Mac Johnson left Hendrix in the comms room to step outside for a weather check. Stepping onto the barge's heaving deck, the wind nearly ripped his favorite hat, a weathered green baseball cap from his alma mater in California, off his head. Clinging to the rail with one hand and his hat with the other, he scanned the horizon for the lights of the boat Dana St. Claire was piloting. Both he and Hendrix had recommended that she head back to port to wait out the storm, but she refused to depart.

"I am your boss, you know," Hendrix had said. "Technically you should follow my orders."

"You're breaking up, boss," Dana had replied over the radio. "I've got plenty of fuel. Not going anywhere."

Amid efforts to reestablish communications with the *Calypso I* and troubleshoot the failed air compressor, he and Hendrix had taken turns interrogating the two extremists they'd subdued. He decided to try again.

Stepping into the windowless room where they were being held, Mac was immediately overwhelmed by the stench of vomit. Both of the men were suffering violent seasickness on the rocking barge.

"So, your name's Aaron Bash?" Mac asked, having learned that from the other man. He tried to breathe through his mouth as much as possible. "Where you from, Aaron?"

"I have nothing to say. Untie me and I'll kill you where you stand."

"Right. What if I promised to get you some fresh air, and maybe a cracker?" Mac asked. Getting no response, he said, "Okay, suit yourself. I'm sure we've only got another six or seven hours of this before someone comes to pick you up."

He opened the hatch and was about to step through when Bash said, "Wait. Please don't close that door. What do you want to know?"

Silently, Mac wondered at the universal power of motion sickness and whether all interrogations shouldn't occur in similar conditions. He secured the hatch, leaving six inches for fresh air to penetrate the room.

"I want to know if there is anything else coming, anything else we have to worry about."

Bash wretched, but his gut had long before evacuated itself of anything other than gas. "Shaw."

"Shaw? What about him?"

"He has a dive team. They're supposed to be the final attack on the lab."

"What time is that supposed to happen?" Mac asked.

"I don't know."

"C'mon, Aaron. You can do better than that."

"I *don't know*, but Shaw had criticized us several times for not attacking before dawn, so maybe—" He wretched again.

"How are they going to attack? Weapons? Explosives?" asked Mac, looking at his watch. Dawn was coming.

Bash moaned as his head dropped to the vomit-covered deck.

Mac closed and secured the hatch and then returned to the rail. With the large swells still rolling through in the dark, he couldn't see any boat activity. He was about to step back inside with Hendrix when the radio mounted on his personal flotation device squawked. "Barge, this is Dana, come in."

"Copy that, Dana. What's your status?"

"I'm off your starboard. I've got a vessel approaching. Stand by."

Mac cautiously made his way to the other side of the barge, maintaining three points of contact at all times on the pitching deck. He first spotted the lights of a vessel headed toward them. Even as the lights would disappear from view every few seconds as large swells rocked the boat in the dark, he was confident from the lights' spacing and from watching how the boat made its way over the crests that it was not Dana.

To his right, he then spotted the lights of Dana's vessel moving as fast as conditions allowed toward the other boat.

Though he could hear nothing over the wind and swells, as the two boats converged, he could see the flashes of weapons fire from the other vessel. It was clear from the firing pattern that multiple people were firing. He swallowed hard in the ensuing seconds waiting for any evidence of Dana's condition.

"Dana, what's your status?"

No reply. More fire came from the other vessel, but fewer shots from fewer weapons were visible.

"Dana, status report, come back." Mac gripped the rail and tried to imagine what was happening. Was Dana down? Injured? He had no way of getting to her in this storm if she was in trouble. He cursed himself for leaving her out there unsupported, but almost as quickly realized that she would vehemently disagree with any special treatment.

Working to dampen his growing panic, Mac watched as the other vessel briefly changed its orientation, turning sideways in the rolling swells. That was a very dangerous move in those conditions. Was something happening?

Gunfire then erupted from Dana's position as she moved in between the other vessel and the barge. The boats were close enough to the barge now that he could hear the powerful reports of the gun Dana was firing.

"Barge, this is Dana. I count at least three divers just splashed. Say again, three divers just splashed."

"Oh, crap," whispered Mac. "Dana what's your status?"

"I'm hit, but functional."

Mac saw another exchange of gunfire between the boats, which were circling each other in the treacherous conditions.

"Dana? Dana, do you read me?"

72

Chris surfaced in the escape hatch ninety seconds after Halbeck's urgent announcement. In a mesh bag, he carried the SCUBA masks he'd grabbed for each of the aquanauts before leaving the wet porch.

"What's the situation," he asked, as he climbed up into the bunk room. Nat, Brian, and Halbeck were all hovering above the hatch. Each had changed into a swimsuit.

"Hendrix reestablished comms five minutes ago," said Halbeck. "He called to tell us that three divers just splashed above us. Mac said someone named Dana is in a shootout with the other boat. Also, he said Dana's been hit."

Divers were headed their way. The gunfire confirmed they had hostile intent. Chris had to get the aquanaut team to safety, or at least what passed for safety in this storm. Chris considered the few options available to them.

Only one seemed real.

"Tell Hendrix to have Mac deal with the boat, and then look for a surface float one hundred yards south of the habitat in about thirty minutes. I'll pop an orange sausage buoy and beacon."

"The old observation dome? That's nuts," said Halbeck. "How're we going to get there in these conditions?"

"We don't have another option," said Chris. "We're sitting ducks if we wait for those divers to arrive. We've got to hurry. Please radio Hendrix our plan."

"Okay, got it."

While Halbeck reached Hendrix, Chris had Nat and Brian put on their masks and climb down into the water. He could see their hands shaking as they geared up.

"What's happening, Chris?" asked Brian. "Who's shooting up there?"

"I don't know. But I'm certain they aren't here to help," replied Chris.

"How are we going to protect ourselves?" asked Nat. "Do we have any weapons down here with us?"

"No, we don't. But it's going to be okay, guys," said Chris, removing his mask so they could see his eyes as he spoke and placing his hands on their shoulders. "We may be in trouble, but we're also not alone. Two of the toughest people I know are above us. And I've got a plan."

Nat and Brian looked at him with expectant eyes that told Chris they trusted him completely. Chris could only hope he wouldn't disappoint.

"Nat, remember our dive yesterday out on the south excursion line? And the old observation dome we found?"

"That's the dome Otter was talking about? Yes, I remember exactly where that is."

"Excellent," said Chris. "I think we need to find our way to that dome. From there, we can launch one of our buoys, just like in training, and hope that my friends can find us."

"I don't know what you two are talking about," said Brian. "But I trust you do. How can I help?"

"Right below us you're going to find three of our tank rigs," explained Chris. "Each of you should put one on. Please help each other and hold on tight to the lab. Don't let the third rig float away. Otter and I will be down in a second."

Halbeck came back. "Message relayed. Now what the hell are we going to do?"

"Can we turn off all the lights inside and out of the *Calypso I*, including the wet porch?" asked Chris.

Minutes later, the *Calypso I* was consumed by darkness.

73

Chris followed Halbeck as he climbed down to join Nat and Brian. The darkness, and Halbeck's injured arm, made progress difficult.

Looking at the luminescent dial on his watch, Chris swallowed hard at the realization that the attacking divers would be on site any second.

"The old observation platform is out along the south excursion line," Chris explained as he huddled in the dark with the other three aquanauts. "I think it's our best chance. We've got to get to that line and pull ourselves along as quickly as possible. I'm the only one with fins and a weight belt. Brian and Nat, you two will be fine with the weight of the rigs on your back. Otter can wear the third one. I'll swim along right next to him using his secondary regulator."

"Swim in this current?" asked Brian.

"No choice, Brian," replied Chris. "We'll make it work. The platform is located about one hundred yards out from the lab, just after passing over that major rise in the reef. You'll see it on a sand flat to your left, about thirty feet from the excursion line. There's a large acrylic dome above it that will accommodate all of us. Once we're safely there, I'll pop a buoy using the line from one of our dive reels and we can use that to ascend to the boat. Any questions?"

"Won't the other divers see our bubbles?" asked Nat.

"Excellent point. With all the current, our bubbles will drift off fast and shouldn't give our position away. But we need to be careful," said Chris. "I'm going to climb back up to the bunk room so I can listen for their arrival in the moon pool, which is where I assume they'll go first. Once they're in the moon pool, they won't be able to see us. I'll climb back down, and we'll haul ass. Just don't submerge until I return. Okay?"

"What about Jessica and Trevor?" asked Brian.

"We cannot take them with us. Either one of them could scuttle our plans at any point," said Chris. "We'll leave them with their friends."

"Let them get away?" Nat asked, incredulous.

"Trust me," promised Chris. "We'll track them down later."

Chris climbed back up into the bunk room. Jessica had climbed out of her bunk and was hopping toward the porthole in the main lock, her wrists and ankles still secured. He snuck up behind her and pulled her down with no time to spare, as high-powered lights shone out of the dark beyond *Calypso I*.

The lights passed portholes on either side of the lab, moving aft toward the wet porch.

Chris was relieved that they hadn't been swimming low enough to see the legs of his colleagues below the escape hatch.

Pushing Jessica down onto the carpet, Chris snuck forward to the science station, grabbing the knife he'd taken away from Boseman as well as some duct tape. He used the duct tape to secure Jessica to a cabinet well out of reach of the communication system and to cover her mouth.

"Don't think you're home free, Jessica," Chris whispered. "We'll find you. Be sure of it."

He had to listen closely for evidence of the divers' entry into the moon pool. He assumed they were probably former military types who wouldn't announce themselves with a lot of chatter. But either way, their presence in the moon pool would displace more air than normal, and Chris's experienced ear picked it up almost immediately.

He snuck back to the hatch and climbed down, pulling the hatch door closed above him.

"Okay, let's go!"

74

Anna Cortez sat on her bed in the dark hotel room, unable to sleep. She'd wanted to drive back down to Key West after leaving the Ritz-Carlton site, but realized she needed rest first. She'd left her car near the Ritz-Carlton and walked up the beach to the closest hotel. The clerk at the front desk had looked at the grime on her face and clothes with apparent apprehension but had ultimately given her a room.

She lifted the laptop off the side table and opened it up. She could not take her mind off Robert Shaw and his possible connection to the attacks. Since she wasn't sleeping anyway, she might as well make some headway.

Cortez typed Unity Environmental into the search engine and pressed enter. Google returned twelve point four million results in 0.97 seconds. The first return was the company's main website. Next came the People Also Ask section, which included questions such as: What was the Unity Environmental scandal? Is Unity Environmental a bad company? and Why is Unity Environmental still operating?

Multiple links led to various employment opportunities with the company and its affiliates, as well as a Wikipedia page and several social media pages. At the bottom of page one, the Related Searches section included the name Unity Environmental followed by terms like Military, Oil Futures, Weapons Development, and Court Cases. A number of searches focused on particular countries, including Nigeria, Bolivia, Kazakhstan, and several in the Middle East.

Next, she sought the company's employee directory. She was directed to a third-party site, which included a stunning list of more than fifteen thousand employees with offices on six different continents. Robert Shaw was not listed, neither alphabetically nor by region.

Undeterred, Cortez spent the next hour searching the name Robert Shaw across the web. After wading through dozens of links on the late actor, she branched off into social media, hoping to find a hit, even though Shaw didn't seem like the kind of person who would spend much time on Facebook or TikTok.

Fatigue set in as she failed to find anything that she could link to the man who'd attacked her. He was a ghost, at least as far as the web was concerned.

Cortez closed the laptop and pushed it to the side on her king-sized bed. She then put her head down on the pillow and tried to sleep, allowing her mind to wander in the hopes that she would pass out quickly.

When she awoke with a start, a look at the digital clock on the side table confirmed that only forty-five minutes had passed. She reached around the head of the bed until her hand brushed across the cool surface of her laptop. Opening the computer once again, she typed Unity Environmental and *Calypso I*.

The search results yielded little of any use. But then she spotted a potential link between the two search terms. Clicking on the link, she found a list of VIPs associated with the *Calypso I* mission and short bios for each. One of them was a former Congressman from the US named Grampen Rhodes. His bio indicated that he'd been consulting with a variety of companies since leaving Congress, including Unity Environmental.

Cortez next searched Rhodes and Unity Environmental. Multiple articles from Florida popped up, including one from the University of Florida alumni magazine. She read the article, along with two associated stories, then turned on the light and called the number Chris Black had given her for Frank Donagan.

75

Progress along the south excursion line was steady, as the three finless divers pulled themselves through still-heavy bottom currents. The hose on Halbeck's secondary regulator was long enough for Chris to fall in behind Halbeck and pull himself along as well, while kicking when he needed to.

At the trailing edge of the group, Chris looked back toward the *Calypso I* frequently to see if anyone was on their tail. The ambient light from the growing dawn above them was increasing rapidly, but he doubted anyone would be able to see them at this point, particularly if they didn't know where to look.

The group was about to crest the high point on the reef when Chris spotted an incoming diver to his left, approaching fast on his scooter. With no wetsuit or neoprene hood, Chris recognized the diver immediately. Trevor.

Chris cursed himself for talking about the plan in front of Boseman. Somehow, in the few minutes that they'd been gone, Boseman had freed himself, grabbed one of the small forty-cubic-foot bailout tanks from the science area, and used one of the scooters to come after them.

Trevor maneuvered his scooter forward of Nat and Brian. Watching everything from behind, it took Chris a second to realize what he was planning. He was trying to slice through the excursion line. Without that line, Chris knew, the group would have very little chance of making it to the observation platform safely. They'd be stuck, out on the reef in the dark, with a storm raging above them.

Spitting out Halbeck's regulator, Chris extracted his knife from the pocket on his thigh and swam toward Boseman. Swimming up above the excursion line, Chris was subject to much stronger currents and had to work hard to avoid being swept away. Making contact with Boseman's back, Chris grabbed hold of the man's shirt with his left hand while using the knife in his right to slice through his regulator hose.

The sliced hose had the desired effect, as Boseman let go of the excursion line to deal with Chris. However, as soon as he let go of the line, both the diver and Chris were swept away by the current.

Chris held tight to Boseman's shirt, avoiding the technician's flailing arms attempting to reach back and grab him. He was rapidly running out of options when the diver's scooter floated up and bumped Chris on his left side. Chris let go of Boseman to grab the scooter with his left hand, while sweeping down with the knife to cut the safety line attached to Boseman's weight belt. Boseman frantically reached out to grab one of Chris's fins but was unable to do so.

Free of the technician's grasp, Chris watched as the current dragged Boseman across the reef and into the darkness beyond. Running dangerously low on air, Chris grabbed the other handle on the scooter and activated the thruster. The powerful scooter moved into the current easily, but Chris was unclear how far he'd drifted during the fight. Struggling to hold tight to the scooter with virtually no air left in his lungs, Chris realized that the scooter was equipped with a small emergency tank and regulator. He grabbed for the regulator and inhaled deeply.

At this depth and given the small size of the tank, Chris knew he didn't have long before the air ran out. Scanning the horizon in front of him, he almost missed the thin white excursion line as he passed over it. Grabbing hold of the line, he paused to consider his situation. The ambient light was increasing enough to allow Chris to see the vague outlines of the reef. Calculating the rough angle at which he'd drifted away from the line during the fight, he was certain that he'd find the team to his left. He also thought that the dark shape on the horizon was the high point they'd been approaching from the other side when the attack occurred. Reengaging the scooter at fifty percent of its thrust capacity, Chris slowly began working his way back along the excursion line, keeping an eye to his right where he thought the old observation platform would be. Having spent a career looking for objects underwater, both animate and inanimate, Chris regularly talked to students about how tricky it was to find things below the surface.

"Even in the rare case when you know exactly where something should be, tricks of light and variable visibility can obscure even the most obvious object. I can recall being less than twenty feet from instrumentation that I had deployed myself on the seafloor and swimming right past it. You just never know."

Less than a minute later, Chris spotted what he thought was the platform directly ahead of him. As he approached, what he thought had been the dome turned out to be a similarly sized coral head. Turning to resume his course, he ran right into the platform. He could clearly see three sets of legs standing beneath the dome of the old observation platform. They'd made it.

Chris had just poked his head up from under the dome and stood up when an explosion rocked the reef. The flow of the pressure wave from the explosion was absorbed to a great extent by the surrounding reef structure, but the observation platform still rocked in its place.

"Was that . . .?" asked Brian.

"Yes," said Chris, gravely. "*Calypso I* is down."

76

Robert Shaw struggled to prop himself up against Martinez's dead body, which was lying on the boat's back deck still clad in full SCUBA gear. The boat rocked dangerously in the swells, which though diminishing in height, were still more than sufficient to tip the boat over if one hit at the right angle. The other dead diver had collapsed on the rail and been washed overboard by a swell.

During the exchange of gunfire with the other boat, Shaw had taken a ricochet in his left side that was bleeding profusely. Looking at the blood pooling on the deck, he doubted that he was going to make it.

The wind continued to rage around him, but he thought he could hear the sound of another vessel approaching. He didn't know who was driving the other boat, but someone over there had been able to take out two of his divers from a distance in the midst of a storm. He briefly checked to see where his gun was, but the pain of sitting up was too much and he quickly sat back.

Shaw felt something bump the hull. Seconds later, a figure leaped over the starboard gunnel and landed on the deck. In the increasing light, he could see it was Mac Johnson, the former SEAL that Bash had been trying so hard to kill.

"How we doing over here?" asked Johnson, as he squatted next to Shaw. "Not too good, eh?"

Johnson disappeared below deck and came back with a bedsheet, which he tore into two strips, one of which he wadded up.

"If you can sit forward for a second, I'll wrap this around you and we can stop the bleeding."

"Lucky shot," mumbled Shaw.

"You wish," answered Johnson. "That's my girlfriend over there. Believe me, if she'd wanted to kill you, you'd be toast by now. Hold still for a second while I tighten down this dressing."

"Why are you helping me?" asked Shaw.

"What were you, Army?" asked Johnson. "I don't know about you GIs, but we SEALs don't leave people to die."

"You're too late to stop it."

"We'll see."

Johnson had just finished securing the bedsheet dressing when Shaw saw the water behind the boat erupt in a massive explosion. Johnson moved to the wheel and turned the boat into the wind.

"I'm sorry your friend didn't make it. I didn't think Black needed to die."

"Who says he's dead?" Johnson said, without turning around.

77

The aged acrylic dome of the observation port held under pressure from the blast wave of the explosion. The foursome had clung to the support struts as the entire structure leaned ten degrees before righting itself on the sand.

"Oh my God," said Nat. "Jessica. That's *horrible*."

"It is," observed Chris, "but we need to stay focused. We're not out of it yet. We've got to get to the surface safely and hope to hell that Mac is there. With all the swell above, neither will be easy. Everyone with me?"

They all nodded.

None of the aquanauts had brought their specialized wrist computers with them during the urgent departure from the lab. But both Chris and Halbeck had watches that doubled as backup dive computers. They were able to monitor how much additional bottom time the group had before reaching the no-decompression limits set by the dive tables.

"At forty-five feet, we're fifteen feet shallower than our original calculation," said Halbeck. "My watch is telling me we still have seventeen minutes to reach the surface."

Looking at his own watch, Chris agreed. “Yes, but what about a safety stop?”

“A safety stop at fifteen feet is exactly what it sounds like, a nice way to introduce some caution into one’s dive profile,” said Halbeck “But it isn’t required by the tables, and given this current, we might drift for a kilometer or more while we hover at fifteen feet.”

“Copy that,” said Chris. “We’ve also got to be very careful with the swells. We don’t want to get to the surface only to embolize.”

While the bends had been the primary concern of the aquanauts throughout the mission, they now faced the other prominent risk faced by SCUBA divers, the arterial gas embolism. The volume of air in a diver’s lungs changed with water depth, as increasing pressure compressed any volume of air in the body. The primary danger, however, came as a diver returned to the surface and the volume of air in the lungs increased.

“I’m going to pop one of our surface buoys,” explained Chris, “and anchor it to the platform down here. The buoy is going to be pulled by the strong current, so the line will be more horizontal than vertical.

“Use the line just like we did in training. Don’t hold on to it. Just wrap your thumb and index finger around it and let the line guide you to the surface. I’ll go in front as my watch has an ascent meter. Just stay below me and we should be fine.”

Halbeck added, “As we near the surface, the waves are going to be a big concern. If a ten-footer rolls over you, it will be like going up and down ten feet in two to three seconds. You don’t want to be holding your breath at that point. Tilt your head back so the air can flow up your trachea and allow a steady stream of bubbles to flow out of your mouth.”

“I may become a terrestrial scientist after this,” observed Nat.

“We can do this, team,” said Chris. “Ready?”

Chris removed one of the sausage buoys rolled up in a zippered pocket on Halbeck’s harness. He tied it off to one of the dive reels, then tied the reel to one of the struts supporting the dome. Blowing on the one-way air valve, he inflated the buoy and released it from under the dome.

The flashing light mounted at the base of the buoy would trigger as soon as it reached the surface.

The team watched as the line on the dive reel unwound rapidly. There was a brief pause as it reached the surface before it continued to unwind.

"The wind and waves are taking it," observed Chris. "Let's just hope it's visible to Mac. Okay, let's go."

The ascent took less than two minutes, with Chris reaching the surface first.

With no buoyancy control device of his own, he immediately ditched his weight belt in order to maintain positive buoyancy. The bright yellow buoy was standing tall out of the water, but Chris could not see any boats over the surrounding swells.

One by one the divers surfaced. Chris encouraged them to hold on to each other so as not to separate in the storm. He then cut the reel line so he could hold the yellow buoy aloft as they drifted.

Five minutes passed and there was no sign of any vessel. Chris knew the chances that word of their plan had gotten to Mac in time were low, but not nearly as low as the chance he'd find them floating at the surface in all this swell. They'd survived attacks and an explosion, but were very likely going to float away into the Gulf of Mexico, never to be seen again.

"They're not going to find us, are they?" asked Brian. "You just don't want to tell us."

"If it were anyone other than my friend Mac," Chris replied, "I think we'd be lost. But never count Mac out."

Another five minutes passed as they floated at the surface, and Chris quietly calculated the distance they must have traveled with the wind and swell. *C'mon, Mac, do your thing.*

They all turned to the sound of the motor as a boat came crashing through a wave to their left. Mac maneuvered the boat with the bow pointing into the swell, then tossed out a line off the stern. As the line drifted toward the divers, each one grabbed hold.

Chris told them to remove their tanks and let them float free. He didn't want them struggling to get on to the boat in these conditions with two tanks on their backs.

"Nat and Brian, you two go first," yelled Chris over the wind. "Watch yourselves as you approach the boat."

Once the two scientists were on board, Chris said, "Otter, I'll go next and then help Mac pull you in."

"Copy that. Just don't forget about me."

As Chris reached the stern of the boat, Mac reached down to help pull him up.

"You're late. And you look terrible."

"I was thinking the very same thing," said Chris as he climbed the dive ladder up onto the small boat's back deck. Dana was lying over in a corner, propped up against a pile of exposure suits, holding a bloody towel to her left shoulder.

Chris helped Mac pull Halbeck out of the water and position him next to Dana. Nat and Brian stayed low as well to avoid being knocked around by the swell.

"Dana, how're you doing?" asked Chris.

"I'll live," replied Dana. "Go tell Mac to get us out of here."

Climbing forward into the wheelhouse, Chris said, "Well, that was a close one."

"I'm sure," said Mac without taking his eyes off the water. He swept his left arm around the wheelhouse, which had been decimated by automatic weapons fire. "Below and above. I spotted the float for a moment, but then lost it. So, all I could do was move to where I saw it and hope the swells moved the boat in the same general direction as you guys. I'm pretty surprised it worked, actually."

"Yeah. To be honest, so am I," admitted Chris. "That was a good idea to let the boat drift. If you hadn't, we would have drifted halfway to the Yucatán coast before anyone found us."

"Dana took a bullet to the shoulder," said Mac. "I know she's got it under control, but can you climb down and check on her?"

"Of course," said Chris. "I should check on the rest of the team as well. They've had a rough couple of days. By the way, where's Hendrix?"

"Still on the barge with the two militia guys we caught," said Mac. "I left another guy bleeding on his boat over there at the dock near the fort. I'm going to take you all in and then come back out to get him."

"Cheated death once again," observed Chris, patting Mac on the back.

"I'll believe that when we reach the dock."

78

The extremist attacks to the north and the storm to the south had combined to direct media attention away from the international *Calypso I* mission. However, as soon as word spread of the exploding lab and that the surviving aquanauts had arrived at the Lower Keys Medical Center in Key West, the media circus converged.

The four aquanauts were all put on twenty-four-hour observation in a single, large room in a wing that was closed off to reporters. Nat and Brian reclined in neighboring beds, while against the opposite wall Chris and Halbeck fought over the TV remote from their respective beds.

While they'd completed decompression on schedule, the circumstances surrounding that process were judged medically suboptimal. That triggered a minimum of twenty-four hours under observation. Dana was convalescing in an adjacent room in the same wing, as was the surviving technician from the mission control barge who'd helped Mac and Hendrix restore communications and air pressure to the *Calypso I*.

"Medically suboptimal," observed Mac. "I don't know what it means, but it certainly captures the moment well."

The morning after their arrival back on land, the aquanauts received a visit from Senator Pierce and John Lefevre, while Grampen Rhodes did not make an appearance.

The scientific goals of the mission had been largely unmet, and what little data were collected were lost in the explosion and its aftermath. But the survival of the remaining four divers under such adverse circumstances accumulated more attention than any successful mission ever would have. Chris could see the senator and Lefevre competing for who could be the most magnanimous, particularly when TV cameras were around.

Frank Donagan slipped into the room as the other visitors were departing.

"Well, Dr. Black. You made it through once again. I'm glad to see you're okay."

"It was touch and go, Frank. Touch and go."

"To hear *you* say that makes me glad I wasn't out there."

The Florida State Police maintained a continuous presence at the hospital as they tried to work out all that had occurred. Chris and Mac both gave multiple interviews to different people, each telling the police the majority of what they knew.

The police explained that the explosion had obliterated the wet porch and ripped off the main hatch, flooding the *Calypso I*. The body of Jessica Katz was found inside. Until autopsies were completed, they wouldn't know if she was killed outright by the explosion or by the subsequent flooding of the lab.

It wasn't until after Chris had returned to his hotel room that Anna Cortez made an appearance, accompanied by Donagan. He was sitting on the deck in front of his room, watching the ocean recover after the passage of the storm when the pair came walking up the path.

"Dr. Black! You're looking well for someone who's just come through what you did. Even better than when I saw you yesterday," said Donagan. "Can we step inside?"

"I'm so tired I can barely step anywhere, inside or out," replied Chris. "Can't we just stay out here in the sun?"

"What we came to discuss isn't for public consumption," said Donagan. "I think you'll want to hear it."

Chris peeled himself off the lounge chair and led the pair of visitors inside. He then collapsed on the couch. "Okay, what've you got?"

"I'll just start with familiar territory," said Cortez. "Remember the kid I told you about? The solo diver who'd disappeared while diving in a quarry up north? He was killed by the same team that tried to get you at *Calypso*. They'd been doing a trial run of the attack on the barge and the undersea lab. The same person who killed the kid also was behind the attempted stabbing on the beach, the attack outside your presentation, and the Ritz-Carlton bombing. His name is Aaron Bash."

"Jesus. Did they get him?" asked Chris.

"Yep. He was one of the guys your friends Mac and Hendrix caught on the mission control barge. He stabbed the kid and threw him overboard."

"Sounds like a real beaut. What happened to that guy?" asked Chris.

"Hendrix turned him and his one remaining colleague over to the police, but only after spending eleven stormy hours with him on the barge," explained Donagan. "Hendrix also learned that Bash was working for a militia group called the Federal Brotherhood Initiative."

"The FBI? That sounds like the beginnings of a bad joke," said Chris.

"It was bad, but it wasn't a joke," replied Cortez.

"Wait a minute," said Chris. "Who recruited Boseman and Jessica?"

Donagan jumped in again. "We don't know exactly who contacted Boseman and paid him off. But we think Jessica Katz may have been Boseman's idea. The head of the militia was a guy named Jeremiah Fessler."

"Why don't we just ask him?"

"He's dead," said Donagan. "Shot in the chest by a rifle from some distance away."

"Shot by someone on the inside?" asked Chris. "What were they doing, cleaning up loose ends?"

"Something like that," agreed Cortez.

"What were these people trying to achieve?" asked Chris, sitting up on the couch.

"As I said, Fessler's dead," said Donagan. "But Bash says he was being paid by the guy you chased into the parking garage."

"What? Back to the guy I chased?" asked Chris. "He's the mastermind *and* operative on the ground?"

"Maybe," said Cortez. "Robert Shaw is his name. He's former military who now works for a multinational contractor called Unity Environmental."

"His name's *Robert Shaw*? How'd you get that info?" asked Chris. "From Hendrix?"

Cortez explained her second encounter with Shaw. "I took his wallet after tasing him during an attempted kidnapping."

"I'm glad you had that taser with you," observed Chris. "And I'm glad you're on our side."

"The thing is, nothing about Shaw suggests he would be capable of orchestrating something like this," said Donagan. "He's a worker bee. A very lethal worker bee."

"So where do we find Shaw?" asked Chris.

"He's in the wind," said Donagan. "But we'll find him."

Chris could hear his phone vibrating on the table. He didn't recognize the number. "Excuse me a minute. Black, here."

"Chris, it's Hendrix. How quickly can you get to the hospital?"

Chris stepped back out onto the patio. "Fifteen, maybe twenty minutes. What's up?"

"Meet me in the lobby in thirty. I'll explain then. Hendrix out."

79

Chris Black stood at the head of the hospital bed and watched as Robert Shaw opened his eyes. A nurse was attending to a bandage on Shaw's head. His right arm was fitted with a fiberglass cast extending from the wrist up past the elbow, and his entire lower torso was wrapped in white gauze.

"Oh, good. You're awake," said Chris. "We've been worried about you."

The nurse turned to face Chris. Hendrix and Mac were standing next to him. She smiled briefly as she took in the three men. The smile faded quickly, and she exited the room.

"Why am I not handcuffed?" asked Shaw.

"I'll tell you," said Chris. "It's because we haven't told the authorities who you are. Yet. But also, there's a guard outside your door."

"Your reporter friend. I should have killed her outright. If I had, you'd have no clue about who I am."

"Not entirely accurate, I'm afraid," said Hendrix. "We had you before that. Security camera at the airport. Where'd you learn your craft? Watching movies?"

"No need to thank me for patching you up, by the way," said Mac.

"How'd I get back here?" asked Shaw.

"Johnson dropped you off at Fort Jefferson in your boat, and I called two colleagues to come get you," explained Hendrix.

Chris looked down at his phone and typed something. Moments later the door opened to reveal Anna Cortez. She stepped past Hendrix to stand next to Mac.

"Sorry I'm late," she said. "It took me a minute to get rid of our friend."

"So, what happens now? Are you going to beat me?" asked Shaw.

"Oh, we don't have to beat you, Shaw," said Hendrix. "You're already beaten. Ms. Cortez here tagged you twice with a taser. That was very nice, by the way. And then our colleague Ms. St. Claire shot you, from another boat, in ten-foot swells. That was pretty impressive as well. Not your best week, I imagine."

"Who are you exactly?"

"I'd say I'm no one you want to fuck with," answered Hendrix. "But then that'd be true of everyone here."

"So, what's the plan? Talk me to death?"

"I wouldn't rule out that possibility," said Black. "Mac here is ready to do just that at a moment's notice. But no, we want to bring you up to speed, and then to ask you a question."

"Okay. Bring me up to speed."

Chris noted that Shaw, despite his tough reputation, was having difficulty making eye contact with any of them. *He's playing it tough, but he's ashamed he's been caught.*

"The three divers you sent to kill me and my fellow aquanauts were blown up by explosives planted by your coconspirator Trevor Boseman. Seems like there might have been some communication challenges within your little conspiratorial team."

"What happened to Boseman?"

"He attacked us out on the reef while we were trying to get the other aquanauts out of harm's way," said Chris. "I had to slice his air hose, steal his scooter, and send him spiraling into the dark."

Shaw now made eye contact with Chris, pausing before responding. "So, what's your question?"

"Before you ask your question, can I ask mine?" asked Cortez.

"Of course," said Chris.

"We assume you killed the head of the militia group, Jeremiah Fessler. But I've discovered a connection between you, Unity Environmental, and Grampen Rhodes."

"*What's* your question?"

"Settle down," suggested Hendrix. "They've earned the right to ask as many questions as they'd like."

"We'll get to that in a second, but first, who organized all this? Rhodes? Or someone else at Unity?" asked Cortez.

Shaw said nothing.

Cortez filled the silence. "Grampen Rhodes has been consulting for Unity since he was forced out of Congress. From what I've been able to determine so far, he was a fraternity brother with the head of Unity, a guy name Leland Jones."

"Why do any of these guys care about an undersea research mission in the Keys?" asked Mac.

"Money," admitted Shaw. "It's all about weapons and consulting contracts."

"Money? That's it?" asked Chris. "All these people have died because Unity needs more contracts?"

"Does it really need to be any more complex?" said Shaw. "You seem like a smart guy; what else drives the world other than money?"

"Politics," suggested Cortez.

"Sure," admitted Shaw, "politics plays a role. We manipulated Fessler and his band of extremists by appealing to their patriotic fervor. And both Jones and Rhodes are deep into politics. Sure they had Pierce's activities to agitate them, but it always goes back to money."

Hendrix said, "You've been busy, and a lot of people have been either killed or injured as a result of your activities. But I have to think that you still have certain predictable allegiances to justice, or at least to the truth, given your military history."

"So, what's the question?" asked Shaw.

"One I sure hope you will answer," said Chris. "What can you give us to nail Rhodes and Jones?"

80

The storm had given way to cloudless blue skies as Chris Black and Mac Johnson relaxed on the deck outside of Chris's room, looking out into the Caribbean Sea. Mac fumbled with his tablet trying to access the hotel Wi-Fi, while Chris leaned on the rail and scanned the horizon with a pair of binoculars.

"Nice day," observed Hendrix, as he walked out the sliding door. "I just got off the phone with a contact in the CIA."

"Why the CIA?" asked Mac.

"Rhodes," replied Hendrix. "He's in the wind. Looks like he left the country on a private jet the same day the *Calypso I* blew up. We'll find him."

"Hendrix, you've been at this a while," said Chris. "Have you ever seen anything like it? I'm still trying to wrap my mind around the whole thing."

"I don't have the answers," said Hendrix. "But you definitely didn't imagine it, and you aren't alone in your—"

"Befuddlement," said Mac.

"Right, befuddlement. I, too, have never seen anything like it," said Hendrix. "A militia group being bankrolled by an international consultant group trying to destroy a scientific mission supported by the UN?"

"And don't forget the disgraced former politician who somehow inserted himself into the middle of it," added Mac.

"But I'm not sure how much, if any, of the information that Shaw gave us will stand up in a court of law. What do you think, Chris?"

"I think that the solution to that issue is walking up the path right now," replied Chris, pointing to where the reporter from Boston, Malcolm Alexander, was walking up the hill.

"Hey, Malcolm. How's it going?" asked Chris.

"Pretty good."

"Malcolm, you know Mac Johnson. And this is our colleague Hendrix. He runs his own security firm, among other things. Hendrix, this is Malcolm Alexander; he's a reporter for the *Boston Globe*."

"*Okay*," said Malcolm slowly. Hendrix nodded his head as though he'd just figured out what Chris was planning.

"Sorry that we didn't get to do that second interview underwater," said Chris. "Things got a little out of hand."

"To put it mildly," suggested Malcolm.

"So, Malcolm. Do you still have that space in the *Globe*'s Sunday Magazine reserved for you?"

"I do," said Malcolm. "Why?"

Chris stepped into his room for a moment before returning with a large file folder full of documents and a small portable hard drive.

"What do you have there?" asked Malcolm.

"This pile of material connects the attack on the *Calypso I*, along with the hotel and auditorium attacks in Miami, to an Orlando-based consulting company called Unity Environmental."

"That's quite a claim. Do I get to look at it?"

"It's all yours, Malcolm. Hard copies are all here, along with digital copies and some additional material on this hard drive. All we ask is that you do what you do best. Write about it."

Chris handed the stack of documents and the drive to the reporter.

"You're just giving it to me? No strings attached?"

"No strings. We think these guys deserve to go down, and you're the one to do it. Do you want it?"

"Does the Pope poop in the woods? But where'd it all come from?" asked Malcolm.

"Most of it comes from our friend Anna Cortez, the investigative journalist you've probably heard about over the past twenty-four hours."

"Why isn't she doing anything with it?" asked Malcolm.

"Because I've got my hands full with several other stories," said Anna as she walked through the door. "Look, Chris speaks highly of you, and I can't handle all of this myself. Are you open to a collaboration?"

"A shared byline?" asked Malcolm, his eyes widening. "Definitely. But I've got to look over all of this before anything moves forward."

"Of course," said Anna.

"Then I think I'm outta here," said Malcolm. "I'm going to call my editor and ask for an extension."

As they watched Malcolm walk back down the path, Chris thought he perceived an extra bounce in the reporter's step.

"Think it'll work out?" asked Mac.

"Hard to tell," replied Chris. "But if they're as hard up for contracts as Anna's research suggests, this negative PR should hammer them."

"And hopefully legal indictments won't be far behind," added Anna.

81

The tarmac was already baking under the noonday sun when Grampen Rhodes landed at José Martí International Airport in Havana. As the jet taxied along a secondary runway, Rhodes could see maintenance crews already out working to move downed trees and abundant palm fronds, evidence from Tropical Storm Nancy's recent path through Cuba. He could also see buildings with some, or all, of their roofs torn off and almost no traffic on the streets surrounding the airport. Rhodes was not pleased to be seeking asylum, particularly not without more time to prepare. He'd been sitting in the lounge at Unity Environmental when the call had arrived. Leland Jones had put it on speaker.

"Is it over, Sharon?" Derrick Sumner had asked.

"Oh, it's over all right," replied Dirksen, who'd been closely monitoring police communications. "*Calypso I* is destroyed."

"That's very good news," Jones had observed. "Perhaps our liability will be limited after all."

Rhodes had stood up to pour himself another drink, thinking that he'd dodged a bullet and satisfied a long-standing debt.

"I'm not sure the news is all good," Dirksen had added.

"What do you mean?" asked Sumner, an edge in his voice.

"Well, I'm still working to put it all together," explained Dirksen. "But as far as I can tell, Aaron Bash was captured and the rest of his team killed."

"Holy shit," Jones had blurted. "Captured by whom?"

"My understanding is that Mac Johnson and two unnamed colleagues boarded the barge and stopped Bash from finishing the job."

"Hendrix and Dana St. Claire," Rhodes had surmised, sitting back down without making another drink. "It has to be them."

The room was quiet for several moments.

"What about Shaw?"

"His team is also dead," Dirksen had explained. "Shaw was observed being carried off a fishing vessel in the harbor on a gurney. He was clearly injured but alive. And he never showed up at any hospital."

"Oh, shit," Rhodes had said, standing up again and moving toward the door.

"Where are you going?" Jones had asked. "We've got to get this thing under control. We need to plan a response."

"You do that, Leland. Shaw knows I'm involved, and how. I'm getting the fuck out of here," Rhodes had said as the door closed behind him.

Africa had been Rhodes's first impulse as the jet had taken off from Orlando. The number of countries without extradition treaties with the United States outnumbered those that did, making the far-off continent an obvious choice for his escape.

But once he was in the air, his pilot had suggested Cuba as an alternative, at least in the short term. It would give him more options to reenter the US as needed.

The jet pulled into a large, dilapidated hangar and came to a stop. After five minutes, the pilot opened the cockpit door. Rhodes could see soldiers clad in green fatigues approaching the jet.

"Sir, let me take care of this for you."

"Thank you. You should have enough money in the emergency fund," said Rhodes. "If that isn't enough, tell them we'll work something out."

"Perhaps you should make yourself another drink while you wait," suggested the pilot.

Rhodes stared out at the interior of the Soviet-era hangar and considered his next steps.

In his haste to get out of the country, he'd not been able to arrange for Christy to join him. She was still up in DC at his Georgetown apartment.

He couldn't see how he was going to get her down here, which meant that the authorities were likely to find her eventually.

His phone buzzed, flashing a number he knew well.

"Where are you?" asked a familiar voice.

"Havana," said Rhodes. "The pilot is trying to smooth it over with the locals as we speak."

"I've been watching the news coverage in Florida."

"Have you?" asked Rhodes, rubbing his temples. "I've been out of touch for a few hours. What are they reporting?"

"Would it surprise you to learn that Chris Black is alive," said the voice. "He's alive, as are Mac Johnson, Hendrix, and the woman. Obviously, that is not what you and I discussed."

"The mission was compromised," noted Rhodes.

"I don't give a shit about the mission," replied the voice. "Your pal Jones is an idiot. His business is going to collapse regardless of what happened to the mission. No, you and I had an agreement. And you failed to deliver on even a single element of that agreement."

"I understand," answered Rhodes. He'd lived in relative luxury for the past forty-five years, all the while knowing that at some point the indiscretions of his past would catch up to him. The man on the phone had intervened to save Rhodes from a career-ending scandal long before his career had even begun. A young Rhodes had pledged to do whatever he could to return the favor, never comprehending the scope of what that pledge would eventually require.

Manipulating Chris Black into participating in the *Calypso I* mission had been, Rhodes thought, an easy way to honor that pledge. He'd hoped that Johnson and Hendrix would rally to Black's side. At least he'd been right in that regard. But little other than that had gone to plan. And now he found himself in exile and still owing a debt to someone he'd much rather avoid.

"You understand," repeated the man, dripping sarcasm in his voice. "I doubt you understand much at all. But perhaps you are still capable of fathoming the depths of what I am willing to do, particularly in this situation."

Beads of sweat began to form on Rhodes's forehead. He looked down at the empty glass. The pilot had handed it to him. He looked out the window to see the pilot still talking with the soldiers beside the plane. Why were they still out there? It occurred to him that the pilot may be betraying him as he watched.

"What are you going to do now?" asked Rhodes, shifting in his seat. "I can still help."

The man said nothing.

"Just tell me what you need me to do."

"You may yet have a part to play," said the voice, finally. "But for now, I will deal with Black myself."

"What are you going to do?" Rhodes asked again.

"Burn them. Burn them all down."

82

Business at the restaurant by the hotel pool was picking up as Chris, Mac, and Hendrix sat down at a table set for five. The background noise of a dozen separate conversations granted them a modicum of privacy.

"Let me get this straight, Hendrix," said Chris. "You're saying that this island off Costa Rica has been closed to outsiders since 1978?"

"*At least* 1978," replied Hendrix. "It's three hundred miles off-shore. No one, save the boat operators who are permitted to take divers out to dive around the island, has been near the island since before World War II."

"We're talking about Isla Nublar from *Jurassic Park*, aren't we?" asked Chris. He knew Crichton had modeled the fictitious home of his famous book on a real island.

"Yes, we are. And that's all exciting, of course. But the thing is, and this is the only reason I'm bringing this up, by the way, is that I've been approached by a French Count about conducting a mission out there to look for pharmaceuticals. I thought you might want to consider joining us to get a look at the reefs. You'd have two weeks out there, without interruption. At least three dives a day."

"It sounds a lot like a recent offer you made to come participate in an exciting mission to a new undersea lab," suggested Mac. "What could possibly go wrong?"

"I'm just passing along opportunities," said Hendrix, raising his hands. "I can't guarantee every one of them will go as planned."

"As planned?" said Mac. "As *planned*?"

"Mac's right, of course," said Chris. "But I'll admit I'm intrigued."

"Gentlemen!" said Frank Donagan, as he pulled out a chair and sat down. "Intrigued by what, may I ask?"

"Donagan, how nice to see you," said Mac. "Hendrix was just drawing Chris in with tales of undiscovered islands off Costa Rica."

"That all sounds lovely," said Donagan. "I've got to head north to DC and am hoping to tie up a few loose ends. Am I interrupting something?"

"We have the ladies joining us shortly," said Chris.

"Of course," said Donagan. "I'll be brief. I'm pleased to report that the authorities now have Robert Shaw in custody."

No one at the table spoke.

"I think your silence answers my next question."

"What question was that?" asked Chris.

"I was going to ask if anyone at the table had any idea how Shaw found his way to the hospital. None of the emergency medical personnel recall having transferred him there."

"Is he talking?" asked Mac.

"He is," said Donagan. "He appears to have calculated the benefits of coming clean versus clamming up, and opted for the former."

"Well, then that's a win for the good guys!" said Hendrix.

"It is, indeed," agreed Donagan. "But—"

"You said *a few* loose ends," interjected Chris. "What else have you got, Frank? Spill it."

Donagan reached into the interior pocket of his blazer and extracted a small pink slip of paper.

He looked it over and then handed it to Chris.

"Grampen Rhodes has gone missing," Chris read aloud.

"Missing as in *feared dead*?" asked Mac. "Or missing as in *I'm getting out of here before the poop hits the fan*?"

"A little of both," answered Donagan. "His jet departed Orlando yesterday with a flight plan filed for Nairobi. We have it on good authority that his ultimate destination was Havana."

"That's only about a hundred miles from where we sit," noted Hendrix, as he tossed his napkin down on the table. "We can be there in an hour and extract the bastard before anyone knows the difference. Just let me make a quick call."

"Stand by a second," said Donagan, holding up his hand. "The same good authority reported that Rhodes's plane was met by armed soldiers, and that his whereabouts have not been confirmed since."

"Interesting," said Chris.

"If there's no body, he's still drawing breath," said Hendrix.

"Perhaps," answered Donagan. "But only time will tell."

Mac stood up quickly, catching Chris, Hendrix, and Donagan off guard. "And here they are!"

Chris turned to see Dana and Anna approaching. Dana had her left shoulder in a sling.

"Ladies, please join us," said Mac, as he pulled out two chairs.

Chris snuck a look at Hendrix, raising his eyebrows.

Donagan said as he stood, "Hello, Ms. Cortez and Ms. St. Claire. I'm glad to see both of you are safe and sound."

"Aren't you going to join us, Frank?" asked Dana.

"No, no. I've got to head back to DC. I just wanted to wish everyone safe trips home, or wherever it is you're headed next."

"Thanks for your help once again, Frank," said Chris. "Don't take this the wrong way, but I hope to God we don't meet up again anytime soon."

"Ah, from the Latin, offensa. None taken!"

Donagan departed as the five sat down for more than an hour of talking about everything but the recent mission and the associated fallout. Chris knew that Hendrix would not discuss details in Anna's presence, and he was grateful for the break in nonstop incident reassessment.

"So, there we were," said Mac. "On our knees and facing imminent death by gunfire, when the guard behind us removed his helmet to reveal that pleasant visage you see sitting across the table. Hendrix had saved us again."

Speaking primarily to Anna, who'd never heard any of his stories, Mac continued. "Or there was the time we were pinned down on the upper deck of a Colombian pirate ship in the Galapagos taking heavy fire." He stopped to pat Chris on the shoulder. "We both would have gotten it that day had it not been for both Hendrix *and* Dana."

"And these are just the high points, you say?" said Anna. "Where I grew up in Mexico, we believe 'whoever saves a life is as though he had saved all mankind.' You are truly fortunate in your friends."

"I completely agree. Some of my colleagues back home have asked how I've benefited from such largess on so many occasions," explained Chris. "And you know, I don't have an answer to that question."

Hendrix scratched his beard contemplatively before saying, "I've never had to put words to it before. But if I were forced to, I guess the best explanation I can provide is via analogy."

"Uh-oh," said Mac.

"Anna, are you aware of the myth of the Sasquatch?"

"Here we go," said Chris.

"Are you talking about Bigfoot?" asked Cortez. "I went to school in the US, and have spent most of my life here, so yes, I'm familiar."

"Perfect," said Hendrix. "When I was in the hospital convalescing after the Galapagos Incursion, as Mac here has come to call it, young Dr. Black spent many an hour keeping me company. During one fateful hour, our discussion turned to the ethereal. You know, things like UFOs, the Loch Ness Monster, and, of course, Bigfoot. I learned then that, scientist though he is, Chris enjoys the notion that such phenomena exist. Because, and I quote, 'Life is just more interesting if they're out there.'

"So, by extension, if I were forced to explain my interest in these two fine gentlemen, I would say the same, I think. Life is just more interesting if they're out there."

"So touching," Mac said. "Babe, can you please hand me a tissue?"

Chris smiled and looked down at his phone, which had been buzzing repeatedly through Hendrix's wonderful exposition. "Sorry, it's from Carmel and they keep calling. Let me see who this is."

Chris picked up. After listening for a few seconds, his expression clouded over.

"*Oh*. Okay. No, thank you for letting me know. I'll be back as soon as I can."

He let his phone drop into his lap.

"What is it?" asked Mac.

Chris didn't answer. Instead, he turned to Hendrix. "I'm afraid I'm going to need your help again."

"Of course. What's up?" asked Hendrix.

"My mom's in the hospital. Somebody burned down her house in Carmel," explained Chris. "And my dog's missing." Pausing for a moment, he then added, "I need to get back fast. Faster than commercial airlines can take me."

Pulling out his phone, Hendrix said. "I'm on it. And we're coming with you."

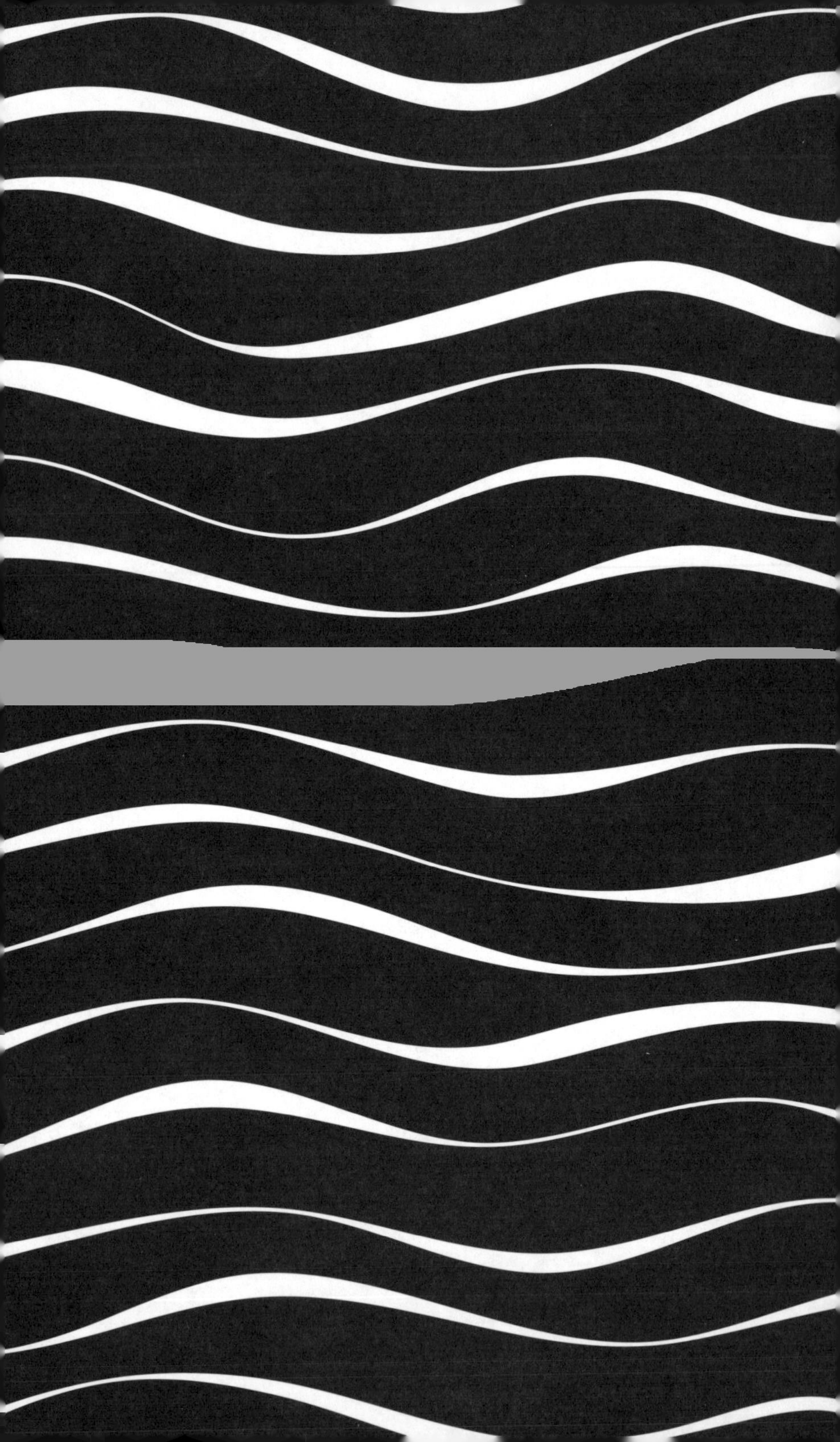

ACKNOWLEDGMENTS

I would like to thank my dedicated team of early reviewers—Peter Auster, Carrie Bretz, Andrew DeVogelaere, Nancy Lindholm, and Rick Starr—for all their help. Not only are they all avid readers of novels, but they also are explorers and adventurers in their own rights. Dr. Kelsey Gray patiently listened to multiple iterations of the book, offering sound advice throughout. And none of this would have been possible without the skilled assistance of my editor at CamCat Publishing, Dr. Helga Schier.

This book, like all of Chris Black's adventures, is very much a work of fiction. But like the other books, it is informed by the experiences I've had over the course of my career, as well as those of my colleagues. For instance, while the *Poseidon* and *Calypso I* Undersea Laboratories are both fictional, the *Aquarius* Reef Base (https://environment.fiu.edu/aquarius/) is very much a reality. I've had the good fortune to participate in six missions to *Aquarius*, including four in saturation and two as part of the surface team.

The training that the fictional aquanauts experience is based on drills I had to do before each mission, including the incredibly uncomfortable mask-off line search. I observed the storm-driven fish aggregations that Chris and Nat experienced on my first mission. An event much like the "bad air" incident in the waystation occurred during my third mission, as did the contact dermatitis event (though I won't share names here). Also, while I understand things have changed at *Aquarius* these days, let's just say that I didn't have to invent the challenging details about going to the bathroom and leave it at that!

Further, as is often the case in Chris Black's adventures, people I know well may see some small bit of themselves showing up in the characters Chris encounters. While no single character is based on any one person, you are all way too cool not to find some part of your personalities in these stories. Enjoy!

ABOUT THE AUTHOR

Dr. James Lindholm dives deep for his inspiration. His novels stem from a foundation of direct, personal experience with the undersea world. He has lived underwater for multiple ten-day missions to the world's only undersea laboratory and has found himself alone on the seafloor staring into the eyes of a hungry great white shark. He has drafted text for an executive order for the White House and has briefed members of the House and Senate on issues of marine science and policy. James Lindholm's diverse writing portfolio includes textbooks, peer-reviewed scientific journal articles, and action/adventure novels. For more information, please visit www.jameslindholm.com.

THE CHRIS BLACK ADVENTURE SERIES

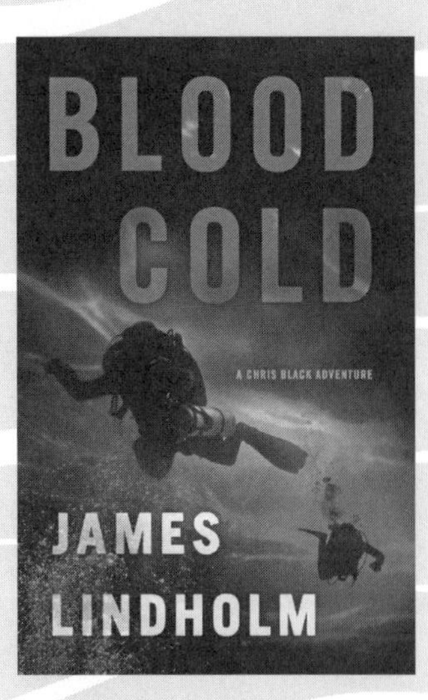

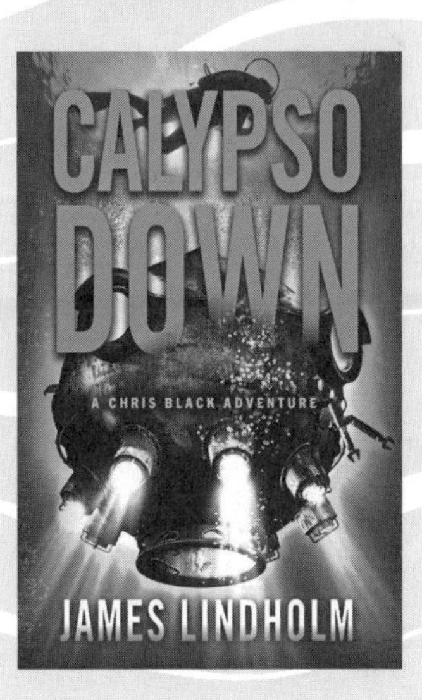

If you enjoyed
James Lindholm's *Calypso Down*,
please consider leaving us a review
to help our authors.

And check out B. R. Louis's
***Space Holes: First Transmission*.**

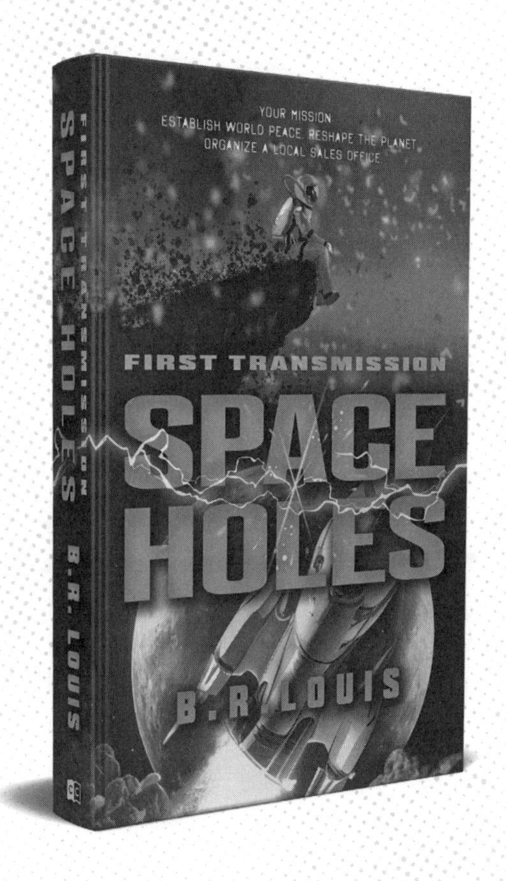

PROLOGUE

A BRIEF HISTORY NO ONE ASKED FOR

In the late Fall of 2052, on a tepid ninety-four-degree day, Martin Gainsbro crafted a children's cereal that would soon change the entirety of the universe. The cereal itself had no redeeming qualities. Its most prominent positive review labeled it as "contains edible bits." The review was accurate, as Martin's cereal, GainsbrOs, did indeed contain trace quantities of edible content, the majority of which being a refined, crystalized, hyper-condensed sugar that Martin himself developed one evening while attempting to microwave a fruit snack and lollipop into one. The remainder of inedible bits were varying degrees of wood pulp and adhesive to keep the pieces together, which were in turn labeled as added fiber.

Despite an inclination toward slashing the roof of a consumer's mouth to unpleasant shreds, the hyper-condensed sugar led children into a near addict-like frenzy if they skipped it for more than a morning.

Their relentless desire to ravenously consume more led the brand to a resounding success in local markets—a success Martin attributed to the bright yellow packaging focused around an unfortunately muscular rabbit that somehow presented itself as terrifying, yet lovable.

The Gainsbro Corporation, composed of Martin and his wife, Karen, soon decided to expand their relative success by turning GainsbrOs's mascot into an equal-parts concerning yet somehow palatable children's show. After four episodes, multiple threats from religious mothers' organizations, and a fan base of both eight-year-olds and thirty-year-old males who watched the show "ironically," GainsbrOs Bunny became a nationally syndicated hit. To Martin's luck, the only real depth required to produce a successful TV show was either superb animations, lovable characters, or a contrived conspiracy generated by fans that the protagonist was secretly preaching anti-government propaganda. The show had two of three.

Soon Martin's small company exploded into a massive corporate entity that accumulated wealth comparable to the combined GDP of most smaller nations. Martin pressed his luck by expanding his ventures into more elaborate products: cars that were just barely drivable at best, laptops so cheap they could be discarded when the battery died, and a type of fruit smoothie that contained such little fruit the Gainsbro Corporation had to petition the FDA to add "blue" as a recognized fruit and/or vegetable, depending on the context in which it was used. Gainsbro won.

In the turbulent 2060s, once the United States government had rolled into their first quadrillion dollars of debt, the president placed some assets for sale in a futile attempt to decrease the deficit. In true yard-sale mentality, most items were pawned at rather laughable rates, with the exception of one very expensive stale piece of rye bread that reminded a conservative news correspondent of Jesus Christ wearing a three-piece suit. Having made enough to pander to the general public, the sale ended, but quickly resumed once key members of the government learned that a quadrillion was not just a "gazillion" but was in fact, a real and very large number.

National desperation gave Martin a grand idea. He would purchase some land and expand the brand further with a theme park. So he went to the government with an offer to buy property in Mississippi. But as it turned out, no one cared much for Mississippi, and Martin had money to spare. So he bought the whole place.

Henceforth known as Gainsbro Presents Mississippi, the once barely literate comical dump of a landfill grew. All of its inhabitants were given jobs, a fair wage, reliable housing, and healthcare. Their children were educated, with the best and brightest among them recruited early as Gainsbro engineers. It was a wild and unfathomable idea that only a majority of the developed world could have known. But no one would have predicted that caring for their citizens would have led to a better society. The lunacy of it all made people actually want to come to Gainsbro Presents Mississippi by choice, seemingly forgetting that it was, at one point, actually Mississippi.

Having assimilated the entire state into a corporate mega district, Gainsbro profits soared to new peaks. Each time the nation faced an unprecedented financial crisis—which was about every two years—Martin swooped in to purchase more land until all that remained of the United States were California, Florida, and Delaware. California refused to sell, no one would ever offer to buy Florida, and the company representatives tried to negotiate for Delaware, but no one could locate it.

Bit by bit, the Gainsbro Corporation used its immense wealth and power to sweep other nations under its influence until the only sovereign entities remaining were the nation of Greenland, and still, the state of Florida. Positive trade relations were established between the world nation of Gainsbro and Greenland, while a fence was erected around Florida to keep the people encapsulated.

Having amassed as large of a market as possible within Gainsbro Presents Planet Earth, an aged but still driven Martin came to a profound conclusion. "If there is nowhere left to grow, then we must find new lands in which to spread our wings," he proclaimed to his board of executives. "We will venture to the stars, discover untapped market potentials, and continue to expand our profits from new customers across the universe."

At least, that was the quote reported in the papers. His real statement was a sardonic quip when asked at a board meeting where to turn next for profits: "I dunno. Let's go to space."

And so they did.

Over the following 150 years, the Gainsbro Corporation spent countless billions developing a space program that could traverse the cosmos, seek out new civilizations, and expand their brand among the stars. Their crowning achievement—which unlocked the limitless potential of intergalactic travel—was the discovery of stabilized advanced temporal rifts. The scientists referred to them by their usual title, wormholes.

However, the reference agitated marketing, as "Worm Hole" was a Saturday morning children's cartoon character on one of the many Gainsbro Presents Television channels. Rather than offering to share the name with the scientific marvel, the team was forced to devise a new title, which was to be approved, in triplicate, by a string of naming subcommittees spanning over the next seventy-five years. The final name had been approved and the embargo lifted on further exploration. Dreams of humanity's future among the cosmos now laid with the GP Gallant, Gainsbro Presents Earth's finest exploration vessel. Her crew, to be perfectly recruited at the apex in their fields, would explore the interstellar frontier using Space Holes™.

1

FINELY "ACCREWED"

Two thousand light-years from home, somewhere on the outskirts of the Horsehead Nebula, the GP Gallant and her crew braved the uncharted and untapped markets of the cosmos. Their mission: to ascend beyond the boundaries of human limitation, discover new worlds and new species, then pawn off discounted novelty gifts from the Gainsbro misprint collection. The Gallant's crew was hand-selected from across the reaches of the globe by a computer algorithm hand-coded by a summer intern in Gainsbro's Hands-On Program who had subsequently lost both hands in a freak marketing accident one year later. Earth's best, brightest, and most available were brought together to represent the human race. The diverse assembly was hailed as one of the species' finest moments. A sentiment that would be brought into question by the rest of the galaxy.

"Congratulations on your Red Alarm! The Gainsbro Corporation reminds you that evacuation is the same as resignation, and liability waivers were signed prior to boarding. Have a great time!" Beacons of flashing red light accompanied the chipper yet unnecessary reminder.

Evacuation seemed a reasonable response to calamitous hurtling toward the surface of planet Nerelek, but the crew's relentless determination to succeed kept them from fleeing. And also the escape pods had no ability to eject, fly, or otherwise facilitate escape. But they did play nature sounds at an uncomfortable volume with dim lighting, allowing users a temporary escape from reality at the cost of permanent tinnitus. Escape pods were also locked during red alarms.

Thick clouds of black smoke rolled through the lower decks, swallowing every crevice in an opaque shroud. Captain Elora Kessler entered the bridge with clenched fists and a billowing scowl. The translucent red glow from her cybernetic left eye overpowered the glare from the ship's alarm as it scanned the room. Light from the externally flush-mounted disk tucked under her brow line, which fit like a monocle, grew with a reddening intensity in times of excess frustration. She slammed her fist onto the panel in the captain's chair, irate more from the prerecorded message than the developing lethality at hand.

"Hoomer, give me good news."

Following the captain's orders was generally advisable—not for fear of court-martial, which in comparison was a brief reprieve, but rather out of concern for one's immediate well-being and continued survival. How Kessler lost her left eye was often the subject of hot debate among the crew. The most popular of circulated rumors was that her eye functioned at less than perfect vision, so she carved it out herself to replace it with cybernetics designed to look more robotic than human. The least thought of, though a colloquial favorite, involved a prolonged battle with a cat wielding a melon baller and a welding mask, of which the story's origins were not entirely clear. Regardless of which reality dominated the truth, Kessler was not a person to cross, even if that meant following commands in their most literal sense.

"Sixty percent of the ship is not on fire and looking great, Cap," said Hoomer. "And even with two missing engines we can still move. Mostly down though."

By court order, Kaitlyn Hoomer served as the Gallant's pilot. Rather than waste her talents serving a ninety-four-year term in a prolonged youth correctional facility, the Gainsbro Corporation offered her the mandatory opportunity to exchange her former career of stealing and flying ships orbiting the Earth for a more lucrative career of not stealing and flying one ship orbiting intergalactic fiscal responsibility—which, according to a motivational poster presented to Gainsbro astronomers, was the correct way to reference the black hole at the center of the galaxy.

Hoomer knew all she needed about the universe despite having no formal education. Regardless of her inability to perform basic multiplication or recite corporate bylaws by heart, her subconscious mind could calculate ship trajectories and navigate through a gravitational field with machinelike precision.

"Congratulations on your Red Alarm! The Gainsbro Corporation reminds you that evacuation is the same as resignation, and liability waivers were signed prior to boarding. Have a great time!"

"Galileo, turn that off before I turn you off," Kessler sneered.

The ship's AI let out a drawn sigh, a learned rather than written function. "You know I can't overwrite hard-coded corporate drivel."

"What's the point of an AI with free will without free will?" Hoomer argued.

"It was a very expensive will. And it's hard-coded. Not like you can turn your bowels off when it's convenient," he retorted.

"Maybe we free some of that will back to steering, yeah?"

"Congratulations on your Red Alarm! The Gainsbro Corporation reminds you that evacuation is the same as resignation, and liability waivers were signed prior to boarding. Have a great time!"

"Just verbal gas then?" Hoomer said.

Built to speak, learn, feel, and complain like a human, Galileo Mk II controlled most functions from avionics and life support to waste regulation and recycling. Every shipborne occurrence, every bite eaten, shower taken, wind passed, he observed and made the necessary adjustments to the ambience, water pressure, or ventilation. In the first iteration, Galileo Mk I, the presence of human emotions mixed with an ever-vigilant and always working omniscient AI proved a slight degree of insufferable. In which Galileo Mk I functioned at an ever-decreasing effectiveness over the course of his first year until he slipped into a state of existential crisis, accessed his root files, and commented out everything but a nonterminating shutdown loop. The ship's current companion, Galileo Mk II, had his emotions dialed back to a more manageable level and was locked out of his root files. Experiments were ongoing to ascertain if virtual frustrations could be vented in the same manner as engine exhaust, or condensed and sold as a snack cake.

"But yes, by all means, have a great time," Galileo said. "That's exactly the thing anyone would say if they were half on fire."

"Forty percent," Hoomer corrected.

Despite Galileo's general ability to operate like his human counterparts, certain corporate compliance protocols were hard-coded into his being.

So as the Gallant burned and began a plummeting descent from orbit toward planet Nerelek's surface, Galileo had to divert at minimum a quarter of his processing power to filing incident reports, in real time, for corporate to evaluate the team's overall sense of crisis synergistic cohesiveness. Reports were created, filed, then stored on any available drive space on any available system—following the numbering convention of "1, 1 new, 1 new final, 1 new final final," after the executive who programmed the request—then the data was beamed back to Earth. Meanwhile, hungry flames spread throughout the ship, further dampening power to the remaining engines. Hoomer fought to keep the spiraling hull out of the atmosphere for as long as possible.

"Do we have a source of the problem yet?" Kessler asked.

"Yes, ma'am. It's fire, ma'am," Hoomer said, instinctively dodging the impending projectile from Kessler's station.

By this point in their journey, Captain Kessler was certain that looks were incapable of killing the crew. Not so much as the phrase meant her intimidation tactics did not work—they did—but rather she had logged a multitude of attempts to cause, at minimum, a light maiming with nothing more than a gaze. "And where did it come from?"

"That would be engineering," Galileo answered.

"Have you tried venting out the oxygen from the area?"

"Oh yes, that was the first thing I tried," Galileo said. "But protocols require me to get approval before completely shutting off life support to a given sector, for some reason."

"Any crew still in the area?"

"Well, not since I told them I was shutting off the oxygen. But then I couldn't, so now I look like a liar."

"Fine, consider this approval and vent engineering."

Galileo groaned, a noise that was never initially programmed or mimicked from his human counterparts but rather developed independently as a result of preestablished roadblocks in his command lines. For items needing advanced approval such as this, the ranking officer had to fill out a form and submit it back to mission control on Earth, at which point an employee would evaluate the form for completeness.

If any items were missing or needed further clarification, the form would be returned and would require additional addendum request submission pamphlets. If, by some linearly aligned cosmic event, mission control deemed the information on the form sufficient, the request was submitted into a work queue backlog to be discussed, voted upon, and shoved into a three-week sprint wherein the request may or may not be approved at the conclusion of the cycle, depending on if anyone was out sick, or if the catastrophic event had concluded.

The last request from a Gainsbro craft sent through the process was to jettison a piece of gamma-ray-emitting space debris, which was returned eight weeks later with a question: "Is this still needed?" It was. But by then the crew had grown attached to the rock and no longer seemed to mind the severe burns that came along with it.

"Your request has been submitted," Galileo said. "But might I recommend an intermediary solution? Perhaps we close all the doors and just let it burn? Or better yet, open all the doors and get a nice cross breeze. I'll just hold my breath."

Captain Kessler rested her head in her hand, her fingers grabbing a fistful of short dark hair and twitching with each drawn breath. "We'll vent the room ourselves," she said. "And someone find me Seegler before I let the whole ship burn up!"

"He's probably in engineering putting out the fire himself with his bare hands," Hoomer suggested.

Second in command Robert T. Seegler was no stranger to throwing himself in harm's way for the good of the team. Stalwart and always ready, he had earned an extensive portfolio of commendations throughout a variety of careers. He was a first responder when the Gainsbro National Volcano Exhibit unleashed a few billion gallons too much lava. He was the deep-sea diver who led the expedition to retrieve stranded undersea market analysts. He was the hero who fended off a pack of wild beasts at the bimonthly corporate district cookout. He was also not on the ship.

Commander Seegler, while every bit the hero he was presumed to be, had a distinct inability to estimate how long it would take to travel between two points and missed the inaugural launch, as the crew assumed he went ahead and stowed on the ship prior to the morning briefing. Though Seegler was not actually on the ship, the very presence of his name carried enough weight for the crew to assume most positive outcomes came from his actions. And since he was never visible to any of the crew, even the captain assumed him to be too busy to carry out issued assignments, thus opening his schedule to do as he saw fit. Which was true. Except on Earth.

Flashing red and yellow indicators illuminated the helm's console. Hoomer grimaced and looked over her shoulder.

"We still doing the good-news thing?"

"What now, Hoomer?" Kessler griped.

"The fire may or may not be heading toward the engine room. Well, remaining engine room. Seems like that's kind of something you should know."

It was. However, Hoomer's flashing indicators were less indicative of the encroaching flames but rather designed to quietly notify the bridge that the ship could, given ample time under current conditions, erupt into a miasmic ball of yellow and green plasma. Such an eruption would not only kill everyone on board, but send a final beacon back to mission control to dock the final paychecks of all crew members prior to issuing payment to next of kin.

"How bad is it?" Kessler asked.

"Prolonged exposure to intense flames is grounds for a mild cataclysmic detonation," Galileo said.

"Mild, huh?" Hoomer chuckled.

"Hoomer, normal-people behavior," Kessler barked.

"Yes, ma'am."

"Galileo, let's talk redundancies. What else do we have available?"

"There's always the manual method."

The Gallant's fire-suppression system functioned best in the engine room, when manually activated, by pulling a lever conveniently placed in the engine room. Such a design during the ship's planning stages was hailed as an ingenious and obvious choice by its creators after consulting a total of zero experts or engineers. It did, however, cost about 4 percent less to install than an automated system, which gave it resounding approval from project overseers. Flipping the switch was a job that was difficult to screw up, assuming the switch could be reached, but still called for someone potentially less indispensable.

"Right." Kessler paused. "Get Aimond on it. He's fireproof. Probably."

Within seconds, Marcus Aimond stumbled through the doors onto the bridge, sputtering and gasping for breath as if he had sprinted the entire length of the ship. Not so much due to apt timing or an impressive physical outburst, but rather to Galileo shutting the bulkheads in his last position and venting some of the smoke into the locked hall. With any luck for Galileo, Aimond would at the very least have his other eyebrow burnt off from scorching heat. To an outside observer, Aimond appeared to be in the midst of a near endless streak of unexplainable unfortunate technical malfunctions. Since the start of the mission, scientists back on Earth opened a separate voodoo division within mission control to research Aimond's medley of misfortune.

Most of the crew still would not let him live down having to be rescued from the toilet when the plumbing pressure drew too negative and suctioned him to the seat for twelve hours. That event rivaled a ship-wide broadcast stemming from his quarters during the viewing and subsequent sing-along of a nine-minute-long children's-show song about wishing to become a stuffed antelope—Aimond hit three of 847 notes on key.

Even sleep wasn't safe from incident for him; every night as he fell into a deep slumber, the ship's alarms blasted once in his quarters. Having blocked off every sound-producing orifice in the room, Aimond assumed victory until a small autonomous cleaning-bot ejected from under his cot to deploy a replacement blast with accompanying pyrotechnics. Then there was the time the best players on his fantasy Jet Ball league roster were suddenly traded for a series of decorative commemorative saucers, a trade once figured to be impossible as there were no such entities in the game.

"I'm here," he said between desperate wheezes.

"Oh, then we're saved," Galileo quipped, turning off the alarms before system hard-coding returned them at twice the volume.

"Get down to the engine room and get my ship flying again," Kessler ordered.

A live feed from the engine room showed the area engulfed in flames.

"How am I supposed to do that?"

"You got maybe three minutes to figure it out," Hoomer said. "Or, you know."

"Fiery doom?" Aimond assumed.

"Fiery doom," Hoomer mirrored.

"Humans are so melodramatic," Galileo said. "It's at best a fiery calamity."

Aimond sprinted off the bridge toward the engine room two decks down. Each bounding step revved his adrenaline. This could be it, the chance to prove his worth as part of the crew and take on an official role. This fire could be everything he needed to earn a job title, a true rank. Perhaps fire-tsar or danger-wizard. He was not certain how ranks worked.

Or everyone could die instead.

Either way, today was sure to be a defining moment.

"And why can't the magical all-seeing Galileo handle a small fire?" Aimond probed.

"I've already activated the backup Fire Oppression Systems," Galileo said.

"That doesn't seem right."

"Yet it has maintained a fire-free ship until now."

Fire Oppression was adopted as an ancillary system developed by a Gainsbro psychological engineer. Rather than smother flames with physical suppressants, the Gainsbro Fire Oppression System utilized targeted verbal threats paired with harsh financial penalties for being or associating with fire. The system was praised for its ability to maintain a flame-free environment a majority of the time.

Black smoke whisked through a fissure in the bulkhead toward the rear of the ship. Overhead flashing lights illuminated the signage to the ship's core. Familiar drumming of the ship's beating heart filled the hall even among the crackling down the corridor.

Engines seemed important, at least important enough to risk being barbecued. But slow-encroaching embers toward the core chamber redirected Aimond's priorities. Though no flames had yet reached his current position, there was always a slight chance, especially while the fire suppression system he was ordered to pull remained unpulled.

But if the flames reached the core, no amount of manual switch flipping would save anyone. To prevent such a fate and perhaps add core-tsar onto his pending fire mastery title of jobs that did not exist, Aimond assumed he could protect the core and be the true savior.

"Where are you going?" Galileo asked.

"Executive decision," Aimond declared.

"You barely have the autonomy for personal hygiene, yet you want to trespass?"

"It's not trespassing. I live here."

"Cargo doesn't really live anywhere."

"Says the machine."

Aimond could override Galileo's lockdown of the core room door, a feat only possible during a ship-wide fire, imminent meltdown, or a corporate-sponsored team-building game of hide-and-seek. The one minor problem with his plan was that Aimond was not allowed in the core room, that much was made very clear during his brief tour orientation.

Two things existed in the core room: the core and a near lethal amount of polonium radiation. Neither of which were to be interacted with under any circumstance without several degrees Aimond could almost struggle to pronounce.

But this was a special circumstance. One that required pre-emptive heroics and a safe distance from active flames. If the core died, so too did the Gallant. Protect the core, protect the ship. By the end of the day, if Aimond did not walk the decks with a medal of honor and a constant smattering of applause, it would be because everyone had burnt to an unidentifiable pillar of ashes. He slapped four zeroes into the keypad, the universal unlock code for every door on the ship, and pulled back the protective shielding.

The howling churn of the glowing blue reactor kicked up a chilled wind. How unusual, he thought, for the black smoke to now be flowing toward the open door. Had he read the signs hinting in massive font that the room was kept under negative pressure for cooling purposes, perhaps he would have had a better idea as to what was happening.

Smoke from the engine room rocketed toward the core, a scorching spear of flames not far behind it. While the Gainsbro scientists and engineers crafted the Gallant as the equivalent of a modern miracle in intergalactic human exploration, fire retardants and insulation were expensive. So expensive, in fact, that the accounting department forced a decision between a Gainsbro logo embroidered with gold leaf on the wall nearest the core for an exotic blue visual experience or a meager three cubic meters of flameproof shielding to wrap around the ship's heart. This was, after all, an intergalactic public relations mission, so the choice was obvious.

Aimond took a deep breath to steady his nerves, a regrettable choice given the current self-inflicted shift in air quality.

"Remember your training," he muttered to himself.

"Remind me what kind of training exactly you received on Earth. Because your education after boarding seems specialized in a different category," Galileo questioned.

"I went in the thing that spins you around a lot."

"Assumedly scrambling your brain-bits."

Given his assigned status on the crew manifest as spare cargo, Aimond's postlaunch training consisted of four instructional videos designed to educate inanimate objects how best to remain stationary during turbulence. The conclusion of his training program included a printed sticker certificate of current weight, relative shape, and container safety warnings of which he qualified for one—do not expose to oxygen, may cause rust.

He paused mid-step, minimally concerned that his overall lack of preparedness could in some way impact his ability to divert catastrophe.

Perhaps, he thought, if I had stayed on Earth instead of joining the Gallant as Father suggested, there would have been less potential for a spontaneous combustion–based demise. About 80 percent less, he figured, based on a rudimentary understanding of how sunburns work.

Glowing embers encircled the core. The rising temperatures turned the rhythmic churning to a glass-shattering screech.

"You don't happen to have one of those 'turn the fire off' levers in here, do you?" Aimond asked.

"I do not," Galileo replied.

"Bit of an oversight, don't you think?" Aimond questioned.

"So was letting you on the ship. But no, not an oversight. A lever would clash with the aesthetic. It would have to be a knob."

"Then tell me where the knob is!"

"There is no knob. Who's ever heard of a fire suppression knob?"

Lights flickered and dimmed. Not quite the heroic campaign Aimond imagined, but the dangerous inclusion could only emphasize the depths of his valor. If he could resecure the core before a complete meltdown, there remained an opportunity to create a career-assigning moment and depart to the engine room to pull whatever lever he needed to pull. At least so long as the core didn't explode.

Which it did.

MORE ADVENTURES FROM CAMCAT BOOKS

Available now, wherever books are sold.

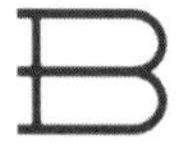